THE EDITED GENOME
TRILOGY

MARCOS ANTONIO HERNANDEZ

CONTENTS

THE EDITED GENOME TRILOGY

AWAKENING

Marcos Antonio Hernandez

For G. Hudson Drakes, who encouraged me to write this story.

For Melissa... you know what you did.

CHAPTER ONE

There's something sinister in the laws of evolution.

Some people, through no fault of their own, find themselves cast below others from the first breath they take. The ones whose parents and ancestors have struggled to adapt are required to scratch and claw for every bit of slack they take from the tether of their existence.

Once technology was created to allow humans to make their offspring happier, healthier, and smarter, a clear split was created between those who could afford the procedure and those who had to wait for nature to catch up.

Edited humans, not wanting their lineage's DNA to revert to the natural state, sequestered themselves in compounds in order to safeguard the wealth they had acquired through generations of increased productivity. The unedited were forced to live in cities and scrape out whatever existence they could while hoping to afford edits to their own children as a perverse retirement plan.

Shada Gray knew she was different because she didn't want children. All she wanted was to play in the league and make enough money to help her sister, Sikya, afford to edit a future child. It wasn't uncommon for professional athletes to set their children up by paying for embryos to be edited before birth, and since Sikya had wanted to be a mother for as long as either of them could remember, it only made sense for Shada to help.

Those dreams were dashed by a five-minute conversation with Shada's coach before practice one summer morning.

"We might have a problem," Coach Patrick said after asking her to sit down across from him at the desk. He was taller than Shada by a head when standing but the same height when they both sat down. Trophies from past victories sat on shelves next to team photos from years past.

"You know how your contract was dependent on your blood coming back clean?"

Shada nodded.

"Well, it appears your levels of hemoglobin are outside the acceptable range."

Shada stared at him, her expression blank.

"Hemoglobin allows for more oxygen to be transported to your muscles," Coach said.

"I know what hemoglobin does," Shada snapped back.

Coach squeezed his lips together and nodded. "I have to ask you this: Have you been blood doping?"

"No! I could never afford it, and even if I could I wouldn't do it."

"So this is natural. This is what we feared. It's why you were dominant in school—"

"Not dominant enough for them to give me a scholarship."

"But dominant enough to get a tryout and make a pro team," Coach said, expressing patience in his now-relaxed face. "It'd be simpler if you were doping. You would be suspended for a few months and could then join the team."

Shada waited for her coach to continue. They'd worked

together for a few short weeks but had already managed to settle into a comfortable coach-athlete relationship.

"But since this is natural, and it falls outside the acceptable range, you won't be able to play professionally. In this country, at least."

Shada got the sense she was falling backwards, like she leaned too far back in her chair and couldn't catch herself. Her mind raced, trying to find a way around this roadblock.

"What if I got it edited into the acceptable range?"

"There can't be any edits whatsoever to hemoglobin levels. League rules."

"So there's nothing I can do?"

"I'm afraid not."

Shada wanted to scream, wanted to launch into a tirade about how unfair the situation was, wanted to demand a solution from her coach even though she could tell from his tone of resignation no solution existed. Instead, she tucked her chin, lowered her head, and took ten deep breaths through her nose and felt the air deep in her belly, a trick she'd learned as a child from her father before he passed away. It had helped calm her down when he died, and it helped calm her down after her dreams were shattered in the coach's office.

Silence enveloped the room before Shada lifted her face. Coach seemed surprised her cheeks were dry; no tears had been shed.

"Thank you for the opportunity," Shada said. She stood up and shook hands with her coach.

"Look into playing overseas. They aren't as strict about genetic differences," Coach said.

"Good to know," Shada said. She was thankful she hadn't put her bag in the locker room before their chat, because now she could walk out without seeing any other athletes and didn't have to explain why she wouldn't be seen at practice anymore.

The sun shone through a cloudless sky and hit Shada's face outside the training facility. She squinted through the ripples of heat emanating from the cars lining the road, most of which hadn't moved in the weeks she'd practiced with the team. Beads of sweat gathered on her forehead as she walked to the train station alongside commuters on their way to work. She pulled out the bag of red gummy bears she saved for after practice every day and ate one at a time. Sikya couldn't stand how much candy she ate, so she took it upon herself to provide Shada with an apple every morning, an apple Shada made a habit to give away to the homeless man on her way to practice.

The train was packed, but Shada found an empty seat next to the window and stared at the buildings that passed by with increased frequency as the train gathered speed. An ad for financed genetic edits by WestCorp, by far the largest DNA editing operation and owner of the island compound just outside the city, was plastered on the side of one of these buildings. She had considered investigating post-birth edits, but they were rumored to cost as much as Shada's entire education. No reason to double her debt when it wouldn't help her get into the league.

The seat next to her opened up for a moment at the next stop before a broken old lady boarded the train and approached. The two tennis balls on the ends of the legs of her walker had been attached for so long that the bright green fuzz was worn away, leaving dull beige rubber to precede each of her uncertain steps.

"Is anyone sitting here?" Tennis Balls asked, pointing to the seat on Shada's left.

Most old white ladies didn't ask to sit next to women with brown skin, they just sat down. Shada shook her head, and the woman managed to sit down right before the train began to move again.

A hand spotted with age gripped the handle of the walker as they picked up speed. "Lovely day today, isn't it?" Her smile was too white and matched her colorless hair.

Shada gave the woman a thin-lipped smile, nodded, and wondered how many of those teeth were fake before she turned to look at the graffiti now passing outside her window. Less than an hour ago she had been making the reverse trip on her way to practice. Her future had almost been secure.

"Where are you heading?" the woman asked.

"Home."

The old lady nudged Shada's backpack, which was on the ground next to the walker, with her foot. "Coming back from school?"

Shada wanted to say something about how, if she was, the class must have started at dawn. Instead, she turned and informed the woman she'd graduated last spring.

"Congratulations!"

"With a mountain of debt," Shada said. Then, under her breath, "And no way to pay it off."

"But nobody can ever take away your education," the old lady said with a twinkle in her eye, as if she was imparting some wisdom on the younger woman.

"But someone did take away my future." Shada told Tennis Balls about the morning's conversation with her coach and how she wouldn't be able to play for the team. "It's all I've ever wanted," she said.

"My grandson's the same way. He's still in high school, but boy does he work hard! Maybe you could get a waiver? It shouldn't be hard to prove you aren't edited."

"The leagues are hell-bent on making sports fair, even if it means some unedited humans are affected in the process."

"Still, it might be worth looking into. You never know what strings the leaders can pull."

Shada marveled at how this woman was able to see the rules as malleable, as if doors could be opened under the right circumstances. She was reminded of how different a worldview could be among people of different races—even if they were both unedited.

"I feel bad. My sister's worked to support the two of us these past few months because my big payday was on the horizon. This was supposed to be our ticket."

"I'm sure she will understand."

Shada looked at Tennis Balls with a sideways glance and ignored the comment. "I'd always wondered if I would test outside the acceptable range. Sports have always been a natural fit for me; I could run and run no matter how intense the game was. I always thought it was because of how hard I worked, but now I know it was just my genetics."

"Don't say that! Just because you were born with the ability to turn the volume up doesn't mean it gets turned up on its own. Do you think edited humans are born with all their knowledge? No, they have to learn. All the edits do is allow them to learn faster. It's not like they don't have to work, it's just that the same amount of work gets them further. Got you further, even though you aren't edited," Tennis Balls said with a wink.

The train slowed down and Shada recognized her stop. She grabbed her backpack and slung it over her shoulder. "This is me," she said.

"Good luck! Trust me, it will all work out in the end."

"Easy for you to say," Shada said as she walked off the train. Through the crowd of people she saw the apple she'd given to the homeless man, shiny and red, on the ground next to the fence alongside his tired beagle.

CHAPTER TWO

"I HAVE SOME BAD NEWS," Sikya said when Shada walked through the door of their shared apartment. She leaned on the kitchen counter with her elbows, typing on her phone.

Shada threw her backpack on the couch and plopped down next to it, grateful for the extra moment before her own bad news was spoken. She looked around their one-bedroom apartment and wondered how long Sikya would be able to afford the rent without her expected contribution. Together they kept the space spotless. The scent of lemon cleaner peaked when the kitchen was cleaned every night and lingered throughout the day. There was enough room for the couch, a coffee table, and a television in the living room, and the counter provided a barrier between it and the kitchen. The sole bathroom could be accessed from the living room or the bedroom, and unless the bathroom was in use, both doors were kept open. Their bedroom had two twin-sized beds and two dressers and left just enough space between the pieces of furniture to walk. All of it could be lost if Shada didn't find a way to help Sikya pay rent.

"What's the news?" Shada asked.

Sikya finished typing on her phone before she set the device down and laid her hands flat on the counter. She took a deep breath. "Tensen lost the election." Miles Tensen had been running for mayor and Sikya had worked on his campaign. After her sister didn't react, she launched into a tirade. "This other guy won't do a thing for the unedited, his entire campaign was paid for by WestCorp!"

"Not the first time the edited get their mayor. Hard to get past all the money."

"And legislators won't approve any limits to donations since their pockets are lined as well." Sikya looked at her phone and checked the time. "What are you doing home so early?"

Shada repositioned herself on the couch. "I got cut."

"Oh my god, I'm so sorry! Today's not a good day for us."

"We're both out of a job."

"What happened?"

"My DNA tested outside the acceptable range."

"What does that mean? Do you have to go through tryouts for a different team?"

"It means I can't play professional sports. Not just for this team, not just for this sport, but for any league in the country."

A flash of anger passed over Sikya's face. "Are you serious? Do they think you're edited?"

"They know it's natural, but the league has limits on all sorts of genetic traits."

Sikya paused for a moment. "Why don't you let me talk to Tensen for you? I'm sure he knows someone who can help."

"There's not much he can do. The leagues are separate from the government."

"But it's discrimination! We can take it to the courts."

"This is the only way leagues can make sure teams with the most money don't get an unfair advantage. Sports are the only thing unedited humans have left."

Sikya stood up and interlocked her fingers behind her head.

"I have one more paycheck coming in from the campaign, but after that we have no income. Is it time to get a job using your degree?"

Shada wanted to sulk and didn't appreciate Sikya bringing up the financial pressure they now found themselves in. "Not sure yet."

"You better become sure. One more paycheck. That's it. I've paid for everything these past few months while we waited for your first check and now it's not coming. We both have student loans, you know."

Shada sat up straight. "Now that Tensen's lost the election, you have no real reason to stay here, do you?" she asked.

"No, I guess not," Sikya said, her eyes wary.

"Coach said it's still possible to play overseas. Why don't you come with me?"

Sikya leaned her lower back against the stove. "Move overseas? I don't know if I can do that."

"Why not? It's not like we have any family left."

Sikya flinched, the memory of their mother's passing too fresh. "There's still a lot of work to do for the unedited people here. I won't stop until edits are free for everyone. It wasn't fair for mom to die because she couldn't afford to edit her DNA."

"We can go somewhere without such a divide between people."

"The divide is what I'm fighting against!"

Shada stared at Sikya. A feeling that her sister was holding back information bubbled up in her stomach. "There's more to it than what you're telling me," she said.

Sikya opened her mouth to deny the accusation then changed her mind. "I can't raise a kid overseas."

"You don't have a kid to raise."

"But I will!"

"You don't even have a man."

Sikya glared at her sister. "Not yet."

"Then let's go!"

"I told you I can't!" Sikya yelled. "There are other reasons too. My friends are here. Tensen said he will make another run at mayor, so there's lots of work to do on the campaign."

"And who's going to pay you?"

"I'm more worried about who's going to pay you."

Both sisters fell silent. Sikya was the first to speak again. "You could go and send the borrowed money back."

"You don't care if I go alone?"

"Or stay and get a job using your degree. I've supported you for months, and now I'm out of a job too. We need money from somewhere."

It was Shada's turn to glare at her sister. "You know going pro is all I ever wanted."

"Then go get paid to play!"

Shada grabbed her backpack and stormed into their shared bedroom. She pulled out her suitcase and began to throw clothes inside. One outfit each for cold and warm weather plus all the athletic clothes she might need.

"What are you doing?" Sikya asked from the doorway.

"What does it look like I'm doing?"

"Packing."

Shada stuffed a handful of underwear into the corner of her suitcase. "There, you answered your own question."

"Where are you going?"

"Overseas. You said it yourself . . . 'Go get paid to play.' So that's what I'm doing! I didn't realize I was such a burden on you. Well don't worry, I won't be much longer."

"I didn't mean go now. You don't even have a ticket."

"I can get one at the airport. I'll just charge it. I have a ton of debt already, what's a bit more?"

Sikya watched her sister finish packing and didn't say

another word until the suitcase was set down next to the front door.

Shada opened the refrigerator and took a long drink of milk before she grabbed her box of red gummy bears from the cabinet.

"I'll send your money the first chance I get," Shada said.

"Don't be like this," Sikya pleaded. "It's been a hell of a day for both of us and I didn't mean to sound like you were a burden. I'm just stressed, that's all."

"No, the message was received loud and clear. You want a return on your investment and don't want to leave. What other choice do I have than to go by myself?"

"Let's just talk to Tensen and see if he can do anything for you." Sikya walked over and placed an apple in Shada's backpack, the second apple she'd given her sister today.

Shada grabbed her bags and stood in the open doorway. "You talk to him and find out if he can help me find a team overseas who won't care about something I can't control. I'm going to the airport," she said over her shoulder before she walked through the front door without another look back.

CHAPTER THREE

_____

SHADA'S WORLD blurred until she caught the homeless man staring at her from against the fence of the train station. She remembered the apple in her backpack she had no intention of eating and handed it to him, the second time today. The homeless man thanked her, and his small dog lifted his head and wagged his tail at Shada. She reminded herself the dog did this to everyone who paid attention to the homeless man, so she wasn't special.

It was just after noon when she boarded the train and headed back into the heart of the city. She again saw West-Corp's advertisement for financed edits, but this time she wasn't able to get the company out of her head. If the edits made her happier, the way they were supposed to, maybe she could find some contentment in a job using her degree. Her debt would double, but her life would have direction.

Shada had to switch trains in the underground hub in order to get to the airport. Flickering lights protected by translucent plastic coverings illuminated the terminal, and the brown tile floor ended at two escalators: one escalator went up and led to the airport, and one descended to the tram, which could take Shada to WestCorp's compound.

On a whim she decided to descend. She still wasn't sure whether or not she wanted to have her DNA edited, but she was curious enough to hear what the company had to say.

After she went down two more escalators she didn't know existed, Shada arrived on the platform that hosted the tram to WestCorp. It was different from the station above. It was bathed in white light thrown down from a track of lights running through the length of its center. Smooth marbled concrete benches and trash cans sat beneath the lights, the benches arranged so passengers could sit facing both directions. There was an information desk at the far end where two blond women, young but not so young they would be dismissed as uninformed, sat waiting.

Shada was the only passenger on the platform. It seemed odd to her, but she continued along the length of the platform towards the two smiling faces and asked what time the next trip would begin.

"You have twenty minutes," one of the women said. Her voice was sweet, its pitch high, and it contained a hint of amusement, as if it was engineered to sound as servile as possible.

"What brings you to WestCorp today?" her partner asked.

"I saw the ads on the train and decided to see what they are all about. Twenty minutes is a long time to wait," Shada said.

"The tram was sent as soon as you stepped onto the platform."

"It was sent for me?"

"Of course! You're the only one here."

"Where's everyone else?"

"WestCorp visitors are always scheduled in the morning. The last one left a few hours ago."

"I just came down to find out more information." Shada

looked at the light blue tiles on the wall behind the information desk arranged in a fractal pattern against a cream-colored backdrop. "Hard to believe this exists beneath the hub upstairs. Don't go through all the trouble for me, I'll just head to the airport."

"It's no trouble at all!" one of the blond women insisted.

"Really, I'll just leave." Shada turned and began to walk away.

"The tram has already been sent. Whether you stay or not doesn't affect its course."

Shada stopped. "Well, I have no place else to be . . ." she said, her voice trailing off.

"Then stay!" both women exclaimed together.

Their excitement was infectious, and Shada found herself wanting to stay in order to be around such positive energy. After the uncertainty of her day so far, it was nice to be wanted.

Shada took a seat on a smooth concrete bench and waited for the tram to arrive. She pulled out her bag of gummy bears and poured herself a handful, then ate one at a time. She found herself thinking about the two women at the information desk, about their happiness. She assumed they were edited—why else would they work on the WestCorp platform?—and if this was happiness, this cheerful disposition, was it what she could look forward to if she were to edit her DNA? Could it be worth the cost?

The tram, a single driverless car, came to a stop in front of Shada without a sound. The doors opened, Shada shouldered her backpack, and with one last look at the two women behind the information desk, who waved goodbye, she boarded the car. The tram's doors shut and the trip began as soon as Shada took a seat.

Shada was carried through a ramrod-straight tunnel and emerged on the outskirts of the city with the bay ahead. A rail extended over the water in the direction of the island on the horizon. Before the tram left land, it passed by a billboard for cologne, a square bottle surrounded by cascading water that claimed Your best you is within reach. Shada wondered how many people saw the billboard in any given week, since the edited humans of WestCorp called the island home and, to the best of her knowledge, never left.

As soon as the tram was over water, a screen descended from the ceiling. The WestCorp logo gave way to a menu, and a voice asked Shada which service she was interested in. In addition to genetic edits there were also sections for donations and business opportunities. Shada wondered what kind of donations WestCorp would be interested in and made a note to ask when she got to the island.

"Genetic edits," Shada said.

"Are you currently unedited?" the robotic voice asked.

"Yes," Shada replied. She felt strange talking to the monitor and looked around the car, grateful she was alone.

A promotional video began, showing a mother and father swinging a young child between them in a field of flowers. The video launched into the benefits of genetic editing, its safety, its efficacy, and thanked Shada for considering WestCorp, as if there was another option available for the same service. Shada couldn't help but think of Sikya and hope this small family was her sister's future.

The video ended with a note about the availability of financing options but didn't elaborate.

Shada looked out the window, to the water around her, and got the sense there was no turning back. It stirred up her rebelliousness, and she launched into a daydream about what would happen if they wouldn't accept her refusal of the genetic edits and held her hostage. What if they wouldn't provide her a ride back to the city? Would she be able to call her sister and tell her what happened? She turned around and watched the city retreat into the distance. She knew how to swim but had never done so in open water and was sure this was farther than she had ever swum before.

The tram began a gradual descent until its track ran onto the island. She passed by manicured lawns and tree-lined roads between buildings of various sizes, both residential and industrial, on her way toward the largest building: a massive square structure that looked like the largest warehouse she'd ever seen, stretching in both directions. Gleaming steel machines dotted the roof, and Shada tried to look inside one of the hundreds of windows before she plunged between two massive doors in the side of the building that opened with just enough space for the tram to pass through.

CHAPTER FOUR

SHADA DISEMBARKED from the tram onto another vacant platform. The aesthetic was the same as the one she left behind in the city except there was no information desk where she could ask for directions. The noisy sound of the bustle of crowds came down from the set of stairs situated in the same location on the platform as the escalator beneath the hub. In front of the stairs sat a security guard, the largest human Shada had ever seen, and he patted her down before he allowed her to pass. After she walked up a set of marble stairs, she emerged in the middle of a glass-covered atrium.

Rays of sunlight bisected by the glass panes spilled down onto the mass of people traveling in every direction, with Shada in the eye of the storm. Planters provided a border beneath the glass, and fernlike leaves dropped down in an effort to collect as much sunlight as possible. Sliding doors on the longest walls were separated by restaurants offering everything from coffee to seafood. Beyond the sliding doors on the corners, buses dropped off and accepted passengers. Shada assumed the four sets of drop-off points indicated that the lines of transportation made a giant X over the island.

The closest thing she could compare it to was the entrance to an airport she remembered from the one flight she'd taken with her university team for a tournament across the country.

For a moment, before she spotted a sign with an arrow in the direction of the lab, Shada debated whether or not to go back down onto the platform and head back to the city. This was her first time around so many edited people, and at first she felt like she stuck out like a sore thumb. But to her surprise, everyone went about their own business without giving her a second thought. She walked through the crowd toward the lab and looked into their eyes, searching for some way to distinguish the edited from herself. She was used to feeling out of place, a brown girl in a world made for white men, but here, to her surprise, nobody gave her a second look.

Maybe this was what set the edited humans apart.

The crowd thinned out near the entrance to the long corridor leading to the lab. Along the corridor were various displays of children's artwork, arranged by age of the artist. The quality of the work increased as the children's age increased, which corresponded to Shada's distance from the atrium. She noticed the same names multiple times and, after realizing this hall's decorations were all furnished by the same cohort, wondered if there were seventeen other corridors of similar length with other children's work on display.

The end of the corridor, another pair of sliding glass doors, came into view just before a group of a dozen or so people emerged from a door painted to match the corridor's wall on Shada's right. As the door swung closed, she spotted a bus pulling away and realized the corridor she'd just passed through was empty because everyone took the bus to different areas of the compound, even areas within walking distance. She followed the group until they went their separate ways through a series of doors arranged in a semicircle.

Shada found herself alone and stared at the unmarked doors, wondering if she should pick a door and press on into what she assumed was the entrance to the lab. The walls were stark white and the smell, a mix of chemicals and plastic, made her eyes water. She turned to go back the way she came and almost bumped into an ancient man in a white lab coat who had materialized behind her.

"Sorry," she said, her eyes downcast. She stepped to the side in an effort to let the man pass, but he didn't move.

"You're not smiling," the man said. He had a white beard, his white hair was parted to the side, and he had the kind of hunch in his upper back that gets more pronounced with age.

Shada forced her mouth into a wide grin and displayed as many teeth as she could. "Happy?" she said. In the city she would have shown the man the middle finger, but in unknown territory she didn't want to cause any trouble.

"I am. But I'm not so sure you are." He leaned in close and whispered, "You're not edited, are you?"

"No, I'm not," Shada said, sounding more proud than she intended.

"Not many unedited come to the island; most visit our office in the city. How did you make it this far into the compound?"

Shada told the man how she'd gotten off the tram, emerged into the atrium, and decided to visit the lab.

"Someone should have been waiting for you when you arrived. Plus, there's an information desk for visitors right across from the stairs. Didn't you see it?"

"No, I didn't."

"Let me show you."

The man motioned for Shada to follow him, and he shuffled in the direction of the atrium. He used his identification card to pass through the corridor doors, and the two of them stepped outside and waited under the sun. The breeze from the water cooled them off until the bus arrived. The old man's card gained him and Shada access to the driverless bus, which took them back to the atrium in a few short minutes. Back among the crowds, Shada noticed their eyes on her and heard their whispers as she was led to the information desk, right across from the stairs, right where the man in the lab coat said it would be. She felt more comfortable with the attention than when she'd walked in anonymity.

The young woman seated at the information desk hung up the phone when she saw Shada and the man in the lab coat approach. She had brunette hair, and her eyes were set deep in her face, outlined by a light shadow. When she recognized the old man, she sat up straight.

"This young lady said she got off the tram and nobody greeted her. Can you explain to me how this happened?"

The young woman flushed red. "I lost her in the crowd, sir."

"I trust you knew she was on her way. You're the one who sent the car to retrieve her, right?"

"Yes."

"Then why weren't you on the platform when she arrived?"

The young woman seemed to be weighing whether or not to explain her thought process. "It was a mistake, sir. It won't happen again."

"See that it doesn't." The man in the lab coat turned to Shada. "Enjoy your visit. And remember to smile!" he said with a satisfied grin before he walked away.

The young woman sat down behind the information desk. Shada expected her to be flustered, but her mood wasn't colored by her previous mistake. "Name?" she said in a cheerful tone Shada thought sounded artificial.

Shada got the sense this was the sort of practiced interaction she would have received if she'd approached this desk when she first walked up the stairs. "Shada Gray."

"Business at WestCorp?"

"I want information about financing genetic edits."

The young woman looked at Shada. "Are you expecting?"

"No, I came here on a whim."

"Not expected. Expecting. Pregnant."

"No, I'm not pregnant."

"So you're interested in post-birth edits?"

"Yes, that's correct."

"OK, wait here."

The young woman called for an escort, and another West-Corp employee showed up right away, as if the escort was waiting around the corner of the booth for the chance to be of service. The escort could have been the twin of one of the women at the information desk on the company's platform in the city. "Where to?" the escort asked the young woman across from Shada.

"Take her to see Alfie."

CHAPTER FIVE

SHADA WAS TAKEN up an elevator just outside the atrium and led down a hallway she guessed led to the lab. But they didn't walk far enough to be anywhere close to the lab, and when they turned off into a series of offices, Shada couldn't have found her way back without stopping to ask for directions. The labyrinth must have made sense to, or been memorized by, her escort, because there was no hesitation about which direction they took.

The escort knocked on the door of one of the offices, and a thin man sporting a gray beard and glasses, about the same height as Shada, answered. The hair on his head was also gray, and it looked as if he'd worn a baseball cap to work and taken it off when he got to the office—matted down against his head with a few thin wisps stuck out at odd angles.

"She's here to see you," the escort said before she turned around and left the two of them alone.

"Come in, come in," the gray-haired man said as he stepped back and held the door open.

Shada walked inside. The bookcases on every wall over-flowed with books, and a window in the back of the office looked out onto the water. Papers on the desk surrounded his computer, and a small picture taped onto his monitor showed a young woman. The picture was bent, and Shada guessed it had been taken many years before.

"Please sit down," the man said as he walked around the desk to his chair, gesturing to one of the two chairs across from his. "My name is Alfie Reynolds-Grant. Head scientist."

"Shada Gray."

"So you're interested in genetic edits?" Alfie said.

"Interested, yes. To be honest, I didn't think this would be such a process. I came here to find out about the financing."

"That's all you wanted? Why did they send you to me?" He sounded exasperated. "The process is straightforward. You provide an egg, we edit it, fertilize it in vitro, then transplant it into your uterus. You could've started the process in the city."

"I don't want to get pregnant. I want the edits for myself."

"Well now. That's a different story." Alfie removed his glasses, placed them in his shirt pocket, and folded his hands on his desk. "Post-birth edits are trickier, and we don't provide financing for the procedure."

Shada took a deep breath to hold back the anger bubbling inside her at having wasted so much time on this trip to the island. "Well, I can't afford the procedure otherwise. Sorry to have wasted your time." She stood up and extended her hand.

Alfie stared at her outstretched hand. "Sit down. I said we don't provide financing, not that there aren't other options available."

Shada's wary eyes didn't leave the scientist as she took a seat.

"Post-birth edits require a twenty-year contract of employment," Alfie said.

Shada's eyes widened. "Twenty years?" She swallowed hard. "That's a long time."

"It's an intensive procedure." He allowed time for the news to be digested. "Can I ask what made you decide to look into editing?"

Shada told Alfie how she'd been banned from playing in the league because her hemoglobin counts were too high. She explained how her future had boiled down to two options—either play overseas or begin a career—and how she hoped the edits would make the career more palatable.

"You already made a team?" Alfie asked. His eyes squinted as his thoughts coalesced.

"I made the team and was practicing with them when the bloodwork came back."

"Well now, this changes things." Alfie leaned back in his chair and explained how a version of this situation had occurred before. "The other guy knew his bloodwork wouldn't pass, so he got us to edit it into the acceptable range, along with the other standard edits. We agreed to provide proof that his edits had occurred before birth in exchange for him being a face for edited athletes. I won't tell you who it was or what sport he played, because he never amounted to anything more than a roster spot, but WestCorp did agree to allow his playing career to count towards his employment."

"That could be an option!" Shada said, excited to have found a solution.

"The only problem would be the failed bloodwork," Alfie said, his voice trailing off.

"I could just say I was blood doping and serve the suspension. After that, I would be free to play."

"That could work," Alfie said, nodding. "There would be approximately four months before your red blood cells could replace themselves and you would test clean. If we time it right, you could be playing professionally before the end of the year."

Shada was so excited she wanted to call her sister and share the good news, forgetting she'd stormed off a few hours before. Now she could pay Sikya back, pay off both their debts, and help Sikya pay for edits for her future children.

A potential problem occurred to Shada, and she was brought back down to earth. "One thing though," she said.

"What is it?"

"Edited players are different on the court. They always have quality technique, and should be good, but the creativity is missing. If we go through with the edits, maybe we just edit my hemoglobin count so I don't lose any of my edge."

Alfie leaned forward and rested his elbows on the desk, his chin in his hands. "Interesting. I've never considered that. Maybe that's why this didn't work the first time. In theory, we could edit you to be more creative. We've isolated the genes, and it's the same procedure."

Shada thought for a moment. "I don't think it's worth the risk. Trust me, I can be one of the greats. I just have to get on the court."

"So we would edit your hemoglobin count and say you've had the standard edits since birth, you play in the league and convince the unedited world that edits don't affect your abilities, and after your career you receive the standard edits and come work for us?"

"I would have to get the standard edits?"

"We don't allow unedited humans to work at WestCorp."

Shada sighed. "Then yes, I would get the standard edits after I retire from the league."

Alfie nodded. "I think this could work well for all parties involved." He stood up and extended his hand. "Could you come back tomorrow? I'll get this cleared with the right people and we can start the process of getting you into the league."

Alfie provided Shada with instructions on how to get back to the atrium, and Shada had to contain her excitement long enough to focus on not getting lost. On the tram back to the city —this time shared with three other passengers—she lost herself in hope. Hope for her career, hope for her future, and hope for her sister. With the money she would earn, she could pay for Sikya's living expenses and allow her sister to fight for unedited rights through legislation. It was the least she could do after her sister had allowed her to chase her own dreams these past few months.

CHAPTER SIX

SHADA STILL HAD a key to their apartment—she'd been gone as long as if she'd gone to a full day of practice—and she let herself in. Nothing had changed in the apartment other than the fact that now it was empty; Sikya must have gone out. Knowing her, it had something to do with Tensen. Maybe she was cleaning out their headquarters after the lost election or convincing voters there was still hope. Her sister came home late that night, exhausted, and found Shada on the couch watching sports news.

"What are you doing here?" Sikya asked. Surprise drained from her face and was replaced with a hesitant smile.

"I didn't go overseas," Shada said. She grabbed the remote and turned the television off.

"I see that." Sikya set her bag down on the counter. "I didn't think you would. Where'd you go?"

"I went to WestCorp."

The surprise on Sikya's face almost made Shada laugh. In a way, WestCorp was the enemy, of her and the rest of Tensen's staff. As the largest and most well-funded editors of DNA, they represented everything wrong with the state of society. Their island compound made them an easy target and provided a rallying point for those looking to advance the unedited cause.

"What were you doing there?" Sikya said, trying to sound conversational.

"I wanted to find out about financing genetic edits."

"You want to pay for edits?" Sikya asked. She leaned her shoulder against the wall outside the kitchen.

"I was on my way to the airport and there was a billboard for WestCorp that said financing is available. Come to find out it's only for pre-birth edits; post-birth edits aren't eligible."

"Headed to the airport? You really were going overseas?"

"I had every intention to when I left here earlier."

Sikya walked to the couch and sat down next to her sister. "So you went to WestCorp and found out post-birth edits aren't available for financing. I could have told you that."

"Well, I didn't know. Anyway, I got lost when I got to the island—"

"Wait, you went to the island? Why didn't you just go to their office downtown? Nobody goes to the island unless they live there and are going back."

"I didn't even know they had an office in the city. You're right, nobody goes. I was the only one on the tram."

"So you went across the water."

"I went across the water, yes. Long story short, I think I found a way to play in the league." Shada told Sikya about the plan she and Alfie had come up with, how they would edit her hemoglobin levels and claim she had been blood doping so she could serve her suspension and get back on the court before the end of the year. "He said he will come up with the paperwork saying I've been edited since birth."

Sikya's silence lasted so long Shada thought her sister would launch into a tirade when she decided to speak again. Instead, she asked, "How much will all of this cost?"

"I have to agree to work for WestCorp for twenty years. But my playing career counts towards the total. Their goal is to have an example of a successful edited athlete."

"There are plenty of edited athletes in the league."

"But none of them have been successful."

"And you will be?"

"I have a better chance at it than any edited athlete! We both know edited athletes are good but they're always missing that extra something."

Sikya continued probing Shada's plan. "And after your playing career? You just show up to work on the island?"

Shada didn't tell her sister about the plan to receive standard edits and become a cog in the WestCorp machine. "They want me to be a recruiter," she said, making up a scenario that would placate her sister. "I'd be in the city office and convince unedited couples to edit their children."

This was not the right thing to say. "You understand we'd be on different sides of the aisle, right? My whole career is dedicated to making edits free for everyone, and you'd be convincing couples to go into debt in the hopes their child has a better life. It's not fair the edited have better access to resources, including edits, when we're all members of the city, whether we live on the island or not."

"It's their choice whether they want to pay for edits or not," Shada said.

"It's their choice, but studies show most would accept the debt to edit their children if they could get approved." Sikya's voice rose in volume and she became more animated. "And do you know why they would carry that burden? Because of the pressure placed on them by the system we live in. The system I work against. And when the parents die, the debt isn't erased, it's passed down to the children!"

"Think of it this way: if I play in the league, I can afford to pay for you to live. You can devote even more time to working with Tensen for unedited equality."

"And if it comes out that my sister, who is working for West-Corp, has gone into debt for edits and pays for me to live, I'll look like a hypocrite. You just don't get it," Sikya said.

"Let people think what they want, your results will speak for themselves."

"And another thing: What's going to happen if you are successful? People will start talking. Why would you be edited at birth and I'm not? And if that's the case, why would we have grown up together?"

Shada thought for a moment. "We can say it was our parents' decision. They're both gone now, nobody could ask them and find out otherwise. Maybe they wanted to run an experiment, one edited and one unedited, and see how the situation played out."

Sikya let the suggested solution digest. "I don't know, Shada, it seems like you're signing a deal with the devil."

"What's not to know! Don't you want to edit your future child?"

Sikya sighed and lowered her head. "Yes, but I want to be able to afford it. I'm not going into more debt, nor will I risk putting my child into debt, just for edits."

"If I play in the league, we will be able to afford it!"

Sikya looked at Shada with tears in her eyes. "Don't do this just for me and a child that doesn't exist yet."

"I'm doing this for us."

"And you'll still be the same, right? You're just getting edits to get your hemoglobin count in the proper range and not the standard edits?"

Shada couldn't remember a time when she'd outright lied to her sister, but she was so close to receiving her sister's blessing

she had to press on. "Just the edits so I can play in the league."
At first.

"OK," Sikya said with an exhale. She leaned in and gave her
sister a hug. "I'm glad you didn't make it to the airport."

"Me too," Shada said as she caught the scent of the city in
Sikya's hair.

CHAPTER SEVEN

SHADA WAITED on the platform to be taken to WestCorp's island compound during rush hour the next morning. There were, she guessed, about forty people there with her, enough that all the concrete benches were taken and the remaining individuals had to stand until transportation arrived. They came from all walks of life: older individuals dressed in business attire stood alongside young adults who looked like they were on their way to the gym. Shada was dressed somewhere in between, having borrowed some of her sister's clothes after Sikya insisted she not wear her normal gym shorts and T-shirt. Sikya had decided on a pair of black pants and a black blouse for Shada but couldn't convince her sister to wear anything but sneakers.

Two women were at the information desk when Shada arrived. None of the commuters bothered to approach them, and they talked to each other with broad smiles, white teeth on full display. From a distance they looked to be the same two women Shada had interacted with the day before, but she never got close enough to be sure. What could they be talking about if they saw each other every day? She imagined she would talk about sports if she was in their position, since there was always news about some team somewhere. Maybe they agreed on which television shows they watched just so they would have something to talk about.

The tram arrived with three cars, enough to accommodate all the travelers. The cars were dark as they pulled up, but a soft white light blinked on the second the vehicle stopped, spilling out onto the mass of people lined up in front of six opening doors. Everyone filed into the tram and found seats. Shada ended up next to a young woman, about her age, with a septum piercing and plenty of metal on the lobes of each ear. Shada's neighbor asked her why she was going to WestCorp as the tram began to move.

"Edits," she murmured, not sure if the woman next to her was edited or not. There was still something about edited humans Shada mistrusted, since they grew up and lived in a different world from hers, and she felt like she was about to enter a beehive full of people who could sting her if provoked. She wondered if Sikya's attitude about the edited taking advantage of the unedited had rubbed off on her.

"Me too," the pierced woman said, nodding. "I'm not pregnant though, nor do I want to be. These are for me." From the sound of it, the woman had made peace with her decision.

"I'm going in for post-birth edits too," Shada said. She kept her statement vague on purpose, hopeful this woman would assume they were the standard edits so she wouldn't have to elaborate.

Shada wondered what the odds were that she'd ended up next to another unedited heading to the island for post-birth edits. From the way Alfie had made it sound, the procedure wasn't as straightforward as the pre-birth edits, and she got the sense it was out of the ordinary. She glanced around the car at the same moment the tram left the underground tunnel, wondering if perhaps all the people whose faces had just been illuminated by sunlight were on their way to the island for the same reason as them. Since she knew there was no discernible difference in structure between the two types of humans, she gave up and turned to watch the island materialize on the horizon, thinking that perhaps everyone on board assumed they were the only unedited human making this morning's commute.

Shada's pierced neighbor laughed at the billboard for cologne they passed before crossing the water. "Nothing could mask the stench of this city," she said. She tucked her chin, turned in Shada's direction, and looked at her fellow passenger through the sides of her eyes. She held out her right hand. "My name's Chloe."

They shook hands. "Shada Gray."

"My name's Chloe Rose."

Her eyes were a blue so faint they could have been white if seen at a glance. Shada wondered if this was her natural eye color.

"Did you meet with Alfie?" Shada asked.

"Who?"

"The head scientist on the island. I came yesterday and sat down with him. He told me to come back today."

Chloe looked at Shada with wide eyes. "You've already been to the island?"

Shada nodded.

"I went to the WestCorp office in the city last week and they set it up for me to come today. I went in to find out about the employment after the edits," Chloe said. She turned forward as the tram continued its trip over the water. "I just got tired of the rat race, you know?"

Shada furrowed her brow. "You want employment even though you're tired of the rat race?" She was surprised at herself for calling out the apparent contradiction; any other time she would have taken note of the discrepancy and left it alone. She was reminded of Sikya, who never let someone off the hook for misaligned statements.

"I've accepted that the rat race is a part of life, but I just don't want to be tired of it anymore. If the edits can make me happy with a lifetime of work, then why not invest in myself?"

Shada took a moment to ponder Chloe's position and recognized the similarity within herself. Her own decision hadn't arrived with such a succinct awareness of motivation, but she recognized the logic.

"Twenty years is a long time," Shada said, both to Chloe and as a reminder to herself. This wasn't a second guess of her decision, just a statement of fact.

"And we're both looking at it. Maybe we can work together!" Chloe said.

"Maybe," Shada said, knowing the beginning of her West-Corp career wouldn't be with Chloe. "I'm not sure how they decide where we work. They just told me that I had to work for WestCorp."

"That's all they told me too. But maybe, if we ask, they can set it up. Even if we aren't good at the same stuff now, they could edit us to be good fits for the same position, right?"

Shada had never considered whether there was any specialization implied with the edits. She assumed the edits were the same for everyone and allowed everyone to succeed wherever they were assigned. Did the edited still have people who were better at math, or art, the way unedited humans did? The difference in quality of artwork in the corridor led Shada to believe such differences existed, but she wasn't sure if the differences survived into adulthood. Maybe edited children all grew up into a shared skill set, but recipients of post-birth edits wouldn't reach the same position since they weren't trained in the same fashion..

"It'd be nice to have a familiar face to work with. Not sure if

I want to see you for twenty years though!" Shada said with a laugh.

Chloe laughed too. "If we're edited to be happy then it won't matter. The time will fly by!"

Out of the corner of her eye, Shada saw the smile evaporate from Chloe's face, as if she didn't have the strength or desire to sustain the expression.

The tram descended onto the island, and both women stared out the window as the greenery flew by. After growing up in the city, a mass of steel and concrete, the onslaught of green was enough to kill their conversation until they arrived beneath the atrium.

"Let's get this over with," Chloe said as the doors opened.

CHAPTER EIGHT

Two MASSIVE GUARDS at the foot of the stairs—where one had sat yesterday—patted down each visitor before they were allowed to ascend into the atrium. Chloe, after passing through security first, waited for Shada before they walked up the stairs together. They arrived in the atrium and both stared at the sea of edited humans passing by in every direction as their fellow passengers came up the stairs, walked past them, and joined the chaos.

Shada grabbed Chloe's arm and began to lead her to the information desk she had been shown to the day before. She expected to see the same young woman, but this time a young man sat in her place.

"Shada Gray and Chloe Rose," a female voice yelled from behind them.

Shada released Chloe, they both turned around, and Shada watched a young woman with dark red hair walk towards them with a clipboard in hand and scowl on her face. "I see you found each other," the WestCorp employee said.

"We did," Chloe said.

Shada wondered if WestCorp had somehow made sure they

met each other, but she couldn't see how it would have been done. Odds were it was dumb luck that drew them to each other —that, or a sort of unedited magnetism unknown to either of them. And what if they had come up the stairs and walked in different directions? Would this woman have had to wrangle them out of the crowd before they ended up somewhere they weren't supposed to be?

"My name is Piper Lawson. Please follow me."

For some reason Shada expected to follow the woman to Alfie's office, or to the lab, but instead they boarded a bus on the opposite side of the atrium. The clouds overhead blocked the sunlight from beaming down on them, but it was still hot enough for beads of sweat to gather on both Shada's and Chloe's foreheads. Piper didn't seem to be affected by the heat.

Nobody made any attempts at small talk, and after a five-minute bus ride they pulled up next to a warehouse. The bus stop was shaded by palm trees, and thin strips of grass lined the front of the building. They were led inside and met by a sea of stainless steel examining tables with fresh white pillows on each.

"What are all these tables for?" Chloe asked.

"Post-birth edits," Piper said from ahead of them. She couldn't have been more dismissive.

Chloe and Shada looked at each other. It was just the two of them, as far as either of them could tell, and they didn't see why so many tables would ever be needed.

Piper must have sensed their confusion because she sighed before elaborating. "We schedule post-birth edits to occur on the same day and knock them out all at once. You two were chosen to participate in a separate procedure."

"Nobody said anything about a separate procedure," Chloe said, crossing her arms.

"You'll find out more in a moment. If you decide this procedure isn't right for you, we will have you come back when the rest of the post-birth edits occur, next Monday. Of course, you'll be compensated for your time today."

"Next Monday? I don't want to waste any more time. I've waited almost a month for this already!" Chloe said.

Shada was surprised to hear how long it had taken Chloe; it had only been a day since she first decided to investigate edits. She knew she was lucky the process took so little time, so she didn't bring up her own objections even though she wanted to get back in the league as soon as possible.

"If you've waited a month, then what's a few days more?" Piper asked as they reached their destination, a room with glass windows at the end of the warehouse. "Please take a seat inside," Piper said before Chloe had a chance to say another word.

There were two tables surrounded by six chairs each and a projector screen on one wall. The rest of the room was bare. Piper pulled out her phone, larger than most, and tapped it a few times before the projector came to life. She shut the blinds before taking her seat. "Before we continue, I must urge your discretion. But even if you were to tell someone, they wouldn't believe you."

"What choice do we have?" Shada said.

"There's always a choice," Piper countered.

"Play the damn thing," Chloe said.

Shada nodded.

Piper pressed play on a series of videos. The footage was raw and looked as if it had been shot during experiments in a facility similar to the one they were in. First, they watched as test subjects learned to control virtual avatars with their minds. Then, test subjects' consciousnesses were shown to be uploaded into lizards, rats, small dogs, then monkeys. Each time, a series of tests was conducted that showed the animals answering a series of questions about math and pop culture by walking onto circles with the correct answer.

Chloe and Shada were watching WestCorp's development of uploaded consciousness.

The last video showed the upload of a man in a white lab coat into a human. Instead of answering questions by stepping onto the correct answer, the human test subject demonstrated fine motor control by conducting a chemical experiment that proved the unconscious man in the white lab coat, in the background, was in control of the host through the wires attached to both skulls. When the upload was reversed, the man in the white lab coat sat up. "It worked," he said through bloodshot eyes.

Shada recognized Alfie, ten years younger, and the reason why she was in the room with Chloe solidified. "They want to control our bodies?" she asked.

"The last footage was simple control of the body, yes. Its original design was for experts to enter dangerous environments without placing themselves in harm's way. Think astronauts entering space with years of specialized training without their physical bodies being put in jeopardy."

"You created people to be sacrificed," Chloe said, her mouth open.

"Don't you see the benefits? With a simple connection it was possible to gain control of limbs much more precisely than any robot could. Paralyzed humans could walk again. Though there was a surprise once the connection no longer had to be hardwired."

"What was the surprise?" Shada asked.

"The uploaded consciousness was able to feel whatever the human host felt. Fear, anxiety, love . . . it led to some less-than-desirable results."

"Like what?" Chloe asked.

"An expert miner felt what it was like to die when his host got caught in a collapse. It drove him crazy."

"Good," Shada said. She wasn't comfortable with what she was being shown and felt like whoever uploaded their mind deserved what they had coming to them.

"We realized the applications we envisioned had to be revisited." The slideshow had ended, and the projector now clicked into standby mode.

"And this is where we come in," said Chloe.

Piper ignored her. "Since emotions could be felt, and the edited humans no longer had the coping mechanisms to deal with the emotions, there couldn't be any situations that would generate a negative response."

"So only good feelings," Chloe said.

Piper glared at Chloe. "In a way. This is still under development, but right now we allow senior WestCorp officials to pay willing participants in order to explore what emotions feel like, since theirs have been edited to be stable at all times."

Shada remembered the screen on the tram had an option for donations and wondered if this was what was meant.

"There are other applications being explored, but this is why you have been brought here apart from the others: to find out if you'd be willing to be paid in order to allow edited humans access to your emotions for one to two hours."

Shada didn't know how she felt about letting her body be used this way, but Chloe sat up and said that as long as the price was right, they could do whatever they wanted.

"What's stopping them from taking over permanently?" Shada whispered, more to herself than to anyone else, but the other two women fell silent.

"We work with a group of unedited humans who register the time you will be taken over and ensure your return."

"How would they know we weren't hijacked permanently?" Chloe said.

Piper winced at the word hijacked but answered the question. "There's an interview, and a series of questions, that only you would know the answers to. As long as you deem the safety check satisfactory, we could upload a consciousness by the end of the week."

"So . . . we agree, get placed on a list, and wait until someone chooses to take us for a spin?" Chloe said.

"No, you've already been chosen. You just have to agree," Piper said.

CHAPTER NINE

SHADA AND CHLOE traveled from the island to the financial district of the city to meet with officials in the Office of Unedited Rights before they gave Piper their final answer. Because of Sikya, Shada knew Miles Tensen had worked here before he made a run for mayor, and she wondered if he'd come back to the same job after he lost the election.

Chloe, Shada knew from their discussion on the trip back to the city, was leaning towards allowing someone to hijack her body. She planned to set aside the money for her retirement, when she no longer had to work and could live outside the city on a farm, away from everyone. When Shada asked why she would want to retire when she would, in theory, be happy working at WestCorp, Chloe replied that she hoped to make enough money to buy the house before she was edited. It would cement her plan for after the twenty years were up, regardless of how she felt at the time.

Shada was surprised Chloe had given her pre-edit decisions so much weight. She herself leaned towards allowing the hijacking as well, but for different reasons. She told Chloe the opportunity was a way to pay back the money she owed her sister, and if possible, pay off both their student debt. What she didn't mention was that if she could go into the league back at financial zero, she would be able to enjoy playing the sport she loved without worrying about money.

The light brown stone of the building Piper had directed them to visit loomed over them, and honking cars sat in its shadow, the evening traffic making movement tedious. Brown marble floors and chandeliers greeted Shada when she passed through the revolving doors. The security guards were dressed in white and wore white-rimmed glasses. Chloe and Shada got into the elevator and rode it to the seventeenth floor. The Office of Unedited Rights was on a corner of the building and had floor-to-ceiling windows overlooking the city. A young Asian man wearing a blue suit and white-rimmed glasses, the same style as the guards below, sat at the reception desk and greeted them when they walked inside.

"How can I help you today?" he asked with a confident smile.

Shada wasn't sure how much information to divulge but didn't have to worry, because Chloe answered for both of them. "WestCorp sent us over before we get hijacked," she said.

A cloud passed over the man's face and blocked the shine of his smile before he regained his composure. Shada couldn't decide if the darkness was pity or the look of a man betrayed. "Of course, we were told to expect you. Please take a seat. Mr. Tensen will see you in a moment."

After they were both seated, Shada whispered to Chloe that Tensen had lost the mayoral election a few days ago and that her sister had worked on his campaign.

"Does she work here?" Chloe said, looking around the office.

"No, she worked for him outside, at election headquarters. Maybe now that the campaign is over she will try and get a job in here, but I haven't talked to her about it and don't know for sure."

"She should try. You see how nice this building is? I bet they make good money here." She used her chin to point to the various desks in the offices visible from where they sat.

"I'm sure they do. I'll suggest it." Shada didn't have any intention of telling Sikya about WestCorp's offer to hijack her body, knowing her sister wouldn't approve. She wondered how she would explain her reason for meeting with Tensen without divulging more than her sister needed to know. Plus, if her sister ever worked here, would she have access to Shada's file? This wasn't something Shada wanted Sikya to find out without her around to explain.

The secretary told "Ms. Gray" that Mr. Tensen was ready to see her.

"Good luck," Chloe said as she leaned back in her chair, laid her head against the wall, and closed her eyes.

Mr. Tensen stood behind his desk when Shada entered the room. After introductions, Shada told him her sister worked on his campaign.

"I can see the resemblance," Tensen said as he took a seat. He was handsome, his black hair parted on the side, and his square jaw emanated a strength tempered by his kind eyes. If Shada had seen Sikya on the street next to this man, she would assume her sister would want to have his child. Even now, knowing their relationship was professional and never having heard Sikya say anything to make her think otherwise, she wondered if Sikya didn't harbor romantic feelings.

"Let me tell you how this is going to work," Tensen began. "We need to come up with a standard confirmation of identity screen. It's mostly stuff from your childhood, things nobody could quantify and search for. After we go through the questions—there are about fifty total—I can answer any questions you may have."

The questions ranged from first crushes to childhood injuries to favorite foods and vacations. Tensen encouraged Shada to elaborate on each, to tell stories about all of them, so that there would be more data to analyze in the event confirmation was required.

As soon as Tensen was finished, Shada began asking the questions she had saved up. "First, how would anyone know to put this test to use? If whoever hijacks my body takes over, couldn't they just pretend to be me and take over my life?"

Tensen nodded. "Good question. Before you undergo the procedure, you let us know the exact times you will be unreachable."

Shada appreciated the euphemism.

"Once the predetermined time is over, we administer a quick confirmation via telephone. We've never had to administer the full confirmation, but to prevent a permanent takeover, we ask that you call in three days later for a second confirmation. Now, if for some reason you are unreachable and we don't find out because whoever has control passes these two tests, we have one final fail-safe. One week after the procedure ends, we call a person of your choosing, someone who knows you well, and tell them we are your therapist checking in on you. We ask if they have noticed anything strange in your behavior or if you have acted differently. If, for whatever reason, they say yes, we administer the full confirmation."

Shada nodded, knowing Sikya would be the person they would contact and grateful they had a cover story already set up. She knew Sikya would appreciate the fact she had a therapist and wouldn't ask too many questions. "And if the confirmation test fails? What then?"

"The authorities will become involved. By law, WestCorp is

required to allow them access to their files. Between you and me, WestCorp doesn't want anyone snooping around their files, so they have no reason to violate the terms."

"The authorities? Which authorities can control WestCorp?"

"They use the procedure as well. Have you ever heard of someone receiving multiple life sentences? Well, those years are accrued by implanting their consciousness into members of death row. Nobody, or should I say no body, has been put to death for a number of years now. Whoever receives a death sentence becomes a vessel for another consciousness who is forced to serve their sentence."

Shada shuddered. "What happens to the consciousness of the vessel?"

"The consciousness of the inmate sentenced to death is forced into the background."

"They're trapped?"

"In a sense. Life imprisonment is less than the death penalty, so in a way, they are having their sentence reduced."

"Or made worse, since their mind is now imprisoned as well."

"I guess it depends on how you look at it."

Shada nodded, not sure of how she herself looked at it.

"Now, who should we contact a week after your procedure?"

Shada told Tensen to contact Sikya and gave him her contact information. Tensen nodded as if he already knew this information but was being issued a reminder.

"OK, you're all set!" Tensen said, leaning back in his chair.

Shada looked at the clock on his wall. Their discussion had lasted a little over half an hour.

"Do you have any other questions?" Tensen said.

Shada looked up and took a breath. "I don't think so . . ."

"Well, if you think of anything, just give our office a call." Tensen stood up and shook hands with Shada. "It was nice to meet you after working with your sister during the campaign," he said.

"Nice meeting you too. I was sorry to hear you lost."

"Me too," he said, his eyes lowering. After a moment he looked up. "Could you please tell Ms. Rose to come in?"

CHAPTER TEN

BOTH CHLOE AND SHADA, convinced Tensen's protection against permanent takeover would take care of them in a worst-case scenario, traveled to the island of the edited the next afternoon. Piper asked them to sit together under the glass ceiling of the atrium and provided them both with credits that could be used at any of the scattered restaurants before she walked away, telling them she would be back. Instead of a typical lunch, Shada bought herself a fruit platter and a smoothie; Chloe got a muffin and a coffee.

"Do you think it will hurt?" Chloe asked Shada with food still in her mouth. A few crumbs fell onto her shirt.

"The procedure? Not sure. I'm curious where I'm supposed to go when I'm no longer in control . . . think it's like falling asleep?" Shada asked. She plopped a piece of melon into her mouth, cut larger than she'd prefer but too small to be taken in two bites.

"Maybe it's like sleepwalking, since whoever is in control will want to walk around and experience stuff."

Shada nodded, unsure if Chloe was as nervous as she was. She stared at the faces of the people walking by and tried to determine if any of them were the ones interested in hijacking her body.

"I wonder how they're going to deal with my anxiety," Chloe said into the silence that had fallen between them.

"What do you mean?"

"I've had anxiety my entire life. I'm used to dealing with it, but an edited person . . . I can't imagine they've ever felt anything like it."

"Piper said the experiences are made to be positive. Puppies and rainbows. No room for anxiety."

Chloe shook her head. "So you've never had anxiety," she said with a chuckle. She took a long drink of her coffee.

"Doesn't it burn your tongue?" Shada asked.

"I always drink it hot," Chloe responded. Her eyes were pulled to something behind Shada.

Shada turned around and saw Piper approach their table, back from wherever she had gone.

"Come with me," Piper said.

Piper led them in the direction of the lab, but instead of walking down the long corridor, she went through a door on the corridor's left and led them to a waiting bus. The bus took them in a straight line to what Shada knew was the end of the corridor, they got off, and Piper swiped her identification card to get into the lab.

"Do these procedures ever become sexual?" Chloe said to Piper's back.

"Sexual? Not with you," Piper sneered without turning around. "Edited humans only have sex with other edited humans. We have no desire to get caught up with the unedited's never-ending drive to procreate. It's part of what keeps us happier than the unedited."

"Sex with your neighbors makes you happier?" Chloe asked.

She looked at Shada with one eyebrow raised, asking wordlessly if the woman ahead of them was crazy.

"The lack of a bio-clock means we only need to replace ourselves. One boy and one girl. Each parent is responsible for raising the opposite gender in order to maintain the gender neutrality on the island."

Shada mentioned that she hadn't seen any children. "Other than their artwork," she said.

"They're on a different part of the island, with the older members of WestCorp. When we are younger we stay focused on our work, and it's only when our physical stamina decreases that we are responsible for raising offspring. The two who want to upload into your bodies no longer have children to raise and are interested in more abstract matters now that they have so much time available to them in their twilight years."

Piper led them into a side hallway, and Chloe was told to wait in one room while Shada was led into the one adjacent.

The room was small, cold, and had just enough room for two stainless steel tables and a collection of wires connected to a monitor between them.

"Take a seat on this one," Piper said, tapping the table farthest away from the door. "Alfie will be in here in a minute," she said before she walked out.

Shada sat down, and a few minutes later Alfie walked in.

"Good morning," he said. He set a manila folder on the second table and began flipping through sheets of loose paper. His gray hair was combed flat, and his white lab coat had been pressed; straight lines ran down each side. The top of his blue button-down, the top button unbuttoned, showed above the lab coat, and a pair of dark brown wing tips sat beneath khaki pants with a slight break.

"Mornin'," Shada said.

"You need to sign a few documents."

Alfie handed Shada a packet of paper. "This one says you spoke with the Office of Unedited Rights."

Shada hopped off the table and used its surface to initial the bottom of each page and sign the last. She was handed another.

"And this one says you are aware of the procedure you are about to undergo."

Again Shada signed, then Alfie took the packet back and replaced it with a third.

"Last one; this one says you agree to a two-hour time limit."

Shada signed then handed the pages back to Alfie. "Do I get to meet the person who wants to take over my body?" she asked.

"Under normal circumstances, no, we keep the uploader anonymous. But this person has informed me the two of you have already met." Alfie double-checked the paperwork and closed the manila folder. "He asked to meet you before the upload. Of course, when he asks, he really means he wants it done."

"I've already met him?" Shada asked.

"You have. He's the head of WestCorp."

Shada felt her stomach drop, as if the ground had been pulled away and she was in freefall.

"The head of WestCorp wants to take my body for a ride? When would I have met him?" Shada said, her voice trailing off.

The door opened, and the old man who'd found Shada walking around the lab on her first visit walked in. Alfie introduced him. "Shada, this is Michael Hollis."

The hunched man with the white beard wore a black T-shirt tucked into black sweatpants. No lab coat this time. "Hello, Shada," he said with a wrinkled smile.

They shook hands. "It's nice to officially meet you," he said.

Shada stared at his face for a moment before she remembered her manners. "Likewise," she said. She made sure not to smile.

"I hope this request wasn't too much," Hollis said.

"Is this your first time being uploaded?" Shada asked.

Alfie and Hollis shared a laugh. "No, we've done this before."

"But never anyone with your athletic pedigree. I'm hoping to feel what it's like to run again, to jump again, to move again." Hollis looked down at his age-spotted hands. "This body has been breaking down for years," he said with disgust. "I started WestCorp when I was young and ignored my body. Now I'm in a position where I can pay for a visit to what could have been if I had been born to different parents."

Shada was surprised to hear that both she and Hollis, opposites in almost every measurable aspect, wondered what life was like on the other side.

Alfie removed his folder from the table and instructed Hollis to lie down. He placed a modified helmet covered with strings of lights over the old man's head before he turned to Shada and motioned for her to lie down as well.

"Does Chloe have to wait until we are through before she gets hijacked?" Shada asked.

"A member of my research team should be over there right now getting her set up. There's a screen between the tables in her room, so she won't find out who takes control."

Shada noticed a thin door in the wall opposite the monitor apparatus where the screen must be kept.

"Hollis is the only person I upload myself," Alfie said. He secured the modified helmet on her head. "You'll feel a tingling sensation before Hollis takes over. Some people report being able to sense the switch through darkness, and some say it feels like they were asleep the whole time. Your body, with Hollis in control, will go through a series of exercises handpicked by Hollis."

"Will Chloe be there too?"

"No, the only person you—or should I say, your body—will come into contact with is me. She will be led to a different area of the compound for a standard visit."

"Filled with puppies and rainbows?"

Alfie laughed. "Something like that. Are you ready?"

"Ready as I'll ever be," both Hollis and Shada said at the same time.

CHAPTER ELEVEN

SHADA GOT the sense the world was a television show and her eyes were the screen. The signal was weak at first; her surroundings were blurred, and she wasn't able to distinguish anything other than the difference between light and dark. A swell of panic arose from somewhere not inside herself—because the connection to her body had been severed—but from the belief she should be panicked. Without the associated feelings, her mind became frantic. In an effort to distill her thoughts using language, she tried to label the situation and settled on "sleep paralysis," though she had never experienced it before. What else could she call the disconnection of her external experiences with her internal dialogue?

Disconnection. She remembered being connected to the machine through the helmet, then . . . nothing. Where did she go, and where was she now? She couldn't feel her body but tried to take ten breaths anyway with the hope of latching onto something, anything. She wasn't able to find air, but the act of counting to ten calmed her mind and allowed the world to come into greater focus.

Shada watched herself be led outside and into the sun by

Alfie. The brightness outside must have affected her body, or its user, because a hand was lifted over her eyes through no effort of her own. She knew someone else was in control but couldn't place the identity of who it might be. It felt like the name was on the tip of her tongue and she could discover the name if she could just regain control.

Her body turned and watched Alfie pick up a frisbee. Shada had never played with one before but knew their purpose. Alfie waited for Shada's body to back up before he tossed the toy. It flew through the air, a white disk against a blue backdrop, before a hand appeared from Shada's periphery and snagged it from the air.

"She's got good reflexes," Shada heard herself say. Up until this point, she hadn't heard anything at all.

"Lifelong athlete," Alfie shouted back.

Shada's body threw the frisbee back to Alfie. The two of them tossed the toy back and forth while Shada groped for a sensation, any sensation, to ground herself with. It was like she was floating in space after being cut from a spaceship, with no gravity to pull her down. Except instead of her body it was her thoughts that had become untethered.

Another count to ten without registering the sensation of breath and she remembered who had control of her body. Hollis, the old man. She assumed he was still back on the table in the small room, unconscious, his body kept alive for no real reason since his mind had abandoned it.

Shada witnessed her attention turn towards a large tire on the grass by the wall of the warehouse. She watched the tire get closer and witnessed herself flip it over. Three flips later and Hollis must have decided he'd had enough, because Shada's body sprinted away through the grass. When he turned her body around and looked at Alfie, the lead scientist smiled as if mirroring Shada's expression.

"Let's see how high she can jump," Shada heard herself say.

Shada's arm reached up high against the wall. Alfie, who had jogged up to come up alongside her, said he would keep an eye on where she reached. Her body jumped and touched as high as possible, but Shada thought she could get higher if she was in control.

"Six bricks," Alfie said.

"See how high you can touch," Hollis-in-Shada commanded Alfie.

Alfie lined himself up against the wall, measured his reach, then jumped, and was able to touch three bricks higher than the one he'd first touched.

"This woman's got some springs," Shada's voice rang out.

After a few more exercises, including an attempt at a handstand, which almost broke Shada's neck but for which she felt nothing, Hollis said he wanted to go to the animal testing building.

"Sir, that's going to be a problem."

Shada saw the world sideways as her head tilted. "Why?"

"Unedited humans get distressed when they see animals, particularly dogs, being tested on. Since you're edited, you don't have the ability to cope with the negative emotions that might arise. Also, the trip there and back would put us too close to the two-hour limit."

"Damnit, Alfie, you're wasting our time by talking so much! Take me there, I can pay her more if we run over. I'm sure she won't mind the extra money."

Alfie shook his head and waved for a small private vehicle to pick them up, unseen by Shada until Hollis turned her head to watch its approach.

Shada was disgusted as her body walked between cages of dogs stacked three high and arranged into long aisles. Some dogs had limbs too small for their bodies, some too large, and some had fur in various stages of mange. She had no awareness of the typical feelings associated with disgust, just the sense she would be disgusted if she was in control of herself.

"What do you feel?" Alfie asked.

"Shortness of breath, tension in the abdominal cavity, a desire to help . . . is this what unedited humans deal with every day?" Shada's voice answered.

"Not every day, just when certain conditions are met."

"I can't control my breath," Hollis-in-Shada said. Shada believed she heard a trace of panic in her voice but couldn't be sure. The dogs stared at Shada with sad eyes, as if they could sense someone was among them who could recognize their plight.

"Her breaths are shallow and fast. Try and slow them down, take big breaths. Closing your eyes might help."

Shada lost her view of the world but could hear herself taking big gulps of air. She focused on the sound and was able to feel herself take a breath, the first sensation she'd felt since control of her body was taken from her. She latched on to the action with long tendrils of awareness but wasn't able to exert any control. A dog barked, and Hollis opened her eyes, ending the spell.

"Let's get out of here," Hollis said in Shada's voice.

"We never should have come."

They rushed back outside and Hollis, in Shada's body, grabbed hold of a tree and pressed his cheek against its bark. He closed her eyes and took a series of breaths unreachable by Shada while she, trapped inside her own body, waited for the edited man to come to terms with the way sadness felt.

"Let's go," Alfie said.

Hollis opened Shada's eyes and she saw Alfie next to her, one arm around her shoulder. Alfie led Hollis-in-Shada to the private vehicle and back to the room where the upload took place.

"Just in time," Alfie said, looking at his watch.

"See, it all worked out," Hollis-in-Shada said without much conviction.

When Shada woke up, aware of her body once more, she took ten grateful breaths through her nose before she opened her eyes. She sat up and looked at the empty table next to her. Alfie was writing on a paper inside the manila folder.

"Where's Hollis?"

"He had urgent business to attend to." Alfie shut the folder and turned to Shada. "How do you feel?"

Part of her wanted to bring up the animal testing she'd witnessed, but the effect it might have on her future payday held her tongue. "Hungry," she said.

Alfie pulled a bag of gummies from his pocket. "Eat these; your body did a lot of exercise, and the sugar will help take the edge off."

Shada ate the red ones and left the rest in the packet. Her phone rang, her identity was confirmed, and after Chloe, who said she'd felt like she was asleep the entire time, met them in the hall outside their respective rooms, Alfie led them both back to the atrium. He was able to inform them their payment would be in their accounts by the time they got back to the city before Piper showed up, whispered something into his ear, and they both rushed away.

CHAPTER TWELVE

When Shada gave her sister the money she owed, and the money for the next few months' rent, Sikya asked how the money had already arrived. They were together in their apartment—the apartment Sikya had paid for over the last few months—Shada on the couch and Sikya leaning against the doorframe of their room.

"You didn't tell me you signed the contract!" Sikya said, excited.

"The money isn't from the team, it's from WestCorp," Shada said. Any apprehension about her sister's attitude toward the procedure had evaporated the second Shada got home and realized how tired she was. Both she and Chloe had stared straight ahead for the entirety of the trip back to the city from the island, and when they parted ways, neither of them bothered to say goodbye to the other. They weren't able to address the exhaustion of the other in case language magnified the feeling in themselves.

Sikya, to Shada's surprise, responded with confusion. "WestCorp paid you? Aren't they the ones who are supposed to get paid? That's why you have to work for them after your playing career."

Shada explained how she had been offered enough money to pay Sikya back and take a sizable chunk from her loans in order let someone take control of her body for two hours.

"You did what?" Sikya screamed at Shada, her eyes wide open.

"Allowed them to control my body," Shada said, her patience wearing thin. "There were two tables, I had to put on a weird helmet, and then someone's mind was uploaded into my body."

Sikya paced the length of the living room. "I can't believe you let yourself be used like that," she said, upset. Sadness, rather than anger, emanated from her frown.

"It wasn't terrible. And the money's good so I don't regret it."

"What was it like?"

Shada didn't want to go into specifics about the experience of watching the world through her own eyes without the associated sensations, so she used Chloe's experience to describe the procedure to her sister. "I fell asleep, and two hours later I woke up. I never saw the person who took over, there was a screen between our tables, and they were gone when I woke up."

"What if some pervert wanted to take control of your body? They could have used you for their sick fetish!"

"It's not like that. The people who pay to be uploaded want to feel what it's like to be unedited. My body was taken through a series of experiences designed to generate positive feelings," Shada said. She thought she sounded like one of the informative videos WestCorp made. "Edited humans don't have the coping mechanisms in place to deal with negative emotions, so it's all puppies and rainbows."

"Sex can be a positive feeling."

"It can be, yes, but that's not the point."

"How do you know?"

Shada told her sister about Piper's explanation of the edited's attitude towards sex and reproduction, including the way Piper looked down on the unedited.

"What if this is their last chance to get their freak on after a lifetime of only having sex with edited people? I don't like this at all. There are other ways to make money!"

"This much this quick? I don't see how. Trust me, they want nothing to do with me sexually."

"Was this a onetime thing?" Sikya said, a flash of protective anger passing over her face.

Shada winced at the thought of going through the experience again. "Nobody mentioned a next time, but if it was offered, I don't see why not. We can use the money."

Sikya shook her head, angry and defeated. She sat down on the couch next to Shada. "This has been one hell of a day," she said, exasperated.

"What happened with you?" Shada asked.

"Tensen told me he can't get me a job at the office he works at. He's offered to keep me as part of his campaign team for the next election, but he won't be able to pay me anywhere close to what I was making."

Shada decided it wasn't the right time to tell her sister about her visit to the Office of Unedited Rights to meet with Tensen. "Then I should try and undergo the procedure again! And if there's this much money involved, I could pay for you to get edited without taking on more debt."

If Shada had slapped Sikya across the face, her sister couldn't have been caught more off guard. "I will never get edited," she snarled.

"You say it like it's the worst thing in the world. Don't you want to have an edited child?"

"About that . . . I'm not sure I can even have a child. I put in an application for a birth license and found out today it's been denied."

"You put one in by yourself? No wonder you were denied. If every person who wanted a kid just went out and had one, there would be no way the city could sustain itself."

"I was making good money and decided to see if they would allow it." Sikya leaned her head back on the couch's top cushion and closed her eyes.

"Without someone else, the financials don't work out. How about you put me down as a co-parent once I sign the contract with the league? There should be enough income between the two of us to afford it."

"Same-sex couples aren't a problem, but I don't know if they would let siblings raise a child."

"Well, once money starts coming in, we could try. Plus, I could afford to edit the child. The WestCorp bump should be good enough to get you a license."

Sikya paused. "I don't want to edit them anymore," she pronounced.

Shada turned to look at her sister and saw Sikya stare at her down the length of her nose. Sikya sat up, and they looked at each other face-to-face.

"Why don't you want them edited?" Shada said, scared of her sister's response but needing to hear it nonetheless.

"You haven't even been edited yet and you've already let them do things I never would have thought you'd allow. Maybe it's better to keep them natural and let them live unburdened."

Shada couldn't help but feel attacked. The edits, and the procedure, were all so she could afford to pay back, then help, her sister. "Do you think I made the wrong decision?" Shada said, her head tilted to the side. Sparks of rage searched for fuel in her stomach.

"I think you've made a deal with the devil."

"Any deals I've made have been for us." The devil threw down tinder.

"I never asked you to do this."

"You didn't ask . . . You made me! Remember? You said I had to make money, and now that I am, now that I can help you get what you wanted, it isn't good enough." Small flames found kindling.

Sikya got up from the couch. "WestCorp is turning you into someone I don't even recognize anymore."

"WestCorp is helping me achieve my dreams! Why won't you let me help you do the same?" The fire burning inside Shada incinerated her exhaustion.

"Because my dream is to have a child and raise them in a world without WestCorp in it," Sikya said, her head bowed.

Shada stood up and her stomach rumbled, the fire ravenous for more fuel. She grabbed her backpack and headed for the door.

"Where are you going?" Sikya cried out.

Shada's plan was to get food, but the devil inside wanted her sister to worry. "Out," she said as she walked through the door, slamming it shut behind her.

CHAPTER THIRTEEN

"COME OVER TO MY PLACE," Chloe responded when Shada finished telling her over the phone about the fight she'd had with Sikya.

"Are you sure? I don't want to impose," Shada said. She hadn't heard Chloe talk about anyone in her life and sensed the woman valued her privacy.

"Positive! Stay here this weekend and we can go to the island on Monday."

Shada put forth a few more weak arguments to ensure she had done everything she could to provide Chloe a way out of the situation in case her friend was just being polite before she agreed, and Chloe gave her the address. "See you soon!" Shada said. According to her phone, the trip would take thirty minutes and require her to take a train to a neglected part of the city.

The closest train station to Chloe's home was on an elevated platform covered in graffiti. Shada could tell the different tags were words but couldn't make out what they said, their letters stylized beyond recognition. She didn't linger in case someone saw her and assumed she had an alliance with a rival. The turnstile at the bottom of the stationary escalator swung loose on its base. No employees were around to double-check if she had scanned her way through even though someone should have been, since the night was young and darkness had just descended. A cluster of tents were pitched below the platform, and dirty children ran around the bodies of passed-out parents beneath flickering streetlights.

Shada was catcalled multiple times on the walk from the station to Chloe's building. She was thankful for her size, knowing she could fight off an attacker if necessary. She gave the groups she passed a wide berth; they sat on the stairs of buildings and stood in the doorways of closed stores she wasn't sure would be open even in the brightness of day. Each time, their dull eyes paid her no attention as she passed, so she allowed herself to exhale but still listened for rapid footsteps behind her. She had a heightened state of awareness on her entire walk, a cycle of contract-relax every time she passed anyone or heard a voice call out to her.

Chloe's building had once required visitors to use the call box to enter, but Shada found a broken doorframe that kept the door open a few inches even when closed. She walked inside and up to her friend's apartment on the second floor. A green turf welcome mat sat in front. She knocked, saw the shadow of someone through the crack at the bottom of the door, then heard the door unlock and a chain slide off.

"Come in," Chloe said after she opened the door. She stepped back and allowed Shada to enter before closing the door and locking both locks.

Shada walked into a studio apartment full of plants. None of the plants had flowers, just green leaves of various size and shape. Shelves held smaller pots, and larger plants were arranged on the floor. The air inside made Shada realize the poor quality of the air she was used to breathing in the city. This air was crisp, cool, and a little damp, like the earth in which the plants grew. There was one bed, a couch, and, to Shada's surprise, no television.

"Make yourself at home," Chloe said.

"This is amazing," Shada said in awe while inspecting a shelf laden with pots. "How long did it take to collect all these?"

Chloe looked up at the ceiling, calculating. "A few years. The hardest part is finding them—there aren't exactly a bunch of plant stores in the city."

"I've never seen one, now that you mention it."

Chloe launched herself onto her bed and propped herself up on an elbow. "That hijack wore me out! I was asleep when you called."

Shada sat down on the couch and set her backpack on the floor next to her. "Sorry about that. I was exhausted when I got home too, but Sikya wouldn't let me rest." Shada again told Chloe how her sister disagreed with the way their money was made.

"She'll come around," Chloe said. With a twinkle in her eye she asked, "Would you do it again?"

"The hijack? Maybe, if someone wanted to pay."

"I was talking to the scientist who did my upload, and she said there are always people wanting to upload. There's a long wait list of people but not enough unedited who know about it."

Shada sat up, leaned forward, and set her elbows on her knees. "We're supposed to be edited this week."

"But what if we ask to get pushed back to the next group? We could get some cash, you for your loans and me for my farm. If we're going to work for the rest of our lives, what's the rush?"

Shada had a reason to rush: the sooner she got back into the league, the sooner her ban would begin. But, Shada thought, a major reason why she wanted into the league was to make enough money to pay off her debt and help her sister. She could do them both without having to wait until she was edited.

"It's not a bad idea. What do we have to do to make it happen?"

"The scientist told me to talk to Piper. I'd rather not, she rubs me the wrong way, but she's the facilitator."

"She does have a way of getting under the skin. Why wouldn't she mention it to us when we were first approached?"

"Maybe she figured we really want to be edited. The lady also said if someone is hijacked too many times, identity loss is possible. But I feel fine, and if we are losing ourselves when we get edited anyway, why not?"

Shada could tell Chloe's mind was already made up, that she'd be hijacked again. Shada still wasn't sure. Just then, a female voice came through a small speaker on Chloe's desk the size of a coaster. A series of numbers followed by a report of suspects getting away on foot towards dock number nine.

Chloe perked up and turned the dial on the small speaker. This time, a male voice could be heard. "Those assholes robbed a liquor store and are running to the abandoned warehouse!"

Chloe smiled and hopped off the bed. "Ready to have some fun?" she asked Shada. Without waiting for Shada's response, she said, "Let's go!"

Shada followed Chloe down the stairs and, once outside her building, away from the train station. The area got more civilized the farther they got from the station, with fewer homeless people and more light. Convenience stores were still open, and there was a bar within a few blocks that Chloe said she went to every so often.

Chloe turned right and ran towards the bay. Shada was surprised at how well Chloe maintained her pace as cop cars screamed by. They arrived at dock nine to find it blocked off by a semicircle of police cars. A series of warehouses stretched off into the distance.

"Can't go any farther, ladies," a cop said, holding up an outstretched hand.

Chloe backed up and beckoned for Shada to follow. Shada hadn't noticed Chloe grab the small speaker, but she pulled it—or another—from her pocket. The low volume required Chloe to hold the device up to her ear, and she told Shada what she heard.

"They followed two suspects and aren't sure which warehouse they're hiding in. Boats are at the far end of the dock, walling them in." Chloe was getting excited. "They are calling in the task force to search each warehouse." She put the speaker back into her pocket. "The search could take all night!"

"All night?" Shada groaned. "Didn't you say you were worn out too?"

"I was, but I can't miss this excitement! Some people go out on the weekends, I listen to the police scanners and try and see all the juiciest stuff in person. A few weeks ago there was a murder close to my house, and I was one of the first ones there!"

Chloe's excitement was infectious, and Shada got caught up in watching the spectacle unfold. Hours into the search, around four in the morning, multiple gunshots cracked out, and they witnessed one man get brought out on a stretcher and another in a body bag.

"That one guy is lucky, usually the task force doesn't let them live," Chloe said.

The next night, Saturday, after Chloe and Shada slept the day away and turned on the police scanner again, they found out that the robber who lived had shot his partner, turned himself in, and shot himself in the confusion.

CHAPTER FOURTEEN

SHADA CONVINCED Chloe to put the police scanner away early on Sunday night, and the two of them were able to get a full night's sleep before they went to the island Monday morning. The day's original plan was to receive their edits, but Chloe had already decided to speak to Piper about another hijack and assumed Shada would come with her.

Dozens of unedited humans were on the underground platform waiting to be taken to WestCorp. She could tell right away because on every one of her other trips, the platform was silent save for a few whispered conversations, none of which lasted long. In contrast, the platform on this day was filled with noisy and energetic unedited humans along with a mix of smells ranging from food to cologne. The normal commuters were present and recognizable by their stoicism, as if the unpleasantness was something to be tolerated once a month. The tram pulled up, ten cars long, and everyone filed inside and took a seat. Shada wondered why no screens descended from the ceiling. She decided it must have been because WestCorp knew why everyone was making today's trip, but they'd had no idea why she'd made her first trip.

The unedited all stared in awe at the massive security guards, who patted them down below the atrium before they were herded up the stairs by a WestCorp employee yelling from the top. He had on a short-sleeved white button-down, khaki pants, and black nonslip shoes.

"Everyone here for edits, this way please!" the young man said, gesturing behind him. With two orange wands in his hand he could have been an air traffic controller.

Shada and Chloe followed the crowd to the top of the stairs and saw a large part of the space in the atrium had been blocked off with velvet ropes. They waited for the last of the unedited passengers to pass before they asked to speak with Piper.

"She's very busy," the employee said without looking at them.

"It's about uploading consciousness into our bodies," Shada said.

The young man looked at the two of them, his eyes narrow with suspicion. "Are you from the papers?"

"No, we got the procedure last week. Can you just tell her we want to talk?" Chloe said.

The young man walked a short distance away, pulled a phone from his pocket, and talked to someone before returning to the two of them. "When I lead everyone away, just stay seated," he said.

Chloe and Shada took a seat behind the black velvet ropes with the rest of the unedited, and when everyone else was led away, they were left alone in a sea of tables and chairs. They stayed there for the next hour.

From what Shada could see, none of the edited humans paid them any attention. She was hungry and wondered if she had enough time to grab food when Piper appeared.

"Sorry, I had to give them the speech," Piper said.

"I thought you forgot about us!" Chloe said with a smile.

Shada could tell the expression on her friend's face was fake.

"Come to my office," Piper said.

They followed Piper through a series of corridors and ended up in a small office with two chairs, one on each side of a metal desk. There was no indication this was anyone's office, let alone someone who facilitated edits, and Shada thought she might have been assigned the space. Chloe took the seat across from Piper, and Shada leaned against the wall.

Piper got right to the point. "You were asking about another upload?" she said.

Chloe spoke first. "Are there other opportunities? I didn't mind the procedure."

"There are, but I must warn you: we have only uploaded multiple times in monkeys, never in humans."

"And what happened to the monkeys?" Shada asked.

"Up until the end, they were fine."

"The end?"

"Their last upload. Some were able to undergo the procedure over ten times, some over forty, before they lost the will to live."

The revelation was allowed to sink in before Chloe broke the silence. "But something like five times should be fine then, right?"

"It would be irresponsible of me to suggest a number, but more than five would never be allowed. Perhaps no more than three."

"How about you upload someone a couple more times and we see how we feel? The money was good, and if we're going to be edited in the end anyways, we want to make some money first," Chloe said, speaking for both herself and Shada.

"I'll make the arrangements. In the meantime, please feel free to stay on the island and make yourselves at home." Piper took Chloe and Shada to a waiting bus then led them to a dormitory. She made them each scan their thumbprint at the door and told them their finger would serve as their key. Chloe rushed into her room and hopped onto the bed. A loud thud rang out, followed by a groan. "There isn't a mattress," she said.

"I have a few questions," Shada said to Piper in the hallway while Chloe tensed in pain.

"I thought you might. You were quiet while your friend talked."

"I've been thinking a lot about employment after the edits. What's it like? Are you really happy all the time?"

Piper smiled. "It isn't so much happiness, it's just the absence of sadness." Her voice lowered. "I was unedited at birth and didn't receive edits until I was your age."

Shada was taken aback. She assumed Piper had been born edited; she didn't expect Piper to be similar to her. In the space of a blink, she wondered how many of the edited humans on the island had been born or made.

"The concept of working my entire life didn't seem satisfactory or desirable. But my parents used their house as collateral to pay for my education, and there was no way I would let them lose their home. Instead of suffering every day of my adult life, I decided to accept my fate. I had to agree to work here for years after, but with the money I make here, I am able to repay my debt and have paid off my parents' house, even though I feel no connection to them anymore."

"You didn't cut off the payments after you got edited?"

Chloe exclaimed how she could see the bay through her window.

"I made the necessary arrangements so the payments would continue to be withdrawn, regardless of the change in my DNA. I don't really have a choice."

Shada recalled Chloe's plan to buy her farm before the edits so her ultimate plan wouldn't change. She wondered about the process required to pay off Sikya's debt and provide for her future child and was grateful the edits wouldn't be undergone before the necessary arrangements were made.

"Most people work until they no longer have any usefulness to WestCorp. It's why there are so many people who want to be uploaded into an unedited body; they have nothing else to do while they wait to expire."

Shada nodded.

Chloe popped her head out of her room. "This is much nicer than my place, right, Shada?" she said.

"The view is, that's for sure," Shada replied.

Chloe walked into Shada's room and remarked how their rooms were mirror images of each other. "Your bathroom is on the left and mine's on the right," she said.

Piper asked if Shada was still on board with allowing an upload again.

Shada nodded, her plan of paying off both her and her sister's debt and providing a cushion for her sister to obtain a birth license before beginning her career solidifying in her mind.

"One more thing," Piper said as Chloe rejoined them in the hallway.

Shada's eyebrows raised higher as she waited for the woman to continue. Chloe looked confused, unaware of the conversation the other two were wrapping up. Piper pulled Shada into her room and shut the door on Chloe.

"Any future uploads you undergo will all be with Hollis. He doesn't like to share."

CHAPTER FIFTEEN

A KNOCK on the door woke Shada up. There were a few moments of frozen panic while she stared at the ceiling and tried to figure out where she was. She sat up, and the sterile room jogged her memory about her trip to the island the day before. Her phone had a notification for a missed call from Sikya. Shada snuck a finger into the thin ray of light that trickled in through the curtains and looked outside. The bay reflected the morning sun, and through squinted eyes she could make out small waves in the distance. The person outside knocked again, more impatient than before.

"Be right there," Shada called out.

She threw a T-shirt on and opened the door enough to look through the opening, bent sideways in order to hide her bare legs. Alfie smiled back at her and handed her a coffee.

"Time to get up," he said. "You're scheduled for upload in an hour."

"You guys don't waste any time," she said. Her jaw wasn't awake yet and words came out slurred. She accepted the black coffee and took a sip. It wasn't as strong as the kind she made herself, but the strength of this cup allowed for the smokiness of the roast to shine.

"Hollis enjoyed his experience last time and wanted to get going as soon as possible. I made him wait this long so you could get nine hours of sleep."

"Nine hours? I'm surprised I didn't jump out of bed," Shada said, shaking her head.

"It takes months to get used to the proper amount of sleep. Based on your vitals, I'd guess you sleep, what, six to seven hours a night?"

Shada thought about the two nights following the police scanner incident with Chloe. "If I'm lucky."

Alfie handed her a plastic card. "This will take care of your meals in the food court. Make sure you eat and are hydrated. Don't overdo it though, we don't want to have to find a bathroom on Hollis's time."

Shada nodded, wondering how she could be held responsible for the timing of her body's functions when she wouldn't even be in control of her body.

"Do you remember how to get to the reception hall?"

"The atrium?"

"Yes, can you get there on your own? All the transport vehicles going towards the center stop there. Even if you get on one going the wrong way, it will loop back around, you'll just have to wait."

"I can figure it out."

"Good, I'll see you there."

Remembering the activities Hollis had preferred on his last upload, Shada put on athletic clothes. She brushed her teeth right before she left. Chloe's door was still shut, and she wondered if her friend would be uploaded into that day as well. Maybe she'd already been woken up and was under someone's control right at that moment . . . If so, Shada didn't want to run into her, but she doubted WestCorp would let a chance encounter happen.

Shada got to the reception hall above the platform and decided to get another cup of coffee. The coffee wasn't the same quality as the cup Alfie had given her; this one was serviceable but nothing special. She got two hard-boiled eggs and a muffin for breakfast. Once she was finished, she surveyed the faces of the people crisscrossing the space while she listened to her body for signs of needing to go to the bathroom. She was in the middle of a roomful of people who all smiled at each other with their mouths but not their eyes, which made every one of them seem cold and detached.

She assumed the people who'd ridden the tram with her were all edited by now, and she was on the lookout for anyone she recognized from the day before. None of them seemed familiar. Maybe they needed time to adjust to their new DNA.

Shada spotted Alfie walking towards her from the direction of the lab. Instead of continuing towards her when their eyes met, he stopped short and waved her over. She drained the last of her coffee and threw her trash away on the walk over to him.

"Ready?" he said. This reminded her of a coach she'd had in high school who used to ask her the same thing before each game.

"As I'll ever be," Shada replied, the standard reply to her coach.

Alfie led her to the same room in which she had undergone the previous upload and instructed her to lie on the table. She sat down instead and watched Alfie turn on the equipment between the two tables. The monitor came to life, and Shada saw two pictures, one of Hollis and one of Piper, recognizable because of her dark red hair. Her physical metrics were listed beneath the photo.

"Piper?" Shada asked.

"She's been uploaded into before."

"By Hollis?"

"By Hollis. Please lie down," Alfie said.

"Isn't she edited? Why did Hollis want to upload into her?"

Alfie programmed the touch screen monitor while he talked. "You ask a lot of questions," he said with a chuckle. "Hollis was born edited and wanted to see what it felt like to upload into the body of a post-birth edited human before he took over an unedited. There was an upload into someone born edited before Piper too."

Shada lay down and folded her hands over her chest. "Why go through all the trouble?"

"We had to make sure his mind wouldn't crack. He's the head of WestCorp, remember?"

The weight of Hollis's position hit Shada, and she wondered why she had been the one chosen to host his mind, not once but twice. "And he was all right after uploading into my body?" she said. Shada felt ashamed of her unedited status and her associated emotions, which could have put the leader of WestCorp in danger of psychosis.

"Better than all right. He was rejuvenated! Right after he got out of your body, he tried to test how high he could jump and fell, almost broke his hip. There's a large bruise there now but it should be gone in a few days thanks to a new treatment still in development."

Shada apologized but didn't know why.

"Nothing to say sorry for, it wasn't your fault. If anything, it's mine. I'm the one who suggested he upload into your body. I thought he might want to feel what it was like to be an elite athlete. After we met, I suggested it to him when I went in to clear the plan we laid out to get you back into the league."

Shada felt a twinge of guilt for not getting into the league as soon as possible and allowing Hollis to upload again. It felt like she was playing with her future instead of playing the sport she loved.

The door opened while Alfie was adjusting the modified helmet on Shada's head, and Hollis walked in with a noticeable limp. "Good morning," he said, his mouth in the shape of a smile but his eyes unchanged.

"Morning, sir."

"Good morning," Shada muttered. She tried to nod, but the helmet kept her head in place.

Hollis lay on the table and put the helmet on his own head. "Shall we?"

Shada didn't have the chance to answer before her world went black.

CHAPTER SIXTEEN

SHADA THOUGHT she saw a faint circle of light far above, as if she was looking up from the bottom of a well. If she tried to focus on the light it would disappear, but by looking into the blackness ahead she could make out the outline of where the light existed. By switching her focus between the darkness and the spot where the light should be, Shada was able to bring the circle into focus. Once she could make out its edges, she concentrated on what was illuminated on the other side. The growing circle pushed the darkness away until it filled her entire field of vision. The brightness overwhelmed her, and she craved the darkness. It heard her desire and the edges of the circle of light constricted.

She reached for a breath in order to calm herself down. When she couldn't find the sensation, she instead counted to ten, some instinctual part of her knowing not to allow the darkness to return.

At the end of her count she saw the world through her own eyes, her body out of her control.

Alfie's arm poked in and out of her field of vision, relaxed as he walked. They were headed to a warehouse, walking through the sun past manicured gardens. Shada's head turned and watched Alfie's mouth move before her field of vision bobbed up and down. She knew her head had nodded in agreement to whatever Alfie said.

The doors ahead opened as they approached. Inside were rows of motionless humans laid out on stainless steel tables. Each human was attached to a blood transfusion machine, which Shada recognized from when her mother was on her deathbed.

Shada's head turned to look at Alfie's hand on her shoulder then looked at the head scientist's mouth. Shada heard herself say, "I'm sure," and a rush of noise flooded her awareness. The low hum of the climate control in the warehouse and the beeping of dozens, if not hundreds, of personal medical devices surrounded Shada's consciousness, and she felt the tug of silence reach out for her. By the time she counted to ten again, her body stood next to the bed of a woman in her early twenties wearing a hospital gown. Alfie grabbed the chart from the end of the woman's bed.

"The edited embryos didn't attach to her uterus," Shada heard Alfie say. Her own eyes stared at the woman's face. Shada realized the point of this exercise was to see if her body would react.

"Tension in the lower part of the throat, facial muscles contracting, urge to close my eyes," Shada heard herself report.

"General response," Alfie said. "Does it have any effect on your mind?"

Shada's field of vision shifted from left to right as she shook her head no.

"Good. Let's continue," Alfie said. They went through the back of the warehouse into a large refrigerator. One wall was filled with small square doors. Alfie opened one and rolled out a cadaver.

"This one died in childbirth," Alfie said. He paused. "Her children will grow up without a mother."

The dead woman became blurry.

"I know edited children don't have the same attachment to parental figures as the unedited do, so this won't matter to her offspring. But it does seem that this body has responded by filling both eyes with tears."

Shada watched a hand approach her face to wipe the tears away.

"And you are able to keep the response separate from your mind, correct?"

Hollis, in control of Shada, looked across the room with unfocused eyes. "No change in my internal state. Given time, I believe I could diminish, if not eliminate, these physiological responses." Shada's head whipped around to look at Alfie. "There's no way she's controlling the body without my knowledge, correct?"

"No, sir, your own consciousness has overridden hers. She's offline, for all intents and purposes."

"Good. I think we've seen enough. We haven't tested the response to torture and death, but I don't think it will be necessary."

"The pain portion is worth examining. It's a quick test."

Hollis-in-Shada sighed. "All right, if it's quick. I want to get some exercise again."

Shada tried to scream but nothing happened.

They went to the warehouse's security room, a room filled with camera monitors showing the rows of inanimate bodies, and Alfie borrowed a pistol from one of the massive security guards. He told Shada to back up.

"Ready?"

"As I'll ever be," Hollis-in-Shada said.

Alfie's head turned sideways, curious, then he shook away

whatever thought had occurred to him. He took aim and fired the electrical weapon.

When Shada regained her sight, she saw Alfie's face above her own, the stainless steel air ducts on the ceiling in the background. "Are you all right?"

Hollis nodded for Shada.

"Any adverse effects?"

"Stiff, sluggish limb control, localized pain in the impact site."

"And your mind? Do you still feel the same?"

"Still able to keep them separate."

Alfie smiled, and Shada got the sense his expression was a mirror of her own.

"This is good. I don't think we have anything to worry about. You should be able to maintain control of your consciousness regardless of circumstance."

"That's good to know. Let's not do that again." Her own hand reached down and pulled the electric darts from her stomach.

Shada agreed with Hollis, even though she never felt a thing.

The exercise Hollis wanted to perform turned out to be lifting weights. Alfie stood by as Hollis-in-Shada chose random machines and tested how heavy a weight the body he occupied could lift.

Shada watched herself in the mirror perform exercises she used to be forced to do with her team. She'd never cared about this aspect of being an athlete and therefore didn't bother to push the limits of what her body could do, so she was surprised when Hollis was able to urge her body to lift more weight than she ever thought possible. Since he could ignore Shada's body's signals about when to stop, he kept pushing past the point of exhaustion. Shada wondered if this weight-training session would affect her on the court but remembered she wouldn't have any meaningful time playing her sport for months to come, so it didn't matter.

It became clear over the course of the workout that Hollis used these machines on his own, because every time he lifted more weight inside Shada than he had in his own body, he remarked how frail his own body had become. He pushed weights around for almost an hour before Alfie coughed and told him it was time to get back to the room and switch back.

Hollis flexed Shada's biceps in the mirror and smiled, enjoying what he saw.

"We have to go," Alfie urged.

When the two of them walked back inside the room where the upload took place, Shada saw Hollis's body on the table taking small, even breaths. He could have been asleep. Without his force of personality he seemed frail, worn out, and cute, the way a grandfather might be. Alfie directed Hollis to lay Shada's body down on the table and placed the helmet on her head.

Shada woke up, back in control of her stiff and sore body, and wondered why she felt so alone even though Alfie and Hollis were in the room with her.

CHAPTER SEVENTEEN

When Hollis sat up on the metal table, his legs almost reached the floor. His back, bent with old age, forced his head forward, and when he spoke to Shada, who was sitting up on her own table, it appeared he was looking up at her from far below.

"Shada, I have to ask you something."

Alfie must have known what the old man had in mind, because he patted the old man's knee. "Sir, I'm not sure this is the right place or time."

Hollis glared at the scientist in response to the unwanted advice. "Damnit, Alfie, I'm running out of time and need an answer!"

Alfie hung his head and muttered, "You don't need an answer, you want an answer. There's already another workable solution."

"Don't waste my time getting hung up on the words I use," Hollis snapped. He turned his attention to Shada. "I'm dying," he said as a statement of fact.

"We all are," replied Shada. She wasn't in the mood to feel sorry for the man who'd agreed to have her electrocuted while in control of her body.

Hollis closed his eyes and tilted his head up. He took a deep breath and said, "I have cancer," with the exhale. "But it doesn't have to be the end." He looked at Shada with a thin-lipped smile pasted on his face.

"This is a bad idea," Alfie said, shaking his head.

"Quiet!" Hollis snapped.

Shada's eyes narrowed with suspicion. "What do you mean, it doesn't have to be the end?"

"It doesn't have to be the end if I could take over, permanently."

Shada looked down at her hands and picked at the cuticle on her thumb.

"I've tested negative experiences," Hollis blurted out. "I know we said the experiences would all be positive, but I had to check if I could maintain my identity under stress in an unedited body. It appears there won't be any problems, short of something catastrophic."

Shada launched into an internal debate about whether to tell the two men she'd been able to witness the tests. She decided to keep the information to herself. "What would have happened if your mind cracked while inside my body?"

"Well, once I got back inside my own body, I wouldn't have been able to have this conversation."

"We think," Alfie interjected. "This is a gray area; there haven't been many tests under these conditions."

Hollis nodded.

"Did you test negative experiences when you hijacked Piper?" Shada asked.

"Piper is edited, so she doesn't have the same emotional responses to misery as you do," Alfie said. "We did see how Hollis's mind responded to pain, and it seemed to be the same as if he was in his own body," Alfie said.

"Did you test the response to pain while in control of me?" Shada wanted them to admit it.

Hollis and Alfie both nodded.

"What did you do?" Shada knew the answer but wanted them to say it.

"Does it matter?" Alfie replied.

"Of course it matters! It's my body!"

"We administered an electric shock," Hollis said.

Shada closed her eyes for a moment before she looked right at Hollis. "Why not take over Piper? You already know it would work," she said.

"My original plan was to live in Piper, but she doesn't have the same physical capabilities as you. The upload into your body was going to be one last experience, for pleasure, before I transplanted my consciousness into her body."

"What about the security guards? They're massive."

"They're bred for size, not the strength of their neural connections. I have already accumulated a lifetime of knowledge. I need creativity. Another reason I prefer to upload into you instead of Piper."

"I'm not creative," Shada said. Between her and her sister, Sikya was the more creative one. She was better at writing and better at drawing. Shada had always been the athletic one.

"Being an athlete is creative. This lack of creativity is why edited athletes never do well in sports leagues. Alfie made me aware of this when he came to talk to me about getting you back into the league as a spokesperson for edited athletes."

"If you uploaded into my body, I wouldn't be able to be the spokesperson."

"That's correct."

Shada had heard all she cared to hear. "Why would I let you take my entire future from me?"

A wicked smirk appeared on Hollis's face. "Sikya."

Shada felt protectiveness rise from deep inside her. As a child she had always been the one to stand up to bullies, for Sikya and for her friends, and now that Hollis had spoken her sister's name, she felt like a child forced to stand up for her younger sister once again. "What about her?" Shada said, ready for a fight.

"She was rejected for a birth license." Hollis searched Shada's face to see how his first strike would affect her. "You knew that, right?"

Shada parried the blow. "She told me."

"She will continue to be rejected, unless you agree."

Shada felt the room slip away. The edges of darkness crept into her field of vision.

"Now, if you agree, Sikya will be approved within a few days of her next application. Guaranteed." Hollis had Shada backed into a corner and knew it.

The age of the two men in the room with her became apparent. Didn't they know an animal with no other options might attack? Shada sized them up and knew she could do a lot of damage, if not kill both of them before anyone could stop her. Hollis was worthless, so she would have to incapacitate Alfie first. Or maybe she could make quick work of Hollis before a more drawn-out fight with Alfie?

What stopped Shada from lashing out was the thought of Sikya never being able to have a child, the one thing her sister wanted in this useless world. She looked down at her palms and saw deep marks from where her fingernails had dug into her flesh.

Both Alfie and Hollis seemed amused as they watched Shada realize how hopeless her situation had become.

"You'll take care of her too? Provide enough money for her

to live with her child and still fight for the cause she believes in?"

"She'll find enough in her account to ensure she never has to worry about money again."

Shada considered the proposal. "All our debts would be paid?" She didn't want a loophole to ruin the plan; she'd seen enough genies grant three wishes to know to cover all her bases.

"Your debt, her debt, all gone. She'd be set for life."

Shada considered the proposal. She wanted to play in the league, yes, and considered the hijacks small setbacks to the initial plan she had formulated with Alfie. She also knew she couldn't face a future where her sister was denied a child.

If Sikya agreed to never have a child in order to keep Shada in control of her own body, Shada would feel guilty.

If Sikya never knew why each and every birth application was rejected, Shada would feel guilty.

Part of her wondered how much power Hollis, and by extension WestCorp, really had. Could they make sure the birth application was rejected? She didn't want to take the chance against such a powerful organization.

"Let me visit her one more time," Shada said.

"Are you agreeing to the transplant?"

Shada withdrew into herself before a thought struck her. "If I don't, could we still edit my blood oxygen levels so I can play in the league?"

Alfie looked at Hollis.

Hollis shook his head no. "Sorry. It's either this or nothing at all."

Shada wondered what she'd done in a past life to deserve this ultimatum. She sighed. "Then yes, I agree. I'll go visit her and come back."

"You'll only make it harder to follow through on your decision," Alfie said.

"If I don't go back, I won't do it at all," Shada retorted. "We got in a fight last time I saw her, and I'm not disappearing on her without seeing her again."

"Then go," Hollis said. "But you'd better hope I don't die before you get back."

CHAPTER EIGHTEEN

SHADA KNEW her future was slipping away. She made it back to the room WestCorp had provided and stopped outside her door, her thumb still on the scanner after she heard the door unlock, wondering where the last five minutes had gone. It was the same way she used to wake up from her daydream as the train pulled to a stop at her station after a grueling day of practice. She left her door open while she collected her belongings into her backpack.

Either Chloe had a sixth sense or Shada made more noise than she thought, because her friend appeared, leaning on the doorframe to Shada's room. Shada knew she was there but didn't want to engage. Chloe watched as Shada packed her bag.

"Where are you going?" Chloe said when Shada stood up to make sure she hadn't forgotten anything.

"Back into the city to see Sikya."

"What's going on?" Chloe said, her eyebrows raised.

Shada had trouble figuring out where to begin. She settled on: "Hollis wants to take over my body."

"Hollis?"

"The head of WestCorp."

"He wants to hijack you? What does it matter, you'll be asleep." A flash of recognition swept over Chloe's features and her eyes narrowed in suspicion. "Wait, how do you know who uploads? They won't let me know who takes over my body. I've asked."

Shada told Chloe how she had known it was Hollis from the first upload, and that he was now the one person allowed to upload into her body. She didn't mention how it didn't feel like she was asleep when her body was taken over. "He's dying," Shada said. She slung the backpack over her shoulder and exhaled. "And he wants to take over my body for good."

Chloe's mouth hung open. "What . . . what are you going to do? Will you let him?" she said when she regained control.

"He said if I don't, he'll make sure Sikya doesn't ever get approved for a child. I can't let that happen, it's all she's ever wanted."

Chloe told Shada to wait and that she was going back to the city with her. "They'll just have to wait until I get back to upload into me again!" she said as she walked out.

Left alone, Shada wasn't sure she wanted Chloe to come but didn't have the energy to put up a fight.

The two of them were silent as they made their way to and through the atrium, waited on the platform, and boarded the tram. Chloe broke the silence as they crossed over the bay. "So you're going to go through with it?" she said.

"I don't know!" Shada exclaimed, louder than intended. The handful of other passengers maintained their silence and acted like they didn't hear.

"You can't go through with it," Chloe said. She put a hand on Shada's thigh. "I have to tell you something."

"What?"

"It's something I've done since the first upload. I didn't trust them, I thought they might want to take over our bodies from the start, so I took . . . precautions."

Shada's suspicious eyes searched Chloe's face for clues. "We both did, at the office."

"No, separate from that." Chloe took a deep breath and took her time exhaling. "I've poisoned myself before each time. When I get back into my body, I take the antidote." Chloe pulled a pair of small vials from a pocket in her backpack, one red and one blue. "The guards never found them," she said. "I think they only look for weapons, maybe recording equipment."

"What if they wanted to upload more than once?"

"The poison has an eight-hour dormant period before it takes effect. As long as I take the antidote within that window, I'm fine."

Shada reached for the vial of red liquid, but Chloe withdrew her hand. "How did you find out about this?" Shada asked.

Chloe put the vials back into her backpack. "My mother was a botanist. She developed organic compounds that could be used as weapons for the military. When she found out the plan was to use them in the event of an unedited uprising, she threatened to go public and was discharged. Then blacklisted by every major company. Those are from her stockpile."

Shada hung her head. "They aren't giving me a choice. If I don't agree, they won't even perform the edits to get me back in the league."

Chloe's confused look prompted Shada to tell her about the plan she and Alfie had come up with for her to be the face of edited athletes.

"So we wouldn't have been working together until your playing career ended . . ." Chloe said, her voice trailing off. "Why didn't you tell me?"

"You didn't tell me about the poison."

They stared at each other, each daring the other to blink, as the train came to a stop beneath the city. "What's done is done," Shada said.

"Agreed."

They disembarked, left WestCorp's pristine platform beneath them, and stopped at the bottom of an escalator that was part of the city's transportation system.

"I need to talk with Unedited Rights and set it up so everything goes to Sikya once I'm taken over," Shada said.

Chloe nodded to the platform on the level on which they stood. "I'm going to run home and grab more vials. I didn't plan for them to let us live on the island."

"Meet me at my place when you're done." Shada took Chloe's phone and put in her address. "I should be there in a few hours."

Shada took the train to the Office of Unedited Rights. Tensen wasn't there, but she was able to talk to another advocate. Without explaining that she would be taken over, not edited, she filled out the necessary paperwork to transfer all future funds to Sikya. While signing the paperwork, she wondered what would happen to Hollis's assets, if they would somehow get transferred to her as well since he'd be dead. If so, would Sikya be entitled to all of it?

The process took twenty minutes, and before Shada knew it she was on the train to her apartment. As she approached her building, she tried to figure out the best way to break the news to her sister. She rode the elevator up, still not sure of the best way to start. Just outside their door, she determined she would make amends before bringing up her own next steps.

Shada walked into an empty apartment. Sikya wasn't home, and there was no sign of when she would be back. Shada sat on the couch to wait and didn't put up a fight when sleep overtook her.

A knock woke her. She wiped drool from her mouth and

flexed her hand to regain feeling before she stood up to answer the door.

Chloe beamed a smile at her before Shada's lack of reciprocation wiped it from her face.

"She's not here," Shada said.

"Did you want to wait for her?" Chloe asked.

Shada thought for a moment before she shook her head no.

"Leave her a note," Chloe suggested.

Shada grabbed a pencil and the pad of paper they used for their grocery list. She hunched over the counter and couldn't think of the right words to say.

Thinking out loud, Shada said, "If I tell her I'm getting the transplant so she can have a kid, she'll get mad at me." She tapped the eraser on the counter. "And if I say I'm getting edited but won't be playing in the league so don't expect to hear from me again, she'll feel abandoned because I could make money playing overseas without leaving her behind."

Shada looked at Chloe and her friend shrugged.

In the end, Shada wrote one word: sorry.

CHAPTER NINETEEN

SHADA GRABBED an apple from the pile on the counter, because Sikya would have wanted her to take one, and grabbed the rest of the red gummy bears from the cabinet. Together she and Chloe walked back to the train station, Shada for the last time. She was about to give her apple to the homeless man and his dog when she saw a pile of pristine red apples behind them, stacked against the chain-link fence. Sure they were the ones she had donated to them on her previous trips, and wondering how they were able to last so long, she kept the apple for herself to see how long it would take to rot. They rode the tram back to the island and were informed that preparations for both their procedures had begun.

Chloe was hijacked into twice in the days Shada waited. Shada assumed, but never asked, that Chloe took the poison before she left each time.

A cleaning lady made sure Shada didn't need anything before she went into Chloe's room during the second hijack. Shada feared it might be a ploy to search Chloe's belongings, and she hoped they didn't find and take her vials of antidote.

Later that evening, Shada heard a thump through their shared wall as Chloe collapsed onto her metal bed.

Piper showed up outside Shada's room while Shada lay awake in the brightness of morning, staring at the ceiling and listening for movement in the adjacent room so she could be sure Chloe was still alive. "Shada, it's time," she said after a crisp knock on the door.

Shada got dressed and gathered the rest of her belongings, not knowing what to do with them since she'd have no use for them once the hijack was done. She made Piper wait in the hall as she banged on Chloe's door to wake her up.

"What?" Chloe groaned.

"I want to say goodbye," Shada said.

Chloe opened the door an instant later. Her eyes were puffy, and indented lines crisscrossed her face from the fabric of the pillow. Chloe looked like she wanted to say something but instead threw her arms around Shada.

Shada imagined the hug was transmitted through Chloe to Sikya via some unknown means of transfer.

Piper coughed and the friends separated. They lingered for a moment, each waiting for the other to say something, but when neither of them said a word they exchanged a nod. Shada turned away and followed Piper down the corridor.

"Another upload?" Piper said.

Shada thought it was a weird attempt at making conversation. "Today's the day," she replied.

"Did you know this was my idea?"

"Alfie said it was his idea for Hollis to upload into my body."

"That was his idea. Uploading consciousness in the first place was my idea."

"Really? I thought Alfie developed it."

"He did develop it, after I asked him if it would be possible. For the idea, I was promoted to Hollis's lieutenant."

They walked outside into the blazing sun. A two-person transport pulled up to them and its door flung open. Shada climbed on board and sat next to Piper with her backpack on her lap, watching the manicured lawns pass by.

Piper interrupted Shada's appreciation of the last moments in control of her own body. "Hollis has uploaded into me too, you know, and he'll be back. You're just the flavor of the week."

Shada realized Piper had no idea the switch was about to be permanent.

"We have a good thing going, so don't think you'll get edited and take over as his second-in-command. I've come too far to let you take this away from me."

"I don't want to work for him."

Piper ran out of ammunition without Shada's engagement. They walked through the atrium and took another small transport vehicle to the side of the island farthest from the city across the water. They got off outside a short cement building with a thick metal front door and no windows. Its roof slanted down towards the edge of the water. There were a few palm trees scattered about, but nothing outside suggested the purpose of the building.

Shada had dismissed Piper's threatening attitude until then, but in this remote corner, she wondered if she meant to harm her.

"This is Hollis's personal residence," Piper said. She grabbed Shada's shoulder and spun her so the two of them were face-to-face. Her index finger hovered in front of Shada's nose. "Don't forget, I won't let you ruin this for me."

Piper let go and walked to the front door. She opened up a hidden control panel and placed her face in front of a scanner. The large metal door groaned to life as multiple locks disengaged. Piper pushed the door open and led Shada inside.

Lights blinked on, and Shada saw a room in sharp contrast

with the exterior. The walls were made of wood and looked like they had been taken from an old wooden ship. There were two sofas, both dark brown leather, and on the walls multiple large fish were mounted in a bent position. The floor was covered with a dense purple area rug. On the wall opposite the front door was a stainless steel elevator door.

"Sit," Piper commanded.

Shada sat on the edge of one couch with her backpack behind her, and Piper sat across from her.

"Alfie should be here to get you soon," Piper said. She stared at Shada with a murderous glint in her eye.

"How many times were you hijacked?" Shada asked, to kill the silence between them. She was pleased to see Piper flinch at her word choice.

"I was uploaded into three times."

"You said yourself multiple hijacks could have an adverse effect. Are you sure it didn't cause you to go crazy?"

If the intensity of Piper's glare could be measured it would be off the charts.

Shada realized that, even though they were the same height, the woman across from her was frail. She laughed as her fear of physical harm dissipated.

"What's so funny?" Piper said.

"Nothing," Shada said.

Faint beeps from the rising elevator got louder as it approached the level where the two women sat. They both stared at the door as it opened and Alfie strode out.

"Shada, good to see you again," the scientist said with a smile. Shada closed her eyes, the weight of her decision getting heavier by the moment.

"Piper," he said with a nod.

Hollis's lieutenant popped up and smiled. She seemed eager and approachable.

"This way," Alfie said to Shada with a gesture towards the elevator.

Piper walked forward before Alfie held up a hand to stop her. "Thanks for bringing her here. You are no longer needed."

Piper looked like she'd been hit in the stomach so hard the air was driven from her lungs. She stammered something about being second-in-command and how Shada was unedited. The disdain in her voice was palpable.

"We need Shada, not you."

Piper didn't move.

"We'll call you if we need anything." Alfie waited for Shada to get onto the elevator before he joined her inside. He pushed the number at the bottom of a column of buttons, a seven, and the elevator doors shut, leaving an angry Piper behind.

"She's upset because Hollis doesn't let her down here," Alfie said, shaking his head.

Shada nodded, surprised at how something could matter so much to someone who had been edited. She thought toxic ambition should be addressed in the standard edits too.

CHAPTER TWENTY

THE ELEVATOR DOORS OPENED, and Alfie led Shada into a large underground cavern. The ceiling above was smooth stone with a grid of light bulbs hanging from wires. Shada stared down a long corridor with white walls that ended at a standard height, well below the level of the stone above. At the end was an open space occupied by a dark brown dinner table, its ends obscured by the walls.

"This way," Alfie said, striding forward with purpose.

Shada followed the scientist past multiple doorways without doors. One room had ancient scientific equipment, analog dials, and beige plastic coverings, all coated with dust. Another room had a television and a couch with a blanket thrown in a pile on one armrest. The third room Shada was led past held exercise equipment, and the fourth held a computer on a desk surrounded by piles of books. If left to her own devices, she would have gone into the study and seen what kind of books the leader of WestCorp kept in his residence.

The table at the end of the corridor was massive, the largest table Shada had ever seen. She took a quick count of the chairs: twenty. Nine on each side and one on each end. She wondered what kind of dinners Hollis had hosted, because she'd never gotten the impression he was one for large social gatherings. A vision came to her of Hollis at one head of the table surrounded by powerful figures from both the city and industry.

On the left of the table was an industrial kitchen full of stainless steel appliances and large open spaces for a chef to work. Two doors on the right side of the room, the only doors she had seen so far, were closed.

"Please take a seat," Alfie told her.

Shada sat down in the middle of the table with her back to the elevator. She set her backpack on the floor next to her, withdrew her red gummy bears, and began popping them into her mouth one at a time. She was intent on finishing the bag before the chance was taken from her by Hollis. In front of her was a bare wall of shiny black rock. The rock wasn't smooth, and its edges reflected the light, giving Shada the impression thousands of small eyes were all looking at her.

Alfie walked over to the two doors and knocked on the one on the left. From the door on the right came the reply. "I'm in here," Hollis called out.

Shada thought his voice sounded weaker than she remembered, but within its feebleness lay a definitive quality she found interesting.

Alfie opened the other door, and Shada saw Hollis lying down on one of two stainless steel tables in a small room. Compared to the other rooms, this one could have been a closet. It was just large enough to accommodate the two tables.

Hollis got up from the table and walked into the room with the large table.

"How do you feel, sir?" Alfie asked.

"Like I'm a hundred. Every bone hurts."

"You won't have to feel that way much longer," Alfie said. His face was unchanged, but the smirk shone through.

Hollis walked toward the kitchen. As he passed Shada, he reached down and squeezed her shoulder. At the same time he replied to Alfie, "I know."

Shada watched as Hollis opened the refrigerator and pulled out a plate covered with aluminum foil.

"One last meal?" she asked. The wavering of her voice embarrassed her, and the faint echo she imagined wouldn't let her brush it off.

"My favorite," Hollis said with a timid smile. "Roast beef, mashed potatoes, and green beans. My mother used to make it for me when I was young."

Even powerful men are sentimental when faced with their own mortality.

After Hollis grabbed a fork and knife, he sat down at the end of the table closest to the kitchen. Shada got the sense he had spent many of his meals sitting at that very spot with nothing but empty chairs for company. Alfie sat next to him.

"You're going to eat it cold?" Shada asked.

"Doesn't matter to me, it still tastes the same," Hollis replied.

Shada and Alfie watched Hollis eat his last meal, having never been offered anything to eat themselves. He was a slow eater, relishing each bite because they were his last. Twice he leaned back in his chair—each time Shada was certain he was done—but both times Hollis leaned forward to resume until the food was gone.

When Hollis leaned forward and rested his elbows on the table with an empty plate in front of him, Alfie asked him if he was ready.

"Let's get this over with."

Hollis didn't bother to clear his used dishes, he just stood up and began walking into the small room. Alfie gave Shada a nod towards the same room and she followed him inside.

"Onto the table, you two," Alfie said. His voice was jovial, an attempt to lighten the mood in what was about to be the end of both Shada's and Hollis's existences as they knew it.

"Will this switch be stronger?" Shada asked Alfie as she climbed onto the stainless steel table.

"Nope, it'll be the same feeling as before."

"And it will be permanent?"

"It will be, because there won't be a switch back. In theory, all of the other uploads could have been permanent too, that's why you had to visit the guys over at Unedited Rights so they could make sure we put everyone back into the body where they belong."

Hollis was the picture of serenity on his table. His head rested on the pillow, his eyes were closed, and his hands were folded on his chest.

Alfie pushed on Shada's shoulder to get her to lie down. Once he deemed her position satisfactory, he placed the helmet on her head.

"What's going to happen to his body? Are you going to keep it alive?"

"He has orders to kill this vessel after the switch," Hollis said. His voice was distant and could have come from the far side of the massive table.

Alfie moved over to Hollis's side and placed the helmet over his head with a delicate touch. The moment they both had their helmets on, Shada felt a surge of energy that had nothing to do with the machine between them. It was as if the whole situation became real in an instant. Her stomach leapt, her heart raced, and her skin crawled, knowing she would be taken over at the flip of a switch.

She closed her eyes and counted out ten shallow breaths while Alfie adjusted the machine between the two tables. She imagined the last time she saw Sikya and hoped the note she left wouldn't cause her sister more pain.

"Ready?" Alfie said.

Shada turned her head and looked past Alfie as Hollis nodded yes. Her eyes met Alfie's and she nodded yes too.

Alfie counted down. "Three . . . two . . ."

At the last moment, at the same moment Alfie said "One," Shada thought of her backpack on the ground next to the table and wondered what would become of her belongings.

CHAPTER TWENTY-ONE

It had taken time for Shada to see the world through her own eyes during the previous uploads, so she was surprised when she was able to witness her surroundings while Hollis, in control of her body, still lay on the table. Through a series of rapid blinks, she saw the ceiling come into focus as the dark circle receded. Her head turned, and she saw Alfie shift his gaze between Hollis's old body and the monitor as if expecting the delivery of an important package. Then, Shada's eyes closed, plunging their previous master into darkness.

"I feel dizzy," she heard herself say. Her voice was pitiful and weak, a voice she used when she was sick and she wanted Sikya to do something for her. Hollis, in charge of her body and therefore in charge of the tone of her voice, had no way of knowing this. He must have taken on this particular inflection in his old age, and it remained after the body his mind occupied had lost decades.

"You've felt dizzy every other time too. This will pass," Alfie said.

Hollis opened Shada's eyes and watched a spike on the monitor between the tables hold Alfie's attention.

"This is the last chance," Alfie said, his face serious. "Are you sure?"

"Let it go," Hollis said from Shada's body.

Inside, Shada could only imagine herself screaming.

A few minutes later, Alfie announced Hollis's body was dead. "No going back now."

"Never intended to. Time to make myself at home." Hollis-in-Shada stood up and looked down at his corpse.

Shada wondered what the sensation felt like and hoped it was more jarring than her own experience of being hijacked.

"Get rid of it," he said with a wave of her hand.

"Do you care how?" Alfie asked.

"How do we get rid of the bodies of the stray dogs? Burn 'em? Do that."

"Will do, sir," Alfie said without so much as an extra blink.

Hollis-in-Shada walked through his bedroom to the attached bathroom. Shada hoped he would turn her head to look at the rest of the bedroom, but he kept her eyes forward, focused on his destination. He stared at her face in the mirror, and Alfie appeared in the open doorway.

"Who else should be allowed to know about the switch?" Alfie asked.

Shada's gaze jerked from the mirror to Alfie. "Nobody! Not a single person. Tell everyone I'm bedridden, too sick to leave my residence."

"So I'll have to burn your body myself," Alfie said, his voice trailing off. "I'll do it tonight."

"Whatever you have to do," Hollis-in-Shada said. He returned his gaze to the mirror and leaned forward, pulling the bottoms of his eye sockets down to inspect Shada's pupils. Shada watched as her eyes crossed then looked far left, then far right. Her mouth opened and Hollis inspected her teeth. "She took care of herself," Hollis-in-Shada muttered.

"Agreed. You made a good choice."

Shada couldn't help but feel a perverse sense of pride at their approval.

"What are you going to do about clothes?" Alfie asked.

"I hadn't thought about it. Let's see what she has in her bag."

Shada's body was taken into the large room, and she watched as Hollis bent down and grabbed her bag. Upon inspection, Hollis found one more pair of shorts and two more T-shirts, each of which had already been worn multiple times in the previous week. He pulled out the apple Shada had taken from home, stared at it for a moment, then tossed it back into the bag.

"We've got to get you more clothes," Alfie said.

"Go topside and grab them," Hollis-in-Shada commanded. He set her bag onto a chair and slid the chair back under the table. "But make sure it's the kind of clothes she'd wear. I don't want anyone to think anything has changed."

"I can do that," Alfie said. He stood still next to Shada's body, his hands resting on the back of a chair.

"Now," Hollis said.

Alfie told Hollis he was planning to do it when he took Hollis's dead body later that night, then he turned and walked to the elevator. The sound of his footsteps fading into the distance echoed off the walls of the cavern. Hollis watched through Shada's eyes as Alfie got into the elevator.

Alone, Hollis-in-Shada went back into the bathroom. Shada watched as Hollis took her shirt and sports bra off to inspect her bare chest, then pulled her waistband away from her body and looked at her tuft of pubic hair. Shada thought she should feel more scandalized, but without any sensations from her body, the inspection seemed scientific. Without words she wasn't able to sense whether Hollis was aroused, and without this feedback there was no sense of shame.

Hollis released the shorts and pulled the shirt back down. He walked into the room with exercise equipment and Shada saw the depth of this room, unknown to her when she'd walked past the first time. There was enough space for every machine he had used the last time he exercised her body, and he got to work pushing himself on the same exercises in the same order.

Towards the end of the routine Shada could hear her body's ragged breaths. Shada expected Hollis to end the routine with another flexing of her muscles, but instead he jumped on a treadmill. Over the next twenty minutes he increased the pace past the point of what she thought possible. In the mirror she could see her own chest heaving and the strain of sustaining the speed on her face. Her own mind couldn't sense the effort her body was exerting, but she tried to count to ten breaths, her standard method of calming herself down when she got too spun up during exercise.

Watching her face to determine the correct timing, Shada counted ten breaths before she began a second count. By the time she reached four, she could sense, in the same fashion she had been able to see the faint circle from the bottom of the well, the presence of her diaphragm. She tried to latch on to the feeling but lost it before she could reach the count of one.

She began another countdown and was able to find her breath without reliance on sight. From ten through seven it tickled the edge of her awareness, from six to three she could identify it, and from two to one she let it take over the entirety of her awareness. It was easy to let it take over since her mind was starved for physical connection, like finding an oasis in the middle of a desert. She exerted control over her breathing, forcing her stomach out with every inhale. She stared at the mirror, looking for signs in her face of whether or not Hollis was aware of her presence. The muscles in her face relaxed as her breath become more controlled, but there was no indication Hollis knew why.

Shada held on to the control of her breathing through the final three minutes of her body's time on the treadmill. The sensation served as a beacon of hope, a tether she could latch on to in the nothingness of space.

Hollis stopped the workout and dismounted. Shada was covered in sweat.

As Shada's heart rate fell and her breathing became more regular, she felt control of her breath slip away. It was a slow descent into the vacuum, but after spending time grounded, it felt like she lost control of her body all over again.

As Hollis-in-Shada took a shower, Shada couldn't help but feel a glimmer of hope. If she could learn to control her body's breathing under normal circumstances, could she one day hope to take over her limbs as well? Then she'd be able to take over her body altogether while still having access to Hollis's resources.

And Hollis would be the one trapped inside.

CHAPTER TWENTY-TWO

HOLLIS HAD PLOPPED Shada's body on the couch and was watching a financial news report when the elevator's gears sprang into action. Hollis didn't bother to move, and he showed no other signs of preparing for a guest, so Shada assumed it was Alfie coming back. She figured the scientist must be one of the few people with access to the space. Now Shada, since Hollis occupied her body, was part of this exclusive list.

A beep rang out as the elevator door opened and footsteps approached.

"In here," Hollis-in-Shada yelled.

Alfie's head appeared around the corner. It seemed as if he wanted to withhold the full arrival of his body until he was sure Hollis was ready to receive him. Shada wasn't sure if this style of entrance was a normal occurrence or if he'd added in the momentary pause because Hollis now resided in a woman's body.

"What are you waiting for?" Hollis said. He sat up on the couch and adjusted the blanket draped over Shada's long legs.

Alfie walked in with a beige fabric bag in each hand. He set them down on the coffee table and withdrew what he brought.

"I brought our standard athletic shorts and T-shirt," he said, pulling these items from the first bag and holding them up.

Hollis-in-Shada nodded.

"And these are some of our other standard outfits." He showed off a dark blue jumpsuit. "This is what the mechanics and gardeners wear."

Shada couldn't sense her face's response, but Alfie responded by stuffing the jumpsuit into the bottom of the bag.

"And this is what we give our people who work in the service sectors." Alfie showed off a pair of khaki pants and a short-sleeved white polo shirt.

Hollis held out one of Shada's hands and accepted the shirt from Alfie. "This could work." He picked up the pants and pulled on the fabric, remarking on their stretchiness. "Give me two more of this outfit, and three more of the athletic gear." He threw the pants and white shirt onto the coffee table and leaned back on the sofa.

"I'll get right on it. How are you feeling?"

"Tired, to tell you the truth." Hollis looked at the clock: 6:00 P.M. "It's still early, but I think I'll get ready for bed soon."

"I'm not surprised, these uploads tend to be exhausting for the host." Alfie stuffed the clothes in the bag and told Hollis he would put the approved clothes into his room and take the other ones topside.

"Did you need anything else?" Alfie asked.

"Yes, as a matter of fact. Two things. One, find a diet for athletes. This body's going to need more fuel than what I used to consume, and I'm not sure where to start. I want to keep her in peak condition."

"You mean 'myself'; this is your body now. I'll get a dietitian right away. Did you want to meet with them or just have the meals made for you and brought down according to their recommendations?"

"Just have the meals brought down," Hollis said. Shada wondered if someone other than Alfie would be coming into the underground residence in order to deliver the food.

"What's the second thing?"

"Bring two women down tomorrow night," Hollis-in-Shada said.

Alfie's lack of surprise at the request suggested to Shada it had been made before.

Alfie glanced at Shada's crotch before he looked up and said, "Will you be participating as well, or do you just want to watch?"

"Just watch," Hollis-in-Shada said.

"Any preferences?" Alfie said.

Hollis paused then told Alfie to make sure they were good-looking.

Shada was disgusted at the nonchalant way these arrangements were made.

Alfie left the room and moments later walked past on his way back to the elevator.

Hollis waited for the beeps to stop before he got up and walked Shada's body to his bedroom. There was a large bed with one dark gray pillow and a matching comforter, a dresser, and a cushioned chair made of dark brown leather that matched the couch in front of the television. On the chair was the bag Alfie had left with the two outfits Hollis had decided to keep, more of the same on the way.

Shada was surprised Hollis's bedroom wasn't larger until she remembered this entire underground chamber was his, and now in a weird way, hers.

Hollis tossed the bag of clothes into his closet—Shada would have winced if she had control of her face, because she detested clothes on the floor—and climbed into bed without taking off any clothes.

Shada heard the elevator descend in the middle of the night. Padded footsteps then walked the length of the corridor and into the kitchen. She assumed it was the meal delivery, so she wasn't curious when the refrigerator opened, closed a bit later, and the footsteps walked back to the elevator.

Her body stayed asleep the whole time. True sleep paralysis. She hated the sensation.

Hollis must have expected the overnight delivery, because the first thing he did in the morning was check the refrigerator. Meals were labeled one, two, three, and four, and each had a suggested time range written on the label. There were three days' worth of food, including that day. When Hollis inspected the day's food, Shada saw meals one, two, and four corresponded to breakfast, lunch, and dinner, and meal three was a lighter snack.

Hollis spent the day the same way he had spent the previous. There was exercise followed by time on the couch watching television. Since he didn't do any work, Shada wondered if this was a planned vacation from WestCorp, intended to give him time to adjust to life inside a new body. It didn't occur to her that this was the weekend and she had glimpsed Hollis's life on Saturday and Sunday.

Alfie showed up during dinner flanked by two women in skintight cocktail dresses. Both showed off long legs. One was blond, with pale skin and high cheekbones. The other looked to be foreign, with olive skin that couldn't be placed and smoky eyes. Both were beautiful, and any man would agree they were of equal quality, just different flavors.

"These are for you," Alfie told Hollis-in-Shada.

Hollis invited the two women to sit down while he finished his meal and told Alfie he would send the women up in two hours, a statement that Alfie interpreted as a dismissal. The two women seemed both confused and impressed that a brown-skinned woman such as Shada had so much power and lived in an underground bunker.

They tried to make conversation by asking how the food was, but Hollis ignored them both while his last bites disappeared. When his meal was finished, he told both women to climb onto the table.

They looked at each other for a moment, a hesitation that caused Hollis to say, "Now!" in Shada's voice.

The women climbed onto the table and kneeled, awaiting further instruction. Hollis told them to make out with each other. He leaned Shada's body back in her chair to enjoy the show.

Within minutes both women were down to their bra and panties, as commanded by Hollis-in-Shada.

Shada saw the way they watched her face, looking for signs of approval. When none came, the blond woman wrapped her arm around the one with smoky eyes to remove her bra.

"Stop," Hollis said. He muttered under his breath. "This body is useless."

"What's wrong?" the blond woman asked.

"It's not working," Shada heard herself say.

"You could join us," the other woman suggested, her smoky eyes glinting with mischief.

"This body has no response whatsoever."

If Hollis could communicate with Shada, she'd be able to tell him she'd never been attracted to women.

"Put your clothes back on and get out," a dejected Hollis told the women. The voice sounded more like Shada's own tone than anything else he had said since the hijack. "You can wait on the couches outside the elevator. Someone will pick you up at the end of your two hours."

After watching the two escorts grab their dresses and shuffle to the elevator, Hollis-in-Shada walked into his bedroom and shut the door. He laid on the bed for a moment before going into the bathroom and looking into the mirror. For the first time, Shada saw herself look frustrated and felt proud of her body for ruining Hollis's evening.

CHAPTER TWENTY-THREE

HOLLIS-IN-SHADA EMERGED from his underground residence on Monday morning and went straight to his office attached to the atrium. It was a massive space that held a solitary wooden desk and two chairs, giving visitors the impression they had a long way to walk from the door to their seat across from him. He had two secretaries: an older man in charge of his schedule and a younger woman who took care of paperwork. They both stared at Hollis, who now occupied Shada's body, as he walked in like he owned the place.

"Good morning," the young woman said. "Can I help you?" She had short brown hair in curls and too much makeup.

From her reaction, Shada could tell Hollis shot her a look of reproach. The older male secretary interjected to diffuse the situation.

"Good morning, Shada," he said. He had dark skin, an African accent, and could have been anywhere from thirty to fifty. "Alfie mentioned you would be joining us from now on." He looked at the younger secretary and his eyes widened.

Hollis looked down at Shada's hand as if reminding himself of his changed outward appearance.

"That's right."

"My name is Ernie, and this is Beth." Hollis-in-Shada introduced himself as Shada and shook both their hands.

"Hollis also said not to walk in on you when you are in the office. If we need you, we can call." The older secretary was reminding his counterpart about the rules that had been established.

Shada saw her world shift up and down as Hollis nodded. Hollis walked into the office, shut the door, and the moment he sat down at his desk he called Alfie.

"I need you to do an assessment," Hollis said.

Alfie paused before he replied. It was obvious he wasn't used to hearing Shada's voice tell him what to do, and the new interaction took a moment to register. "I can do one right after lunch, I'll call when I'm ready. It should be around two," he said. Even though Shada had had limited interactions with the scientist, she could tell he was exasperated after dealing with Hollis the entire weekend, but she wasn't sure Hollis could tell or, if he could, cared.

"After lunch then," Hollis said before ending the call.

Hollis spent the morning doing computer work. Shada had never been good at sitting still, and it seemed Hollis was now learning what it was like to be unedited while trying to do work in an environment optimized for edited humans. The incongruence caused Hollis-in-Shada to walk around in frustration multiple times per hour. Lunch, brought from his residence, was eaten at noon, in accordance with the label. Lunchtime was spent dealing with a lawsuit courtesy of the Office of Unedited Rights.

At one thirty Hollis lamented how time never cooperated, slowing down and speeding up in direct contradiction to what was necessary. Shada heard his complaints and wondered if he'd said them to himself or for her.

Two came and went without a call from Alfie. It wasn't until almost three that Alfie called Hollis's office and told him to come to the lab.

"Sorry, I was busy putting out fires," Alfie explained.

"On my way," Hollis said before rushing out, without acknowledging Alfie's explanation.

Shada's long strides ate up the distance to the transport vehicle that took Hollis to the lab, and soon her body was seated on an examination table. Alfie's disheveled hair and stained lab coat inspired a host of questions in Shada, but Hollis ignored the scientist's physical state.

"What's going on?" Alfie said.

Hollis looked around the room before he began. "Is it possible for this body's previous owner to influence any of my actions?"

Shada could feel another awareness searching for sensation as soon as these words left what used to be her mouth. It was as if by identifying a channel of connection, and looking for its existence, Hollis had created it himself. Shada felt her breath and dove into its steady rhythm, a grounding presence she had missed during her time in isolation.

"What makes you say that?" Alfie asked as he sat down on a wheeled stool.

"Last night, with the girls, I felt nothing."

"Your biological responses won't be the same as before. Shada brought her own likes and dislikes to the table, and you'll have to learn what they are."

"But I still like the same things!"

"You need to reframe your mindset. You are now inside this body. For example: if you liked pickles, and Shada hated pickles, you won't like pickles anymore."

Shada took full control of her breathing while Hollis explored the repercussions of consciousness transplantation with Alfie. She held an inhale for the briefest of moments, to see if it could be done, but released the breath before Hollis picked up on the change.

"But I still think the same!" Hollis-in-Shada said.

"That's the thing! You don't. You're still clinging to old thought patterns and aren't making space for the full spectrum of what you can now accomplish. There's a reason you didn't switch into a member of security; you wanted her creativity. Have you been inspired at all?"

"All I've noticed is that I can't pay attention the same way I used to."

"Because you aren't in an edited body anymore. Embrace it."

Shada stretched her awareness down to her hands. Over the years she'd spent a lot of time developing the grip and coordination of both to help in her sport, so she knew it was possible to bend just the last knuckle of her right pinky finger, if she could find it in the darkness.

"So there's no way she didn't let her body get turned on by the women just because she wasn't into women herself? It was her body's response?"

"Correct. Just because your mind wants something doesn't mean the body does. Interest and arousal aren't the same thing."

Hollis stared at the white wall as he digested the information. "If her body is aroused by men, then that means I'll have to use men for sexual satisfaction . . ."

"And if the thought is repulsive, then you'll just have to forego sexual stimulation," Alfie said.

Hollis exhaled and shook his head. At the same moment, Shada was able to find her hand and bend her pinky finger. She let go right away so Hollis wouldn't find out she was taking back control.

"Is there some sort of test we have to determine if she's

somehow still alive in here?" Hollis said, using one hand to gesture over the entirety of Shada's body.

Alfie pondered then shook his head. "Not that I'm aware of. We haven't had this problem in the others." Alfie took a rapid inhale and his eyes got wider; he'd said too much.

"Wait, there are others?"

"Yes, we've uploaded other edited minds into unedited bodies. A few hours at a time. You know that," Alfie said. He turned away in an effort to be dismissive.

"You said that like there are other permanent uploads. Are there?"

Alfie sighed. "You don't think we'd let the head of West-Corp be the first recipient of a new procedure, do you?"

CHAPTER TWENTY-FOUR

THE OTHER RECIPIENTS of permanent switches had never met before Hollis demanded their assembly. Two of them were brought in from the city, where their edited minds were trying to live in unedited bodies among the unedited. Alfie claimed this was for "research purposes" but never elaborated on what research was being conducted. Three other recipients of permanent switches resided on the island for observation. These were the first three WestCorp had ever produced, edited minds transplanted into edited bodies.

Hollis asked if these three maintained the same position within the company that their minds had occupied, or if the body's previous position was where they stayed. Alfie told him that all the uploaded minds had to stay at the level of the body so nobody would wonder how these people received their promotions.

Five other bodies, filled with five minds, and Shada wondered if any of the original minds were still active. She assumed they'd had enough time to find the light and could witness the world through their body's eyes, but she doubted they would be able to exert the level of control she had over her own body. It had taken her years of deliberate practice to learn how to control her body, and her level of body awareness was rare among athletes, let alone the general population.

Hollis-in-Shada walked through an empty warehouse to a small room in the back, one that could have been used as security but was now empty. It was identical to the room to which Piper had brought Shada and Chloe when they were offered the chance to receive the uploads in the first place. Alfie was already present with the other five, a pen and notebook in his lap. They were seated in a circle of chairs, waiting for Hollis-in-Shada to take the last available seat.

After Hollis sat down and nodded to Alfie, Alfie stood up and spoke.

"We've brought you together today because you six are the first ever edited consciousnesses transplanted into other bodies."

Everyone looked at the faces around them.

"Four of you reside here on the island for observation," Alfie said as he nodded to a broad-shouldered woman of Asian descent, a heavyset Caucasian man with a goatee and ponytail, a weasel of a man with stooped shoulders, then Shada. "And two of you have lived in the city." Alfie looked at a dark-haired man and woman with deep-set eyes who could have been related.

"I won't tell you what the name of everyone's previous body was, or their position, but trust me when I say all of you were once high-ranking officials in WestCorp."

The group looked at one another once more. Shada was curious about what the unedited humans did in the city, and where they lived, but she imagined the uploaded minds all brimmed with curiosity about the former identities of everyone around them, measuring where they might stack up.

"This is the first time we've brought the six of you together, and I'll have to ask that you not contact each other once we leave this room. Other than you two, of course." The two unedited bodies closed their eyes and nodded.

"What are we here for?" the Asian woman said. From the tone of her voice, and the way she felt entitled to an answer so early in the meeting, Shada guessed her mind came from a high-ranking male.

"Think of it as a support group. We want to hear about any issues you might have had so that others here can know what to expect. Not all of you have lived inside another body for so long, and some have found the experience jarring."

At the edge of her vision, Shada could see the man with the goatee look in her direction. She wondered if he had access to more information than the others.

"For those of you who now occupy a body different from your original gender, have you noticed a change in sexual desire?"

Alfie looked at each face in turn. Shada could have sworn he lingered on her face for just a moment longer.

Shada saw the Asian woman's hand raise and saw her own fingers lift while her hands still rested in her lap.

"What happened?"Alfie asked the Asian woman.

"Nothing at all, that's the problem! Women do nothing for me anymore! It's like looking at what I know should be my favorite food and not finding anything about it at all appetizing."

Alfie thanked her for sharing. "And with you?" he said to Hollis-in-Shada.

"Same thing here. I had two women over and there was zero enjoyment. It felt like I was witnessing two mammals, like something I'd see in a zoo. Purely scientific and rational. Completely ruined the experience for me."

"I can imagine it's quite a shock to realize something that brought you pleasure before has no effect on you anymore," Alfie said, nodding as he noted their responses.

Hollis-in-Shada and the Asian woman both nodded in agreement.

"Does anyone else have a similar experience?"

The members of the group all looked at one another before the unedited woman from the city spoke up. "I used to eat meat all the time, multiple meals a day. I knew this body ate a vegetarian diet before I took over, but I figured I would be able to still eat my normal foods. Turns out meat now makes me bloated and sluggish, so I've had to cut it out of my diet."

"Her gut microbiome wasn't prepared for the sudden introduction of meat," Alfie said, looking up and to the left as he riffed on the subject. "You could probably introduce meat slowly into your diet and over time get back to the levels you were at before. You have to give your body the chance the adjust."

"It's not even worth it," the unedited woman said. When she tucked her dark hair behind an ear, Shada wondered if this habit was one from her former edited self or if the body her mind now occupied did it on instinct. Of course, it could have been neither and the hair in front of her face was bothersome.

Over the next hour the group shared various quirks about life in their new bodies that they hadn't expected. Everyone had something to share, and things ranged from needing more sleep than before to a newfound sensation to engage in running as exercise.

During a lull in the conversation, Alfie placed both hands on his knees and leaned forward. "Does anyone have anything else they'd like to share? I'm going to schedule these sessions once a week, so if anything comes up, we can discuss the next time we meet."

The group was silent for a moment before Hollis-in-Shada spoke up. "Do any of you wonder what happened to the mind of the body we occupy? Like, it just sits in there? Are they dead? Could they take back over?"

The rest of the group seemed to look inwards before they directed their attention to Alfie for answers.

Alfie cleared his throat. "Their mind still exists, but it's trapped in a senseless void. The legal system clarified this position when they said the minds of those sentenced to life imprisonment, when uploaded into the body of someone from death row, continue to exist. The person on death row is considered dead."

"That's what the legal system says, but has there been any research on how complete the takeover actually is?"

"We've had no observed cases of the body's original mind taking back control. But this is an interesting topic, worthy of investigation. Let us know if there are any instances when you feel like you lose control so we can study the phenomenon."

"And what if it's discovered they are able to take back control? The prison system could cancel their contract with us and sue, costing us millions," the weasel said. He had the bearing of a man who thought in dollars and cents.

"Well, if we find anything, we just won't tell them," Alfie said, a mischievous glint in his eye.

CHAPTER TWENTY-FIVE

THE OLDER MALE secretary called into the leader's office and requested permission to enter.

"Come in," Hollis-in-Shada told him.

Shada wondered how much Ernie knew, or could guess, based on how she had been transformed into a VIP overnight. His ability to follow protocol with this upstart sitting in his boss's chair impressed her.

"I wanted to go over the details of your trip into the city tonight," Ernie said when he stood across the desk from Hollis-in-Shada.

"Go on."

Ernie laid a manila folder on the desk. "Hollis arranged for you to take the helicopter to city hall for a meeting." He handed Shada a single sheet of paper with the trip's itinerary laid out in bullet points. "You're scheduled to fly out at five, meet with a representative from five thirty to six thirty, and be back by seven. Does this all sound reasonable?"

Shada gained a unique satisfaction from the way the older man talked to her. This would be her first ride in a helicopter, although without sensations from her body, the ride would be more like watching a scene from a movie than an experience. She knew she must have seen this in an action movie at some point in her life but couldn't recall a specific example.

"It all sounds reasonable to me. What will this meeting be about?" Hollis-in-Shada asked.

Shada hoped this wasn't a test by Hollis. She liked Ernie and wanted him to stick around.

Ernie looked apprehensive, the first time he seemed unsure about how much information to divulge. "Hollis never told me what you'll be meeting about, but every other time he's visited, an announcement followed about our technology being used by the city's government."

"Like . . ." Hollis-in-Shada said.

"I'll let them tell you more. I'd imagine Hollis has already briefed them about what you will be talking about. If I had to guess though, it has something to do with your recent uploads."

So Ernie knew Shada had been uploaded into. Shada doubted the meeting had anything to do with her specific experience but appreciated the innocence with which he made the suggestion. It seemed like he was trying his best to find common ground, to include Shada to the best of his ability, but without clear direction from Hollis, his fear of giving the unedited woman too much information held his tongue.

Hollis gathered the papers back into the manila folder and placed it next to his keyboard.

"Did you want Beth to get you anything to eat for the trip?" Ernie asked.

"I already have my meals, but . . . I've got a strange craving for candy. Something sweet and chewy. Could you have her find something in the food court and bring it to me for dessert?" Hollis said.

Shada was proud her body still craved those red gummy bears Sikya hated so much.

Right before it was time for the helicopter to depart, Beth showed up with multiple options of chewy candy. None of them were Shada's old favorite. Hollis-in-Shada selected a single bag of candied peach rings, carried them across the concrete landing pad, then boarded the craft. The bag was empty by the time they landed on the roof of city hall.

A man in a blue suit with an earpiece in one ear stood next to a door that jutted out from a corner of the roof. He gestured for Hollis-in-Shada to come to him. The wind generated by the helicopter's rotors made words useless, so Hollis tapped the back of the pilot's chair twice before he jumped out and ran towards the door.

The suited man's black hair, parted on the side, stood as solid against the wind as his flexed jaw. He held the door open for what he perceived was a woman, gesturing with his head for Hollis-in-Shada to go through first. On the other side of the door was a handsome set of dark brown circular stairs with an elegant railing on both sides. When the door shut behind them, blocking the noise of the helicopter, the man urged Hollis-in-Shada to head down.

"There will be someone waiting for you," he said, all business.

The stairs ended in a waiting room outside the mayor's office. A middle-aged woman with red hair and yellowed teeth sat at a desk outside a pair of double doors with cameras above.

"Good afternoon," the woman said with a close-lipped smile. "I'll tell Mayor Fitzgerald you've arrived."

Although the secretary urged Hollis-in-Shada to sit, Hollis remained standing and looked at historical pictures from the construction of city hall on the room's walls. He lingered on one that showed the laying of the building's cornerstone. It showed a past mayor without a suit jacket, sleeves rolled up and a construction hat on, leaning against a shovel surrounded by numerous construction workers.

"The mayor is ready for you," the secretary said.

Hollis tore his eyes away from the picture, nodded to the woman behind the desk, and walked through the double doors.

The mayor, a small bald man with circular glasses, stood up and shook hands with Hollis-in-Shada. "James," he said with a smile.

"Shada," Hollis replied. "I trust you've been told that I'm here representing Hollis?"

The smile disappeared from the mayor's face. "I was informed."

"Then let's get to it," Hollis said.

The mayor directed Hollis-in-Shada to a sofa and two matching chairs on one side of his office. "Care for anything to drink?" he said, gesturing to a small bar.

"No thanks," Hollis replied. He sat down on the couch, and the mayor sat on a chair.

The mayor informed Hollis-in-Shada that the plan was coming along well. He kept telling his guest that her boss would be pleased with the progress.

Hollis launched into a description of the plan, which Shada assumed was to demonstrate to the mayor how informed his guest was. "Since you seem to be skirting around the specifics, I'll give you a sense of my level of involvement. I know you have been denying birth licenses to all unedited humans who don't plan on editing their children pre-birth."

The mayor waited for Hollis-in-Shada to continue.

"WestCorp will offer post-birth edits at reduced rates for those who are denied birth licenses multiple times. These will be marketed as a fix to their biological clock, a chance through science to be content without having children. These reduced rates haven't been rolled out yet. Nobody has recognized the mass denials, as far as we know, and the purpose of this meeting is to see if there has been any recognition among the unedited of their new reality."

Shada knew Sikya was a victim of this plan.

The mayor leaned forward in his chair and rested his hands on his knees. "That's where Hollis and I left things last time he was here."

"So has there been any news?"

"There have been a few grumblings by those who want to have unedited children, but receiving post-birth edits isn't on their radar, as far as I know. They want to have unregistered children."

"Is that even possible?"

"In theory, yes, but they'd be kicked out of the city. Not many people are willing to risk the wilderness to have a child."

"So these grumblings are pointless." Hollis-in-Shada leaned back on the sofa and stared at the ceiling.

"For the most part. The lawsuits are still trickling in."

"Good. We'll wait until they're desperate before we announce the cheaper post-birth edits as a solution to their frustration."

Shada felt helpless knowing there was no way to communicate with her sister. If she could, she would tell her not to fall for the trap and to alert the people she knew who fought for unedited rights. She reached for her breath in order to calm down, not caring if Hollis discovered her control.

Hollis was too busy formulating ways to make the unedited people even more desperate in order to speed the process along to notice the change in breathing. He was insistent WestCorp be seen as the great savior from the evil City's government, with promises of increased funding for the mayor and the city.

"We haven't seen any money yet," the mayor complained.

"Your money will come once people begin post-birth edits. That's what we agreed on."

"Hollis said all of the money from the post-birth edits will come to us." The mayor shifted in his seat. "My only question is, why does WestCorp care if people edit themselves post-birth if they won't make any money on it?"

"Because, mayor, within a generation we can rid the city of all unedited humans once and for all."

CHAPTER TWENTY-SIX

THE MAYOR HAD a fruit and cheese plate brought in, and between bites he reported on other business ventures WestCorp was involved in with the city. The life sentences of prisoners, increased advertising, and better transportation options for WestCorp employees still living in the city were all discussed with minimal awareness on Shada's part as to what was being said.

Shada couldn't stop thinking about how WestCorp wanted to force all humans to be edited, to annihilate the unedited population—not right away and not against their will, but by making them suffer so much they gave up the part of themselves that made them human.

By the end of the meeting, Hollis-in-Shada had demonstrated such intimate knowledge of WestCorp's inner workings that the mayor seemed to be at total ease with his guest. "You'll fill Hollis in on all we've talked about today, right?"

"That's correct," Hollis-in-Shada said.

Shada saw her hand rise to display a small electrical device the size of a thumbnail. "This has been recording our entire conversation. I'll have him listen to it when I get back to the island."

"It's too bad he couldn't be here today, but I'm glad to have gotten the chance to get to know you," the mayor said. He switched seats and sat next to Hollis-in-Shada on the couch.

Shada had been around men long enough to know when their minds transitioned to their base instincts. She doubted Hollis knew the signs.

The mayor leaned in close, and Shada could smell the cheese on his breath. This was the first time she'd smelled anything since before the hijack. The scent thrilled her even though she had a sense of how repulsed she would be if she were in control of her body. The smell of the rest of the room flooded her awareness, and she was aware of the faint smell of glass cleaning solution, of musty carpet, and stale cologne. With the addition of a sense of smell came a greater awareness of her body. She was convinced she could move her entire arm if she wanted.

Hollis wasn't aware of the mayor's intentions until his hand fell on Hollis-in-Shada's leg. Hollis scrambled away. "What are you doing?" he said in Shada's voice.

The mayor wasn't deterred by the reaction. "Now that business is over, how about a little pleasure? This isn't the first time Hollis has sent a woman over."

Shada took control of her body and punched the mayor in the face. Hollis stared at Shada's hand for a moment before launching into a tirade. "Did any of those women ever talk to you about business? Get your head out of your ass, I am—" Hollis grew quiet.

The mayor rubbed his cheek and smiled. "You're what?" he asked.

Hollis-in-Shada stood up. "Leaving," Hollis said. He left the office, ignored the secretary, and began the climb back up to the roof.

Shada found joy in knowing her face would forever be attributed to punching the mayor's face, even if it was just between the two of them. Little did the mayor know that all of his future dealings with "Hollis" would be with her. She felt a prickle of awareness as Hollis grasped in the dark for her.

He had to know she was inside and could guess it was her who threw the punch.

Shada tried to retreat, but when she pulled back her own awareness, the hand she had taken control of to punch the mayor froze. It now served two masters. The hand was about to grasp the rail, and without the support, Hollis-in-Shada stumbled on the stairs.

"I knew it!" Hollis screamed in Shada's voice.

Shada tried her best to retreat, and even lost awareness of her body's breathing, but the hand remained motionless.

Hollis stared at the hand, trying to get it to move. He slammed it against the wall then banged it on the railing. It didn't reanimate. Desperate, he sandwiched his right index finger between the thumb and palm edge of his right hand. "I'll break it," he said.

Shada thought it strange that he threatened her with damage to a body that no longer belonged to her. In a surge of focus, she took back control of her breath and stopped his next inhale.

When Hollis realized he couldn't breathe, he looked around the stairwell as if his attacker could be on the ceiling. The right index finger was released, and Shada took back full control of the hand. She pointed her index finger and shook it from side to side, telling Hollis no. She allowed her body to breathe again.

Hollis used the left hand to support himself on the railing and gulped air. While he was preoccupied with breathing again,

Shada took over the rest of her body. She stood up straight, breathed twice through her nose, and said to the air around her, "How does it feel?"

She climbed the stairs and prepared to head back to the island to destroy Hollis's work.

When she reached the top of the stairs, she realized Hollis had taken control of her breathing. He was using the same method to take back control that she had used to find control in the first place. He stopped her breathing and Shada fell to the ground.

Hollis stood Shada's body up, back in control, and opened the door. The helicopter pilot spotted him and turned on the rotors. Hollis rushed past the security guard with the stationary hair as the craft came alive.

Shada had allowed Hollis into her body so Sikya could have a child. Hollis would stand by that statement, he would allow Sikya to have a child, so long as it was edited before birth. A condition Sikya wouldn't agree to.

Shada wanted revenge.

Hollis didn't make it halfway to the helicopter before Shada was able to take back control. In that moment, she decided to destroy Hollis once and for all. Her body veered to the left, and she forced herself to walk towards the edge of the roof but was stopped when Hollis stopped their body in its tracks.

On the roof of city hall, two consciousnesses took turns controlling different parts of the same body, one with the goal of jumping off the roof and the other wanting to board the helicopter. To those witnessing the struggle, it looked like two stop-motion animations had become interwoven.

It became clear Shada was winning the fight, because her body kept inching closer to the edge of the roof. In a rare moment of near-complete control, Shada was able to use one leg to hop towards the edge while Hollis used the other as an anchor. She was able to win because she fought not only for herself but for her sister and future niece or nephew. She was convinced if she could kill Hollis, she could save them all.

Shada was tackled a few steps from the edge of the roof. She saw the blue suit of the security guard on top of her.

"Tie me in and take me to Alfie," Shada heard herself say.

Shada continued to struggle, but the guard was trained to manipulate those who resisted.

The guard looked confused but relayed her words to the pilot. He nodded in understanding before the two of them tied Shada to one of the rear-facing chairs in the helicopter and they took off.

Over the bay, Shada discovered that as long as she stayed in control of her breathing, she could trap Hollis inside for good.

CHAPTER TWENTY-SEVEN

SHADA WAS LEFT in the helicopter while the pilot ran to get reinforcements. Through the headset covering her ears she could hear the blades overhead slowing down. The waves of the bay rolled into shore while Shada focused on her breathing. She could feel Hollis fighting to regain control, but she didn't allow any space for him to find footing in her diaphragm.

The pilot returned with Alfie and two security guards. By then Shada was covered in sweat from the heat inside the black helicopter. Alfie removed the headset from over Shada's ears and asked, "How do you feel?"

"I feel fine," Shada said, trying to mimic the impatient way Hollis sounded when he spoke with her voice.

"The pilot said you had an episode before takeoff."

"I did. Not sure what happened, but I'm back to normal now." Shada attempted her best commanding tone. "Untie me."

Alfie gave her a quizzical look. "I will, but we're going to have to go to the lab for an assessment."

Shada continued her impression of Hollis. "That won't be necessary. I have a lot of work to do, no time for assessments." She didn't pay as much attention to her breathing; her efforts were spent impersonating Hollis instead. In the space that opened up, Hollis grabbed hold of a breath before Shada forced him back into the darkness.

Hollis's attempt to take back control showed up to Alfie as a startled gasp. "What's wrong?" he asked, now on high alert.

"Nothing, nothing," Shada said. "The heat is getting to me."

Alfie flashed a knowing smile before he untied Shada. He instructed the two massive guards to accompany them to his office. "Each of you place a hand on one of her shoulders; I don't want another episode of what happened on the roof."

Alfie thanked the pilot, telling him that he'd done well in making sure Shada was secure on the return trip, before dismissing him.

The party of four took a transport vehicle back to the atrium and walked through, the guards flanking Shada the entire time, before they ended up in Alfie's office. He told the two guards to stand outside.

"Take a seat on the table," Alfie said to Shada when they were alone.

"Really, I'm fine. This isn't necessary," Shada said.

Alfie looked at her, a stern look beneath raised eyebrows, and Shada acquiesced. She climbed onto the table and looked down at her hands. Still aware of every breath, she flexed each finger joint in turn, starting with her right pinky finger and working her way to the left. Meanwhile, Alfie pulled up both her file and Hollis's on the computer before sitting down on his circular stool on wheels.

Alfie took a quick trip through Shada's major joints, asking her to move each one. Ankles, knees, hips, then shoulders, elbows, and wrists. After Shada demonstrated control of each, Alfie asked if she felt any of them were slow to respond.

"Nope," Shada said. "Everything seems to be working fine." She impressed herself at how much she was able to invoke

Hollis in her voice this time, sounding both exasperated and commanding at the same time.

"Do you have any concern that your host was able to take back control? Or was fighting for control?" Alfie asked. His pen hovered over the file in his hand.

"You mean because of the incident on the roof? I wanted to look at the city from above and stumbled on my way over, that's all." Shada continued to count her breaths in the background.

"The pilot said it was more than a stumble. He said it looked like you were fighting against yourself. His words. And the last time you were in here, we were talking about your concern that the host was able to take back control. Now, I didn't witness the event, but it sounds like you were fighting to keep control of this body."

Shada tilted her head to the side. "I can see how it could look like that, but I'm telling you I'm fine!"

Alfie jotted something down in the file before looking back at her. "And tell me how you feel."

"I feel great," Shada said. She lowered her chin. "Ready to get back to all the work I have," she growled.

"In time, in time. I understand this is frustrating, sir, but this is important. The pilot swore you were going to jump off the roof. You tell me, does this sound like someone who is fine?"

"It does when I'm telling you I am."

"OK, OK. There's just one more thing we have to do." Alfie stood up and withdrew a modified helmet from a cabinet on the wall.

Shada watched as Alfie plugged it into the computer. She didn't want to ask what he was going to do, because she didn't want her ignorance of the procedure to tip him off that Hollis was no longer in control. She tried to come up with possible uses for the device, wondering if there was a chance her consciousness would be pulled out and placed back inside.

If this was the case, should she leave Hollis inside and hope her body would stay unconscious until she returned?

Or should she allow Hollis to be withdrawn by allowing him to take back control at the last possible moment, so he could be pulled into the machine while she stayed in her own body? She wasn't sure she would be able to relinquish control on command, in which case it would be a coin flip to see which of them would be withdrawn.

While she tried both these options on for size, she counted her ten breaths over and over again in order to keep Hollis at bay. Alfie asked her to lie down, and Shada wondered if Hollis had learned to see through her eyes. She doubted it.

Alfie explained the process as he placed the helmet on Shada's head. "Since our last discussion I've been thinking about how to measure if the host is able to control any body processes, and I think I've come up with a way to measure. Before we can transplant consciousness, we have to scan the mind that will be transplanted. That's really what this device does," he pulled the helmet straps tight. "Creates a map. What I'll do is create a new map of your mind and look for inconsistencies in the connections between neurons. If the host has taken back control of anything, they should show up as dark spots."

"Will I be unconscious?"

"No, you'll be awake the whole time. The only way you can lose consciousness is if there is another body to switch into, but since none are hooked up, there's nowhere to go." Computer keys clicked as Shada waited for the scan to begin. "OK, lie still. This will take a few minutes," Alfie said.

Shada took extra care to focus on the exhale of each of her next ten breaths. She began a second round and got to two more exhales before Alfie said the scan was complete.

"Any inconsistencies?" Shada asked.

Alfie stared at the screen, his head blocking Shada's view. He searched every corner, and when his head moved, Shada could see a series of white dots with thin white lines stretched between them. He nodded his head. "I don't see any dark spots," he said. He sounded surprised, as if he'd expected some part of another's consciousness to show up on the screen.

"So I can take this thing off?"

Alfie rolled over and helped Shada take off the headgear.

"So I can go?" Shada asked.

"Yes, sir. Sorry to hold you for so long, but I had to be sure."

When Alfie said "sir," Shada remembered she'd forgotten to talk as if she was Hollis. The leader of WestCorp would never ask to go; he'd inform Alfie that he was leaving. She stood up and walked out of the room, hoping the scientist didn't notice that something about the end of their interaction wasn't quite right.

CHAPTER TWENTY-EIGHT

SHADA STARED at Hollis's computer while she sat in the high-backed chair behind his desk. She had memorized his password, so getting into the system wasn't a problem, but she had no idea how to begin the large-scale sabotage she envisioned.

It was the morning after her trip into the city, and she had woken up in a panic, worried Hollis had been able to take back control of her body. After a quick body scan and a series of purposeful breaths, she knew she was still the one in charge, though she sensed Hollis in the background. She guessed that as long as she was asleep, Hollis had no sensations to ground his attempt to retake control.

Shada clicked on various folders and stumbled upon files for every employee at WestCorp. At first, she clicked random names and checked to see how much money they made, but she stopped once she realized the information was useless to her. She opened his email and couldn't find a single reference to his plan with the mayor for the city's unedited inhabitants.

She had no idea where the sensitive files were. Even if she had, she wasn't sure whether she should corrupt them, delete them, or send them away to some outside entity who would be able to exact revenge.

"The movies make it look so easy," she said to herself.

She gave up her quest for a smoking gun and stared at the bay through the window. Waves continued to roll onto the island; their perpetual motion made Shada realize her attempts to subvert WestCorp would be like trying to stop the tide. No matter what happened they would keep coming, and the only way to end them once and for all would be to remove their source.

The source was trapped inside her.

She knew she could keep Hollis trapped, but only as long as she kept control of each and every breath she took. This was no way to live a life. Something in the depths of the water called out to her, and she knew she had to follow through on the plan she'd first come up with on the roof. Hollis must be killed, and the only way to do it would involve sacrificing herself.

Ernie called into the office in the middle of Shada's daydream about the best way to kill herself. Shada put him on speaker and was informed Alfie was there to see her.

"Send him in," Shada said. She felt like Alfie was on her turf now, even though the office belonged to Hollis.

Alfie walked in, followed by Chloe. Based on her lack of recognition, Shada guessed her friend's body was occupied by another person's consciousness.

Shada did her best to avoid the eyes of her friend, reminding herself that Hollis would have no reason to care about this random unedited person. This preoccupation almost made her lose track of her breath. Shada sensed Hollis at the periphery of her awareness, waiting for the opportunity to retake control.

"I wanted you to see the first person uploaded into four times," Alfie said from behind Chloe. He placed a hand on her shoulder and beamed with pride. "Your host was friends with her."

Shada leaned back in her chair and assumed a nonchalant air as she played along. "Four times? Has she shown any signs of degradation?"

"I'll let her answer that," Alfie said, turning to a stone-faced Chloe. "Did you notice any resistance? Does there seem to be any lag?" Alfie asked.

Chloe squeezed her lips together and shook her head. "Seems like every other time," she responded.

"Her body accepted the upload at the same rate as before," Alfie added.

Shada stood up and walked around the desk to where Chloe and Alfie stood. She circled Chloe, assuming Hollis would do the same if he was in control. Chloe was smiling when Shada returned to her front.

"Is it really you?" Chloe said.

Shada was surprised by the question. She looked at Alfie for direction, wondering if this could be Chloe taking back control. Nothing in the scientist's face suggested he was worried. All he did was smile.

"It's really me," Shada said to Chloe, trying her best to sound confident. She was herself, after all.

"I always knew you could do it. Interesting choice of body though," Chloe said. It was her turn to inspect the other, and her eyes went from head to toe and back again.

Shada shot Alfie a look that asked, "Does she know?"

"I told her," Alfie said with a nod.

Confused, Shada withdrew into counting her breaths in order to maintain her composure.

"Are you OK?" Chloe asked.

"I'm fine. I've found that focused breathing keeps me grounded," Shada said. She hoped somewhere inside Chloe's body her friend heard her words and would reach for these important first steps of taking back control.

"Who do you think this is?" Chloe asked Shada.

"I'm . . . I'm not sure," Shada replied. Alfie's knowing smile tempted her to punch him in the face.

Chloe brushed Shada's cheek with the back of her hand. "It's Ruby."

Shada had no idea who Ruby was, but she knew the response this type of touch should elicit. She also knew edited humans didn't feel attachments to the same degree as the unedited, so she felt she could delay an emotional response in favor of a rational one.

"What were you thinking?" Shada said to Alfie.

"Relax, it's just me," Ruby-in-Chloe said.

"She's the only one I told," Alfie explained. "I told her before she uploaded."

"I made him tell me!" Ruby-in-Chloe said. "When I heard about the incident on the roof, I got worried. Alfie said we should upload my mind into this girl and see your response. I think he fears your host was able to take back control."

Alfie glared at Chloe. "You weren't supposed to tell him that."

"Oh, what does it matter? You said he passed the inspection in your office."

"And this was another test. Worthless, now."

Shada returned to her chair on the far side of the desk and left the two visitors standing.

"Make sure you let me know how the host does once the procedure has been reversed," Shada said, dismissing them.

"Of course," Alfie replied.

"I'll come see you in my own skin," Ruby-in-Chloe said.

"Don't bother, I have lots of work to do," Shada said. She was pleased to see Chloe's face fall at the dismissal.

Alfie guided Chloe towards the door. Before he left, he told Shada the report about Chloe's condition post-upload would be sent over that afternoon.

Alone again in the office, Shada returned to the computer and looked up Ruby. There were three individuals on the company payroll with that first name, but one of their last names was Hollis. Shada clicked on the file and began to read.

She discovered Ruby Hollis was Michael Hollis's wife. Still married, but separate primary residences. Her birth date made her the same approximate age as the leader of WestCorp, but the photo attached to the file showed a middle-aged woman instead of the advanced age that would be expected. The file didn't reference a date of marriage; instead, a date of assignment was listed from when Hollis was thirty. Two arrival dates were listed, one year and three years after their assignment, and Shada assumed these corresponded to the birth dates of their children.

Shada typed out a message to Alfie telling him to kill Ruby when the upload was reversed. She wondered if the message, without justification, would be enough for Alfie to follow through with the orders. If Alfie was convinced Hollis was still in control, he might have listened, but the lingering doubt he harbored, evidenced by testing Shada with Chloe's body, made Shada think the orders wouldn't be carried out.

Shada deleted the message. One Hollis death would be enough to make her happy.

CHAPTER TWENTY-NINE

ALFIE ASKED SHADA, assuming it was Hollis, to come to his office. "There's something I have to show you in person," he said. He wouldn't elaborate over the phone, regardless of Shada's insistence.

Shada guessed Hollis would resist going to Alfie's office—it would have something to do with power dynamics, she was sure —and might even make the scientist wait until the next day, but her curiosity got the best of her, so she agreed to the meeting. She assumed it was about Chloe.

Alfie's office was flanked by two security guards. Shada walked in, unannounced, the way she imagined Hollis might do. She caught Alfie seated at his desk, deep in thought. The faraway look of a man whose thoughts are somewhere else evaporated when his eyes focused on her, replaced by a deep fatigue set in darkened eye sockets. On his desk was a grid of eight vials, standing vertical in two rows of four.

"Please take a seat," Alfie said, gesturing to the chair opposite him.

Shada told Alfie she had been sitting all day and would rather stand. She wondered if Hollis would ever do the same.

"I need to give you an injection," Alfie said, not wasting any time.

"An injection? What for?"

"I designed this to keep your host from taking back control. It took me all night." He withdrew one of the vials and rolled it between his fingers.

Shada weighed her options. Hollis, fearful of Shada, would accept the injection without question in order to keep her consciousness under his thumb. Shada knew she was in control at the moment, but for how long? If this injection served to keep him silent, then she could have Alfie continue production for her to use it long-term, allowing her to eliminate Hollis without killing herself.

The injection seemed like a good idea.

Shada sat down and laid her bare arm over Alfie's desk. Alfie withdrew a needle and syringe from a desk drawer and injected the clear liquid. He gave her a cotton swab to hold over the injection site.

"Give it a few minutes to kick in," Alfie said, exhausted.

"What was it?" Shada asked.

"A modified form of LSD. It makes the subconscious conscious."

Shada's eyes got wide, and she stared at Alfie. The scientist seemed to be carrying a massive weight on his shoulders that didn't allow him to sit up straight in his chair.

"I thought you said it would help keep him under control . . ."

She realized too late that she'd said him.

Alfie closed his eyes and exhaled. "I had a feeling you were back," he said. "I wanted to have a conversation with whoever's in the background. I'm not sure it will work, but I didn't know what else to do."

Shada felt strings of panic pull her down and focused on her exhale.

"I had a feeling before I brought Chloe over with Ruby trapped inside. She ruined the test by telling you, but I still couldn't shake the thought. Hollis and Ruby were never close—edited relationships are different from what you're used to in the city—but there was nothing to suggest you even recognized the personality of the woman you were paired with for over two decades."

Shada felt reality slipping away from her, and counting breaths did nothing to slow its departure. Hollis was coming back and there was nothing she could do about it. It wasn't the same as before, when one had control and the other had to sit in the background. It was more like they both shared the same space, two halves of the brain who had access to one body. For now she could keep her mouth shut, but she wasn't sure for how long.

Alfie didn't seem to care about Shada's silence. He continued telling Shada how he'd arrived at his conclusion.

"I came back into my office after Ruby left Chloe's body—both women are fine, by the way—and took a look at the mapping of your neurons. I was looking for the dark spots, certain I had missed something. It didn't even occur to me that you, Shada, would be able to take back complete control. But then it hit me. Why would Hollis know how to control parts of his body that weren't his? Once he lost control, it would be the most natural thing in the world for you to shut him out. That's why there weren't any dark spots."

Alfie turned his computer monitor around and rested an elbow on his desk. The screen showed two images side by side, each a series of white dots connected by thin white lines. They were the same type of picture, but it didn't take a scientist to know they were different. Alfie pointed to the one on the left.

"This is the map we made last night. Notice no dark spots?

This is why I assumed there was no loss of control."

Shada tried to nod but ended up jerking her head left and right.

"The one on the right is a map I had of Hollis's brain from his initial upload. We don't have a map of your brain; well, we didn't before last night. I think it's clear these two aren't the same. Now, the way the uploads work is that we take one neural mapping and transpose it onto another brain. There are paths of least resistance present, from the previous occupant, but the machine we designed is able to highlight these connections and negate them, while amplifying the correct ones, allowing the upload to take hold. Imagine it like this: we are able to turn on and up every neuron and connection in a brain, making it into a block of marble. Then we chisel away the necessary parts to sculpt the statue we are trying to create."

Shada put her head in her hands and tried to focus on her breath.

"That's all a mind is, a series of firing neurons and their connections. Right now, we have the ability to copy one map onto another, but in time we hope to design our own minds from scratch. In a robot, this would be called artificial intelligence. In a human, we call it the Vitruvian Man."

Shada lost control of her breathing. The drug didn't make her hallucinate, which she'd expected, but instead allowed her to feel a connection to the world around her, a sense of wonder that allowed her to view Alfie not just as a person but as a wonderful example of life. The wood of his desk seemed to call out to her, its smooth edges a marvel of human ingenuity. Without a firm hold of reality, Hollis took back control.

"That bitch tried to kill me!" Hollis-in-Shada said. The words didn't come out in one smooth statement but between facial spasms.

Alfie displayed a tired smile. "Welcome back, sir."

CHAPTER THIRTY

"You're going to pay for that one," Hollis said to Shada's reflection in the bathroom mirror. He was back in his underground bunker after spending the last few days under Alfie's direct supervision. Together they'd determined how often the low-dose LSD had to be administered in order for Hollis to maintain control over Shada's body. One injection every fifteen hours was the minimum, but they shortened the window to twelve hours to be on the safe side.

Hollis stared at what was now his reflection and made a show of holding his breath. His cheeks puffed out, and he put his hand on his throat, holding onto his air for so long his face turned red. His loud exhale was followed by a maniacal laugh.

"There's nothing you can do!" he said.

Shada didn't try to retake control of her body's breathing. There were a few times during Alfie's observation when she thought it might be possible, but a new dose of the drug would take away her ability to focus. It would create a sense of wonder and appreciation for the world around her, a content sensation that got snapped away from her as soon as Hollis retook control. She went through this cycle of attraction and repulsion to retaking control a few times before she gave up. Now she stayed in the background, watching and hearing the world through what used to be her eyes and ears.

Hollis disclosed to Alfie that he'd had no sensations while Shada maintained control. He never knew where he was and couldn't hear a thing. He said it was like being in a dark room, alone with his thoughts.

Shada thought forever in solitude would be a fitting end for such a despicable human.

Hollis pried himself away from the bathroom mirror and went into the kitchen. He withdrew one of the premade meals and began to eat it cold.

"I'm not sure you can hear me, but I'm going to pretend you can," he said through a full mouth.

Alfie and Hollis had never gotten Shada to speak about her experience being trapped inside her own body. They assumed she experienced it the same way as Hollis but couldn't be sure.

"Your sister, I forget her name, hasn't received a cent."

Shada knew her blood would boil if she had access to a body.

"And it's your fault. The transfer was set up, but we wanted to wait to make sure the upload was permanent. You can thank Piper for that idea. There's a phrase I had to say to Alfie, but you took back control so soon I never said it."

Hollis stopped chewing and stared at the cavern above, listening for a response that would never come.

"Are you curious about what the phrase is?" Hollis took another bite and listened once more.

"Well, you'll have to stay curious, because I'm not going to tell you. What if you are able to retake control?"

Hollis shoveled food into Shada's mouth, not taking any extra time to chew. "You only have yourself to blame," he said.

Shada knew she couldn't kill herself, and therefore Hollis,

before Sikya received the money. If she did, it would make the hijack pointless. There had to be a way for her to take back control, but even if she did, she wouldn't know the phrase.

The shores of hope, once in sight, had disappeared, and she was left alone to drift in the sea.

She thought back to when she'd had control of Hollis and was alone with access to his computer. She hadn't even thought to check on Sikya. What kind of sister was she? Even if Sikya never got the windfall Hollis had promised, Shada could have done something, even if it was just sending a message telling her she was all right.

She had a long time to come to grips with the oversight.

Hollis finished his meal and threw away the silverware along with the disposable container. He walked back into the bathroom and opened the bathroom mirror, exposing shelves empty except for a small box of razors. From the box he withdrew a single razor blade and left the rest of the box next to the sink.

Hollis closed the mirror and leaned forward, leaving Shada's face an inch from the surface. Her eyes were so close that the flecks of black inside her brown irises were easy to distinguish.

"I want you to cry for your sister," Hollis said.

Shada watched her own hand, a razor squeezed between her thumb and forefinger, rise to her face and hover just below her right eye. Her own lips parted in a grin as the corner of the blade pressed against the lower part of her eye socket and continued straight down until even with the base of her nose. The parting of the red sea recreated in flesh.

Hollis admired his handiwork.

"I spent a lot of time thinking of ways to punish you. As an athlete, you prize your body. But now that this body belongs to me, anything I do to it would just be a punishment for me too!

But then I thought how useless this pretty face is. Anything, or anyone, I want, I can afford to buy myself."

Hollis stared at Shada's reflection for a moment before bringing the razor up to her left eye. "I'm a sucker for symmetry," he said as he repeated the procedure on the other side of her face.

Blood dripped from the two wounds. Each drop strengthened Shada's resolve to make Hollis pay.

"Wipe away those crocodile tears!" Hollis said. Shada couldn't tell if he was angry or joking. He contorted Shada's mouth into a dramatic frown and stammered, "But my sister!" then slammed a fist onto the counter.

He looked down. Drops of blood joined previous neighbors, pooled together, and covered the sink's edges. Hollis made no attempt to move Shada's head so the blood dripped closer to the drain. He lifted Shada's head enough to see the tops of her eyes.

"You did this to yourself," he said.

CHAPTER THIRTY-ONE

THE WOUNDS on Shada's face required stitches, but Hollis didn't address them. He went about the rest of his day as if nothing had happened, ignoring the pain. The few times he caught his reflection in the mirror, he smiled at the gashes. When he did, the corners of Shada's eyes crinkled up and distorted the straight lines running down her cheeks. Hollis didn't seem to register the pain, or if he did, he enjoyed it.

In bed that night, without any bandaging, the open wound on his right cheek scabbed over and became fused with the pillow. When Hollis opened his eyes the next morning, he couldn't lift his head.

Shada, her consciousness bathed in darkness while Hollis slept, became aware of the room as soon as her body's eyes opened. She couldn't feel her face attached to the pillow, but when Hollis cursed, she knew something was wrong.

Hollis began to count. "One...two..." he said in her own voice.

On the count of three Hollis ripped his face from the pillow. Shada's right hand rose up, touched her right cheek, and came away covered in blood.

Hollis didn't inspect the damage. Instead, he went into the kitchen and devoured the day's first meal.

Alfie came over to administer the day's first dose. Their agreed-upon schedule was eight in the morning and eight at night. Shada could tell, but she wasn't sure Hollis recognized, that Alfie did his best to avoid looking at her face.

"Any adverse effects?" Alfie asked as he withdrew the needle from Shada's arm.

Hollis shook his head. "Haven't heard from her since the first injection."

"That's good. What happened to your face?"

"Oh, these? I just wanted to decorate," Hollis said.

"Decorate your face?"

"What, you don't like what I've done?"

"Sir, let me remind you that this is your body now. Any harm you do must be considered self-harm. With this treatment's potential for psychosis, it will have to be reevaluated."

"No!" Hollis yelled. "I'm fine. I did this so she would see who's in charge now," he said with disgust.

"There's no doubt about that anymore." Alfie said, exasperated. "We'll continue the injections, but I'll be looking for alternatives. In the meantime, don't show your host who's in charge again. I'm worried you'll go too far."

"Like you said, it's my body. If I ruin this one, I can always get another."

"You can't think like that. The further you get from your own body, the greater the chance of degradation. You are in charge, you don't have to show her."

Hollis thought while Alfie gathered up his trash and threw it away.

"Why don't you bring some girls over here tonight? I'm sure she won't like that."

Alfie turned towards Hollis-in-Shada and looked at him with crestfallen eyes. "I can do that."

"Two. Young."

"They'll be with me when I come back for your evening injection."

Hollis waved Alfie away. With the scientist gone, he went into his study. His day was spent behind his computer, working from home, looking over his company's operations.

Shada was too busy trying to take back control to pay attention to his work. Each time she tried to focus on her breath, which had worked so well before, she would be struck by a disorienting sense of wonder at the world around her. She felt connected to the environment, as if she could sense the life that once was in this underground chamber. She couldn't decide which physical form the life took, which creatures were killed or driven out by the creation of Hollis's residence, but knew that the enormous length of time it had existed held a certain power. Her focus was drawn away in this fashion every time she tried to take back control of her breathing, meaning she never succeeded in holding on for more than a moment. It was like trying to pull herself from dark water by clawing at slippery rocks, never gaining enough traction to lift herself out but not losing herself inside its depths.

Shada was shocked at how young the two girls Alfie brought back with him were. They couldn't have been more than teenagers. She thought to herself how wrong this was and wondered what perverse intentions Hollis had for them. How would he show Shada who was in charge?

The girls watched Alfie administer the second injection of the day, all four of them seated at the expansive kitchen table. When Alfie left, they sat still, awaiting instruction.

Shada felt the increased awareness of the world around her

that came with the drug's administration, the strange wonder at all living things. These two girls in the room with her, they had their whole lives ahead of them. An awareness of their beating hearts informed her they were unedited, and she was filled with an overwhelming sense of connection with their vitality. As Shada listened, the two girls' hearts began to beat in sync.

All of this occurred in the time in which Hollis inspected his companions.

From deep within the cavern of her consciousness, Shada felt a sense of her own heartbeat synchronizing with those of the two young girls. The resonation of the three hearts reverberated off the cavern's walls. If she took a second to think about what she sensed, she would decide it wasn't possible by the laws of physics for any of these feelings to be proven, nullifying their power. She ignored rationality and maintained the awareness of life in both herself and the room.

Shada focused on her own heartbeat and found a sense of peace. At the same moment, Hollis instructed the teenagers to take off their clothes.

The two girls stood up and began to disrobe.

Shada focused on her own heartbeat and felt her awareness travel alongside her blood to every corner of her body. It began in her chest and spread out, down to her toes and up to the crown of her head. She felt herself swallow hard, Hollis's doing, and realized she could control her mouth. Not because she'd trapped Hollis deep inside, but because she accepted his attempts at control and decided not to allow them. Like wanting to eat but deciding to skip the meal, aware of hunger but not giving in.

"Stop," she said in a hoarse whisper.

The two girls stood still, their dresses pulled down to their waists and their shoes on the floor beside them.

Shada could feel Hollis's panic. He was still able to send signals to her body, but now the body wasn't responding. When he'd lost control before, he was banished to the darkness. Now, he lived in the light.

CHAPTER THIRTY-TWO

SHADA SPOKE AGAIN, this time with more force. "Stop. Put your clothes back on," she told the girls. While she controlled her mouth and vocal cords, Hollis was able to communicate with the rest of her body. She hadn't been back in control long enough to stop him.

Hollis threw her right hand onto the table and with the left gouged one of the wounds on her cheek. Three fingernails dug into her flesh, causing her eyes to roll back into her head.

The girls were terrified. Shada could sense their racing hearts and, using the resonation of her own heartbeat with theirs, was able to take back control of her hand and end the searing pain. She found her legs, forced herself to stand up, and walked into the bathroom.

"Don't go anywhere," Hollis snarled. He was able to take back control of Shada's voice while Shada was preoccupied controlling her movement.

Shada could feel Hollis try to retake control of her legs. The sensation was similar to a leg being asleep; she could still stand and move, but her body's response was slow.

When Hollis realized her legs were out of his reach, he took over her arms. She could tell when his attention switched to a different part of her body, but she wasn't fast enough to get there first. Hollis grabbed the backs of chairs, which fell over, and held onto the edge of the doorway in an attempt to stop Shada from reaching her destination. Shada's legs continued to march, and with some help from her momentum, she was able to continue despite Hollis's best attempts to stop her.

In the bathroom, Shada stared at her face in the mirror and focused on her pounding heart. At first, it felt like she was chasing Hollis from limb to limb, but once she accepted the impulses in totality, she gained a relaxed control over her entire body. Her fingers grazed the gashes on her cheeks. "Never again," she whispered. The marks had a new meaning now, that she was back in control of herself, constant reminders of the harm that could result from allowing someone else inside.

Shada felt Hollis try to blink and negated the signal. She heard a voice the world had lost during the upload: Hollis's. He muttered, "I can't even blink."

Shada smiled. "Didn't you tell me to smile more?" she thought.

"What are you talking about?" Shada heard. Her lips never moved.

She communicated via thoughts with the voice inside her head. "When we first met in the lab, you told me I should smile more. So here you go." Shada looked in the mirror and grinned, showing off as many teeth as she could. She allowed Hollis to see through her eyes without worrying if he could control where she looked.

Shada enjoyed Hollis's struggle. His attempts to find and control her limbs grew frantic, but none of the signals were anywhere near strong enough to overpower her. Her smile, forced at first, became genuine.

"What's the phrase to send the money to Sikya?" she thought.

Hollis refused to acknowledge her words and stayed silent. Shada knew she didn't need him to admit the phrase to her; she could read his thoughts. It wouldn't be hard to probe his memories.

She pried his mind open with little trouble. The process reminded her of trying to give her childhood dog his medicine, the insertion of a finger between teeth and a controlled effort to open his jaw wide enough to insert a pill. An initial struggle with no real threat of failure.

While Hollis's memory was under attack, he made no effort to control her body. It was as if his mind was frozen while under inspection.

The dancing dwarf.

"Thank you," Shada said to herself in the mirror. "I never would've guessed that."

Shada spent the next few minutes, an eternity for her, stopping Hollis from controlling any part of her body. She accepted his desires as she did other sensations, reducing him to a series of impulses. The process was similar to what all children undergo when learning to control their response to stimulation. Shada had learned to control her impulses once; it was easier to do as an adult.

Shada wasn't sure of the science behind what she was experiencing. She thought she'd understood after Alfie's explanation, but this new development didn't make sense. How could it be possible to experience both consciousnesses inside the same mind? The only explanation she could come up with was that Hollis's attempts at control were like flashes of light, or an entire mapping of lights, that she was able to extinguish at will. As long as she kept the flashes of light as short as possible, she could maintain control over her own body.

She wished she could tell Alfie so he could do further research and provide more clarity, but she would never reveal her secret. The injections would have to continue so Alfie didn't grow suspicious. Shada knew she could always find her own heartbeat's resonation with the world around her, aided by the low-dose LSD injections.

The injections didn't keep her mind in the darkness. They opened her awareness.

Shada, satisfied with her level of control, walked back out and told the girls, who hadn't moved in the half hour Shada had been gone, to put their clothes back on. She walked them back to the elevator and rode it to the surface with them.

Both girls stared at Shada's face during their vertical trip. It seemed like they were aware of the change in Shada, that this was another young girl in a strange place, just like them.

Shada felt a burst of energy and recognized another of Hollis's attempts to retake control. Shada couldn't tell if these attempts were becoming less powerful or if she had less of a reaction to them, but she was confident they wouldn't register in the near future. She dove into his memories. He tried to block her, but she was able to neutralize his resistance with brute force. She remembered, through Hollis's eyes, when he sat in Alfie's office and told the scientist the phrase he would have to say to release the funds. She wasn't sure how probing his memory served to freeze him, but she didn't care. All she cared about was that it worked.

One of the girls asked Shada what happened to her face.

"My shell cracked," Shada said. She flashed them a mischievous smile.

The girls seemed to understand what she meant and nodded in unison. All three hearts skipped a beat.

CHAPTER THIRTY-THREE

"I BET you're wondering how I got these scars," Shada said to the support group. Shada looked at the five members of the group and smiled at each one in turn. She wanted them to see she wasn't ashamed of the new additions to her face. The narrowing of her eyes tugged at the scabs on her face, causing pain on the upper part of her cheek.

She'd been in complete control of her body for a full two days. She'd asked Alfie to call the group together, telling the scientist it was so she could tell them what to expect if their host took over.

Shada did her best to place herself in Hollis's shoes before she spoke. "I did this to remind my host who's in charge." She flashed her best wicked grin.

The weasel-looking man, an edited mind placed into an edited body, leaned in. The others shifted in their seats. Not one of them offered words of support.

Shada thought the others didn't understand. Their silence pulled more words from her. "She tried to regain control and kill me!" she exclaimed.

The dark-haired man and woman, edited minds transplanted into unedited bodies, didn't look surprised at the news. The other two edited minds placed in edited bodies, the Asian woman and the man with the ponytail, shook their heads. "That isn't possible," the weasel said.

"Well, it happened to me!" Shada said, imagining herself to be Hollis telling the world about his struggle.

"To be clear, she's not suggesting you go to these lengths," Alfie clarified. "This response was uncalled for; we had already been able to suppress the host with an injection."

Shada nodded in agreement but thought Alfie was seeking acknowledgment for his serum. She wasn't going to give it to him. "Of course, there's no reason to go to this extreme. I just wanted to call out the elephant in the room." Everyone stared at Shada as if they didn't understand the metaphor.

"The reason I asked Alfie to bring everyone together again is because there are a few tricks I learned to maintain control, and I want you to be aware of them." She looked at the weasel, the Asian woman, and the man with the goatee. She doubted the edited minds trapped inside would be able to grasp the importance of what she was about to share but figured it wouldn't hurt them to listen, if they could. Her message was intended for the unedited whose bodies had been taken over by edited individuals, the same situation she herself faced with Hollis. She had to assume the unedited minds trapped inside had been able to see and hear the world of their bodies. So, while she looked at the three edited humans, she was really talking to the two dark-haired unedited people with deep-set eyes.

"Everyone close your eyes," she instructed. The group obeyed.

Alfie's questioning eyes stayed open, but he didn't object.

"First, we're going to imagine what it's like to have contact with your body taken away from you. Imagine you're at the bottom of a deep well. The circle of light in the distance, it's calling to you. Don't reach for it, allow it to take over your awareness. The process might be slow, but don't rush."

A few moments later, the broad-shouldered Asian woman opened her eyes. "I don't see anything. How's this supposed to help?"

"Trust me," Shada said.

She closed her eyes again and bowed her head.

"Then, once you've been able to find the light, allow the sounds of the world to rush in. It might take some time to find—"

"I'm still not seeing the light," the dark-haired man said.

"It's OK, this is just practice in case you find yourself losing control," Shada said, believing the unedited consciousness inside him knew what she was talking about. She closed her eyes and could sense the heartbeats of the two unedited humans, faint thrums she would miss if she wasn't looking for them. Even with her recent injection, it was difficult to maintain her awareness of them.

"Everyone open your eyes. So now, you're able to see and hear the world around you. I call this waking up." Shada didn't need to keep the group isolated from one another anymore. If the trapped minds heard her, they would be able to follow along in the background while the minds who had control were present in the room.

"But you'd still be trapped inside. The next thing to do would be to gain awareness of a background process without your host finding out. Take breathing, for example. Nobody gives it any thought, but thousands of times a day means a lot of opportunities for the trapped mind to find something to hold on to."

Alfie's eyes burrowed into Shada. She ignored the impulse to cater her explanation to him.

"With awareness comes control, and with control of a physical process, it isn't long before the rest of the body can be manipulated."

"We already have control of these bodies, we don't need to learn," the man with the goatee said.

"You're right, I just want you to be aware of the threat posed. But if your host ever tries to take back control of their bodies, you can use these strategies to maintain the status quo."

The heartbeats of the dark-haired man and woman grew louder. Now Shada couldn't miss them if she tried.

Shada did her best to sound as commanding as Hollis. "If it does happen, make sure you get into Alfie's lab as soon as possible so he can use the serum he developed to put them back in place."

The three edited humans looked confused. Shada guessed the edited minds inside their bodies would never pose a risk of taking over. But the other two, their hearts began to race.

Shada assumed they had found their breath and were over-joyed at the prospect of removing the chains of the edited mind. She allowed her heartbeat to resonate with theirs, slowing them down. "All this is to say: don't take drastic action against your body, like putting two gashes into your face," she said with a smile.

"Don't cause massive self-harm, got it," the weasel said. "Can we go? I've got a lot of work to do."

Alfie looked at Shada, telling her to field the question without saying so. "We're almost done. Last question: Is anyone suspicious their host is trying to take back control?"

The two unedited humans raised their hands. The woman's hand shot back down, and she stared at it hanging useless by her side. The man stared at his raised hand, and it was clear he was exerting a large effort to keep it aloft.

"At least two hosts here are trying to take back control. Alfie, get the serum."

The three edited humans gawked at the two members of the group who were struggling to keep control of their hands. Shada couldn't sense their heartbeats and determined they would forever be silent. Edited minds in edited bodies posed no risk to be lost.

Alfie injected both unedited humans with the serum, and a wave of relaxation washed over each of their faces. "I've had a sense of foreboding for some time now," the man said.

"And when they found out there was a serum to keep them in the darkness, they had to show themselves," Shada said. She took a weird pride in having the edited minds present believe she was on their side. While she smiled in their faces, she was also resonating her heartbeat with the two unedited, showing them the true path to subversion. Soon they would be able to follow their blood, the path to accepting the implanted mind as another part of themselves, giving them the ability to take back their bodies without struggling to keep a separate mind silent.

The entire group watched the two unedited humans, in possession of edited minds, to see if there were any signs of struggle. They looked at the group around them and smiled.

"Nothing?" Alfie asked.

"Nothing," they said, shaking their heads.

Shada alone knew the unedited minds trapped inside were now learning to listen to their own heartbeats, and it was just a matter of time before they hatched.

CHAPTER THIRTY-FOUR

THE TIME HAD COME for Shada to make sure Sikya received the promised funds, but doing so meant she would have to do her best impression of Hollis. It had been some time since Hollis had tried to take control of any part of her body, but she knew he was aware of her actions, a constant presence on the periphery of her awareness.

Shada took a big breath outside Alfie's office to calm her nerves. She walked into the scientist's office and sat down. "First things first. Let's get the money sent over to the host's sister," she said.

Alfie leaned back in his chair and steepled his fingers. "Are you sure you want to do that?"

"The dancing dwarf," Shada said. She made sure it was said both with confidence and in an offhanded way, a simple matter of business they needed to address.

Alfie smiled before he leaned forward and typed on his computer. "We should go for a walk," he said when he finished. He led the way back to and through the atrium then outside, towards the lab. He didn't call a transport vehicle. "Nobody can hear us out here."

"Who is listening inside?"

"I don't want any record of this conversation, even on my own devices," Alfie said. He turned to Shada and stared into her eyes. "Welcome back," he said with a smile.

Shada pretended she was Hollis. "I've been back since the injection!"

Alfie nodded and continued to walk along the outside of the building. Shada followed.

"I told the people at accounting to release the funds to your sister, so you don't have to worry about that hanging over your head. Would you like to call her and confirm?" he said.

"Why would I want to talk to an unedited?" Shada tried to sound disgusted at the thought, although to the best of her recollection Hollis didn't speak about them in this way. He'd known she was unedited when they first met and was nice enough to her. Still, the tone seemed right.

"Hollis didn't have a negative view of the unedited. In his eyes, he thought he would be helping them by offering them the ability to become edited. It was pity, not disgust."

Shada didn't know what to say. How would someone respond if they were told their own views on a topic? Alfie spoke again before Shada could probe Hollis's thoughts.

"Shada, I know it's you." His eyes stayed forward. "I thought you'd be the one to do it."

Shada refused to admit she had taken back control of her own body, scared Alfie would come up with another serum. The palm trees swayed in the breeze brought in by the bay. An automated lawn mower in front of a warehouse in the distance turned on a dime and began another straight line over the grass.

"The serum was my best attempt at keeping you subdued. Correct me if I'm wrong, but now that you've been able to overpower Hollis despite the injections, there's really no chance he's coming back. What's the secret? How'd you do it?"

They took a dozen more steps towards the bay in the distance before Shada responded. "I learned to listen."

Alfie waited, but Shada didn't continue. "Very well, don't go into specifics. Just know that I won't do anything more to stop you. If you were able to pry the phrase from Hollis's mind, there are levels to this I don't understand. Maybe one day you'll trust me enough to share."

"Why would I trust you?" Shada said. She felt comfortable saying this because she still didn't have to admit it was her, not Hollis.

"You shouldn't. But this has been my greatest experiment. I tried five times before you and none of them showed any promise. It wouldn't surprise me if one of them tried to retake control after your tutorial."

"The serum will put them back," Shada said.

"It will, but my hope is that you told them enough to overpower that too. My real experiment, the one WestCorp doesn't know about, was to see if a mind could be consumed by another human. Not under their control—we do that every time someone uploads for a few hours at a time—but in a way that allows their entire database of knowledge and experiences to be retrieved at will. By telling me the phrase, you proved it was possible, although to what extent I don't yet know."

Shada felt Hollis try to take control of her voice, to scream at Alfie, then her hands, to attack him. Fueled by rage, these impulses were more powerful than his previous attempts, but they were still received by Shada as nuisances to be ignored. She had stopped walking for a moment, and Alfie looked back at her from a few steps ahead.

"Like watching a storm pass," he said in admiration.

Shada nodded, took the few steps to close the distance between them, and they continued to walk.

"Do you get constant input from two sources of knowledge?

Or is it more like you have to retrieve Hollis's knowledge, like a massive encyclopedia you must search every time you have a question?"

"Two inputs would be overwhelming," Shada said, still wary.

"So you have to know the question you want answered before you dive into his mind. Fascinating."

Alfie pointed to the building behind the lawn mower. "What's that building used for?"

Shada dove into Hollis's memories and knew the answer in less than the time it took to blink. "It's where edited children go to primary school." If Hollis was still in control of her body, he would know the answer, so she had no reservations about answering the question.

Alfie pointed to a smaller building near the water. "And that one?"

"The administration offices for the marketing department."

"They're the ones who advertise to the unedited. The reason you came, if I'm not mistaken."

Shada nodded. "Will you upload an edited mind into an unedited body again?"

"Of course! What kind of scientist would I be if I didn't produce repeatable results?"

Shada shook her head, unwilling to speak up for the future victims of the procedure.

"There's another option as well. One that I believe you are uniquely suited for," Alfie said.

"And what is that?"

"We upload another mind into your body. You've regained control once, doing it again should prove no more difficult."

Shada was unable to control her first impulse. "Why the hell would I let you do that?"

"Think about it. Multiple minds, multiple databases, all

searchable in an instant. You already have all the resources you could ever want, but their resources would be yours as well. You could have multiple lives' worth of knowledge at your fingertips. A true superhuman."

Shada stopped walking and stared at Alfie. "I'm going back," she said. She turned around and left the scientist alone in the realm of possibility.

CHAPTER THIRTY-FIVE

SHADA COULDN'T SHAKE Alfie's suggestion to probe Hollis's memory when viewing the world around her. As she entered the atrium, she half remembered its initial construction. It had been sterile and empty when the foreman led Hollis into the space and announced the project's completion. The tram station underneath, a direct line to the city, had been completed soon after. Before that, there had been a ferry that brought employees to the island. They were more isolated then and liked it that way, a small group of visionaries trying to change the world with technology. Hollis had ignored their grievances when he connected them to the outside world.

On the way to Hollis's underground bunker, she remembered a time before the automated vehicles ran between buildings. They used to have to walk! Hollis's memory included a time being caught in a rainstorm, and a massive swell flooding the underground cavern before it was complete.

Shada was aware of Hollis's memories everywhere she went, small tidbits of information about the world around her. If she wasn't careful to ground herself in reality, to pay attention to her surroundings, it was easy to get caught in a sense of nostalgia about a world long since passed. She cursed Alfie for opening up Pandora's box.

The underground bunker took on a new significance once Shada became aware of Hollis's reason for creating the space. Numerous death threats had been made against him for his work editing unborn children. A fanatic from the city had come to the island and hid until the middle of the night, well after the tram stopped running. Hollis woke up to find the man holding a knife to his throat while Ruby slept next to him; his children, a boy and a girl, were in rooms down the hall. He'd had the bunker created and moved in alone in order to protect his family.

Feeling sorry for Hollis felt wrong, but Shada couldn't help it. His own story, now present as she moved through the residence, made her appreciate all he had done. When faced with a similar situation, she might have done the same.

The black wall behind the long table between the kitchen and the bedroom drew Shada's gaze. She remembered the hours Hollis had spent in front of that wall. It wasn't just his actions Shada remembered, but also his thoughts, and she became aware of how Hollis had found the black wall comforting while he pondered his status as edited, wondering if there were aspects of life he was missing out on because of his inability to feel sadness. It reminded Shada of a child's curiosity when looking at the stars, the light bouncing off the textured rock filling him with wonder at the unknown.

Shada called Hollis's office.

Beth answered the phone after the first ring, prompting Shada to wonder if she knew the call was from his living quarters. If the secretary was surprised to hear Shada's voice, she hid it well.

"Can you please send Chloe Rose down to Hollis's bunker? She's unedited but is staying on the island for testing," Shada said. Shada wondered if she would ever be comfortable claiming Hollis's belongings as her own, though she knew she had to continue to pretend they belonged to him as long as people didn't know his mind resided in her.

"Chloe Rose, got it," Beth replied, sounding as if she was writing down the name.

"Tell her I'll be waiting behind the outdoor structure, next to the water."

Beth said she would relay the message right away.

Shada went back outside and walked to the water's edge. There was no sand. Instead, the ground dropped away a few feet where water had eroded the island, exposing soil that extended into the water. The water was too dark to see anything beneath. The wind picked up speed, keeping Shada cool beneath the setting sun. She dove into Hollis's memories and discovered a time when he had been a young edited member of the island community. He'd wanted to explore the depths of the ocean even though he was assigned to explore the depths of the mind. Shada felt pity for young Hollis, born into a society that took away his right to determine his own future.

"Hello?" Chloe called from behind her.

Shada turned around and was greeted by an apprehensive Chloe. She no longer had the jewelry in her pierced septum, but her earlobes, exposed by the wind blowing back her hair, still showed numerous pieces of metal.

Shada closed the distance between them with a few long strides. "You're not hijacked right now, are you?" she asked.

"No . . ." Chloe said.

"Then who am I?"

"You're Hollis, inside Shada's body."

"So you remember my name. That's good," Shada said with a laugh.

Chloe didn't even smile.

"It's me! Shada!" She threw her hands out as if to put herself on display.

Chloe's head turned sideways. "You're Shada?" She got defensive. "What is this, some kind of trick? Your body was taken over by Hollis."

"It was. But he's in the background now. I taught myself to take back control of my body."

"I don't believe you. What did we do the first night you came over?"

"We followed the police scanner to the warehouses."

Chloe thought for a moment. "They could have been following you." She still wasn't convinced.

"That's true." Shada thought for a moment. "What about the poison you inject yourself with before each upload? If Hollis knew about that, there's no way he would allow you to host his wife's mind."

Chloe's eyes grew wide. "Holy shit, it is you!" She rushed forward and gave her friend a hug. "What the hell happened to your face?"

"Hollis wasn't happy I took back control of my body. He left these before I was able to make my control permanent."

Chloe leaned in close to inspect the two thin lines. "Well, they look cool," she said with a smile.

Shada dismissed the compliment with a wave of her hand. "Let's go inside. I want to show you how this guy lived."

From the moment they got off the elevator, Chloe rushed from room to room. "This was all his? It's all yours?" Chloe asked as she stood in front of Shada in the kitchen after her inspection of the residence. "How does that work? Do you call everything yours now, or do you still think of it as his?"

"I still think of it as his," Shada said. She leaned her lower back on the counter. "And it was all his. This was his home."

Chloe looked up at the roof of the cavern in awe. "How'd you do it?"

"Take back my body?"

Chloe nodded.

"Have you been able to see or hear the world while being hijacked?" Shada asked.

"Not until the most recent one. I saw you, and heard your voice, but was so sad knowing you were occupied by another mind and would never be the person I remembered. I had to convince myself you were dead."

"Good, that's the first step."

"Pretending who you see is dead?"

"No, seeing and hearing the world while you're hijacked."

Chloe pulled a chair from beneath the table and sat down. "And what do you do after that?"

"Well, I started by finding my breath and controlling it. It leads to one level of control by shutting off the hijacker's mind. It's hard to maintain though and requires constant focus on breathing."

Chloe held her breath even though she wasn't hosting another mind. She exhaled and displayed a sheepish grin. "So are you focusing on your breath right now?"

"No need, I don't have to keep Hollis muted." Shada was struck by the thought that Hollis's residence could have listening devices but an instant later was calmed by the knowledge, from the owner himself, that Hollis valued privacy too much to allow their installation. "He's with me all the time."

"How'd you do that?"

"Listened to my heartbeat. It led to an awareness of every part of my body. Now, even when Hollis does try to take over, I can brush his attempts away."

Chloe became silent, and Shada could tell she was trying to detect her own heart.

"That seems hard," Chloe said.

"The injections helped," Shada said. She went on to explain how the low dose of LSD had helped her become aware of the life in everything around her, a sensation that tore away her ability to focus on her breathing but opened a new avenue for her to explore.

"So what are you going to do now? Live down here and become a recluse?"

"No way, I'm leaving. We just came down here because I wanted you to see the way this guy lives and to get my stuff."

Shada went into the bedroom and grabbed her bag. She changed out of the WestCorp clothes and put back on her shorts, sports bra, and T-shirt. They all smelled like stale sweat. At the bottom of her backpack was the apple she'd taken from her apartment, still red and shiny. Thoughts of Sikya bubbled up in Shada's mind and she felt a wave of homesickness in her stomach. Shada shouldered the backpack and walked back into the kitchen.

"Are you going back to the city?" Chloe asked.

Shada nodded. "I need to see Sikya. Are you going back to the dorms?"

"Only to get my things. I'm coming with you."

CHAPTER THIRTY-SIX

CHLOE AND SHADA left the bunker and were greeted by the last remnants of the day. The waves lapping against the shore underlined the purple, orange, and red hues created by single rays of sunshine. They took the transport vehicle Chloe had used to get to the bunker back to the atrium.

"I'll have to come back. I still need the money," Chloe said during the ride.

"I've got all the money you'll ever need," Shada said. "All of Hollis's accounts were signed over to me."

"That's a nice offer, but I can't accept. It's your money. Use it for yourself, and Sikya."

"Sikya got money too. We have more than we need. Let me help you," Shada said. "Plus, you've already been hijacked more times than anyone else. It's not safe to do it again."

"I'll be fine," Chloe said. She sighed. "And it's not just the money. Part of me wants to know if I can do what you did. I know it's not a competition, but I think I can control a mind that's been transplanted into my body. What if we take over multiple people? We could each have access to not only their funds, but lifetimes of knowledge. Imagine what we could do!"

Shada turned to stare at Chloe. "There's no guarantee it can be done again. What if I just got lucky?"

"Well, let me be the one to find out. If your method works, we don't have to be the only ones. Imagine all the edited minds we could capture! It would be a double blow. Unedited minds becoming more powerful while taking out the edited humans at the top. We could flip the world."

Shada knew Chloe's logic was sound but didn't want her friend to risk being lost to the world forever. She stared out the window and could sense Hollis's anger at his helplessness. They arrived at the atrium while she listened to the captured consciousness inside her.

"Go get your stuff and meet me above the steps at the entrance to the station," Shada told Chloe from outside the transport.

Chloe nodded, told Shada she'd be right back, and the vehicle pulled away.

Shada walked inside. In the seating area, with a tray full of food in front of her, was Piper. The edited woman stood up and walked towards Shada, leaving her food behind. A furrowed brow was perched on her contorted face, and each step was further evidence of her iron resolve.

Piper stopped in front of Shada. The two of them stood at the entrance to the island's coffee shop. "Where has he been?" she demanded to know. When Shada didn't respond right away, she placed both hands on her hips and stared as if her eyes had the power to force someone to talk. "Well?" she said.

"What makes you think I'd know?" Shada said. Her calm exterior hid how ready she was for Piper to strike.

"I spoke with Beth and Ernie, all they'll tell me is he isn't in the office. You and Alfie are the only two allowed into his residence, and Alfie won't see me."

At the mention of Alfie's name Shada was struck by one of

Hollis's memories. Alfie, it turned out, was Hollis's son. The scientist had changed his name when he received his doctorate, a practice Shada learned was common among the scientists.

Lost in a fog of the past, Shada tried to walk away from Piper and leave the conversation behind. Piper grabbed her arm to stop her. Shada was pulled back to the present. She stared at the hand and knew it would be easy to overpower the woman.

Piper let go.

"He's been sick in bed, if you must know. The only reason I go down there is so he can upload. It gives him the chance to move around."

"That's it? He's not having you do anything else?"

"What else could I do? I'm still not edited," Shada said. She knew Piper was worried about being replaced as lieutenant.

It took a second before Piper appeared to believe Shada. Her face relaxed and she let out a sigh. "I feel like he's up to something. I haven't heard from him for over a week now . . ." Her voice trailed off.

Shada could tell Piper wasn't satisfied with the response she got, that she wanted more information and was trying to gain Shada's trust to find out what she wanted to know.

"Nothing I'd know about," Shada said.

Piper's eyes narrowed in renewed suspicion, but there was nothing else she could do. She walked away without another word.

Shada took a seat near the steps that led down to the tram station and set her backpack on a chair next to her. She watched the edited humans visit the various restaurants, wondering if they ate every meal in the food court or if any of them cooked their own food. Hollis didn't seem to know the answer; when Shada probed his consciousness, she found out the leader of WestCorp had been brought all his meals precooked. He didn't know or care about the rest of the island's occupants.

An older woman, near seventy, caught Shada's eye. She carried a tray with a covered plate on it and was given a wide berth by all the edited humans in her vicinity. Hollis remembered the woman and Shada discovered her identity: Ruby, Hollis's wife.

Shada was flooded with memories of their time together. She already knew they'd lived in a spacious house on the island next to the water, where they raised their two children. After Hollis moved to the underground bunker, the two of them had drifted apart and never lived together again. Hollis harbored no ill will toward the woman; they'd just fallen out of their routine and never got back into one that involved the other.

Chloe came from behind Shada and sat at the table with her. "You just missed Piper," Shada said.

Chloe pretended to be upset. "No! I really wanted to catch up." She laughed. "What did she want?"

"Hollis was planning to upload into her before I came along. She thinks I have some grand plan to take over the company and wanted to double-check I wasn't becoming his number two. She's got a weird protective thing about him."

Shada could sense Hollis wanted to look at Ruby again, and she obliged. "Do you see the old woman over there?" Shada asked, gesturing with her chin towards Ruby.

"The one sitting by herself?" Chloe said, turning away from Shada to look at the topic of their conversation.

"That's Ruby Hollis," Shada said.

Chloe stared at the woman who had taken over her mind. "She's a slow eater," Chloe said.

Shada watched Ruby take two bites. Each one took minutes.

Ruby must have sensed their eyes, because she lifted her own, looked in their direction, and stared at the two of them. The fork with her next bite hovered in front of her face. Chloe turned back around, but Shada didn't avert her gaze.

Ruby never took the bite. She set the fork down and beck-oned for someone sitting at the next table to come to her. The man who came to her side had a mustache. When he leaned over, Ruby whispered something into his ear. The man turned and looked at Shada and Chloe.

"Shit," Shada said.

"What's wrong?" Chloe asked.

"We have to go." Shada stood up and slung her backpack over her shoulder.

Chloe followed Shada's lead.

"What's wrong?" Chloe repeated.

"You said you were able to witness the visit in Hollis's office, right?"

"It was the first time I wasn't in complete darkness."

"So you know Ruby knows that Hollis transplanted his mind into my body." As Shada said this, she led the way to the stairs and took them two at a time. The last thing she saw in the atrium was the man with a mustache beckoning for the men from the surrounding tables to come to him.

"There's no reason for Hollis to be in the atrium," Chloe said.

"And even less of a reason for him to be seated with an unedited, unless I've been able to take back control. She knows."

CHAPTER THIRTY-SEVEN

SHADA AND CHLOE weaved through commuters waiting to go to the city for the night. Although there were more people on the platform than Shada had seen before—their exodus coincided with the end of the business day on the island—there was enough room to pass through the crowd without jostling anyone. They were careful not to maintain a brisk walk so they wouldn't garner suspicion as they put as much distance between themselves and the staircase as possible.

Shada kept looking behind her to see if they were being pursued. Each time she looked at the staircase, all she saw were the two security guards, one on each side of the bottom step. She worried they would receive orders to stop her and Chloe, but from their unaffected stare, she could tell the two of them would be staying put.

On the far end of the platform, they stopped to wait for the tram to arrive. A few tense minutes later, a low grumble came from the tunnel that extended towards the center of the island, soon followed by a pair of lights. A rush of air in front of the tram blew through the crowd until the tram's first car stopped in front of Shada and Chloe. Chloe brushed the hair from her face, and Shada clutched the straps of her backpack while her eyes still watched the staircase.

The doors opened and they boarded. As the doors shut behind them, Shada allowed herself to exhale. The tram began to move. Shada took one last look at the staircase and saw the mustached man reach the platform. He seemed to be in no rush whatsoever. The two security guards lifted their massive frames from their seats when they recognized the man who'd missed the trip into the city. Shada saw the mustached man lift a finger in their direction before she left the station and the tunnel's wall blocked her view.

The tram then came to an abrupt stop. Everyone on board was thrust forward when their momentum was interrupted. One man, whose hands weren't fast enough to catch himself, smashed his face into the seat in front of his own. He yelped in pain and sat back up with blood dripping through the hands covering his face.

Shada probed Hollis's mind. "They are able to stop and reverse the tram," she whispered to Chloe.

Chloe searched the area around her, and Shada presumed she was looking for a weapon. Not finding anything to use for defense, Chloe took out a vial of the poison and offered it to Shada.

"Just in case," Chloe said.

Shada shook her head no.

The tram began to continue on towards the city. It inched along as if it was unsure of its trajectory. It soon picked up speed, and moments later the passengers found themselves passing above the bay in the reflected light of the moon.

Shada's first guess was that Alfie had had something to do with the tram not going back to the island, but the scientist would have no way of knowing she had left. After further consideration, she came up with the theory that after the mustached man had stopped the tram, Ruby had overruled the reversal and allowed her to escape. She felt her instincts were correct but had no idea why Ruby would interject on her behalf.

Shada leaned back in her seat but was unable to relax. She refused to believe she had been able to escape the island until the city was close enough for her to distinguish individual buildings in the night, and even then she wasn't convinced. When the tram descended into the tunnel below the city she became nervous, knowing her destination was close. She believed that once she got into the city, her nightmare would be over and she could disappear into the mass of unedited.

She could tell Hollis, his mind trapped in her body, was excited about the prospect of living among the unedited. He relished the opportunity to see firsthand how they lived. Shada knew he held out hope that he would one day regain control of her body, and his time among the people would allow him to further understand those he wished to eliminate as part of his company's grand vision.

Chloe seemed to share Shada's reservations. It was obvious she was on edge as well, waiting to see if they would be allowed to reach the city.

The tram pulled to a stop below the hub of the city. Shada and Chloe stood by the door, and as soon as it opened they fell onto the platform, the first passengers to disembark. Free from the long reach of WestCorp, they gave each other a hug. They didn't care that the rest of the passengers stared at them.

Shada and Chloe went up a level to the city's transportation system. Shada assumed the two of them would be parting ways, but Chloe announced she was going with Shada.

"I want to make sure you get home," she said with finality, as if this phrase was enough explanation to put the matter to rest.

Shada didn't put up a fight. Chloe allowed Shada to have the last open seat on the train and stood over her as they rode to

Shada's stop. They got off, and Shada saw the homeless man with his dog. Remembering the apple in her backpack, she took it out. Its skin was still shiny, red, and tight. Instead of giving it away, which she didn't want to do because she knew the homeless man would just set it off to the side, she took a bite.

The apple was rotten on the inside, dark brown and mushy. Now that its skin had been pierced, a putrid smell wafted out, covering the area around her. She spit it out onto the concrete below her.

"What the hell," Shada said. She spit, trying to get the taste from her mouth, but it didn't help.

Chloe looked at the apple in Shada's hand. "Why'd you eat a rotten apple?" she said.

"It didn't look rotten!" Shada said in defense. She turned the apple to show Chloe the fruit from the unbitten side. Its color was still bright red, but now that its skin had been pierced, the rest of the skin was wrinkled, like a drum that had been cut.

"How old was it?"

Shada threw the apple over the fence and onto the track below, which ran perpendicular to the station. "A few weeks, I guess. It's the one I took from the apartment."

"And you expected it to still be good?"

"It looked good on the outside." Shada spit on the ground again. "This is why I stick to gummy bears."

CHAPTER THIRTY-EIGHT

SHADA KNEW Sikya was home as she and Chloe approached the apartment door. She didn't have a specific reason why she knew—there was no audible activity behind the locked door—and couldn't elaborate her reasons if she had to, but deep down she knew her sister was there. Call it a sister's intuition. She didn't consider what Sikya thought about her last disappearance until she was about to knock. She wondered if her sister would be upset when they saw each other again after she'd left just a one-word note as her final goodbye and had had no contact since leaving. She got the urge to turn around and walk away, to save the reunion for another time, but didn't move.

Chloe, perhaps sensing Shada's reservation, told her friend, "Sikya's going to be happy you're back."

"I don't know. She probably wasn't happy I left."

"Trust me," Chloe said.

Shada knocked twice, even though she had a key.

A shadow passed beneath the door. All of a sudden, the locks were disengaged and the door flew open. A breathless Sikya stood in the doorway, concern written on her face.

"What happened to your face?" Sikya asked.

While Shada stumbled to find the right words, Sikya rushed out and wrapped her sister in her arms. Sikya squeezed tightly and pushed her chin into Shada's neck, a pressure that disarmed Shada and assuaged any concerns she'd had about any imagined animosity her sister might have felt. The two held each other a long time before they parted and Sikya held her sister at arm's length.

"Are those lines supposed to be some sort of tattoo?" Sikya asked.

Shada shook her head and laughed at her sister's naivety. "It's a long story."

Inside Shada, Hollis felt a sadistic pride at leaving his mark on what he considered his property. Shada didn't bother to correct him about who her body belonged to.

Sikya introduced herself to Chloe and told the two of them to come inside.

"I can't stay for long, I just wanted to make sure she got back all right," Chloe said.

"Well, thanks for bringing her back!" Sikya said, turning it into a joke.

Shada tossed her backpack on the floor next to the couch and sat down, the weight of her time away hitting her and pressing down, making even the weight of gravity intolerable. Chloe chose to stand with her lower back against the counter.

Sikya sat down next to her sister. "Where were you?" she asked.

"On the island."

Sikya let the information sink in. "I thought you went overseas."

"My playing career is over," Shada said. She hadn't really thought about it before that moment, but without the need for money, there was no incentive to fight for the chance to play in the league. Her love for the sport was still there, but she didn't want to fight against an unfair system.

Reminded of money, Shada told Sikya to check her account.

"It says there's a pending transfer," Sikya said, trailing off. A moment later she gasped and set down her phone. "Shada. What did you do to get that much money?"

Shada ignored her sister's question. "That's just the money for you. I have my own, much more than that."

Shada explained how Sikya's money had come from Hollis's payment for uploading himself into her body. When Sikya said she knew this, Shada had to tell her it was meant to be permanent. That it was permanent. "His mind is in my body right now," Shada said.

Sikya's eyes grew wide. "You said sorry because you weren't coming back." She grew agitated. "What were you thinking!"

Shada watched her sister stand up and pace in front of the couch. "It's not important. I'm back now," she said.

Chloe had heard enough. She cleared her throat and announced she was leaving, going back home.

Shada stood up. "Promise me you won't go back."

Chloe smiled. "I promise."

The two friends hugged each other and Chloe left. As soon as the door shut behind her, Sikya announced Chloe was lying. "You could see it in her eyes."

Shada was surprised Sikya was able to tell, since they'd just met each other for the first time. "Agreed. She thinks she can capture another edited mind. Then we'd both have access to a lifetime of knowledge and resources."

"You know everything the guy inside your head knows?"

Shada nodded with a sly smile on her face.

"Is that why you did it?" Sikya said. "Like a robbery?"

"No, I had no idea I could take over again. I thought I would be effectively dead."

"And you still followed through with the procedure! What's wrong with you?"

"I left you a note!" Shada said. It was meant to be a joke, but Sikya didn't find it funny.

Shada struggled with whether or not to tell her sister her ability to get a birth license was on the line. "I did it so you never have to worry about money again. But having been on that island all this time, and seeing what WestCorp plans to do, you have to promise not to edit any child you have."

Sikya grew suspicious. "What does WestCorp plan to do?"

"They are going to force all births to be edited. The mayor and everything's involved."

Sikya sat back down on the couch, the new information and her own weight too much to bear. "What's going to happen when people refuse?"

"They will be offered cheap post-birth edits so they won't feel the pain of being childless."

Sikya let this revelation soak in before she spoke again. "So I won't be able to have an unedited child," she uttered, her sadness filling up the room.

"As of right now, no. Not officially at least. But we have all the money we could ever want, so there has to be someone we can pay."

Sikya shook her head. "I don't want it if others don't have the same opportunity." She set her jaw, and her eyes narrowed with determination. "We have some work to do," she said.

Sikya had every reason to turn her back on the people of her city, but she chose to fight for them, even though her sister would have preferred to leave them to their fate. Without people like Sikya, people who fought against the natural order, the world would never evolve.

With technology creating such a clear line between those with and without edits, the ability to get inside the minds of those on the other side was a distinct advantage. Capturing the mind altogether, as Shada had, could, Sikya hoped, serve the same purpose.

The laws of evolution didn't account for adaptations being passed on instead of passed down.

CHAPTER ONE

TIME DEVOURS ALL THINGS.

The decay of a physical object is easy to identify. Time exacts its toll whether the object in question is alive or dead, evidenced by the presence of rust, the growth of mold, and the eventual return to the earth.

The decay of memories is subtle in the way it presents itself. There is no dust to be measured, no lack of color to be scrutinized. Instead, it is measured by what is missing. A lack of coherence, of completeness, creeps in over time until what remains is the skeleton of what was once alive.

Chloe surveyed the photo on her dresser of her grandfather and his dog and realized she had lost a small part of the memory from the last time she saw him. She could picture him in her mind as he picked an orange from the tree on his farm, she could hear his voice as he explained the way to tell whether the fruit was ripe, but she couldn't find the comfort the memory used to bring, couldn't feel his presence beside her anymore.

Was it because she had let people's minds occupy her body for money?

This question haunted her. Even if she had taken the time to recall the memory before she had been hijacked and compared it to the memory she now possessed, she wasn't sure she would have been able to tell any difference. By any measurement she could come up with, the memory was the same as it had always been, but the missing feeling, the diminished comfort it brought, made her wonder if she would lose even more of it if she captured someone else's mind inside her body.

Chloe knew she didn't have a choice if she hoped to invert the power structure.

She had returned to the city days before, after spending time on the island off the coast of the city. While there, she had been paid well to allow edited minds to take control of her unedited body. Chloe was the first human to have been uploaded into five times, an achievement bestowed upon her by the cordial enemy, WestCorp. The accomplishment was a source of conflicted pride.

Her friend Shada, also unedited, had had an even more historic experience on the island. While Chloe was relaxing between sessions of two-hour uploads, Shada had been trying to take back control of her body after she became the first person to accept a permanent upload. Michael Hollis, the leader of West-Corp, was dying and had made Shada an offer she couldn't refuse in order to allow his consciousness to live inside her body. Everyone assumed Shada would be lost forever, trapped inside her own body behind the mind of the edited man.

Shada had other plans.

It took time, and a few false starts, but Shada had been able to regain control of her own body, to everyone's surprise. What nobody had ever thought possible was that she would be able to access the mind of the leader of WestCorp, making his knowledge and memories her own.

Chloe had found all this out when she'd left the island with Shada. Neither of them was sure who in WestCorp knew about the theft of their leader's mind, but since they were allowed to leave the island, they both assumed there would be no repercussions.

Shada was back at home with her sister, in control of all of Hollis's assets. Hollis had assumed he would begin another life in her body, so he had transferred his vast wealth to her. Control of the company was another matter. While Hollis had control of Shada's body, and that body was still on the island, he still ran WestCorp, but everyone thought he was sick in bed and she was his mouthpiece. His terminal illness wasn't common knowledge, but his absolute control was never questioned, so the edited employees took orders from Shada without a second thought. Corroboration by the lead scientist, Alfie Reynolds-Grant, helped assuage any reluctance.

Now Chloe planned to go back into the power vacuum of the island, to capture a mind for herself. She wanted what Shada had, the resources and knowledge from a lifetime of work on the island. This was how she would invert the power structure, to bring herself and the unedited humans, or at least some of them, to a level above the edited.

She surveyed the dozens of plants that lined every surface in her studio apartment. In preparation, they were all watered, and the ones that needed sunlight the most were placed in front of the window, whose iron bars cast vertical shadows into the room. She debated making her bed but decided against it. She never made it anyways and didn't want to place extra importance on her trip. She had been in communication with Reynolds-Grant, who insisted she call him Alfie, and together they had made plans to replicate Shada's capture.

When WestCorp's lead scientist had contacted her, she didn't know if she should trust him. She knew Shada's opinion on the matter, that she should stay away from the island and be grateful for making it out alive, but the scientist said he needed to recreate his results. Since Chloe had been uploaded into before, she was the best candidate, and the fact she had talked to Shada and heard about how her friend had regained control of her body added to her qualifications.

Alfie had told her, "We both stand to gain from this," and he was right.

Chloe climbed over her unmade bed and reached an arm down through a small space between the mattress and the wall. There was enough space for her to withdraw a small safe. She entered in the code, her grandfather's birthday, and when the door unlocked, she withdrew two vials, one red and one blue. There were still four of each left in the safe, the last remains of a poison and antidote combination that took effect after eight hours. There had been many more vials, the last remnants of her mother's military research, but before each time she uploaded she took the poison then took the antidote when she returned to her body. She didn't trust the edited.

It had taken Shada days to first gain control of her body, so Chloe knew she wouldn't be able to take the poison before the consciousness was transplanted; she'd run out of time before she could take the antidote. She packed the vials with her as a kill switch. If she couldn't regain permanent control, she would find a window of time when she could take the poison and eliminate both herself and the edited mind inside her body.

Chloe put the two vials in separate pockets of her backpack so the edited mind inside her head, when it got there, would have no idea an antidote existed. Her plan seemed shaky, even to her, but knowing a kill switch existed made the prospect of losing her body to an edited mind more palatable.

She packed a change of clothes and zipped up her backpack. After turning to take one last look at her room, she decided to bring along the framed photo of her grandfather, throwing it in her backpack and closing the door on the plants. She promised them she would be back before they wilted.

CHAPTER TWO

THE COLORS of the city shed their typical washed-out gray hue and became more vibrant during Chloe's potential last walk to the train station. The bright wrappers of single cigars and broken balloons left behind from the night before seemed like the remnants left behind by beloved siblings. The smell of stale alcohol enveloped Chloe as she passed by an alley filled with broken bottles, an aroma she would rush by on normal days but one she savored now while walking at a steady pace. She shook her head at the mischievous antics of her neighbors.

She greeted the homeless men and women on staircases outside abandoned buildings and they scowled at her, no doubt wondering why she'd chosen this day of all days to acknowledge their existence.

This was a run-down, crime-infested part of the city by night, but the light of the day showed the shadows left behind by the darkness, shadows Chloe had never thought she'd miss.

The train ran on an elevated track. Below the track was a tent community composed of multicolored fabrics and structures made from various recycled materials. This was where the homeless children lived, their parents doing what they could to provide some semblance of roots. As far as Chloe knew, this was the largest concentration of homeless people in the city. She could afford to live in another part of the city now that she'd been paid for accepting the edited minds into her body, but she chose to stay in order to save money for her ultimate destination: a house outside the city, in nature, with orange trees, just like her grandfather's.

Chloe watched the children invent a game with a stick, a modified form of tag where whoever was "it" used the stick to extend their reach. One of the rules seemed to be that runners had to be hit on the legs, and when one boy broke this rule and hit a young girl on the back, the rest of the children surrounded him. They yelled at him, and were about to hit him, until one of them spotted a frog in a trash-filled puddle. The group of children all surrounded the amphibian, and the boy who broke the rules picked it up. Chloe climbed the rusted, grated metal steps up to the level of the train so she wouldn't have to witness whatever game the children came up with, not wanting to see the death of the frog.

The turnstile was stuck open, so Chloe walked into the train station without paying. A security guard, the lone person responsible for this station, was busy forcing passed-out individuals to wake up and either leave the station or get onto a train. None of the sleepers appreciated being woken up, but the guard, a no-nonsense older man, thin and wiry and sporting neck tattoos, wouldn't back down. In the end, some of the sleepers gathered themselves and left to lie back down on the other side of the turnstile, and some of them sat on the bench to wait for the next train to arrive.

Chloe leaned against a metal pillar and drank in the sight of the station she had been to so many times before but never appreciated. The billboard across the tracks, which would be hidden by the train whenever it arrived, displayed an advertisement for the current mayor, James Fitzgerald. The sign had been put up months before, during the beginning of his campaign, and now the bottom right corner was turned up, showing the bottom of the previous ad, a bright pink background for a product Chloe remembered as being marketed towards women. She couldn't remember what the product was. Graffiti artists had covered the mayor's face; some tags Chloe knew were local, and some she didn't recognize.

In the center of the platform was a large, broken analog clock. It had been broken for as long as she could remember. The time showed 3:41. She considered it lucky if she happened to be on the platform at the same time as what the clock displayed, and all but one time that it had happened had been during the day. Her nighttime witnessing of the correct time had occurred when she had missed the last train and slept on the platform, only to be woken up by the security guard in the morning. She'd stayed on the platform instead of walking home because the people who lived in this part of the city couldn't be trusted at night, and she was too inebriated to defend herself.

The train pulled up, empty. It had come from the depot at the end of the line. This was the farthest station from the center of the city, and with its reputation, one of the least used. Chloe boarded the train and took a seat beneath Mayor Fitzgerald's gaze. For the first time, she wondered why the candidate had chosen to waste his advertisement in this type of neighborhood. His smiling face was left behind as the train began to move.

While the train traveled into the heart of the city, stopping and starting with regularity to allow more people to board for their morning commutes, Chloe thought about what she would do after capturing the mind of the edited island-dweller. The first thing, of course, would be to go see Shada, to share the news with her friend. Not to throw it in her face, but to convince her it was possible for others to capture minds and, in the process, eliminate edited humans. Chloe wanted to turn the process Shada had discovered into an advantage for all the unedited. Plus, her friend would be able to provide insights about keeping a consciousness under control while it struggled to exert its will over a shared body. Since Shada was the person who'd developed the method, which revolved around learning to control the breath then listen to the heartbeat, it was important for Chloe to be aware of any of Shada's further insights.

Shada was a guru in Chloe's eyes, even though she shunned the responsibility.

Chloe got off the train at the center of the city. She descended two levels down to a platform nobody used unless they had specific business with WestCorp.

The difference between the public platform above and the private platform below was immediate and all-consuming. The public area above was decades old, and the accumulation of time and the passage of millions of passengers had rubbed smooth every surface and infused the space with dense, musty air. In contrast, WestCorp's private platform was bright, clean, and modern, with plenty of room to sit and attendants on the far side willing to help in whatever way possible. If WestCorp didn't have such a negative reputation in the city, more people would visit the space just to get away from the bustle above. But their reputation did exist, and couldn't be changed, so the few people present had more than enough space for themselves.

As Chloe waited for the tram that would take her to the island, she thought about how she wanted her house outside the city to have the same ambience as this space. The money she had made for the previous uploads ensured she had a comfortable life, but if she could pull off this heist, she could buy the house of her dreams and escape the rat race altogether.

CHAPTER THREE

Chloe boarded the tram bound for the island, along with the morning's commuters. One older gentleman, dressed in a suit and tie and carrying himself in a way that made Chloe believe he was playing businessman for the day, stared at her as the tram began to move. She had gotten used to the sideways looks ever since she'd begun wearing numerous piercings in her ears, but people began to hold their gazes longer when she got her septum pierced. She smiled at the man, and he didn't return the gesture, instead pretending to look out the window behind her, as if he wanted to watch the walls of the tunnel pass by.

A display at the front of the car told passengers it would be eleven minutes before they got to the island. There weren't any other stops on their route, so it would be a straight shot. It also displayed the time—just after nine in the morning—and Chloe thought about the stark difference between the digital display on board the tram and the broken analog clock at the train station closest to her home.

The tram left the tunnel beneath the city and began a steady climb onto an elevated track above the bay. Chloe wondered how much energy was required to maintain the tram's speed as it ascended and how much was their momentum being used to carry them to the greater height. With the bay extending on both sides of her car, she could see far into the distance, until the clouds overhead met the water on the horizon. As the city receded, she visualized coming back with someone else's mind residing in her body. Failure wasn't an option.

The other passengers on board didn't share her relaxed demeanor. They either seemed to be on their way to conduct business, based on the way they were dressed, or seemed nervous, if they were dressed as if they'd come from the standard population of the city. Numerous pairs of searching eyes, not seeking to judge but seeking to connect, peered at other passengers. Chloe could tell these people were unedited and were headed to the island to become happier, healthier, and smarter.

Chloe felt a connection to the unedited on their way to the island, appreciating their bravery for crossing the chasm that separated the two types of people. She had been one of them, once, but it felt so long ago. On her trip to become edited herself, a procedure that would launch her into a career with WestCorp, she had met Shada. Shada had been more vocal about the apprehension they both shared, but each other's presence helped calm their nerves.

The tram came to a stop below the center of the island. When the doors opened, the people she assumed were there for business lined up at the doors, waiting for them to open, and the ones Chloe assumed were unedited stayed seated, as if to delay their arrival. The man she had caught staring at her face was the lone passenger who didn't follow this pattern. When he stayed seated, Chloe wondered if he'd dressed in a suit and tie not because he had important business with the company, but because the unedited part of him was here to die, and this was how he wanted to be dressed in the coffin.

Everyone filed out when the doors opened. Before anyone could go up the stairs, they had to be searched by the pair of massive humans posted on each side of the staircase. The travelers formed two lines on their own, each line waiting for one of the guards, and since each search was quick, both lines stayed moving. These guards, Chloe knew, were designed this way, made to be laborers for the company. They towered over everyone present and reminded Chloe of trolls from the fantasy stories she'd been read as a child. The searches seemed to be a formality, evidenced by the fact that the large humans continued their conversation the entire time, and Chloe assumed they were looking for something specific, like firearms. She had passed through the checkpoint with numerous vials of poison and antidote the last time she came to the island and the guards never found them, or if they did, never bothered to withdraw them from her backpack.

When it was Chloe's turn, she stepped forward and was dwarfed by the immense amount of flesh next to her. It could have been because they recognized her, or maybe they deemed her to be no threat to the members of the island, but a cursory pat down and quick peek into her backpack was all it took before she was waved through.

She climbed the wide staircase and found herself in the large, glass-covered atrium. This was the hub of the island, the central location where the edited humans could take transport vehicles to any corner of the island. Seen from above, the transportation system was a giant wheel, the paths of the vehicles the various spokes. This was also where the food court was located, the only place someone could purchase food on the island. Most WestCorp employees ate their meals here. As such a central part of the island, this space saw most of its inhabitants on any given day.

There were numerous restaurants offering a wide variety of food. Locations for coffee, pastries, seafood, and ethnic cuisine stood out to Chloe, all staffed by employees with white shirts and pasted smiles. She wondered if any of the food had been brought from the city or if it was all engineered by local scientists. If they could transplant consciousness, the creation of artificial food was well within their wheelhouse.

Chloe already knew where she had to go. The businessmen who were on the tram with her each searched the sea of faces for their contact, the unedited humans huddled together until a WestCorp employee gathered them together and took them in the direction of the lab, and Chloe went straight to one side of the space, to an elevator that would take her up to the head scientist's office.

She wasted no time walking, her long strides eating up the ground beneath her. She was eager to get the transplant over with so she could begin to take back control of her own body. In her head, she rehearsed the process Shada had described to her: find your senses, control your breath, and, with the help of a serum created by Alfie, listen to your heartbeat. By following the flow of her blood from the central station of her heart, she would be able to regain control of the furthest corners of her body.

CHAPTER FOUR

ALFIE'S OFFICE was locked when Chloe arrived. After a knock and a few moments of waiting, the door opened and the gray-haired scientist stood in front of her, smiling. He wasn't wearing his usual white lab coat; instead, he had on well-fitting jeans, a crisp white button-down, and brown wing tips, a look that distinguished him from other company employees Chloe had interacted with during her previous visits to the island. Their khaki pants, white polos, and stiff demeanor gave them a country-club, elitist sort of distance from the island's visitors.

"Come in," Alfie said, stepping back from the door and gesturing inside.

Chloe stepped into his office. Books with slips of paper between their sheets were scattered on every surface, on the bookshelf, the desk, even the floor. His white lab coat hung beneath a baseball cap on a rack in the corner. There was a steaming cup of coffee next to a half-eaten scone in front of his computer.

"Were you eating breakfast?" It was just after ten.

"Late start today. Ruby wanted to talk to me this morning.

She's in charge now that Michael is . . . incapacitated," Alfie explained. He walked around the desk and sat down.

Chloe knew the mind of Ruby's husband was in the city, occupying Shada's body. She didn't press the issue. "Did you want me to come back?" she asked.

"No, no, go ahead and take a seat. As long as you don't mind if I finish while we talk."

Chloe indicated that she didn't mind. She pulled the chair opposite his from beneath the desk and sat down, setting her backpack on the ground next to her.

He took a bite of scone then a sip of his coffee before typing on the computer. A few dozen keystrokes later, he returned his attention to Chloe. "Today's the day," he said.

"It is?"

"I thought we agreed on that. Did you want to push it back a day? It shouldn't be a problem."

"No, we can do it today, I just thought I might be set up with a place on the island before the procedure."

"Well, you won't need it once the mind is uploaded."

Chloe nodded. "Very true."

"Did you have any other questions?" Alfie asked.

Chloe racked her mind for anything she might need to know. When nothing came to mind, she shook her head.

Alfie's voice got serious. "You didn't take any . . . substances, did you?"

Chloe pretended to be baffled by the question, but they both knew what he was talking about. She'd assumed her pre-upload ritual had been a secret because he had never mentioned it before.

"I know about the poison. It takes hours to kick in, and you took it before all five uploads. I won't bother asking how you got it, we all have our secrets, but don't take it before this procedure.

You won't be able to take back control of your body in time to take the antidote."

"You knew?"

"From the first time. The system found it right away, but since the uploads were only going to last two hours, I didn't have a problem with you having your own insurance policy. But now I have to advise against it."

"Advise against or restrict?"

Alfie smiled then took another sip of coffee. "Restrict," he said over the rim of his cup. "I was trying to be diplomatic."

"I didn't take it," Chloe said with a half smile. "Since it took Shada a while to take back control. She told me how she did it. You'll be giving me the serum, right?"

Alfie was surprised at her request. "The serum? You want the serum?" Alfie leaned back in his chair. He steepled his hands for a moment before reaching forward for another bite of scone. He swallowed and asked, "The serum helped? Interesting. I wonder how?"

Chloe shrugged.

"I still have some left from when she was on the island, and it's easy to make." Alfie turned around and looked out the window behind him. "The serum helped . . ." he said, his voice trailing off.

"So who's going to upload?" Chloe asked, interrupting Alfie's reverie.

Alfie spun back around. He opened a drawer and withdrew a manila folder. Opening it, he began to read. "Ben Fisher. Seventy years old, retired. Former administrations specialist, still on call in case of emergencies." Alfie took a break from reading to add, "He worked closely with Michael Hollis." Continuing with the information in the file, he said, "Uploaded once before, enjoyed it. Minimal imagination and was content with predetermined activities."

"What kind of predetermined activities?"

"Sad movies, comfortable chairs, time alone to reflect. We make a safe place for them to cry. As an edited human, he never had access to these feelings, and in his old age he finds them fascinating."

Chloe nodded, and Alfie shut the folder.

"I've told him this would be an upgraded experience, longer and more intense. He has told the office not to contact him for the next two weeks, plenty of time for you to take back over."

"What's going to happen when he doesn't come back?"

"I'll tell them he went into the city and disappeared. I can make up a reason, maybe something like he was abducted by organ farmers. Nobody will care; there hasn't been a single need for him for years even though he's been on call the entire time."

Chloe felt sorry for the old man. She hoped he was never aware of how useless he had become. But she knew that even if it had crossed his mind, he didn't have the circuitry to be anything other than happy. The lack of emotion insulated him from the pointlessness of his existence.

Alfie finished his scone and drank down the remaining coffee, cooled by this point, in one large swig. "Shall we?" he said before he stood up. "I'll tell him to meet us there."

"Let's get it over with."

Alfie called Ben Fisher and told him to be at the lab at noon. He took Chloe back through the atrium, onto a transport vehicle, and into the lab. Once there, he navigated through a series of hallways until they were far from the entrance. "The uploading room," he announced.

There were two stainless steel tables inside, each equipped with a modified helmet, and a small machine on a table between them. When Alfie got word Fisher had entered the building, he instructed Chloe to lie down on the table farthest from the door and turned on the device. It emitted a low hum next to her head.

"We can't let you see him. His identity is supposed to be anonymous, and he is serious about his privacy."

Chloe laughed. "Doesn't matter to me. Guy's about to have the ride of his life."

Alfie smiled. "If this works, imagine what it could mean—" He shook his head. "Let's not get ahead of ourselves. Good luck."

"Don't forget the serum."

Alfie tapped his pocket and told her not to worry. He pulled the curtain between the two tables, blocking the rest of the room from Chloe's view.

The door to the room opened within minutes, and Chloe heard Alfie greet a man with a gruff voice. A slow shuffle of feet against the floor ended at the other table, and Chloe heard the old man lie down on the second table. There was movement on the other side of the curtain, and Chloe assumed the helmet was being placed on Fisher's head. They exchanged a few words, and the man confirmed that his office knew he would be away. Alfie poked his head onto Chloe's side of the curtain and asked Chloe if she was ready.

Chloe wanted to tell him to hurry the hell up but nodded instead.

Alfie double-checked with the other man as well, who said he was looking forward to it.

Chloe couldn't help but wonder if she could beat Shada's time to capture the mind.

Alfie withdrew to the far side of the room. The curtain bisected his body and he was able to see both patients. He counted down.

"Three . . . two . . . one . . ."

Alfie flipped the switch, and Chloe's whole world went black.

CHAPTER FIVE

CHLOE AWOKE to the familiar darkness around her. She had no sense of gravity, no concept of time, and the black of a vacuum was the entirety of her experience.

The first time she'd felt this sensation, during her first upload, she tried to panic, but without control of her body she never got past its initial stages. She was caught in a purgatory between states, the mind knowing what should be felt but without control of a body to follow through with the emotion. Each time the hijacks ended and she found herself back in control of her own body, she forgot how unpleasant the experience was. She considered herself lucky her short-term memory allowed her to forget; it made the following uploads easier to bear. There had been three more periods of being consumed by darkness—her first four hijacks—before her final upload and the first time she was able to find the light.

Chloe allowed herself to relax into the darkness, to accept it, and when her mind quieted down and withdrew from the brink of panic, she witnessed a small circle of light in the distance. It was so far, and so faint, that she couldn't focus on it or else it would disappear into the black, like a distant star. Instead, she had to look in its vicinity and allow it to grow large enough to hold its shape under her full attention.

Her first time finding the light had been while Ruby Hollis had control of her body. This woman had been chosen in order to get a response out of her former husband, Michael Hollis, whose mind was inside Shada. Something about being in Shada's presence had made Chloe aware of the light, and by the time she learned to relax enough to allow it to take over her awareness, she could hear Shada's voice. The light turned out to be her vision, but it was as if her mind had taken residence at her feet and had to wait to drift up and lodge itself between her eyes before she was able to witness the world around her.

Chloe waited for the light to take over her awareness, to see through her own eyes again while her body was under Ben Fisher's control. After she ignored it long enough, her mind began to rise, and she was able to watch the light's approach. She anticipated seeing the room the upload had occurred in, but by the time Alfie's voice reached her, she knew they were no longer there.

Once she could see through her own eyes again, she discovered Alfie was walking next to her through the lab's hallways.

Chloe felt paralyzed with sensory input from her eyes and ears but unable to control any part of her body. It was strange, because she knew she was moving around and could see the halls she passed through with Alfie, but none of it was due to her control. Like a dream, or a movie, she followed the action, trying to take Shada's next step: regain control of breathing. It took a number of scans before she found her diaphragm, but while the two men walked, she was able to sense it in the background and within minutes had learned to speed it up past her body's natural rhythm.

Alfie led Chloe's body, controlled by Fisher, through the atrium and onto a transport vehicle while Chloe practiced breathing. Not a single breath was taken by her body without her being aware of the air filling her lungs. The scientist kept asking how Ben felt, and with Chloe's voice he answered, "Fine!" every time, like a child being taken on a day trip to an amusement park.

Chloe believed he did feel fine. Anyone would feel fine if they'd had decades removed from their body. She wondered what would happen to the shell of the body Fisher used to occupy—if they would dispose of it or if they would keep it running in case of his return. She had to make sure the mind never returned, to prove to Shada it was possible for other unedited humans to capture edited minds.

The two of them got off the transport vehicle outside the dorm rooms Chloe had stayed in during her previous trips to the island. Alfie led Ben-in-Chloe to the same room she'd occupied during her last stay.

"Why can't I go back to my own room?" Ben asked, in Chloe's voice.

"Uploaded individuals aren't supposed to leave the prede-termined experiences," Alfie said, as if his expertise was beyond reproach. "This is where you will get used to the body. There are other activities planned, but they don't begin until tomorrow."

Chloe took this to mean she had until tomorrow to take control back from the mind inside her body.

Alfie told Ben there was one more step necessary for an optimal upload experience. "A simple injection, it helps keep the body's original mind from fighting back against the upload."

Ben stuck out Chloe's arm, and Alfie administered the serum in the crook of her elbow. It took mere moments to act. Chloe felt control of her breath slipping away from her grasp. It wasn't long until she stopped being able to sense her breath at all.

Alfie told Ben he would be back with dinner in the evening and in the meantime to get used to being inside the unedited body. "Don't let your emotions get the best of you," Alfie warned.

"I won't," Ben-in-Chloe said. "I'm so curious about what you have planned!"

Chloe almost felt bad for the old man. He was so naive and had no idea their plan would leave his mind trapped inside her body for the rest of another lifetime.

Alfie smiled and left, shutting the door behind him.

Ben sat Chloe's body down on the bed, testing the mattress, before he got up and locked the door to their room. He went into the bathroom to inspect his mind's new residence in the mirror.

First, he leaned forward in front of the mirror and looked at the numerous piercings in her ears and nose. He gazed at her eyes, a light brown, and played with her hair.

Chloe searched for her breath and was frustrated when she couldn't find it. Every time it would show up in her awareness, she tried to use the same strategy, relax until it grew, but it never grew. It stayed on the periphery and wouldn't budge.

What did grow was her sense of connection with the world around her. Even inanimate objects seemed to emit a life force that called out to her and interrupted her attempts to focus on her breath. She felt a sense of wonder at her own reflection, an awareness of her own existence.

Ben stepped back and began to take off her clothes. Her body didn't respond to Ben's fascination with seeing her in just her bra and panties. Chloe sensed her heartbeat on the fringes of her awareness and focused on the sound, finding it easy to appreciate its resonance. It was then that she remembered the final step of Shada's plan, to feel her heartbeat and follow its flow to her limbs, and she chastised herself for forgetting. She gave herself a pass because she'd assumed she would still be able to control her breath, that finding her heartbeat would build on the previous step and not replace it.

Ben took off Chloe's undergarments, and he used her fingers to feel every inch of her most intimate areas. The resonation of Chloe's heart extended to every limb, and with little effort, Chloe was able to gain control of her hands to stop their exploration. Ben looked at Chloe's face in the mirror, confused. Chloe took control of her mouth to smile.

It took a few hours, with numerous false starts and attempts to regain control by Ben, but by the time Alfie returned with dinner, Chloe had mastered keeping Ben's consciousness from taking control of any part of her body, all while standing naked in front of the mirror. After hearing Alfie's knock, she bent over and picked up her clothes, putting them back on before answering the door.

"Hey, Alfie," Chloe said with a smirk. "I could've taken the poison after all."

CHAPTER SIX

Alfie couldn't believe Chloe had been able to take back control in just a few hours. He quizzed her about previous uploads, asked her questions about Shada, and even asked her to demonstrate physical tasks, like balancing on one foot, as proof.

Chloe answered each question without hesitation and was able to balance with minimal effort. "He's trying to take back control," she said after both feet were planted back on the ground. "It isn't hard to block him if I concentrate."

Alfie opened and closed his mouth, looking like a fish gasping for air while searching for words. In time, he managed to find the words he was looking for. "You're better at this than Shada."

Chloe blushed. "She told me how to do it. I wouldn't have any idea where to start if it wasn't for her. Hell, it took me until the fifth upload to get back my hearing and sight."

"Even after she took back control, she wasn't able to maintain it so well," Alfie said.

"I'd imagine keeping hold of a man like Hollis would be harder than keeping this guy in check," Chloe said. She walked over to the couch, sat down, and pulled the coffee table with the meal Alfie had brought on it closer to her. Dinner consisted of chicken, mashed potatoes, and green beans, a homestyle meal Chloe hadn't eaten in years. She hadn't seen a restaurant in the atrium serving this kind of food and wondered if there was somewhere else the edited on the island got their food.

"This was Ben's requested meal," Alfie said. "We took his order for meals before he uploaded, made it part of the experience. Looks like we won't need the rest of his orders."

Chloe nodded, her mouth full of food. "You want some?" she mumbled, gesturing with her fork to the meal in front of her.

"No thanks, I already ate."

Chloe devoured the meal. Alfie sat down and watched her eat.

"What's the plan?" Chloe asked when she finished.

Alfie shook his head and laughed. "Didn't think you would get here so soon. I guess tomorrow we will run some tests. I do want you to stay here for a few days and see if you can access Ben's mind, his memories and knowledge, in a continuous stream. Shada said she wasn't able to probe Hollis's thoughts without a direct inquiry, but I think it might be possible to have a constant awareness of his thoughts without too much difficulty."

"She said Hollis is with her all the time. I assumed his thoughts were in the background and she could listen in if she wanted, but maybe she meant she could always access his data if she knew what to look for."

"Like an encyclopedia she carries with her. That's what she told me. Over the next few days, I want you to find out if you can let Ben see and hear the world, listen to his thoughts, but still not allow him to control your body."

Chloe grew silent as she withdrew into herself. She tried to sense Ben's mind, but it felt out of reach, covered in darkness, like he hadn't yet figured out how to sense the light from the bottom of the well. She wanted to find out what he knew about Alfie, to remember previous interactions the two of them had had, but without anything to grasp, she was left with her own limited knowledge about the scientist.

"I can't even sense his mind at all. It's like he isn't even there." The effort of trying to sense Ben drained Chloe, and she felt a wave of exhaustion wash over her. Her eyes struggled to stay open.

"Well, he has to be somewhere." Alfie looked up, as if his thoughts were written on the ceiling. "Hollis had a stronger mind, I'm sure that had something to do with it. I hope Ben's mind isn't lost in there for good." He brought his gaze back down and looked at Chloe. "That's what you can work on the next few days, giving him space to exist without being able to take back any control."

Chloe nodded and confessed to Alfie she couldn't begin until tomorrow because she was about to fall asleep. Alfie told her the events of the day had taken a toll on her and to come find him whenever she woke up tomorrow.

"I'll probably be in my office," Alfie said as he walked out the door.

Chloe didn't bother taking off her clothes before climbing into bed. Her eyes gave up their fight, and a breath later, she was fast asleep. She felt anxious when she woke the next morning, as if the events of the previous day had coalesced while she was asleep and stayed behind instead of marching forward in time to meet her. She couldn't recall dreaming the night before, and she feared her own consciousness had descended into the darkness alongside Ben's, allowing room for him to take over her body while she slept. This thought terrified her, and she made a mental note to ask Alfie to monitor her while she slept. She hoped she wouldn't need to be tranquilized or restrained in the future.

She shook her head to clear her mind of these thoughts, stood staring at herself in the mirror, and reminded herself to stop catastrophizing before she left to find Alfie, wearing the same outfit as the day before.

Since she'd stayed in this building during her previous time on the island, she knew how to get back to the atrium. From there, she could try to find Alfie in his office, or if he wasn't there, she could take a vehicle to the lab. The day was clear, and from how high the sun was in the sky, she guessed it was late in the morning, though without seeing a clock she couldn't know for sure. Chloe looked out over the bay and wondered if her own mind was like the water, drifting out at low tide and allowing the island that was Ben's mind more space to maneuver.

The atrium was less busy than when she'd passed through the day before. She guessed everyone had eaten their breakfast and it wasn't quite time for lunch. From the clock over the transportation hub, she found out it was eleven, and some quick math revealed she had slept more than ten hours the night before.

As she walked along one side of the atrium, headed for the elevator, she saw Piper, the woman who had introduced her and Shada to uploading, walking towards her from the opposite direction. At a glance, Chloe was reminded why she didn't like the woman. It was her overall demeanor, the way she held her head and seemed to look down at everyone around her, both edited and unedited alike. She'd traded in her humanity for success in the company, and the result of her bargain was her proximity to Michael Hollis. In return, Hollis received her fierce loyalty.

Chloe wasn't sure Piper even remembered meeting her and hoped they would pass without acknowledgement. Piper's gaze was locked straight ahead when they were a few feet apart, unaware she was granting Chloe's wish.

Chloe's hand shot out and grabbed Piper's arm the moment they were next to each other. Chloe knew right away Ben had taken back control, and she cursed herself for getting lost in her own thoughts. The space her lack of focus created had allowed Ben to lie in wait and lash out at a time most advantageous to him.

"Michael Hollis is trapped inside Shada," Ben, in control of Chloe's body, said. "Took him into the city."

Piper stood dumbfounded, caught off guard by the statement. A flash of recognition, followed by rage, passed over her face as she looked at Chloe and her jaw dropped. "I knew it! I'm going to kill her."

Chloe knew Piper was protective of Hollis but had no idea why her first reaction was a death threat. She took control of her body back from Ben, let go of Piper's arm, and rushed away while Piper called after her.

"Hey! You, come back!" Piper called out, never using Chloe's name.

Whatever distance Shada had placed between herself and the island would soon be eaten up by Piper, who Chloe could tell wouldn't rest until Shada paid for capturing her leader.

CHAPTER SEVEN

CHLOE HAD no intention of going to Alfie's lab. First, she left the central building at the exit she needed to leave through if she was going to get a transport vehicle to the lab. There, she found one of the smaller pods waiting for its next passenger. She hopped in, said she wanted to go to the lab, and exited as it started to move. She wasn't sure if the vehicle would continue without its passenger and was grateful when it didn't slow down or stop. With her false trail laid, she jogged around the building in the midday sun and entered the central space from the opposite side. All told, she was outside for almost ten minutes, and by the time she went back inside, beads of sweat dotted her forehead. She looked at the spot where she'd encountered Piper; the intimidating WestCorp employee wasn't there. She searched the rest of the open space for the woman's face and was relieved to not find it. In a flash of inspiration, she popped back outside to see if the edited woman had followed her around the building and didn't see her there either.

The area around the entrance to the tram's platform beneath the atrium was occupied by a handful of people. Chloe wished there were more, so she could blend into a crowd, but her luck had already proven to be bad that day. She took a deep breath and walked with confidence towards the train station, hoping her efforts to ignore the people around her would result in everyone ignoring her.

She made it past the two massive guards and onto the platform without anyone looking at her twice. There was one other person waiting for the next tram, a forgettable man wearing an ill-fitting blue suit. Chloe guessed he had come for an early business meeting with someone on the island. His attempt at a stylish hairstyle looked like it was a remnant from his college days well over a decade ago, completing the look of someone trying to sell something inconsequential, like shower curtain rings. Chloe tried to search Fisher's memories to see if he somehow knew the man, but after his successful takeover of Chloe's body moments before, he had retreated back into the darkness.

She tried to give Fisher enough space to take back her right arm while she waited for the tram, but the edited man never took the bait. She knew she had to practice controlling the implanted mind, but how could she learn to stop his attempts at control if he never made them? She feared a repeat of what had happened with Piper, a coordinated all-out attack at a moment when she was lured into a false sense of security. In addition, she knew she would never be able to establish a consistent stream of his memories if she wasn't able to access them at all. It was like Fisher was engaged in guerrilla warfare, hiding in the recesses of her mind and waiting for the right time to strike.

When the tram came, Chloe remembered that the trip would be made without Alfie's serum. After Shada's insistence on the substance's importance, and her own experience being under its influence, Chloe knew she would have a tough time retaking control if Fisher took over while she was in the city. She wondered if the mind inside her had heard her and Alfie discuss the capture; if he hadn't, he might return to Alfie if he was able to take back control from Chloe. If that happened, Alfie could administer more serum and welcome Chloe back from the abyss. She didn't want to make plans for the worst-case scenario —if he didn't go back to Alfie at all—believing this might bring about its actualization.

The train pulled up and Chloe boarded. She was hit by a sobering thought: What if Fisher was able to hear her thoughts? If so, she would have to find a way to change her self-dialogue. Maybe she could follow her instincts without consciously considering them? Even if Fisher was able to sense the same bodily sensations, he wouldn't know which course of action Chloe would take, giving her a modicum of secrecy.

Chloe grew envious of Shada as the train carried her back to the city. It seemed more straightforward for Shada to be aware of the implanted mind, to know what it thought and experienced and sensed, instead of the open-ended questions associated with Chloe's silent passenger. All the while she wondered if Fisher, inside his own black box, was able to hear her concerns, or if they were both in separate black boxes, cut off from each other.

The train pulled into the hub below the city, and Chloe transferred onto one of the city's trains, into a seat much less comfortable than the one she'd occupied on her ride back from the island. The train had a layer of grime that made every surface appear sticky, with a stale, sweet smell to match. It was as if the train car had been left in the heat, and now that its services were required, the air-conditioning was turned on but no attempts were made to air it out. Chloe rode the train to Shada's stop, walked to Shada's apartment building at a speed just below a jog, and when the elevator took too long to descend, she ran up the stairs to the sixth level where the sisters' apartment was located.

A breathless Chloe knocked on the door and Sikya answered.

"Chloe?" she said.

"Where's Shada?" Chloe said as she stormed into the one-bedroom apartment. The room had minimal decorations and minimal furniture, one couch and a television, with nothing on the walls.

Shada walked out from the bedroom. The scars on her face, two thin vertical lines descending from each eye, were almost healed and were now thin pink slivers. They were the result of her loss of control to Hollis after the first time she had taken back control of her body, before she'd learned to use the serum to her advantage. Chloe rushed over, grabbed both her shoulders, and turned her around.

"Go pack a bag, we need to get out of here," Chloe said.

Shada wriggled free. It wasn't hard; she was much larger than Chloe. She turned around and looked at the fear in Chloe's eyes.

Chloe was struck by how weary Shada looked. It was as if her eyes alone had aged decades, the result of over a century of combined lived experience.

"What's going on?" Shada asked.

Chloe took a deep breath before relaying the events of the previous two days. When she finished, Shada looked at Chloe in awe.

"You've got a mind uploaded into you? And you took back control in less than a day?"

"Don't be impressed; he's stopped trying. That's why I wasn't ready when we ran into Piper! When I ran into Piper."

Sikya, who had been listening the entire time, said, "I don't know why you guys think it's a good idea to mess around with these WestCorp people! I've devoted my life to helping the unedited, and the two of you get into bed with the people trying to keep us down! Now look what you've done: we've got some crazy woman saying she wants to kill Shada, and Chloe has no way of knowing when someone else's implanted mind will turn up and ruin things!"

Shada laughed at her sister before turning to Chloe. "She's got a point," she said with a turn of her head. Her expression turned serious. "I'm pretty sure Ruby knows I left with Hollis uploaded into my body. If they were going to come after me, wouldn't they have done it by now?"

"Ruby's in charge of WestCorp now. They think Hollis is in the bunker, sick. As long as he's out of the picture, she can be in charge, but if they find out Hollis is really dead, then the next person in line will take over."

"Piper," Shada said, chewing on the word. "Now that she knows Hollis still exists inside me, she could kill me, prove he's dead, then take over."

"That's why we need to pack a bag! I came here right after Fisher told Piper."

"And where do you suggest we go?" Shada asked.

Chloe shrugged.

"I know someone who can help," Sikya said, shaking her head. "I can't believe I'm getting caught up in this."

CHAPTER EIGHT

CHLOE, Shada, and Sikya took the train to the heart of the city, the more affluent business district and home of the Office of Unedited Rights. Their alertness never wavered during the entirety of their trip, looking out for WestCorp agents sent to eliminate Shada. The sisters sat edged forward on their seats with their backpacks still on their backs so they could make a hasty retreat if necessary, not trusting the other passengers.

Chloe was grateful the sisters appreciated the severity of the threat but couldn't help chuckle to herself about their lack of options in the cramped car. Where did they think they could go?

Sikya led the way from the train station to the office building. They walked past elevated gardens surrounded by smooth rock, and each open space in front of the buildings they passed had a fountain in the center surrounded by people milling about. Each of these people represented a potential threat, and Chloe scanned each face, searching for murderous intent. Sikya dealt with the threat by setting a blazing pace to their destination, walking so fast she could have been in a race.

Sikya led them into the light brown stone building. Before

the guard could stop them, Sikya told him they were "with her." The guard waved them through without a second thought.

Chloe was impressed at the level of familiarity Sikya displayed and realized she had underestimated Shada's sister. This feeling grew when Sikya went straight to the reception desk on the seventeenth floor and asked if Tensen was in.

"He is, should I tell him you're here?" the young Asian man said. Chloe recognized him from the last time she'd been here with Shada, when they'd set up the safety net for the initial hijacking of their bodies by WestCorp, but he didn't seem to know who the two of them were. It was clear he knew Sikya though.

"Is there anyone in there with him?" she asked.

"No . . ." the young man said, unsure or disliking the implication of her question.

"We'll just go in," Sikya said with finality.

She waved for Chloe and Shada to follow her. The receptionist stood up but never moved his feet, the index finger on his outstretched right hand attempting to create space for him to interject, but the three women ignored him.

Sikya pushed the standard wooden office door harder than necessary, and the three of them stormed into Tensen's office. The former candidate for mayor looked up from the papers on his desk and blinked, every other muscle in his body still. His phone rang, and he pushed the button to answer it on speakerphone.

"I'm sorry, sir, they just barged in."

Chloe heard the voice from two places at the same time, live from the room behind her and through the speaker in the office.

Tensen laughed. "It's OK, we both know she can't be stopped."

Hearing this, Sikya lost some of her edge. It was as if the acceptance of her disposition by the candidate whose campaign she'd poured herself into quelled her desire to cause a ruckus. Chloe could see why he was an effective politician.

Tensen ended the call, leaned forward in his chair, and rested his elbows on his desk. "What brings the three of you in today?" he asked.

Sikya cut right to the chase. "We believe someone at WestCorp wants to kill Shada and we need someplace to hide."

"From what I remember, the two of you went to the island for a procedure," Tensen said, addressing Chloe and Shada.

Sikya looked at her sister, confused that she'd been in this office before.

Chloe appreciated his discretion but thought it odd he withheld his information when Sikya had been so forthcoming with hers. She nodded, and so did Shada.

"And did everything turn out all right?" Tensen asked.

"For the most part," Chloe said. Shada stayed quiet.

"Then why would they want to kill you?" Tensen asked Shada.

"She took something that belongs to them," Chloe said, answering for her friend. "After their leader hijacked Shada's body, she retook control and left the island with his mind inside her."

"Hollis's mind is inside you right now? No wonder they're pissed." Tensen took a moment to digest. "But wouldn't killing you kill their leader too?"

"It's complicated," Chloe said in an attempt to stem the flow of information.

"He was dying anyways, and the plan was for him to transfer everything over to me and live a second life from inside my body. I had other plans." Shada showed a mischievous smile, and Chloe wondered if capturing the leader's mind had been her plan all along.

"That still doesn't explain why they want you dead. Wouldn't they want him back?"

"There was someone being groomed to take over when Hollis died. Right now, everyone assumes he's sick in bed, so his wife is running the company. I'd imagine the wife's trying to find a way to make her position permanent."

"And which one of them wants to kill you?" asked Tensen.

"Piper, the one who was supposed to take over when Hollis died," Chloe said.

Tensen nodded.

"Why doesn't she just tell everyone Hollis is already dead?" Sikya asked.

"Because he isn't. As long as he still exists in my body, it would be possible to upload his mind to yet another body, or back into his old one if it still exists. Hollis is the one who built the company into what it is, and everyone on the island knows it."

Chloe began thinking out loud. "And if that ever happened, Ruby could claim she was keeping the company safe until her husband returned. She has a way out no matter what."

"Piper needs Hollis gone for good before she can show her hand," Tensen said, summarizing the situation. "So we need to find somewhere for Shada to hide."

Sikya groaned. "That's what I told you in the first place!"

Tensen smiled at her with a warmth that begged forgiveness for his need to understand the entirety of the situation. "I'll help, but I have a request," he said.

"What is it?" Sikya asked.

"It's not from you. It's from her," he said, pointing to Shada.

Shada looked at Tensen with the gaze of an elder seeing the totality of the person in front of them. He grinned, appreciating the attention, in no way shy of being seen for who he was.

"You said Hollis transferred everything over to you?"

Shada nodded, and Chloe was struck by the thought that her friend had known what his request would be before they walked into the room.

"There's a lot of good we could do with those kinds of resources. Would you be willing to donate to help the unedited people of the city?"

"And by helping the unedited people, do you mean donate to your next campaign?"

Sikya looked at Shada with the bright eyes of a young, hopeful child. The prospect that her sister would become her life's work's most significant benefactor had to have crossed Sikya's mind before then, but based on her reaction, Chloe guessed the topic hadn't been discussed.

Tensen flashed his politician's smile. "Who better to help the unedited than me?"

Shada looked at Sikya, smiled, then turned back to Tensen. "Of course I'll donate. We can discuss after I stop having to worry about a crazy edited person coming to kill me."

Tensen slapped his desk and made a fist in celebration. "Give me one second," he said.

He picked up the phone, dialed, and told whoever was on the other line to be at the office in half an hour. "We need a locker," he said before hanging up.

CHAPTER NINE

W‌HEN THE STERN-LOOKING man dressed in black emerged from Tensen's office, he had been with the politician for all of ten minutes. On his way in, he had ignored the three women in the reception area, but now he walked up to them, his face relaxed and deferential, and introduced himself.

"My name is Richard Rees," he said before shaking each of their hands. He was tall enough to be imposing but not draw attention, handsome enough to disarm but not draw stares, and his smile was warm without flashing too many straight white teeth. In short, he was made to blend in.

The three women stood, introduced themselves in turn, and waited for instruction from Tensen, who had emerged from his office and stood in its doorway. "Richard here will take you to the safe house," he said.

Shada and Sikya grabbed their backpacks from the floor and slung them over their shoulders.

"The car is waiting in the parking garage," Richard explained, moving towards the door.

"I'll be in touch with you once you're settled in," Tensen said.

Richard led the way to the elevator, down to the parking garage, and into an idling black SUV. Chloe, Shada, and Sikya climbed into the back, and Richard got into the passenger seat. The driver had an olive complexion similar to Richard's, a shade hard to attribute to any particular heritage. They spent a silent hour in the car, and Chloe had to look through the front windshield to see where they were going because the rear windows were too dark to see through. She believed they were still inside the city's limits but in a more suburban area, where single-family houses were the norm. The SUV pulled into one of the gated driveways, waited a moment for the gate to swing open, and parked inside the garage of a nondescript ranch-style house.

"We're here," Richard announced.

Everyone, including the driver, climbed out of the car and walked inside.

"This house has constant surveillance," Richard said. He pulled open the cabinets and refrigerator to inspect their provisions. "There should be enough to last today," he said, gesturing to the driver, "but Tony here will be back either late tonight or tomorrow with groceries and anything else you need."

When Tony smiled, Chloe wondered how such a charming face had ended up hidden behind the steering wheel for whatever group the two men worked for. "Just let me know what you want," he said. His voice was soothing, like aloe on a burn. She got the sense he was the kind of person she'd want by her side if events took a turn for the worse.

Richard looked at Tony and gestured with his head back towards the garage. "He'll be back," Richard said.

The two men began to leave, and Chloe announced she was coming with them. "I need a ride back to the central station," she said.

Sikya was stunned. "Where are you going?" Sikya said, her apprehension palpable.

Shada wasn't fazed. "Back to WestCorp," she said.

Chloe explained. "I still need to get control of Fisher. Which means I need the serum from Alfie."

"What about Piper?" Sikya said.

"She can't be everywhere at once. Avoid her on your way to Alfie, and he should be able to take care of you," Shada said.

"You support her decision? She should stay here with us!" Sikya lamented.

"Without control of Fisher, she's still a threat. What if he takes control while she sleeps and tells Piper where we are?" Shada said to calm her sister.

"She could give us away on the island too," Sikya argued.

"But if she's on the island, she can use the serum to keep control. Without it here . . ." Shada trailed off, not wanting to speak the worst-case scenario into existence.

Chloe was hit by a wave of self-consciousness, and she inspected the two men dressed in matching black outfits. She wondered if they'd been too cavalier by talking about the details of their situation in front of people they'd just met.

"Your secret's safe with us," Richard said, all business, interpreting Chloe's look.

"Can you take me back?"

"Of course," Tony replied.

On the ride back downtown, Richard sat in the back seat with Chloe. "Tensen told me WestCorp wants Shada dead because she captured a mind important to them. Why aren't they hunting you if you've captured a mind too?"

Chloe was apprehensive, but something in the man's voice convinced her to trust him. "I'm not sure I've been gone long enough to warrant a hunt. Plus, the person I captured isn't important; it was more of a test to see if it was possible."

"To see if what was possible?"

"If another unedited person, besides Shada, was able to capture an edited mind," Chloe said.

"And you captured this Fisher guy?"

Chloe turned and stared at Richard, measuring the man. His continued questioning made her second-guess his intentions.

"Hey, we're on the same side here," Richard said. "I've devoted my life to equality for unedited people." He pulled out his wallet, withdrew a picture, and handed it to Chloe. It showed him in a park with two young children, one in each of his thick arms. "These two are mine. I don't want them to live as inferiors just because we couldn't afford to edit them."

Chloe marveled at the devotion to his family. When she exhaled, she realized she had been holding her breath. "Yes, I captured Fisher. But I wasn't able to keep control, that's how Piper found out Hollis is trapped inside Shada. I'm the reason all this happened." Her gaze fell, and she looked down at her shoes, embarrassed.

"Don't be so hard on yourself! You've done something incredible. And now you're willing to go back into the lion's den. It's commendable."

Chloe was grateful for Richard's kind words. "Thanks," she said, not feeling as brave as he made her sound.

"Do you think the procedure could be done again?" Richard asked.

"Like capture a second mind inside my body? If I could get control of this one, I don't see why not. I bet Shada could do it."

"No, could it be done again to another person?" He paused. "Do you think Alfie would agree to upload a mind into me?"

Chloe was shocked. "If it doesn't work, you'd leave your children without a father," she said.

"But I wouldn't be able to rest if I knew there was a chance to weaken WestCorp and I didn't try. They would understand."

242

"They're too young," Chloe argued. She returned his picture, and he put it back in his wallet.

"Not anymore." Richard's mood darkened. "This picture was taken years ago. Their mother took them and left, said she was tired of how much I worked. But if my work resulted in a mortal blow to the corporation responsible for them being second-class citizens, it would all be worth it."

Chloe shook her head. "I'm sure they'd prefer to have their father instead."

"It's too late for that," Richard lamented.

Tony honked the horn at a car that had cut him off. Chloe looked through the front window and realized they were close to the train station.

"Let me talk to the scientist and see if he wants to run another test," Chloe said.

"Perfect, let me know."

"How can I reach you?"

"Tensen and Tony both know how to get a hold of me."

Chloe nodded, unsure how she felt about sharing the internal process to taking back control. Shada was the one who'd created the framework, she should be the one to guide him. But Shada had objected to Chloe's attempt to capture an edited mind, and Chloe believed she wouldn't want to risk someone else. Then again, Chloe thought, maybe Shada had objected because she and Chloe were friends. Since she'd just met Richard, she might not care whether or not he attempted the procedure.

The conversation never resumed, and Chloe considered Richard's request. In the end, she decided she would be able to describe the steps necessary for Richard to take back control, provided Alfie agreed to perform the procedure. Hadn't she been able to regain control of her own body faster than Shada had?

Tony pulled the car to a stop and a car behind them honked. He turned on his hazards and rolled down his window before sticking an arm out, waving traffic around him. "We're here," he said.

Chloe took a deep breath before she got out of the car.

"Let me know," Richard said again before the door shut and the SUV pulled away.

CHAPTER TEN

CHLOE TRIED to appear casual as she looked around the crowded atrium in the center of WestCorp's island. It was past business hours, and the tables were packed with people eating dinner. She was one of a few people who had come to the island at this hour; in contrast, the island's platform had been filled with commuters heading back to the city for the night. They piled onto the train as soon as she got off. Her fellow travelers hadn't paid attention when she lingered on the steps, letting them all go ahead of her. They entered into the island's bustle without pause, leaving her alone to peek over the railing and scan the space for Piper.

It had been hours since Fisher had taken control of her mouth to spill Shada's secret, and Piper's reaction to the information still hadn't revealed itself. Inside her mind, she couldn't find any sign of Fisher, but she stayed vigilant so the captured consciousness wouldn't be able to reach out to anyone else.

Convinced the atrium was Piper-free, Chloe stood tall and climbed the final stair. She passed tables filled with WestCorp employees and thought she felt a spike of awareness from Fisher, but the sensation was so quick that she doubted its existence. She was hit by a wave of nausea at the thought of losing control once more and wanted to get to Alfie as soon as possible so she could get another dose of the serum. Part of her was grateful so many people were around, so she could blend in, but if she gave in to her desire, she'd begin running at full speed.

Chloe realized she was sweating when she got to the elevator that would take her up to the level of Alfie's office. The events of the day had fried her nerves, and this most recent rush of adrenaline pushed her over the edge. She felt exhausted and missed her bed, both the one on the island and the one in her apartment, and wished she could retreat to the comfort of sleep. She knew that without the serum this wasn't possible, in case Fisher was somehow able to retake control while she slept. She became aware of how little she'd eaten throughout the day. She didn't eat much on most days, but most days weren't filled with the level of nervousness and constant awareness she had dealt with since the morning, draining her energy.

Alfie wasn't in his office. The door was locked, and when she put her ear to the door, she heard nothing inside. She had no idea where he lived, and the other place he could be, the lab, would require her going back into the crowded food court, a daunting prospect.

She closed her eyes and felt for Fisher. She wanted to know if he was going to make an attempt at her body so she could deal with it while she was alone, but there was silence on his part. She took a deep breath and exhaled, aware of her diminished capability to find and focus on her heartbeat. She needed the serum.

When Chloe entered the food court, she stayed on the edges of the space, hoping to use the perimeter to avoid prying eyes. In reality, she knew there was just one person who cared if she was on the island, Piper, so the slinking around and worrying was unnecessary. In addition, the first time she'd run into Piper was on the edge of the atrium, in front of a restaurant, but keeping a low profile helped Chloe believe she was being proactive instead of just hoping for the best. She made it to the waiting transport vehicle outside and hopped in, hoping Alfie was in the lab. If not, she could be in for a long, sleepless night.

Special identification was required to get past the waiting area of the lab. She had seen Alfie raise the badge on his right hip to the small black box next to the frosted glass double doors, but she'd forgotten that the lab required permission to enter. She milled about in front of the doors, her desperation growing, while she wondered how she could contact someone inside to let her in and help her find Alfie. She looked up and saw a security camera. Without a second thought, she hopped up and down and waved her hands, hoping a guard would see her and investigate. Her hope was to convince them she had forgotten her pass and they would let her in.

She paced the room, trying to assume the air of a frustrated scientist kept away from her work, as the minutes crept by. The door opened just as she was about to give up.

"What are you doing?" Alfie asked with a laugh. "The guards said some crazy lady was out here and asked if you were one of mine."

Chloe felt a flush creep up her neck before anger at her body's natural response settled in. "Where were you?" she said, as if Alfie was the one who'd left the island, not her.

"I've been working, like always," Alfie said, tired. "You were supposed to come find me hours ago. No way you just woke up."

"I didn't just wake up." Chloe nodded towards the camera overhead. "Can we go talk inside?"

Alfie understood and tilted his head back, gesturing for Chloe to follow him. He led the way through an empty series of halls and offices until they were quite far from the entrance. Chloe knew she would have trouble finding her way out alone.

"In here," Alfie said, opening a door for Chloe.

The room was much larger than Chloe had anticipated based on the size of the door. There were three stainless steel tables, and stainless steel counters surrounded the perimeter. It had numerous machines she had never seen before, some made of exposed wires and gleaming metal, others made of dark gray plastic. There were multiple computer monitors hooked up to various machines, and in a fume hood was a full set of glassware and small ceramic containers. The walls were unfinished, and every corner of the room was illuminated by bright lights overhead.

"Is this where you work?"

"Most of the time. This is where I built the machine to transplant consciousness."

"You have an office and this whole room?" Chloe said in awe. She realized how important Alfie must be to the company if he was the sole user of both spaces, and she wondered how the loss of the lead scientist would affect their operations if anyone ever captured his mind.

"The office is for theoretical work. In here is where I bring my ideas to life."

"And you use this all by yourself?"

"I have a team who helps me here and there, but for the most part, yes, I'm in here alone."

Chloe walked around and looked at the various pieces of equipment, curious about what they all did.

"Where were you?" Alfie asked.

"I left the island."

Alfie smiled. "I know that. What did you do in the city?"

Chloe told Alfie about her run-in with Piper and how she went to warn Shada. She kept out the parts about visiting the Office of Unedited Rights and relocating Shada and Sikya to another part of the city, unsure of how much she could trust the scientist.

"I spoke with Piper earlier today, as a matter of fact," Alfie said, as if to continue their conversation.

Chloe felt her bottom jaw drop and rushed to close her mouth. "About what?" she said.

"She inquired about editing for increased physical strength."

"I knew it! She's getting ready to go after Shada!"

"Perhaps," Alfie said, his voice trailing off.

"What did you tell her?"

"I told her the truth: that it would be hard but not impossible."

"You can't do it!"

Alfie's face turned to stone. "I can. But I won't. It's easy enough to test new procedures on people from the city, but if I ever got caught testing on employees, I'd be removed from my position."

Chloe appreciated the euphemism for unedited and edited people and wondered if "removed from his position" meant killed. "Did she mention anything about me? About me capturing a mind?"

"She didn't say anything about you or Shada, just asked about the edit. She wouldn't share that information with me though; she has to know I'm involved, since Hollis is the one who was captured."

Chloe stayed silent, imagining the interaction between Piper and Alfie. "But do you think she suspects?"

"Maybe she thinks you and Shada had a falling-out? There are any number of reasons why you might have told her; I don't think she would just jump to the conclusion you captured an edited mind. It's only happened once before, ever, so I doubt it's a viable consideration for her."

"I can't lose control again. Do you have more serum? I haven't had any since last night."

"I was finishing another batch of the serum before the guards asked me if I knew who was outside the lab." Alfie walked over to a large stainless steel container that reminded Chloe of a refrigerator. From the third rack from the top, he pulled out an array of vials. "This should last us a while. Long enough for you to figure out how to read Fisher's memory."

"I don't know if it's possible; he stays far from my awareness," Chloe said, picking up and inspecting a vial.

Alfie took out a needle and syringe, filled them with the serum, and told Chloe to give him her arm. When she did, he injected her in the crook of her elbow. Within moments, she felt the associated flood of awareness of everything around her, in particular Alfie, since he was the sole living entity in the room. She found her own heartbeat and felt the flow of her pulse to each of her extremities. There wasn't any sign of Fisher.

CHAPTER ELEVEN

CHLOE WOKE up the next morning to sunlight spilling into her room through the window facing the bay. A sense of calm emanated from her and was aided by the sight of water outside. She watched the small waves rolling into the island, and instead of drawing the curtains closed and climbing back into bed, which was her initial plan, she left them open and started her day.

There was no way to measure whether her body had belonged to her the entirety of the previous night, but without a hint of anxiety, she was confident Fisher had stayed inside the dark corner of her mind he had decided to make his home. Nothing surfaced when she tried to remember her dreams from the night before, making her wonder if her mind had descended into the darkness and joined him.

She dressed and was about to leave when she was hit with a sense of déjà vu, like she was reliving the morning from the previous day when she'd run into Piper and put Shada in danger. Her stomach grumbled, its way of reminding her of its requirements. She didn't know where to get food without going to the atrium and wished she had a way to contact Alfie. If she was careful, could she make it to his office without being seen? She cursed the fact that all transport vehicles ran through the center. She could always walk, but that would attract unwanted attention at a time she needed to lie low.

She sat down on her bed to think and the mattress called out to her, begging her to climb back under her blankets. Her stomach urged a different agenda once more, wanting her to leave and find something to eat. In the end, her stomach won, so she prepared to go to the food court. No way was she going to be caught without a plan this time. She would rush in, get food from the restaurant closest to the door, and leave right away, minimizing the time she could run into Piper.

When Chloe opened her room's door, she found a tray with a covered plate on the floor in the hallway. She grew suspicious of her neighbors, wondering how whoever had left the tray there could trust the people around her. She wondered if the other rooms were empty. She and Shada had been given rooms straightaway, she had been assigned the same room when she came back to the island, and she never saw anyone else. She made a mental note to ask Alfie about it later.

Chloe brought the tray into her room and sat it on her bed. Under the cover was a bowl of thick oatmeal and a banana. "Standard," she said to the empty room around her. She decided whoever had brought the meal must have left it within the last hour, because the oatmeal was still lukewarm and dots of moisture dotted the inside of the cover. The bowl was empty in minutes, consumed in large, rapid spoonfuls. Chloe stood and stared out the window as she ate the banana, looking for signs of life outside. She wondered what kind of security WestCorp had put in place outside the island's borders. There was no way they trusted water, their natural border, to keep everyone out. She imagined a private coast guard, but since she had never once seen a boat near the island, she decided they couldn't exist. She guessed there were underwater sensors looking for trespassers, equipped with mines for protection. If she slept in her room for enough nights, would she be woken up by an explosion from the bay?

Her daydream ended with the last bite of her banana. She put the peel into her empty bowl and carried the tray with the intention of leaving it where she had found it. This was what people in movies did when they had room service, so she guessed it was standard practice on the island as well. She used her hip to hold the tray against the wall, threw the door open, and used her right foot to stop the door from closing. There was a piece of paper in the hallway where she'd first found the tray. She set the tray down beyond the paper—if there was anyone else in the rooms with her, they would just have to walk over it—and picked up the paper. On it were instructions from Alfie:

USE THE TRANSPORT VEHICLE OUTSIDE THIS EXIT, IT WILL BRING YOU TO ME - ARG

This was underlined by an arrow pointing to the right.

Chloe stuffed the note into her pocket, looked back in her room, decided she didn't need anything else, then made her way to the exit Alfie had indicated. Outside was an unpainted single-seat transporter. It looked like it was a private vehicle, not one of the company's. Chloe guessed it belonged to Alfie, maybe Hollis. The leader wouldn't have any use of it anymore, even if his body had been kept alive. Chloe climbed in, and the vehicle began to move. At first, it headed down the path leading to the atrium, and Chloe worried she had been tricked. Then, all of a sudden, the vehicle lurched with the sound of changing gears and left the path, cutting through the manicured grass lawns between buildings. The open windows of the vehicle were small, and even though there wasn't any material between her and the outside, it would have been hard for anyone to see her face if they happened to see her renegade vehicle break the mold of traditional island travel.

The trip ended in front of the small building with a slanted roof, a single door, and no windows that Chloe knew was Hollis's bunker. Shada had shown her the residence of West-Corp's former leader before they'd fled from the island. The front door led to a room with an elevator, and below the island was Hollis's bunker, with multiple rooms and plenty of privacy.

The front door opened, and Alfie strode out. He met Chloe just as she was climbing out of the transport vehicle and gestured for her to follow him.

"This was Hollis's personal residence," Alfie said. The way he said it left space at the end of his statement, a sort of vacuum for Chloe to fill with her disbelief the leader would live in such a small building.

"I know, Shada showed it to me before we left."

Alfie seemed surprised, then angry, and his emotional journey ended with him being disappointed. "So you already know this is just the room where we catch the elevator?" he asked as they walked through the front door, his surprise ruined.

Chloe nodded.

They rode down in silence. When they got to the underground cavern, Alfie led her to what Chloe knew was Hollis's study. At the end of the hallway was the dinner table, so large it had to have been built in the space, and on the far wall was the inky black stone that served as the far end of the residence.

Alfie injected Chloe with another dose of serum before the two of them got straight to business. He was seated behind Hollis's desk when Chloe told him about the member of Tensen's team who wanted to upload an edited mind. "I can upload a mind into Richard, but I can't be held responsible for the results," he said.

"He understands that, he just wants to be a part of the testing," Chloe said. She was standing, leaning against the wall next to the door.

"And he knows about the process to take back control of his own body?"

"Not yet, but I'll tell him."

Alfie nodded. His demeanor become more personal. "What do you think about it? Will he be able to take back control?"

"I think he's stubborn enough to try. Once I tell him how he should be able to do it."

"But both you and Shada had been able to plug back into reality while hijacked, before your permanent uploads. It took you multiple times to do it."

Chloe liked the way he described the process as plugging back in. "Richard could be just as good as Shada, for all we know."

"True, but I have the feeling you and Shada are exceptions to the rule. We've been doing uploads for over a year now, and the two of you are the only ones who were able to witness their world while hijacked."

Chloe paused for a moment. "But you'll still go through with it?"

"Definitely. I want to find out for myself if an unedited off the street can capture an edited mind. I just wanted you to appreciate the risk."

Chloe was reminded of the two children Richard used as motivation.

"Let's discuss the reason I wanted to talk down here, in private: I need to find out if Piper told Ruby about Shada capturing Hollis."

"You don't think she suspects?" Chloe thought about the discussion she, Shada, and Sikya had had with Tensen but kept it to herself, wanting to hear Alfie's version of how the situation might unfold.

"Suspecting and knowing are two very different things. If she knows for sure, there could be . . . repercussions for me, which also means future uploads won't happen. And I don't know how we could get you the serum. It's easy enough to produce, but why would WestCorp scientists bother?"

"We also need to know if Piper knows I've captured a mind myself," Chloe said, thinking out loud.

"If she confided Hollis's situation to Ruby, she might have also told her about you. Either way, we need to find out."

"How will we do that?"

"You're going to be Ruby's personal assistant."

CHAPTER TWELVE

ALFIE'S PLAN was simple enough. In order for Chloe to work for WestCorp at all, she would have to be edited.

"No way I'm going to edit anything now, I've got Fisher in here," Chloe said, tapping her head. She thought maybe she should have tapped her stomach, or her heart, instead.

Alfie shook his head. "You misunderstand me," he said. "We will forge the record."

Chloe flashed a wicked smile, appreciating the scientist's willingness to subvert the establishment.

"The one problem is the money," Alfie said.

"How so? You can't just put it into the system as paid?"

"The money has to come from somewhere. If you could access Fisher's memories, you could transfer his assets to yourself and pay for it, but since he's been uncooperative, that won't work."

"Can you access his account?"

"In theory, yes. But it'll look strange if he paid for you to get edited, since you two aren't supposed to know each other."

"We could say he took a liking to me after he uploaded and decided to become my sponsor."

Alfie's head turned sideways, and Chloe was struck with the realization she'd said "we," as if she would be explaining anything to anyone.

"Who would look into it?" Chloe asked.

"The people in accounting are hawks, they don't miss a thing. What it comes down to is whether I want to pay for it out of the lab's budget or take it from Fisher. I can't decide which would seem less suspicious."

Chloe paced the length of Hollis's study. She knew what she was about to say didn't make sense, but she couldn't think of another option. "I've got some money from the previous uploads," she said, thinking out loud. "But I don't want to use it."

"It won't be enough anyways," Alfie said.

"What if we tried another dose of serum? If it increased my awareness, I might be able to find Fisher then transfer his assets to me."

"I'd rather not. Too much could leave you unable to distinguish the difference between your inner and outer realities." After a moment's pause, he asked if she would be willing to go into debt for the procedure. "It would legitimize the process," he said.

Chloe didn't want to tell him no right away, but she knew she didn't want to go into debt. Her previous five uploads had given her a sizable windfall, which she knew was almost enough to buy her home away from the city. She didn't want to put her future at risk.

Alfie, witnessing her hesitation, told her that whenever she was able to control Fisher, she would be able to transfer all his assets to her. "It would be more than enough to pay off the debt and have quite a few more zeroes than you were able to make with the uploads."

"What if I never find him?" she said. It was a fear that had been rolling around in the back of her head, and as soon as she said it out loud, she realized the nervousness she would live with if that turned out to be the case.

"You think that's an option?" Alfie said. He looked at her with the tenderness of a father who wants his daughter to believe in herself. "I pegged you as the type who wouldn't give up."

Chloe's gaze dropped. She was ashamed her confidence had wavered. "You're right, it's only a matter of time until I figure him out."

"That's what I think too."

Chloe agreed to take on the debt so she could undergo the procedure, although since she wasn't going to receive any genetic edits, she was going into debt for nothing. They made plans to meet at the lab later, in the afternoon, which would give Alfie time to set up the trail of paperwork that would keep the accountants happy.

"Can I use the off-road transport vehicle again? I don't want to have to go through the center of the island," she said.

"Of course. It's voice-controlled, just say where you want to go and it will get you there."

Alfie said he had some things to do in the underground bunker and that he would see Chloe that afternoon. He gave her a sack of vials filled with serum and instructed her to dose herself every morning and night. She left without going into any of the rooms, though she was curious to see if anything in the residence had changed since the tour Shada had given her. Her best guess was that Alfie had taken over and made the space his own, but this was just a gut feeling and had no basis in anything she'd witnessed.

She spent the rest of the morning bored in her room, waiting for the time to leave and meet Alfie. Inside the bathroom, while staring at the mirror, Chloe tried to sense Fisher lingering deep inside her consciousness. Twice, she thought she sensed his awareness of her, but instead of trying to fight back, which Chloe hoped he would do, he shut down and went back into the dark. She slammed her fists onto the bathroom sink, ran her fingers through her hair, and wished there was something she could do to force his hand. She would have been satisfied even if she lost control of her body, but it was the anticipation that got beneath the top layer of skin and picked below the surface where she couldn't scratch.

Alfie was outside the lab when Chloe arrived. He waved at her vehicle as it approached, and Chloe was struck at the way he had developed into a quasi–father figure for her. He led her inside.

Chloe was anxious, as if she was waiting for a moment of pain. She imagined she would sign a paper and that would be the press of a button, signifying her acceptance of the debt. Instead, when they were alone, Alfie told her everything had already been done. "You now have a twenty-year employment contract, unless you pay off the remaining balance yourself."

The lack of buildup was appreciated.

"One thing to keep in mind: if you were edited, you would be happy with your situation on the island. If you paid off the debt, you would have to leave because it would be suspicious that you ever desired more than what the island could provide."

Chloe thought about the implications while Alfie continued.

"Of course, once you get control of Fisher and have the money to pay back the debt, you should leave the island anyways. I just want you to keep in mind how WestCorp views the situation."

"Believe me, I don't intend to stay," Chloe said.

Alfie led Chloe to a large white cylinder with windows made of thick clear plastic. It was bisected by a cushion with a pillow on one side for a person's head. There was enough space inside to accommodate even the security guards, the most massive specimens of human Chloe had ever seen.

"This is what we use to edit DNA," Alfie explained.

"Much more involved than the helmets used for uploading," Chloe observed.

"Funny enough, the process is much simpler. It just requires more equipment. The upload is much trickier, but we only need access to the brain, so the helmet is the only thing people see."

"If I'm not getting edited, what are we doing here?"

"I still need to run the machine. I can duplicate the results of the procedure from another subject, but there's no way to get past the required surge of electricity." Alfie pulled a mechanical lever and the cylinder peeled open. He closed it right away, the cylinder still empty, then turned to Chloe.

"Ready to get edited?" he said with a smile.

Chloe nodded, and Alfie pushed the button.

The white cylinder creaked to life. It sounded like there was something spinning inside, and once it got going, a low whir filled the room. While the machine ran, Alfie explained their next steps.

"Ruby already knows you will be her personal assistant and is expecting you tomorrow."

"What happened to the one she has now?"

"Turns out she's the exact blood type we need for an experiment. Her assignment was changed, and she'll be reporting to the lab starting tomorrow."

"Ruby didn't care?"

"Everyone at WestCorp knows science is our main focus. The whole company was built on the backs of our experiments; if the lab needs something, or someone, then we get it. The best thing Hollis ever did was instill an appreciation for what science can do."

"What can you tell me about Ruby?" Chloe asked.

Alfie looked at the ceiling and his face turned thoughtful. "Nothing much. When you meet her, remember you're supposed to be edited. No more attachment to unedited people. In fact, you should learn to look down on everyone not on the island. And pretend to be happy all the time, of course."

"What if I see Piper while working for her?"

"It's not if, it's when," Alfie said. "Working for Ruby will give you a certain amount of protection. Piper wouldn't dare do anything if you work for the woman in charge."

"She could find out where I've been staying," Chloe countered.

"Nobody knows that but me," Alfie said with finality.

When the cylinder stopped buzzing, Alfie told Chloe to take the transport vehicle back to her room. "In the morning, tell it you want to be taken to Ruby. Her position is on the island's grid, and the vehicle can take you wherever she is."

"Wait, is everyone connected to the system? If I told the vehicle to take me to you, it would do it?"

Alfie laughed. "Yes, but why would you want to see me?"

CHAPTER THIRTEEN

CHLOE TOOK a deep breath and knocked on the door to Ruby's office. She donned a reserved smile, the one she had practiced in front of the mirror the night before, hoping to appear genuine without looking too happy.

"Come in," a high-pitched voice from inside the office replied.

The door opened without a sound, and Chloe strode in with feigned confidence. Slivers of bright yellow walls were visible between numerous hand-drawn pictures of birds. Their feathers were painted with watercolors, but it didn't help any of them appear lifelike. If there had been one or two, Chloe would have thought they were the work of a daughter or son, but the fact they were displayed with such prominence, and that there were so many, led Chloe to believe Ruby had drawn them herself.

Ruby noticed Chloe's inspection and sat up in her chair. "Do you like them?"

"They're a great addition," Chloe said. They weren't professional quality, but they served to hide the overwhelming yellow beneath.

"Just something I do in my free time," Ruby explained. She

gestured towards the chair in front of her. "Please take a seat," Ruby said. There was no indication that she recognized Chloe.

Chloe sat down, and Ruby began telling her the expectations associated with being her personal assistant. Ruby didn't mind if Chloe came to work after her in the morning but required her to stay until she left for the day. "In case anything needs to be done last minute," Ruby said as an explanation.

Chloe stared at Ruby's hair while the woman reviewed which correspondences needed to be sent to her and which Chloe could answer herself. It was an artificial gray, as if she had chosen a reasonable color to hide white beneath instead of pretending her hair was still the color of her youth. Her wrinkles were well hidden beneath layers of makeup, but the lines around her eyes appeared when she talked.

"Did you get all that?" Ruby asked.

Chloe rattled off the few names that Ruby required her to forward and mentioned that she would ask about any names not included on the list.

"Good," Ruby said with a smile, deepening the wrinkles at the corners of her eyes. The smile disappeared and she grew serious. "There's something I need you to do. Think of it as a sort of test."

Chloe appreciated Ruby's straightforward manner. "What's that?"

Ruby leaned back in her chair. "I understand you edited yesterday. Before that, you participated in a fair share of uploads."

Uncertainty made Chloe's nods slow and measured.

"One of those uploads was me. Did you know that?"

Chloe scrambled to act surprised. "I had no idea. Did you enjoy yourself?"

"Don't lie to me, girl," Ruby said. Her eyebrows narrowed,

bringing out the wrinkles in her forehead. "I know you and Shada were close. She must have told you."

Chloe doubled down and gave Ruby an icy stare. "She didn't mention you," she said.

Ruby seemed to doubt she wasn't important enough for Shada to discuss. "It doesn't matter, that's not what I want to discuss. The woman who organizes the uploads, Piper. Do you know her?"

Chloe felt her stomach drop, and her blood ran cold. She considered saying she didn't, but one lie was enough for the day. "I do."

"Good." Ruby leaned forward in her chair. "I need you to kill her." Ruby then stared at Chloe, measuring her reaction.

While Chloe concentrated on what she should say, she felt the stirrings of Fisher in the depths of her awareness and had to fight to keep her focus in the room.

"I don't know what to say. Can I ask why?"

"You can."

Chloe waited for Ruby to elaborate then realized she never did ask the question. "Why then?" she said.

Ruby smiled like a teacher whose student just realized the correct answer. "I don't trust her. Never have. I used to tell Michael all the time that she was manipulating him so she could take over the company, but he wouldn't listen. Now I fear she is trying to capitalize on his illness."

"Makes sense," Chloe said.

"Of course it does," Ruby snapped. "And for what it's worth, I don't trust you either. All of a sudden Alfie needs my old personal assistant and you come waltzing in to take her place? Sounds too convenient. This is how you can prove your loyalty."

"Do you have a suggestion how you want it done?"

Ruby thought for a moment. "No, I don't care how you do it. I'll leave that up to you to decide."

"What happens if someone finds out I did it?"

"Well, you'll just have to be careful! But even if you aren't, I should be able to tell whoever investigates to ignore you since you have no reason to want her dead."

Chloe held her laughter inside.

Ruby got up from her chair, walked around her desk, and motioned for Chloe to follow. She stopped at the desk outside her office door.

"This is where you will work. Like I said, it's OK if you get here after me because I often keep strange hours and get here early. But once you get here, make sure you let me know you've arrived."

With that, Ruby went back into her office and shut the door.

From then on, Chloe was at her desk by eight in the morning. Some days Ruby was there before she arrived, and some days the office door was still locked and Ruby would come into the office around lunch. One day Ruby didn't come to the office at all. On this day, she called Chloe and had her reorganize an entire cabinet of paper files behind Chloe's desk, all over five years old. Chloe sensed her boss didn't have anything pressing and was looking for work she could do, regardless of Ruby's insistence that the organization was a priority. When Ruby showed up the next day, she never looked at the files, either trusting Chloe had completed the work or not caring whether or not she did.

In between completing tasks for Ruby, Chloe tried to come up with how she would eliminate Piper. It wouldn't be hard for her to use her transport vehicle to find out where Piper lived, she thought. She could then show up in the middle of the night, but she doubted she was strong enough to kill the woman with her bare hands. It wasn't her style and would put herself in harm's way.

She considered using the poison she'd brought to the island with her, but she had no desire to get close enough to administer a dose and had no idea when or what Piper ate. The risk of poisoning the wrong food was high, and when the toxicology report was returned, Alfie would know right away who committed the murder. Chloe couldn't pinpoint why she cared if Alfie knew she killed Piper, but she knew she wanted to keep it a secret from as many people as possible. There was also a chance someone else would see the report, and she didn't want to force Alfie to cover for her.

Drowning was also out of the question. From what she'd seen, the edited never approached the water.

As her days passed at the desk outside Ruby's office, she continued to daydream about a solution to her problem. She tried to probe Fisher's memories but found them still beyond her reach. The more she considered her problem, the more she came to believe that the answer was dependent on her ability to reach into Fisher's mind. The two tasks became interwoven, the success of one dependent on the other. She never considered the reverse, that killing Piper would allow her to harness Fisher's mind.

CHAPTER FOURTEEN

WORKING for Ruby came with its fair share of perks. For one, Chloe was given access to the files of every employee in the company. She wasn't expected to do anything with the information, and her work never required her to access the data, but it came with her clearance. She had stumbled upon the information by accident one day while trying to kill time when Ruby was in a private meeting with a food vendor from the city looking to become one of the restaurants in the food court. Chloe was curious about the company Ruby was meeting with, Sunshine Foods, and searched her computer for information about it.

The operating system returned multiple results, from both the internet and local files. Chloe read about the company online first and found out it specialized in vegetarian smoothies and snacks. If it were to establish a location on the island, it would be the lone restaurant of its kind. There were two mentions in local files. The first was a calendar event, Ruby's meeting. The second was inside an employee's file, inside software Chloe had never used before. The file said that the man, Lane Onza, who was still under contract with WestCorp, was also employed at Sunshine Foods. Chloe couldn't imagine why WestCorp would want a presence in such a specific company not even in the technology sector.

Without a second thought, Chloe then used the software to search for an edited person of great interest to her, Ben Fisher. It turned out there wasn't much more to his tale than what Alfie had mentioned. He'd spent his entire career as an administration specialist, and after his utility had worn out, he spent his time playing online chess and poker. His file also included his income as well as his net worth. If she could ever access the funds Fisher possessed, Chloe could pay off her debt and afford to leave the city behind.

Ruby escorted her guest out while Chloe took a shot in the dark and tried to find the mind trapped inside her. She had no luck.

"Do you have a second?" Chloe said before Ruby walked back into her office.

"Sure," Ruby said with an artificial smile. "What's going on?"

Chloe wondered if she should lie about how she'd stumbled upon the employee's file but decided against it. "I did a quick search for Sunshine Foods and found out one of our employees also works there."

Ruby nodded. Then waited in silence. "That's a fact. Did you have a question, or did you stop me just to tell me something I already knew?"

"I assumed you knew," Chloe blurted out, not wanting Ruby to think her time was being wasted. "Why is he there? Were you using him to set up this opportunity?"

Ruby laughed and shook her head. Her hair stayed in place. "No, not at all. A lot of companies find our edited employees more useful than the unedited." Ruby said unedited with such disdain that Chloe felt her blood boil. "They can't afford a whole company staffed with edited, but one or two is rather common. If you were to look into the employees of most large companies in the city, you'd find they have at least one."

"I see," Chloe said. "I never realized our reach extended so far."

"You have no idea," Ruby said before walking back into her office.

Chloe wondered how deeply the edited had infiltrated into the city's society. Could they also be a part of the government? She wouldn't be surprised.

A short while later, Ruby popped her head out of her office. "Can you go grab lunch?"

Chloe felt her stomach drop and hoped she would be sent to a kitchen to grab a meal made just for Ruby.

"I've got a taste for a burger today. Go to the Cheeseburger Chalet and tell them I sent you, they know my order. Don't bother standing in line, and get whatever you want as well."

Ruby was back in her office before Chloe could agree or come up with an alternative that wouldn't put her into contact with the island's inhabitants. Chloe slid her chair back from under the desk, stood up, and began her march to the atrium, dread at the possibility of seeing Piper making each step laborious. Her small hope was that her time in public would be short, since she didn't have to stand in line; she could be in and out before they came into contact with each other.

Chloe scanned the sea of faces as soon as she walked into the island's atrium. There were dozens if not hundreds of people, filling every table, and more standing in line at every restaurant. No sign of Piper. She went to Ruby's restaurant of choice and walked right by the line of people waiting for their chance to order. If any of them had a problem with her jumping ahead of them, they didn't say anything. She assumed they knew she was there on orders from Ruby. She told the cashier that she wanted Ruby Hollis's typical order, and the young man turned around and told the cooks he needed "one of Ruby's."

"Anything else?" he said.

Chloe told him she wanted the same thing but with chicken instead of beef.

The cashier turned around and yelled, "And another but with chicken." He then instructed Chloe to stand off to the side with a small group waiting for their meal.

Every other order was typed into the computer at the front. The cooks in the back would reference the computer in order to determine what needed to be made. Chloe marveled at the efficiency of the employees, at their lack of wasted movements. They churned out orders, and the people who had been waiting for their food before Chloe dwindled until she was next.

The cashier waved her up and handed her a bag. "Tell Ruby to have a great day," the cashier said.

Chloe wondered if he was edited or if he'd commuted from the city. "Will do. Do I owe you anything?"

"No, you are good to go."

There was a moment's pause when Chloe debated whether she wanted to ask about why Ruby got this sort of treatment, but instead of opening her mouth, she turned around to leave. She then came face-to-face with Piper, and her mouth opened on its own.

"Chloe, right?" Piper said, pretending they hadn't met.

Chloe closed her lips and tilted her head to the side. She didn't want to believe the woman she was tasked with killing had just walked up to her.

"You're going back to Ruby's office, right? I'll walk with you."

Chloe felt Fisher's awareness perk up and closed her eyes, found her breath, then her pulse, and made sure she was ready if he made another attempt to reach out. She started back without consenting to Piper. She wondered if the cashier had told Piper she was there, if every person working at the restaurants had been told to alert Piper when Chloe showed up. At least Piper knew Chloe worked for Ruby; this would make sure the woman didn't try anything stupid.

Piper didn't say a word until they left the noise of the atrium. She waited until they were in the hallway between buildings to speak. The people passing them would receive mere snippets of their conversation.

"I understand you're close with Shada," Piper began.

Chloe kept her eyes forward. Her mind was torn between three conflicting goals: monitoring Fisher, protecting Shada, and completing Ruby's assignment. She knew she couldn't make any moves in broad daylight, but if she decided to, two of her problems would be solved.

"I know I spoke with the two of you, but I imagined your relationship with each other was due to convenience. But after you told me such intimate knowledge of Shada's . . . capture, I realized you have her confidence."

Piper waited for Chloe to speak and continued when she didn't.

"I don't know, nor do I care, why you told me. But I have a favor to ask."

"Why would I do you any favors?" Chloe said, the words dripping like poison off her tongue.

"Why not? I never did anything to you."

Chloe had a sudden realization. From Piper's point of view, the two of them had had minimal contact, and the information Chloe had divulged could be seen as a sort of olive branch. It didn't seem far-fetched that Piper believed them to be comrades.

"What do you want?" Chloe said, exasperated.

"I need you to help me locate Shada." Piper paused, then said, "She's in trouble, and I'm the only one who can help her."

Chloe didn't care about Piper's reasoning, but curiosity got the best of her. "How is she in trouble?"

"Ruby wants her dead. If she can kill her, and make sure Hollis is gone for good, she can take over the company."

Everything inside Chloe wanted to scream how Piper was the one who wanted Shada dead, that she had to protect Shada from her, but she kept her eyes forward and took one step at a time. Fisher knew he didn't have an opening.

An idea took hold, and Chloe stopped walking. Piper took two more steps before she stopped as well.

"What is it?" Piper asked.

"Would you like me to take you to her?"

Piper nodded, her expression grave.

"Tomorrow's Saturday. I had planned on relaxing on the island after a hard week of work, but I can take you to her instead."

"What time?" Piper asked.

"Meet me at the platform at nine in the morning."

CHAPTER FIFTEEN

CHLOE WAITED until Ruby was finished with her meal to tell her boss she'd talked with Piper.

"You talked with her?" Ruby said, amazed. She was seated behind her desk while Chloe gathered the trash from lunch.

"I turned around with our lunch and there she was." The burger's wrapper had some meat juice on it, and Chloe folded the paper and put it into the bag without a drop getting on the desk.

"You're supposed to take care of her, not talk to her. What did she say?"

"She wanted to know about Shada." After a moment, Chloe said, "For some reason."

Ruby stayed silent, a thoughtful look on her face.

"I'm not sure if you need me for anything on Saturdays, but I won't be on the island tomorrow."

"That's fine, I'll have no need of you," Ruby said. She was still lost in her thoughts.

"If Piper disappears from the island, will you make sure there's no investigation?"

Ruby's attention snapped back to the conversation. "You

plan on killing Piper in the city?" she said.

Chloe nodded.

"Good, we can pin it on the unedited scum."

Chloe felt her face flush red and kept her eyes down as she reached across the desk to gather an empty Styrofoam container. "That's what I was thinking," Chloe forced herself to say.

Ruby waved Chloe away. "I don't want to know any more details. Make sure it gets done."

Friday afternoon dragged by. Chloe was assigned few tasks, and the ones she did receive were done right away, each taking a few minutes of the slow-moving hours. Ruby decided to stay in the office later than usual and didn't leave until after six, which meant Chloe also didn't get to leave until after six. Ruby told Chloe on her way out that if she wanted food that evening, she could tell the workers it was for her.

"Don't do this unless I give you permission. Tonight I won't be eating dinner, so you can take the free meal in my place."

Chloe thanked Ruby and watched her boss walk out with the air of someone in a rush to take care of an urgent matter. She organized her desk and turned off the computer before she left. She decided against taking the free meal because she didn't want to deal with the crowd. Her personal transport vehicle took her back to her room.

In preparation for the next day, Chloe spent Friday night staring at her reflection in the mirror, trying to find and control Fisher. Her evening dose of serum coursed through her veins, allowing her to be aware of her heartbeat and follow it to the furthest corners of her body. She searched for Fisher for hours, wondering what it would take to find him and gain access to his memories. By the time she left the bathroom, the sun had left the sky, leaving darkness behind in her room's window. She glimpsed her reflection in the window and imagined Fisher's entire experience was something similar, looking into the darkness and seeing his reflection. If he hadn't figured out how to see or hear the world through Chloe's eyes and ears, how could he ever show up? Chloe lay down and fell asleep wondering how she could allow Fisher to see the world.

The next morning, Chloe got to the platform below the atrium fifteen minutes before nine. She took a seat on a cement bench to wait. A tram, filled with people in fewer cars than during the week, pulled to a stop, and Chloe watched the passengers disembark. She wondered how the number of cars in the tram was decided and if there was ever a situation when there wasn't enough room to fit everyone wishing to make the trip. The tram pulled away, into the belly of the island, and a digital display flashed that it would return fifteen minutes past nine.

Piper showed up right at nine, and Chloe wondered if the woman had been waiting in the atrium above for the exact time of their meeting.

"Good morning," Piper said. The woman flashed a duplicitous smile.

Chloe squeezed her lips together before uttering, "Morning."

Piper sat down to wait next to Chloe.

"Does Shada know we're coming?" Piper said after a few minutes of silence went by.

"She does," Chloe lied. "She said she's grateful you're willing to risk your neck to tell her about Ruby."

Piper smiled, giving the impression she wanted to help. It was as if she'd forgotten her own threat against Shada and expected Chloe to do the same. Chloe made a mental note to look into the effect of edits on short-term memory.

The tram emerged from the direction of the center of the island. It had one less car than before. Nobody else but Chloe and Piper were headed into the city, so Chloe assumed the number of cars was dependent on how many people were expected to take the return trip. Were the passengers now waiting on the platform below the city, or was the number of cars a guess based on historic trends?

Chloe took a seat right inside the door. When Piper went to sit right next to her, a cold look from Chloe made her reconsider, and she sat in the seat across. They were silent during the trip.

Once the tram made it into the city, Piper followed Chloe's lead without a word. They went up to the main transportation hub and waited on the aged platform for the run-down train. Chloe took the train she had taken numerous times before, to the station at the end of the line, the one that she used to get to her now-abandoned apartment. They got onto the crowded train and were able to get two seats next to each other. At each stop Piper turned her head to Chloe, her body language questioning if it was their stop, and each time Chloe stayed still. Passengers got off each time, leaving fewer and fewer people on the train.

An announcement rang out over the train's speaker. "The next stop is the end of the line."

Piper turned her head to Chloe, and Chloe told her the next stop was their destination.

The empty train pulled away, leaving the travelers on the platform. Piper stared at the graffiti on the walls, the dilapidated billboard, and the trash on the ground. Chloe felt home.

Chloe told Piper to stay where she was. "I'll call Shada and make sure she's still there." She walked a few steps away and pretended to make the call. She saw Piper notice the broken clock and tilt her head sideways, since it claimed the time was after three. She withdrew her own phone to check the time and laughed to herself.

Chloe reapproached Piper and told her Shada had moved

locations. "We'll have to get back on the train," Chloe said.

If Piper was annoyed, she didn't show it.

A gust of wind blew through the station, causing the lighter pieces of trash to tumble past them and onto the tracks. A screech could be heard in the distance, getting louder with each passing moment, signaling the approach of the train. Chloe took the smallest step back as she turned to investigate the sound she knew so well.

The headlights of the train appeared, and Chloe felt her heart flutter for a moment before it settled into impassivity. She assured herself she was making a donation, that the world would be better for her actions.

The front of the train passed the first edges of the platform. Chloe took another small step back and noticed Piper was staring at the approaching train as well. Chloe made it a point to stare at the billboard across from them and furrow her brow, pretending to be confused. Piper followed her gaze and stared at the mayor's smiling face.

When the train was mere feet from where they stood, Chloe pushed Piper as hard as she could. She had intended for the train to run over Piper, but the timing caused the woman's body to be in midair when the train hit her. It wasn't moving fast enough to kill her right away, or so Chloe thought, but it couldn't slow down fast enough to avoid running over Piper when she fell onto the tracks.

A sickening crunch of bones rang out as the train screeched to a halt, and Chloe looked down and saw pieces of Piper in the small space between the platform and the train. She turned and ran before anyone could stop her. She stopped in front of the tent community below the station.

"There's meat on the tracks if anyone wants it," she said.

Hungry eyes of all ages peered at her. As she ran away from the station, numerous people ran towards free food.

CHAPTER SIXTEEN

CHLOE RAN for as long as her lungs allowed. She had covered most of the distance to the next station before she had to stop in the middle of a block of restaurants. It was still early in the day, so the restaurants were all closed; they would be opening up for lunch. Once Chloe's pace slowed, the looseness in her legs caused her to almost trip twice—both times catching herself before she fell—because her feet weren't lifted high enough to clear small bumps in the sidewalk. As she tried to catch her breath, she felt another consciousness viewing the world around her. It was an out-of-body experience, witnessing of a witness.

"That was messy," Chloe heard Fisher say.

A surge of panic coursed through Chloe. She stood stock-still and tried to regain control of her breath. The few people who were walking in the same direction went around her and shook their heads at her sudden stop.

"Don't worry, I'm not going to take over. Right now I'm just enjoying seeing the world again."

"How long have you been watching?" Chloe asked. She didn't say the words out loud, instead thinking the words of their conversation.

"I saw you push her. I sensed I could take over if I wanted, but I was stuck in darkness so long the light blinded me."

Chloe focused on her heartbeat. It wasn't hard to locate, since it was racing, but finding the beat and allowing it to resonate were two different things.

"It's nice to see the world again," Fisher said. Chloe looked around, inspired by Fisher to take in her surroundings. Trash from the night before was piled on the side of the street, filled with holes from where rats had tried to harvest leftover food. The restaurants were between one to three stories high, but much taller apartment complexes rose up behind them. The restaurant Chloe stood in front of, a hole in the wall serving pizza and wings, had numerous stickers stuck to the inside of its front window. Where there was a bare bit of glass, there was a layer of grease that prevented outsiders from seeing more than a blur of what was inside.

"How long has it been?" Fisher asked, regarding his time in the darkness.

"A while," Chloe answered, not trusting him. She started walking again.

When Fisher fell silent, Chloe assumed he was enjoying the sights of the city. They passed the remaining blocks before the next train station in silence, though Chloe kept a vigilant awareness of the mind inside her. A sign for the station pointed straight ahead, and Chloe found the municipal concrete building in the distance. She asked Fisher a question that had plagued her for days. "Why did you tell Piper?"

"I saw an opening to take back control, and I took it. I almost told her I was uploaded into you but knew that would be too much to explain. You have no idea how invested Piper is in Hollis."

"I know she was set to take over when he died."

"Then you know she wouldn't be able to let that information go without following up."

"Then you disappeared. Why?"

"I was waiting for the upload to be reversed. In the darkness, I started thinking through my situation and came to the conclusion I'm in here for the long haul. That's why Alfie had me take so long off work. Do you know if my body still exists?"

"No idea, Alfie never mentioned it."

"And that serum you have just leaves me jumbled. Whenever you looked for me, I just went further from the light. Then, when I felt your heart skip today, I saw a window of light in the darkness. I'd thought I lost my ability to come back, you know."

Chloe said, out loud, "Have you been in the city before?" Chloe searched Fisher's memory and knew the answer before he said it.

A mother and young son walking by saw her talk to the empty air around her. The mother wrapped a protective arm around her child and they rushed by.

"Never. I spent my whole life on the island. I find it fascinating."

Chloe probed Fisher's mind once more and witnessed a memory of him in school, staring up at a teacher inside a room full of attentive children. There must have been close to a hundred, and they looked to be of different ages, all sitting straight up with perfect posture, attentive and ready to learn.

She was still walking and almost stepped off the sidewalk into traffic. A loud honk pulled her from the memory.

"It's not polite to stare," Fisher said. He said the words as if he was disappointed in her.

"Alfie was bugging me about searching through your memories. I won't do it if it bothers you." Chloe couldn't believe she was considerate of the edited mind's feelings. But then again, he'd be in there for the rest of her life, and she might as well make peace.

"Don't dig into the personal stuff. I've got no problem with you looking up facts for reference."

"How can you tell?"

"Because I get thrown into the memory too. These aren't things I think about most of the time, so it's jarring, to say the least."

"That's fair," Chloe said. She couldn't think about the last time she'd immersed herself in a memory. If someone else made her do it, she wouldn't like it at all.

Chloe crossed the street during a break in traffic, turned left, then crossed once more and approached the entrance to the station. Without questioning Fisher, or seeing his past in her mind's eye, she knew he was curious about the city's train system and had never been this close to cars. Through her new lens, it was like she was seeing the city for the first time. Dilapidated buildings between those in use, chain-link fences with trash captured in their many corners. Each aspect of her surroundings, which she had taken for granted all her life, now became a question of whether or not Fisher had seen something similar in his past on the island. He hadn't.

Chloe couldn't shake the constant input of "No" to her standing question of "Have you seen this?" as she waited for the train, boarded, and took her seat.

Each person's face was searched, and some of them reminded Fisher of a person he knew, or had known, on the island. Fisher never said so outright, but there was a sense of the fact from a feeling deep inside. It was like Chloe knew without being told. Overwhelmed, she closed her eyes and found her breath, then her heartbeat, just to be sure she was still in control.

"Better?" Fisher said. He didn't have a chance at taking over any part of Chloe's body.

"Much," Chloe said out loud. All but one of the passengers ignored her. The one who looked at her was a young man who Chloe would have taken interest in if she wasn't stuck inside her mind. From his attention, it seemed he had deemed her worthy of his interest as well.

Chloe transferred trains at the hub instead of going back to the island. She had to wait on the platform for a long time for the next train on one of the city's slower lines. When it arrived, she climbed aboard and, after a few underground stops, emerged into the sunlight. The landscape changed into a perpetual suburban sprawl, each house looking like the next. The train passed vast lots filled with cars in various stages of decay, causing Fisher to comment on all the wasted assets. As much as Chloe wanted to leave the city, she preferred to stay in its urban area over becoming one of the masses in an overpriced home, dealing with small yards and terrible commutes. Either she was leaving it all behind or staying in the thick of things, no half-assed exit for her.

The last stop of the train was a full twenty minutes' ride past the previous stop. Chloe knew Shada's hideout was somewhere close but didn't remember where. She called her friend.

"Hello?"

"Sikya? It's me, Chloe. I need a ride to your place."

"I'll see if Tony can come get you, he's in the city now. Where are you?"

"At the station."

"Which station?"

"Sinbad Landings."

"That close! You're practically here. I'll come get you myself, there's a SUV here we can use in case of emergencies."

"This isn't an emergency," Chloe said.

"It'll take two seconds," Sikya replied before she hung up the phone.

"Sinbad Landings," Fisher said, as if committing the name to memory. "It's like all these people sailed away from the city in order to live on their own isolated island, together."

CHAPTER SEVENTEEN

"You should stay here," Sikya said when they were back in the safe house. "You don't need to keep playing with fire on that island."

"I can't stay," Chloe replied. "I just came to tell you, in person, that Piper is no longer a threat."

"What did you do?" Sikya asked.

"She killed her," Shada said from the kitchen table. Her eyes stayed closed while she took slow, measured breaths. It was clear she was listening to the sensations of her body, keeping Hollis from taking back control.

Chloe could sense Fisher's awe at seeing Shada for the first time. He wanted to communicate with Hollis but never tried to gain control of Chloe. It was a desire without an outlet. Chloe became aware of Sikya's stare boring into the side of her head, as if Sikya was in the presence of a monster.

"What?" Chloe snapped.

Sikya frowned. "Did you really kill her?"

"What choice did I have? She wanted to kill Shada."

"I know, but still . . ." Sikya looked at Chloe's hands.

"I didn't choke her," Chloe said. "I pushed her in front of a train."

Sikya's mouth opened. Chloe looked at Shada and saw the hints of a slow nod.

"It's done, no point in getting hung up on it," Shada said.

"Does that mean we can leave?" Sikya asked. She turned, opened a cabinet, and pulled out glass. "Want some water?" she asked.

Chloe nodded, and Sikya grabbed a second glass before filling them up with water.

"No, we still don't know what Ruby's planning," Chloe said.

Sikya placed a glass in front of Chloe before downing half her glass in two large gulps.

"You should have never uploaded that mind into you," Sikya said when she pulled the glass away from her lips.

"Don't bring this up again," Shada said from across the room. She opened her eyes, stood up, and joined the women in standing, her lower back against the counter and arms crossed. "You better get used to it. There will be more."

Sikya looked at her sister in disbelief. "More! The two of you have caused enough trouble. Why would you want more?"

"I don't want more. She does," Shada said, using her chin to gesture towards Chloe. "She and Alfie."

It was Chloe's turn to be surprised, but she wiped the look away with a hardened determination. "It wouldn't hurt to have a few less edited in the world. If we can make an unedited smarter and better off financially, even better."

Fisher, hearing Chloe mention finances, knew Chloe would search his mind for the necessary codes and passwords to transfer all of his assets to her. He resigned himself to the fact and in that moment realized he'd been given a second life. Not one he controlled, but the chance to share in the future of another. As someone whose entire career had been spent in an administrative role, he felt at ease acting as support.

Sikya paced back and forth in the kitchen. Chloe and Shada let her go, waiting for the thoughts swirling in her head to coalesce. "They didn't choose to be the way they are," Sikya said, her voice soft.

"But it doesn't change the fact they're the ones holding all the power in the city."

"WestCorp holds the power. Holds power over them too. They're just not able to be upset by the imbalance."

"So we're putting them out of their misery!" Chloe said.

Sikya glared at her.

"Most of the people on the island were born that way, right?" Sikya said.

"I suppose, I don't know the numbers," Chloe replied.

"Let's assume," Sikya said. She glanced at Shada, and her sister raised her eyebrows in expectation.

"So their parents chose for them to be edited."

"They were probably edited too," Chloe said. She scanned Fisher's memory and found out he had been born edited to edited parents.

"And keep going down the line to the first edited humans. They didn't know what they were doing. They were using technology to try and improve the world, not ruin it."

"So we should feel bad for the edited?"

"No, I'm not saying we should feel bad, but rather understand that it isn't their fault. This goes back generations."

"Wait," Chloe said. "Aren't you super involved with the advancement of the unedited people of the city? Why are you arguing for the edited all of a sudden?"

"I want the unedited to be equal to the edited humans. That means elevating our status, not tearing them down from the inside, one quasi-murder at a time."

"He was dying anyways," Shada whispered.

Both Sikya and Chloe waited in silence for her to continue. They didn't have to wait long.

"He's the one who wanted to take over my body. He never imagined I'd be able to take it back. Hollis only has himself to blame." The volume of her voice never raised more than necessary for the other two women to hear, and her tone stayed consistent throughout her statement, as if she was relaying facts.

"I wasn't calling you a murderer," Sikya said to apologize.

"If anything, he wanted to quasi-murder her!" Chloe said. "They brought this on themselves."

"And what did your guy do? Did he convince you to upload as well? Did he even know what he was getting into?"

Chloe turned around, closed her eyes, and found her body's breathing to keep from losing her temper. When she turned around, she found Sikya's eyes. "He thought he was going on an extended upload. He just didn't know how extended it would be," she said with a small laugh.

Sikya cracked a thin smile, and the tension in the room evaporated. "All I'm saying is we shouldn't punish the child for the parent's decision."

Chloe brushed off Sikya's parting shot. "Too late, their time has run out."

Shada chuckled and changed the subject. "Did you hear about what's going on with the mayor?"

"No, I've been on the island the whole time. It's like living in a bubble," Chloe said.

"I know, that's why I'm asking if you've heard," Shada said.

Sikya shook her head. "Smart-ass."

Shada told Sikya to tell her.

"The mayor's resigned. There's going to be another election, and it looks like Tensen has a good chance of winning. He was a close second last time," Sikya said with pride.

"Resigned? What happened?"

Sikya told Chloe about the scandal that had rocked the mayor's office. It all came down to an assassination. A lawmaker had been on his way to propose a law to decriminalize drug use, turning it into a mental illness. "The politician was murdered by drug dealers."

Chloe took a second to digest the information. "Why would the drug dealers want him dead? If addiction isn't a crime, their business would skyrocket."

"Part of the plan was to provide state-sponsored rehab clinics. As more people got healthy, fewer would be looking to score."

"And how was this all linked back to the mayor?"

"It came out the drug dealers were sponsored by WestCorp. Apparently, WestCorp had a deal with the mayor to use incarcerated unedited to test their post-birth edits. With fewer people being locked up due to drugs, they would have fewer test subjects and the value of their government contract would go down."

"A lot of people didn't want this law to get passed," Chloe mused.

"When it all came out, the mayor didn't even put up a fight, he just resigned. I'm surprised nobody talked about it on the island."

"I told you, that place is a bubble. To be honest, I'm not sure they care who's in charge, they'll just bribe the next guy."

"Tensen's different. He's one of us."

"That's assuming he wins the election," Chloe said, skeptical.

"The mayor's entire party has been caught up in the scandal. There's money passing hands everywhere, kickbacks and contracts that shouldn't exist. Nobody else stands a chance."

"It's really just a formality," Shada added.

When Sikya was sure of a thing, Chloe found herself doubting. But when Shada knew a thing to be true, Chloe never gave the fact a second thought and accepted it as a fact.

"Didn't you donate to Tensen?" Chloe asked Shada.

Shada nodded. "He made sure I sent the money as soon as the mayor resigned."

"What's going to happen when someone finds out Hollis's money is sponsoring the next mayor?" Chloe asked.

The blood drained from Sikya's face.

Shada smiled. "You've caught on. Nothing happens in this city without WestCorp."

CHAPTER EIGHTEEN

RICHARD AND TONY showed up Saturday evening. They brought food with them: Chinese takeout, ice cream for dessert, and groceries for the next few days. They were both surprised to see Chloe there.

"We would have brought you," Tony said.

"It's OK, it was a last-minute thing." She didn't mention the business with Piper, and neither did the sisters. She tried to leave before the four of them ate dinner, but they convinced her there was enough food for all of them and she should stay for the meal.

"Just leave with us after dinner," Richard told her. "We'll give you a ride back."

Chloe agreed, and Sikya pulled out five plates. Tony opened containers of fried rice, lo mein, beef and broccoli, and cashew chicken and left them on the counter. Everyone took turns making a plate. Chloe, Shada, and Sikya sat at the kitchen table while Tony and Richard stood to eat.

During their meal, Chloe found out what the sisters had been up to to pass the time. Sikya had spent her days working on Tensen's campaign, cold-calling potential donors and following up with her contacts from the previous campaign. In the evenings she watched made-for-TV movies with Shada, low-budget romantic comedies. When Chloe asked Shada what she did while Sikya worked, Shada informed the group she was learning all she could about the history of WestCorp by combing through Hollis's memories.

"They've been busy through the years," Shada said. When asked by Richard to elaborate, she said there was nothing he needed to worry about at the moment.

"Well what about a future moment? Anything I need to know about then?"

Shada looked at him and in seriousness told him, "When you need to know, I'll tell you."

Richard's laugh didn't do much to cover his frustration.

Everyone helped clean up when the meal was over. The two men lingered for a while after, long enough for Chloe to get anxious about her trip back to the island for her nighttime dose of serum. Without probing Fisher's mind, she heard the mind inside her say he wouldn't try to take over her body.

"Look, the way I see it is we're stuck in here together. No reason to piss you off," Fisher gave as his reason.

Chloe still didn't trust him.

Richard's phone buzzed on the counter. After he picked it up and read the message, he looked at Tony and used his head to signal it was time for them to leave.

"We'll be back on Monday or Tuesday. Let us know if you need anything before then," Tony told the sisters.

Chloe hugged the sisters goodbye and left with the two men. She sat in the back seat, Richard in the front, and Tony drove into the city. Once the three of them were alone, Chloe told Richard that Alfie had agreed to perform the procedure on him.

"I was going to ask you about that," Richard said.

"I'll have to go over Shada's process to take back control," Chloe said. "It isn't the easiest thing to do."

"You can fill me in on the way to the island."

The way Richard said this planted the seed in Chloe's mind that they would be heading to the island together, but not at the current moment. When she looked out the window, she saw they weren't heading to the city's center. Instead, Tony was taking them to the eastern side of town, close to the water.

"Where are we going?" Chloe asked.

"You'll see," Richard said.

Chloe expected him to turn around and flash a smile, to let her know it was a pleasant surprise, but when he didn't, Chloe's mind turned towards darker possibilities. Could they be working for WestCorp as well? She kicked herself for not searching for their names in the employee files. Like Ruby had said, there were WestCorp employees all over the city. Could these be some of them?

Half an hour later, Tony pulled into a row of warehouses and parked outside the one farthest from the street. The massive parking lot was empty except for the spaces near their car, where there were a dozen or so other vehicles parked. Tony and Richard got out and told Chloe to come with them.

Chloe followed, grateful for the presence of other people. Her belief in their status as WestCorp employees had solidified in her mind, and when they arrived at the warehouse, she thought she would be interrogated. She couldn't figure out why they would go to such lengths, since she'd answered their every question right away, without lying, but her distrust of people forced her to prepare for the worst.

The door to the warehouse was up a set of metal steps to the left of a loading dock. She expected to see a massive space with high ceilings and concrete floors when she got inside. Instead, she found herself in a single room with a standard-height ceiling, the floors still concrete. She guessed a door opposite the door they'd entered led out to the warehouse. Chairs lined the walls of the room, and most of them were occupied by serious-looking individuals, all dressed in black and seeming to be in excellent physical shape.

Richard turned to Chloe. "These are all of my coworkers who are willing to receive uploads. We all work for Tensen," he said.

Each member of the group nodded. Chloe did a quick count and determined there were thirteen in total, including Tony and Richard.

"Alfie only agreed to upload a mind into you," Chloe said.

"And once that works, we can convince him to upload into everyone else. These are all highly trained, educated unedited. Imagine what we could do with the knowledge and resources an edited mind could provide."

"There would be a shift in power," Chloe said. It was a personal thought she shared out loud.

"We are the resistance," said a pretty brunette woman, her hair pulled back in a ponytail.

The group had the same agenda Chloe had advocated to Shada. Unedited humans capturing edited minds in order to both weaken WestCorp's position and increase the uniteds' power. Seeing it made real reminded her of Shada's desire to step away from the struggle and Sikya's insistence that uploads weren't the appropriate course of action. By being in the presence of a more radical group, Chloe was forced to adopt the stance of a moderate; in contrast, when she was in the presence of the more passive sisters, Chloe was transformed into the voice for action.

"We don't even know if uploading into you will work. Let's see how that goes," she said to Richard. She didn't like being the voice of reason.

"Why wouldn't it work?" Tony said. "You and Shada did it."

"We had already been uploaded into before. Both of us were able to see the world through our eyes while under control from another mind, Shada on the first upload and me on the fifth."

"We will learn to do it too."

"You're trying to run before you can crawl," Chloe said. She didn't mean to sound condescending, but being forced into action in front of the resistance made her lash out.

Richard's eyes read Chloe, and he took steps to defuse the situation. "She's right, let's see how my upload goes before we make plans for everyone else."

"What if you aren't the best possible candidate? It could fail for you but work for all of us," a large man with neck tattoos said.

It was Richard's turn to push back. "That's a risk we have to take. The scientist agreed to upload into me first."

The large man leaned to his side and grumbled to his neighbor.

"If you have something to say, say it to the group," Richard said, ice in his voice.

From the way the rest of the group watched the exchange, Chloe could tell the tension between these two had been seen before.

The man sat up straight in his chair. "I said they don't know what you look like. We could send any guy here and say he's Richard. Hell, any woman could be a Richard too, he doesn't know."

Tony jumped in. "Look, Richard's the one who got us this opportunity. Let's stick to the plan, and when his upload works, we can start the process of uploading into everyone else."

Chloe marveled at how her help in their plan was taken as a given.

Tony and Richard looked down at the seated man, and after a few tense moments he raised his hands in a display of surrender.

"Now let's move on to the reason for the meeting tonight," Richard said. "Does Tensen have any idea we're the ones who took care of the legislation?"

Fisher laughed, and Chloe knew she was right to assume the worst. These people were killers.

CHAPTER NINETEEN

RICHARD CALLED an end to the meeting just before ten at night. The group filed out, leaving Tony, Richard, and Chloe behind. Richard and Chloe were first out the door, walking down the steps while Tony lingered behind to turn off the lights and lock the door behind them. Chloe wondered how many of the group's members had keys to the space.

"Want to stay in the city tonight and head back tomorrow?" Richard asked.

Chloe couldn't say no fast enough. "I need to get back to the island," she added, thinking of the vial of serum in her room.

Tony's eyes searched for Richard's response, and the leader nodded. They all climbed into the car and began the trip to the center of the city.

While the three passengers rode in silence, Chloe's personal passenger tried to convince her he wasn't worth worrying about. "I'm not going to try to take over," Fisher said in the space they alone had access to.

Chloe wasn't in the mood to argue. "I still don't trust you," she said to the voice in her head.

"When you take the serum, it feels like I'm turned upside

down," Fisher said, taking a different approach, trying to garner Chloe's sympathy. "I don't want to lose my view."

"Then you'd better remember how you found your sight in the first place. I'm not going to risk sleeping with you inside my head, able to take over while I'm unconscious."

"I could take over now," Fisher countered.

Chloe tensed up, searching every part of her body for signs of Fisher's control. After a few moments she realized it had been quite a while since she'd blinked. She focused and forced her eyelids to touch. "That wasn't funny," she said to Fisher.

"Relax, I am well aware you can negate any attempts I make."

Chloe didn't reply and let her awareness of Fisher fade.

"We need to make a quick stop," Richard informed Chloe.

"Quicker than the last stop, I hope," Chloe muttered. She had wanted to say, "It'd better be," but knew the threat would be meaningless. As long as she was in the car with them, she was at the mercy of their haphazard scheduling.

"It will be, I just need to grab my overnight bag. It's already packed," Richard said.

The extra stop made sense to Chloe, but it didn't mean she had to like it. It was one more thing delaying her nighttime injection, and without the serum, she had to stay more alert to her body in case Fisher tried to take another stab at control. She took a second to feel the breath entering her body and closed her eyes during her extended exhale.

Richard mistook her long breath as a sigh. "I promise it'll be quick. The meeting went longer than anticipated, sorry for that."

Chloe opened her eyes but didn't say a word.

Tony parked the car in front of a high-rise apartment building and turned on his hazard lights. Richard jumped out of the passenger seat and ran inside. He returned less than five minutes later with a black duffle bag slung over his shoulder.

"Told you it would be quick," he said, out of breath.

"Any longer and I would've walked," Chloe joked.

A few minutes later, Tony stopped outside the station.

Before Richard got out of the car, he grabbed Tony's forearm, and his colleague returned the gesture. The two of them locked eyes, their expressions saying what words could not. Chloe tried to climb out of the car in order to give their moment its space, but she wasn't fast enough, and the moment ended while she was still inside. Tony drove away when Richard and Chloe were on the sidewalk outside the station.

They paid to get into the city's train system then descended to the bottom level. The few people they passed on their way down appeared to be homeless, riding the rails and taking advantage of the indoors before spending the night out on the streets. The platform that hosted WestCorp's tram was dark and empty when the two of them arrived, but when they took their first steps onto its surface, lights began to pop on, starting at their location and extending off into the distance until the entire area was illuminated. A display screen came to life, telling the two of them the tram would be arriving in sixteen minutes.

Chloe assumed this was the exact time it took to travel to the island, that the tram had sensed their presence on the platform and deployed itself to pick them up. She sat down on a concrete bench with Richard and tapped the spot next to her, urging him to sit down. He said he preferred to stand.

"Well, we need to get you caught up with how you're going to take back control of your body," Chloe said. She went through the process of getting uploaded into, describing the room and equipment he would soon experience. Then she told him what it would feel like trapped in the darkness of his own mind.

"Like existing in the vacuum of space," she said.

Richard hung on to every word.

The empty tram arrived, and they climbed on. They sat down, and Chloe continued her lesson, telling him how to find his vision for the first time.

"Don't look right at it; it will disappear as soon as you try. Instead, look past it, around it, like trying to see a dim star. Let your peripheral vision see the dim light, and over time it will take over your vision." Part of Chloe hoped Fisher was listening, to help him after she took the serum.

Richard nodded, but Chloe had the sense he wasn't appreciating the nuance involved with this crucial step.

Chloe continued. "I'll be honest, I'm not sure when or how the hearing comes back. It just shows up when you can see the world through your own eyes again."

"Do you think it's possible to hear first?" Richard asked.

Chloe shook her head no. "The closest thing I can relate the experience to is floating to the top of a well. From the bottom, you can see the light, but the narrowness of the space makes it impossible to hear a thing. If you're patient, the light gets brighter, like you're getting closer to the top. Then, when you can see the world, it's like the sound is no longer being blocked by the well's walls."

"So the light from your eyes is the light at the top of the well? I have to float up from my feet?"

"In a way."

"Then the light should be off and to the side, not a single circle up top."

"Then think of it like your mind is a tiny dot in the back of your skull," Chloe said, reaching out and touching the back of Richard's head.

"Wouldn't there be two circles of light then?" Richard asked.

Chloe glared at him.

"What?" he said, taken aback.

"Ignore the metaphors, just remember the instructions. Wait for the light to take over your awareness, and you'll begin to hear the world around you."

The tram came to a stop beneath the island. Chloe, remembering the guards, grew concerned. "Do you have a gun on you?" she said.

"Of course," Richard replied.

"You'll be searched. Be ready to give it up."

Richard hesitated, then nodded. "That's fine. But they'd better give it back when I leave."

They walked off the tram and were stared down by the large humans posted on each side of the staircase leading up to the atrium. One of them held up a hand as they approached. "Stop," he said, his voice booming.

After they both obeyed, Chloe was waved forward. The guards gave no indication they remembered her, but their cursory search led her to believe they knew she wasn't a threat, by memory or instinct, she wasn't sure. Both guards participated in Richard's search. One withdrew a small computer and a knife from his duffel while the other took two pistols off his person, one from his side and one from his leg.

"These stay with us," the guard who searched the duffel said before shoving the lighter bag at Richard's chest.

With a look from Chloe, Richard nodded, and they both began climbing the steps.

CHAPTER TWENTY

CHLOE's personal transport vehicle was still parked where she had left it, outside the atrium. She climbed in first, holding Richard's bag on her lap as Richard climbed in. The vehicle was made for two, but the space was cramped. The trip to Chloe's room took no time at all, and the whole time she was imagining taking the serum. She injected herself as soon as she got into her room.

Richard, watching Chloe's face relax after the serum, asked what was in the vial. "Something Alfie made to help me make sure the mind inside doesn't take back control."

"It helps you see the light?"

"Not exactly," Chloe said. She sat down on her bed, and Richard leaned against the bathroom doorframe. She went on to explain the importance of finding the body's breath after seeing the light, how controlling it led to greater control of the entire body.

"And where does the serum come in?"

"It makes it possible to block the edited mind from taking back control." She twirled the empty vial between her fingers. "The serum allows you to sense your heartbeat resonating with the world around you. It's a much more powerful anchor than breathing."

"Why not just find your heartbeat without it?" Richard asked.

"Try it."

Richard stayed still. Chloe could see his breathing become regular and knew his heart rate would lower as a result.

"I just lowered my heart rate," Richard said with a smug grin. "They taught us how in training."

"The trick isn't lowering the heart rate. It's allowing it to resonate throughout your body so you can find every limb and maintain control. The serum allows us to do that while at the same time scrambling the edited mind inside."

Richard nodded. Chloe wondered if he was doing it to make her happy.

Chloe felt how tired she was after the conclusion of Richard's lesson. She informed him she was going to sleep. She appreciated that Richard assumed he was sleeping on the floor and as a reward gave him her comforter, despite his objections.

"I'm leaving it on the floor. Use it or not, it's up to you," she said.

In the darkness, with the serum coursing through her veins, she could sense the pulse of the world around her, including Richard's heartbeat. As she fell asleep, she felt him lower his heart rate on purpose before he was asleep, and she worried he had missed the point of the day's lesson.

Richard was already awake when Chloe rolled over the next morning and looked at him. He was staring at the ceiling.

"Morning," she said.

"Good morning," he replied without looking at her.

There was enough room next to her bed for Chloe to step off without Richard having to move, but she had to shuffle sideways in order to get to the rest of the room. Once she had more space, down near Richard's feet, she leaned back and stretched her back, cracking it twice in the process.

"Those were good," Richard said. Thin rays of light shone through the curtains, illuminating parts of his torso. His face was kept in shadow. He'd slept clothed and hadn't used the comforter, using his arm as a pillow instead.

A surge of guilt rose through Chloe when she saw the two pillows on her bed. She could have spared one, she just hadn't thought about it. She grabbed a vial of serum from the desk and took it into the bathroom to inject herself without Richard watching. He hadn't moved when she came out.

"So what's the plan?" Richard asked.

Chloe began to get dressed. "Well, Alfie doesn't know you're here, so I need to talk to him, tell him you're on the island."

Richard sat up. "And what am I supposed to do?"

"Whatever you want."

"Let me come with you. It'll be good for me to see the island."

"No, you need to keep a low profile."

"It's Sunday, nobody will give me a second look. I'll just act like an edited zombie."

"They aren't zombies," Chloe shot back. "If anything, they're happier than most. It's like a weird mix of aloofness combined with blind optimism."

"OK, I'll act like that then." Richard stood and opened the curtains. Sunlight poured into the room. He turned around with a wide grin pasted on his face.

Chloe couldn't contain her laughter. His expression went against everything she had come to expect. When she was able to talk again, she agreed to bring him to see Alfie, but they would have to come right back to the room afterwards.

"Deal," Richard said. This time, his thin-lipped smile was

genuine.

They took a moment to put the room back in order before they left. The transport vehicle, when told to bring them to Alfie, went to the lab. On their way, Chloe told Richard about the purpose of the buildings she knew and realized there were a lot more she had no idea about.

Richard seemed intrigued by the concept of a large space with rows of tables where post-birth edits were performed en masse on unedited humans. "They do them all at the same time?"

Chloe thought back to the pod Alfie had shown her in his personal lab, the one made for one human at a time. There was no way all the humans got edited on the tables, she realized.

"I think they are prepped in the large room then taken to a chamber where the edits actually take place," she said. "Piper said all those tables were for post-birth edits, but I guess she didn't feel like elaborating."

The transport stopped outside the lab, and the two of them climbed out. Chloe knew they would be stuck outside the entrance to the lab, since they didn't have the cards the scientists used to get past the locked doors, but she figured Alfie would be out to get them soon after being alerted to their presence.

They waited longer than expected.

While they waited, two scientists Chloe had never seen before swiped themselves into the lab. After the first one—a young woman with short hair—went in, Richard was about to try to catch the door behind her when Chloe put a hand on his arm to stop him. The scientist pulled the door shut. When the second scientist swiped himself in, Chloe asked in her most polite voice if the older man could tell Alfie he had someone waiting for him in the lobby. The scientist ignored her.

"Do people always work on Sundays?" Richard asked.

"I think a lot of their projects require daily attention. They probably take some extra time off during the week."

"Or just work all the time."

"Being artificially happy makes it easier, I'm sure."

No one entered or exited the lab for long enough that Chloe got nervous. Maybe Ruby had gotten wind Richard was there? Or Alfie had changed his mind about uploading the edited mind into Richard? Her stomach was in knots, and she got up to leave. She planned to take Richard back to her room and come back alone.

That was when Alfie came out with Ruby. Chloe stood up right away at the sight of her boss, and Richard followed her lead.

"So this is our second subject," the older woman said, looking at Richard with hungry eyes.

Chloe could feel Richard's eyes boring into the side of her head, searching for a clue about how to handle the current situation. She wanted to look at Alfie, to get a clue for herself, but doing so risked being witnessed by Ruby. She played along with Ruby instead. "This is him," she said.

Alfie placed a hand on Richard's shoulder. "You're brave for volunteering," the scientist said. His eyes were devoid of any emotion, a look Chloe found chilling. There wasn't even a hint of the happiness that was supposed to be edited into his mind.

"Thanks?" Richard said.

Alfie stepped aside and gestured for Richard to walk through the lab's doors. Chloe, still dazed from trying to figure out what was happening, tried to follow him, assuming she was going into the lab as well. Was this all part of Alfie's plan? Or had this been designed by Ruby?

"Chloe, can I have a word?" Ruby said, as if her assistant had any choice in the matter.

Alfie followed Richard into the lab and the door shut behind them, leaving Chloe and Ruby alone.

CHAPTER TWENTY-ONE

"Let's hope he can repeat what happened with Hollis and Shada."

Chloe's mouth dropped, betraying her disbelief at Ruby's open discussion on the topic. So Ruby knew about Shada but didn't know about Chloe, since she referenced Richard as the second subject.

"Oh, you didn't think I knew about that? About Michael's illness? The man doesn't have a body, I'd say that qualifies as an illness."

"That's why you had me kill Piper," Chloe whispered.

"And to prove yourself. Now that she's gone, I know where you stand."

Chloe's head spun trying to keep track of who knew what.

"The city will be looking for you soon, so it's time for you to move here permanently. I'll take you to your apartment in my personal helicopter to gather your belongings."

"I thought you said you'd convince them not to investigate me!" Chloe blurted out.

"I will, just give it a few days to die down. Right now, you need to get anything you want to keep out of your apartment."

Ruby led Chloe to the atrium, then through a series of tunnels that ended in a vast underground chamber. A black helicopter sat on a circular slab of concrete. A white circle was painted around the slab's edges, with a large white H painted in the middle. A crack in the middle of the roof above the chamber allowed a thin line of light to spill in. The two women climbed in, joining the pilot, who was already in the cockpit.

At a thumbs-up from the pilot, the helipad began to elevate. At the same time, light spilled into the chamber as the roof above opened. All motion stopped when the landing pad was level with the ground. The edge of the slab ended right at the start of the lawn around them. Without prior knowledge of the chamber, any onlookers wouldn't know about its existence below.

The pilot flipped a series of switches and the helicopter's rotors began to spin. Ruby handed Chloe a headset, telling her to put it on.

"Can you hear me?" Ruby said after placing her own headset over her ears.

Chloe nodded. She assumed the pilot could hear her too, but he didn't make any gesture to confirm.

The craft took flight, and Chloe felt a wave of butterflies in her stomach. She had never been in a helicopter before, and its rapid maneuvers unsettled her. They took off in the direction of the city.

When they were over the bay, Ruby began talking about her plan for the future direction of the company. "If Richard's upload is successful, we'll be able to give our senior employees a second life," she said. "Alfie said Shada was an anomaly."

Chloe stayed silent. At least Alfie knew for certain that Ruby was aware of Shada's procedure. She wasn't sure she wanted to know Alfie's plan for Richard. She had assumed he would help the unedited man take back control of his body from the edited mind, but the way Ruby talked, she wasn't sure whose side Alfie was on. The picture of Richard with his children flashed through her mind.

"Of course, we'll have to retrieve Shada when the time is right."

Chloe almost screamed that Ruby would never find Shada, but at the last second she remembered she was supposed to be edited. "She's still in the city, I'm sure."

"Does Richard know where she is?"

Ruby's straightforward question caught Chloe off guard. She decided not to lie. "He does."

"Good. Once he's been taken over, he can tell us where she is."

If Richard couldn't regain control, it would be a repeat of the Piper situation. Would she have to kill him too? It would be much harder than killing Piper. She shuddered at the memory of the loud thud of the woman's body against the front of the train.

Chloe wondered if Ruby ever thought about using her to find Shada.

Fisher crept into Chloe's awareness. "You're playing a dangerous game," he said. "Don't underestimate this woman."

Chloe blocked him out, knowing she needed to save her full attention for Ruby.

Ruby sighed. "Look at the city. So many unedited," she said with sadness, as if she was the sole person who cared about their future.

"There are a lot of them," Chloe replied. She kept her words about WestCorp being responsible to herself.

"Not for much longer, if I have anything to do with it."

"What do you mean?" Chloe asked.

"I'm going to offer free adaptations." The wrinkles at the corners of her lips deepened when she clenched her jaw.

Chloe was stunned. This would be an enormous cost to the company. "Free? Why?"

"To get rid of them," she snarled. "Filth like Shada have no place in the world I want to create."

"Will they all work for WestCorp?" Chloe asked.

"God no. I'm not editing them to become one of us. I'm going to edit them to become angry and impulsive. Then, I'll convince them that Shada has become the leader of WestCorp, that the negative edits were her, and Michael's, idea. It won't take long for them to rise up against her."

Chloe took a deep breath and reminded herself she was supposed to be happy. She smiled. "Then why bother trying to find her with Richard?"

"So I can tell the unedited hordes where to find her! I'll make sure they know what she looks like before letting them loose," Ruby said. Her wicked smile came with a dash of pride.

Chloe forced herself to smile back. When she looked out the window, she recognized the area of the city they were over. "We're close," she said.

Ruby looked out the window. "You live here?"

"Lived," Chloe corrected.

The pilot landed the helicopter on top of Chloe's building. Chloe began to climb out, and Ruby made no sign she would be joining.

"Make it quick. Ten minutes, tops," Ruby said.

Chloe exited the helicopter and rushed across the roof. The door to the roof had been broken as long as Chloe could remember; it hung loose on its hinges and never shut. She threw it open and took the stairs two at a time down to her floor. She surveyed her room once inside. It was just how she'd left it except for the plants, which had succumbed to neglect, their leaves brown and withered. She almost took the time to water them but knew it would be a waste of time.

She went to the closet, retrieved several large bags she used for groceries, and began stuffing clothes inside. It seemed pointless since WestCorp provided the island's inhabitants with uniforms, but she didn't plan on staying there forever. She looked at the spot where the framed photo of her grandfather once stood and remembered it was in her bag on the island. It had been too long since she'd seen his face, and she didn't want to forget her ultimate goal, to leave the city behind and live in a house in the country, far away from this mess. The items she wanted most, the vials of poison and antidote created by her mother, she withdrew from her safe and stuffed into the pockets of a pair of jeans. By returning to the island on the helicopter, she wouldn't have to get them past the guards. She left the safe open so anyone searching her room wouldn't have to bother opening it.

There were a few toiletries Chloe wanted from the bathroom, and some books, like 1984 and Catcher in the Rye, that she had kept for so long she couldn't imagine not owning them, so she grabbed these and put them into the bags as well.

Chloe took one last look at the plants in her room, her surrogate family, and regretted breaking her promise to be back before they wilted. She turned away from them before she got emotional. "Edited humans are always happy," she reminded herself.

With the bags in hand, Chloe left her apartment behind.

Ruby beckoned for Chloe to hurry across the roof when she was in sight of the helicopter. Chloe walked as fast as she could without running.

"You have everything?" Ruby asked when Chloe climbed up and sat down, her bags on the floor by her feet.

Chloe told her she did.

Ruby pulled out her phone and sent a message as the helicopter ascended. She saw Chloe looking at her phone and explained. "I just informed the authorities you were a suspect in Piper's murder. They'll be at your place soon."

"They didn't know yet?" Chloe yelled. She was furious.

"Relax, you won't be a suspect for long. I'll make sure whatever evidence they collect gets misplaced. I just needed you on the island permanently."

Chloe took several deep breaths. Fisher reminded her Ruby was a snake. "She'll bite you the first chance she gets."

"For now, you can't go back into the city. But there's plenty to do on the island," Ruby said.

"They can't come get me there?"

Ruby laughed. "On my island? No way! It's part of our deal."

Chloe couldn't believe the situation WestCorp had created for themselves. At first, she marveled at Ruby, but she knew Michael was the real architect. She was both impressed and scared of the power the company wielded.

They were over the bay when Ruby told Chloe about her new role. "Every morning, I need you to meet with the new unedited recruits. Make sure they feel welcome, answer any questions they have, and get them into staging before their edits."

Chloe grew nauseous at the thought. "Similar to the role Piper filled when I first arrived . . ." she reminisced.

"Whose fault is it she won't be there to perform her duties?" Ruby said, one eyebrow raised.

Chloe squeezed her lips together for a moment, resigning herself to her fate. "Have the free edits already begun?" she asked.

"They are set to begin tomorrow. Your first day of work!"

CHAPTER TWENTY-TWO

CHLOE WAITED in the atrium for the first wave of unedited humans from the city to arrive. She had been informed by Ruby that she was to take care of the recruits in the morning then go to Ruby's office in the afternoon to complete her personal assistant work. The long hours expected of her loomed over her like a dark cloud, and she knew Ruby wasn't the type of person to cut Chloe's workday short because of her increased responsibility. In the city, Chloe would have refused to comply, or at the very least voiced her displeasure, but part of being edited was supposed to be the feeling of happiness, regardless of the situation. Knowing this, she did her best to paste a smile on her face and settle into the long days ahead.

She had made a sign and placed it on a stand right above the stairs, telling the people coming to the island for edits to walk to the left and sit down in a sectioned-off portion of the seating area. Instead of waiting inside the area herself, she stayed back, near a restaurant, so she could watch the people she had to deal with before they knew she was in charge.

The first arrivals climbed the steps, their eyes wide with awe. They stopped in front of the sign then followed its instructions, taking seats at separate tables. As more people emerged from the platform, they had to sit down at tables already occupied, engaging in small talk while they waited. Chloe waited a few minutes after the last arrivals sat down before approaching. Her stomach was in knots knowing these people had been tricked into getting edits that could make their lives more difficult, that their edits wouldn't bring about the positive changes they hoped.

"Welcome to WestCorp!" she said as she walked up, loud enough for everyone to hear and with as much command as she could muster. A script hadn't been provided for her. "We are honored you chose to trust us with your future."

There were murmurs of greeting from the crowd. One of the men seated in the middle of the group looked at a woman by his side, his eyes telling her how upset he was to be there, before she elbowed him in the ribs. She tapped his leg twice as an olive branch.

"Now, if you'll follow me . . ." Chloe said.

The island's visitors all stood up and lined up behind the space in the partition.

Chloe led the group out the back entrance, the same path she'd taken with Shada. It felt like forever ago. Somehow, the transit system on the island knew to provide a larger transport vehicle, and one the size of a bus sat waiting for the group of new arrivals. Nobody thought twice about the absence of a driver, and as soon as the last member of the group sat down, the bus began to move.

It took less than five minutes to arrive at the warehouse. The group was quiet except for the few whispered, private conversations of people who'd come to the island together. Chloe, in the front seat, informed them they had arrived when the bus stopped outside the warehouse. She stood outside the door of the bus as everyone climbed off, then took a look inside to make sure everyone had disembarked. There was a solitary woman in the back seat, tears streaming down her face. Chloe walked back and sat down in the seat next to her.

"I can't do it," she said.

"Come on now, we're already here," Chloe said, drawing on all the sweetness she possessed.

"I left my kids with my mother. I was convinced I was doing the right thing, creating a future for my children. But now I can't help but think I'm abandoning them!" The woman didn't cry out, but tears streamed down her face anew.

Chloe sat, waiting for the woman to continue. Pretending to be edited was hard, but pretending she wasn't one of them, unedited, was harder. She wanted to take this woman under her wing, to tell her there were steps being taken to topple the company for good, to help this woman as well as unburden her own mind.

"It's for the best," the woman said after a deep breath, finding her resolve. She nodded as if convincing herself of the fact. "For the best," she repeated.

"It is," Chloe said. Her skin crawled at how easy it was for her to help WestCorp manipulate the unedited.

The woman stood and walked off the bus, joining the people milling about outside the warehouse. Chloe, having joined the crowd, stood on tiptoes and called out, "This way, everyone!"

Inside the warehouse were rows of stainless steel tables. There were enough to accommodate many more than were with her, so she told the cohort to each take a table but bias towards the front of the room. "There will be more people joining you shortly," she yelled out. "Please be patient. Bathrooms are in the back"—she pointed to the far wall—"and there is reading material present near the door we entered through. Please don't try and leave the premises, or the alarm will sound and you'll be escorted back by security. I can't guarantee you won't be restrained."

Chloe searched the faces, trying to determine if anyone else would get cold feet. The crying woman appeared resolute. "Any questions?" Chloe asked.

The husband who'd given his wife a look raised his hand and began to speak without being acknowledged. "How many more people will there be?"

"I've been informed there are three waves coming in today. So, most of these tables will be filled before we begin." The group looked at the empty tables around them, and Chloe took their distraction as her opportunity to leave.

She rode the bus back alone and walked into the atrium to find a group already waiting for her. WestCorp ran like clockwork. She repeated the procedure twice more and left the warehouse for the final time that day with most of the tables full, just like she'd said.

When Chloe returned to the atrium for the final time, she raced to the bathroom and washed her hands. She stared at her face in the mirror for a long time, disgusted at herself for helping WestCorp. She felt Fisher try to communicate with her, but she blocked off his access to her, not wanting to deal with the edited mind. She was angry at the edited, and she lumped the mind inside her body along with them even though he'd had no involvement in the distribution of the free negative edits.

She walked out of the bathroom, intent on getting food before starting the second half of her day, but stopped short when she saw Richard.

He was wearing the WestCorp business uniform, a white polo and khaki pants, and walked around the food court as if seeing it with fresh eyes, a newfound appreciation for the world around him. She knew without speaking to him the edited mind was still in control.

"It's only been a day," she told herself. She closed her eyes and focused on her breath. She wanted to follow Richard but knew it was no use. He had no idea who she was.

Fisher, in the background, told her to stop worrying about him. "And Shada, for that matter. They'll be fine," he said.

"Be quiet," she thought, focusing on her exhale.

"If your goal is to live outside the city alone, it doesn't make sense to forge ties with people. You'll have to walk away from them eventually; just stop caring now so it isn't so hard," Fisher said.

Chloe tried to lie and tell Fisher she didn't care about Richard but wasn't able to silence her true thoughts. If she had to lie with her words, she could've done it, but thinking a lie, hiding it from herself, wasn't something she was able to do.

"I knew it," Fisher said.

Chloe walked in the opposite direction to Richard, in search of food. "You should be worried too," Chloe said to Fisher inside her mind.

"And why is that? He isn't my friend."

"If Richard tells anyone about your upload into my body, we'll both be in trouble. It's not like you have a body you can go back into."

Fisher was quiet while Chloe purchased a bar and a smoothie from the coffee shop. She devoured them both with minimal time spent breathing. She began the walk to Ruby's office.

"Realistically, what can they do to me? My body is already dead, so what if my mind goes too. But you . . ."

Chloe stopped in the hallway, waiting for Fisher to continue.

"They could put your mind into a different body and kill you. Then I'd have free reign." Fisher twitched Chloe's thumb, and Chloe, instead of stopping him, allowed it to continue.

"I'd never leave my own," she said.

"You wouldn't have a choice."

Chloe knew Fisher was bluffing. Every upload had to be voluntary, or else there wouldn't be complete transference. It was part of the briefing Alfie had gone through with Fisher before his own upload. Chloe's access to his memories made it so Fisher couldn't sustain any deception for long.

"It's only been a day," she repeated to herself, hopeful Richard had been paying attention when she'd told him how to find the light.

CHAPTER TWENTY-THREE

CHLOE FOUND Ruby luxuriating in her office, her feet on the desk and head resting on the top of her leaned-back chair, staring at the ceiling. The head of WestCorp didn't move when Chloe entered.

"How was it?" she asked.

Chloe pasted a smile on and reported her first day in her new assignment had been "wonderful."

"Did you need something from me?" Ruby asked.

"No, just wanted to let you know I arrived."

"Noted. Shut the door on your way out," Ruby said.

Chloe retreated and shut the door behind her. She cursed the older woman under her breath, then cursed herself for sticking around when she wanted to leave, the rebellious streak in her coming out. There wasn't any work for her to do. Instead of turning on her computer and pretending to work, she stared at her reflection and descended into Fisher's memories, looking for previous interactions he'd had with Ruby.

The two of them had never had direct contact with each other. The memories Chloe could find were times when Ruby was present in the front of a room as Michael's wife, smiling and seeming to agree with everything the previous leader of West-Corp said. Ruby once spoke by herself to Fisher's team, a few dozen people, outlining the importance of their work and thanking them for a job well done. The memory was infused with a sense of gratitude because the group had had minimal recognition from the leaders of the company. This time, they were thanked for their ability to organize a massive influx of candidates for editing, the first time the company had rolled the service out to the public, and Fisher's group had worked day and night to get the work complete. The warehouse filled with stainless steel tables had come from this project.

Chloe stumbled on the memory of a rumor from a time before Michael and Ruby were married. They had been selected for each other—or rather he'd selected her—but there were rumblings within the company that Ruby's family had poisoned her name. Ruby's father had run away from the island, leaving his wife and a young Ruby behind, to go into the city and be with an unedited woman. This was before WestCorp had their current reach, and there was nothing the company could do. They'd kept tabs on him, plotting how they could get back at the man. The whole company was aware of the trajectory of his life; Fisher couldn't remember if the company told everyone or word got out through loose lips. Either way, they found out when he became mayor of the city. This news was the last Fisher had heard of Ruby's father. By then, Michael had ignored the members of WestCorp who disagreed with his selection and married Ruby. From then on, WestCorp had been involved with every major election, making sure their preferred candidates were the ones elected.

A siren rang out, pulling Chloe out of Fisher's memory. She now knew why Ruby hated the unedited so much: they had almost cost her a future.

The siren didn't stop. It was earsplitting and seemed to

come from every corner of the room. Chloe questioned Fisher about what it meant.

"Emergency," he said. "You need to exit the building."

Chloe jumped up and walked into Ruby's office without a second thought. "What's going on?" she yelled, loud enough for her boss to hear.

Ruby was in the same position Chloe had left her and showed no signs of moving. "No idea," she said with a shrug. Her words came in a space between siren blares.

"Do we need to leave?" Chloe asked.

Ruby didn't move. "I'm not going anywhere. Go find out what this is about, then come back and tell me."

Chloe didn't know how she heard Ruby's words over the noise of the siren. "What if it's a fire?" Chloe asked. Part of her was impressed by the woman's nonchalance.

"That's a different alarm."

Chloe shrugged. "Good to know. I'll be back." She shut the door behind her when she left.

Years of fire drills as a child had made Chloe associate loud indoor sirens with leaving the building, so she found the nearest exit and walked out into the sunlight. There were other people outside, all streaming to the left, towards another side of the building. The same siren seemed to be blaring from every adjacent building, but outside, the noise wasn't so overwhelming. She caught the sound of her heavy breathing, took a moment to calm down, and followed the crowd.

Chloe turned the corner and saw the backs of a large group of people. There was a space near the center of the mass enclosed by the semicircle of people and the wall. On the opposite side of the space, emergency services forced their way through the crowd, towards what everyone was gathered around. Chloe had never seen people wearing this uniform, but their dark shirts, matching dark baseball caps, and commanding air made it obvious they were there to take care of the situation. When they made it to the center of the crowd, their hats disappeared as they ducked down to inspect the source of the commotion.

It seemed every person but Ruby had exited the building. The crowd swelled, and more people came from surrounding buildings. Within minutes, Chloe was near the center of the mass. She searched the sea of faces, hoping to see Richard. If she could get near him and talk to him, she could find out if he had been able to switch. Maybe she could find her own heartbeat and allow it to resonate with his. She thought of Shada, knowing her friend would be the one who could pull off a maneuver like that with so many people around; there was a massive chance noise would be introduced to the experiment. But she could try.

She worked her way forward, keeping her eyes on the faces across from her, looking for Richard. She got to the open space, looked down, and found what she was looking for.

His body was bent in awkward, rigid angles, reminding Chloe of a cubist painting. His ear rested on his shoulder, and there was a space between the bones of his neck where two corners of broken bone pushed against the skin. It struck her how important that space was, how it signified his death more than the blood running down from his mouth.

"He jumped," a woman told the two men and the woman with dark baseball caps. "And landed just like that."

"We heard," one of the dark hats replied.

The sirens stopped blaring, but the voices of the crowd took their place as an incessant noise, a constant buzzing in Chloe's head. She turned and walked away, numb, making it back to Ruby's office without realizing where she was going until she arrived.

"What happened?" Ruby asked when her door was opened.

"The second upload test was a failure."

Ruby sat up. "How do you know?"

"He just jumped off a roof. He's dead outside." Chloe stared at the rolling waves in the distance through Ruby's window on the back wall.

"Damn," Ruby said. She looked down and away, thinking. "We'll need to run another test."

Chloe remembered Richard's children and a wave of nausea swept over her. She dreaded putting another life at risk.

"Alfie better get it right this time," Ruby said.

"Agreed," Chloe said, and she meant it. There was no reason for anyone else to die.

Ruby stood up and looked out her window, blocking the bay from Chloe's view. "I know he's using Michael's underground bunker as another lab, but he doesn't know I know." She turned around with a grin on her face. "I monitor the electricity usage of the space," she said.

Chloe appreciated Alfie's caution when forging her edits, how he'd run the machine just to consume the electricity. The man knew what he was talking about.

"I need to keep him around long enough to perfect the process. I wonder if he botched this one on purpose . . ." she said. She shook her head no. "No, he wants this to succeed as much as I do. He wouldn't."

Chloe stayed silent, marveling at the stream of Ruby's thoughts.

"I'll need to replace him eventually though. I can't have someone on the island working behind my back, even if he's my son." Ruby leaned on her desk and tapped her fingers. She looked at Chloe. "What would you do if someone took away the person you loved?"

Chloe guessed where Ruby's mind was headed and wanted to get to her conclusion first. "Do you want me to kill Alfie?" she asked. Although she was still numb from seeing Richard's dead body, she was surprised at how her question didn't come with any emotions. Maybe being around the edited had made her less emotional even without going through the procedure.

"No, if anything I'll send him to the city. We still need him for now. We just need to keep in mind that he has an agenda of his own. Can't give him too much power until we find out what it is."

Chloe nodded and, after asking if Ruby needed anything else, excused herself. She was amazed the woman didn't realize Chloe had her own agenda as well.

CHAPTER TWENTY-FOUR

"Ruby wants to get rid of you," Chloe told Alfie in his office. It was night, and she was exhausted from her first day filling two roles in the company. She'd willed herself to come see the scientist, to talk to him, even though she wanted to curl up in bed and sleep. Seeing Richard's dead body on the lawn had strengthened her resolve.

Alfie sat back before looking up and to the left. His eyes returned to Chloe. "She does, does she? And what makes you say that?"

"She told me herself."

"And did she share her reasons why?"

"Wants to get back at you for uploading Michael into Shada."

Alfie smiled. "Well, I'm right here."

"She won't do it until you have the chance to upload an edited mind without the unedited host taking back over."

"It seems I was close. Richard must have been worried he wouldn't take back over for good, even with the serum, and decided to jump off the building instead of being trapped inside."

Chloe shifted in her seat. "If he was able to get that bit of control, why not try again later? The first bit of control is the hardest."

"Maybe he realized he was in over his head. Or he didn't like the sensation of losing control of his body. For someone like him, it had to be unsettling."

"Has there been any news about him telling anyone that I was uploaded into as well?" Chloe asked. She didn't want to say his name; referring to Richard as "him" was more tolerable.

"I was going to ask you the same thing. Did Ruby receive any news while you were there?"

"I was only there for the second half of the day; the first half was spent guiding unedited recipients of the free edits to the warehouse where their procedure would take place."

Alfie thought for a moment. "Did Ruby act weird at all?"

"Very. She was staring at the ceiling and didn't move for a very long time. Now that I think about it, she could have been digesting the information, deciding what to do having found out about Fisher in my body."

Chloe felt Fisher's awareness spike at the mention of his name.

Alfie let the revelation settle before offering his thoughts. "Without definitive proof Richard was able to take over, it's hard to believe the edited mind even thought to probe his memories. Even if it was considered, and attempted, it's my guess Richard was still too deep to access. I'd guess your secret is safe, but we need to monitor Ruby closely to make sure she doesn't have any idea about you."

The scientist's logic seemed sound to Chloe, and she felt better after hearing his assessment.

"I do have something for you," Alfie said. "Richard gave it to me before his upload." He opened one of his desk drawers, withdrew the picture of Richard with his children, and handed it to

Chloe. "He said if anything happens to him, he wants this to get back to his family."

Chloe's hand shook as she accepted the photo. She avoided looking at it and put it in her pocket. "I can't go into the city right now, the authorities are looking for me in connection with Piper's murder."

Alfie didn't bat an eye; he must have known she was the one who killed her. "Ruby told me you were involved. Said the edits worked well when I met with her yesterday."

"Is that all you two talked about? I was furious when I saw her walk out of the lab with you."

"Among other things. She came right out and said she knew I'd uploaded Hollis into Shada. I thought she'd be more upset than she was, but it sounds like she's taking time to set up her revenge."

"She's a snake," Fisher said to Chloe. Chloe relayed the sentiment to Alfie without attributing it to the edited mind inside her.

"Too calculating for her own good, I'd say. If she just came out and told me what she wanted, I could help her."

"You'd help her get rid of you?"

"Well, maybe not, then," Alfie said with a smile. "But even if she took away my access to the lab, I could continue working in Hollis's bunker."

"She knows about the underground lab too."

Alfie shook his head and cursed under his breath.

"What else did you two discuss in your meeting?" Chloe asked.

"Not much else. She said she wanted to perfect the process of uploading, and that's when I told her about the next test we would be doing, on Richard. She seemed pleased to hear I was already working on the project. The whole thing was rather quick. And unexpected. She just showed up."

"So you're trying to make it so the unedited mind can't regain control of their own body? Am I and Shada going to be the only two who end up this way?" Chloe said. She felt her blood pressure rise.

Alfie leaned forward in his chair. "I could lie to you and tell you no, that I'm on your side, trying to allow the unedited to take over edited minds. But the truth is that I want to be able to do both successfully."

Chloe glared at the man.

"You have to understand. I'm a scientist. If I told you it didn't bother me that my initial hypothesis was incorrect, I'd be lying."

Chloe stood up. "Were you trying to make it so Fisher would take over my body?" she yelled.

Alfie asked Chloe to sit back down. "No point in getting worked up," he said.

She sat down and crossed her arms, waiting for the scientist to continue.

"Truth be told, I didn't know what was going to happen. I had to try again, repeat the conditions of the first experiment and record the results. It's not like I can run large trials of this procedure. I had a feeling you would be able to take back control, but I wasn't sure."

"Shada's the only reason I was able to. If she didn't tell me how to do it, I doubt I'd have figured it out."

"Well, the process didn't work for Richard. I'm assuming you told him the same steps to take."

"I did."

"And now we know there's something else required. Maybe it's because you are both female and he was a male? I could test it on another male, see if I can get the same results. But in an ideal world, I'd test two males, one with instructions from you and one from Shada, seeing if the instructions are the differentiator. Then, your history with uploads comes into play. Did your prior experience with the uploads set you up for success when the stakes were higher? What about Shada allowed her to take control after her first upload? Is one upload sufficient prior experience?"

Chloe's head spun trying to keep track of the possibilities, and she informed Alfie that she understood the point.

"So what I'm after is repeatable results. Science is what matters to me. The mind that ends up in control at the end of the day is just data to be analyzed."

While Chloe didn't like Alfie's uncaring attitude about the people involved, she did appreciate the dedication to his work.

"There is one question I'm dying to find the answer to . . ." Alfie said. He seemed hesitant.

"What?"

"If it's possible to capture multiple minds in the same body."

Chloe thought for a moment. Fisher said he thought it was possible right away. "If the person in charge of the body could keep them organized," he said in Chloe's mind, "I think it could be done. Not sure how much access everyone would have though."

"Fisher said he thinks it's possible. It'd have to be Shada," Chloe told Alfie.

Alfie's eyes betrayed his curiosity.

Chloe continued. "Do you have an edited candidate in mind? Maybe someone who wouldn't be too much to handle?"

"I do have someone I'd test in an ideal world, but they'd be a handful." After a pause, he said, "What if we got Ruby and Michael back together?"

Chloe laughed, then, when she realized Alfie was serious, her jaw dropped.

"Shada wouldn't have to worry about Ruby trying to kill Hollis once and for all, and Ruby would be out of our hair."

"Who would take over WestCorp?" Chloe asked, wondering if this was Alfie's attempt at taking over the company himself.

"Shada, in possession of Michael and Ruby Hollis," he said without hesitation. "The whole world would find out what WestCorp is capable of."

"If the world doesn't turn on you first. Ruby's free edits are to make the city's inhabitants angry and impulsive; once word gets out, the city will clamor for retribution."

"They'll come for the one who designed them," Alfie said, his head lowering. He had accepted his fate. "That's also what we were discussing yesterday. She wanted to make sure they were ready."

Chloe could have jumped across the desk and strangled the man. "You're helping her!"

"I had to prove my loyalty. You of all people should understand the importance of that."

CHAPTER TWENTY-FIVE

"MRS. HOLLIS?" Chloe said from the door to her boss's office. It was Friday, the end of a long week of corralling unedited newcomers to the warehouse every morning.

Ruby took a moment to respond, choosing to finish reading her computer screen before acknowledging her assistant. When her eyes did find Chloe, she seemed to be far away, as if she had something else on her mind.

"Have you told the police to stop investigating me for Piper's death?" Chloe asked.

"No, I meant to do it yesterday. I'll take care of it." She looked back at her computer monitor, trying to end their conversation.

Chloe wasn't done. "Could you make sure you do it before tomorrow? I need to go back into the city."

Ruby didn't hesitate on her screen this time. "Into the city? What for?"

"Richard, the second test, had a picture he wanted returned to his family. Alfie gave it to me to bring back to them."

"A picture of what?"

Her gut reaction was to ask her boss why it mattered, but she humored the curious woman instead. "Of him and his two children."

Ruby shook her head. "Sentimental nonsense. Go, if you must."

Chloe wasn't asking permission. She had never been told she was expected to work on the weekends, so she felt that time was hers to use as she saw fit. She just had to make sure she wasn't going to be arrested before she went.

"So you'll take care of the police today?" Chloe asked.

"Yes, I'll take care of it today. If for whatever reason you are stopped, you can always just tell them you live on the island. Working for WestCorp has its benefits."

Chloe marveled at Ruby's confidence. She wanted to believe her, to think the company gave her a sort of immunity, but her years spent in the city, seeing the way the police targeted the underprivileged, made her doubt the effectiveness of this protection.

Ruby finished work late on Friday night, and Chloe had to sit at her desk with nothing to do until after the sun had gone down. She skipped dinner and went straight to bed, exhausted from the week and wanting to have a full night's rest for her trip. She woke up on her own on Saturday, groggy.

Her trip into the city was uneventful. The policemen at the city's transportation hub didn't give her a second look. It was a relief to stop pretending she was happy all the time now that she was off the island, and her face reverted to a neutral, borderline unapproachable look.

Chloe had no idea where Richard's family lived, so she went to the Office of Unedited Rights, hoping Tensen or someone else there could provide her with more information. The building had bare-bones security and was otherwise empty.

Chloe walked into Tensen's office and found it in the process of moving. Boxes were piled near the door, and movers were filling more. Tensen recognized Chloe when she walked in and came right over to her when she arrived.

"You're moving?" Chloe asked.

"To the mayor's office. It became official yesterday," Tensen said with a smile.

"Congratulations!" Chloe said. It was easy to slide back into pretending to be happy when in reality she didn't care.

"What brings you in?" Tensen asked.

"I need to find Richard's family. Do you know where they live?"

Tensen's eyes narrowed. "Not offhand, but I can find out. Why? Did something happen to him?"

Chloe informed the now-mayor that Richard was dead, leaving out the part where an edited mind had been uploaded into his body. Tensen's remorse knocked him sideways, causing him to put one hand on his barren desk for support.

"When did it happen?"

"Monday," Chloe replied.

Tensen shook his head. "First they roll out the free edits without telling us, now they don't report when a resident dies on their island. Seems they're trying their hardest to end our relationship."

Chloe wanted to remind the mayor the deal had been made with snakes, to not be surprised when he got bit, but she kept her mouth shut.

"Do you know where his wife and children live?"

"Ex-wife, if I remember correctly. Why?"

"Richard wanted me to give them something. A picture he carried with him."

Tensen nodded. "Understood. Let me find out."

Tensen waved away a mover who was about to unplug the computer, stopping him just in time. After some typing, he printed out the address and asked Chloe if she could inform them of Richard's passing. "It would save me the trouble of bothering them twice," he explained.

Chloe thought bother wasn't the best choice of words but agreed to tell them. She wished Tensen good luck in his new position before saying goodbye.

"Let me know if you need anything else," Tensen called out to her as she left.

Chloe kept walking, trying to determine how she would ever be able to contact the mayor of the city in the event she did need anything else. She was convinced he said that to everyone, always looking to gather votes.

A car accident had just occurred outside the building. There was a police officer in the street, directing traffic to go around the two vehicles involved. Meanwhile, the drivers of the vehicles were arguing about who was at fault. A crowd was beginning to gather on the far side of the street, watching the incident unfold. Seeing all this, Chloe realized how much she missed the city and its chaos.

At a break in the traffic the police officer looked right at her. He seemed to recognize her and put his hand to the radio clipped on his uniform.

Chloe's heartbeat quickened, and Fisher brought himself to the forefront. "Bet Ruby didn't bother to tell the police to end the investigation," he said. "Shouldn't have trusted her." If he had a head to shake, it would be moving left to right.

"Shut up," Chloe thought. She could have blocked him out but didn't want to put forth the effort. She assumed more police officers were already on their way and knew she had a limited amount of time before they showed up. She turned away and heard the officer yell for her to stop. Her rebelliousness peaked, and she thought about how, for the second time in a span of minutes, a man had yelled at her back, telling her what to do, as she walked away. A surefire way to make sure whatever it was they wanted never happened.

She didn't stop, continuing through the building she'd just left and leaving through a back exit. She began running to the closest train station a few blocks away.

"Not suspicious at all," Fisher said.

Chloe laughed to herself, appreciating his sarcasm. "They're showing up for an accident. I'm just a lonely woman late for an appointment," she said, in her mind, to Fisher. Thinking this made Chloe believe it herself, and her facial expression was one of someone who was exasperated at themselves for running late yet again.

"Sorry to burst your bubble, but if they did send out a report that you were here, they'll be looking for you," Fisher said.

Chloe ran faster.

Inside the train station, she looked at the address. She referenced her phone and found out it was a few stops before Shada's hideout. Keeping an eye out for officers, and avoiding the station's employees, she boarded the next train in that direction. She kept her head down against the seat in front of her, looking at her feet, risking a quick look at each stop to see who got on the train and if any of them were looking for her.

Chloe got off the train and called a car to take her to the address she'd been given. The houses she passed were small, a front door and a few small windows wide, packed together so tightly there couldn't have been much privacy from the neighbors. The car pulled up to her destination, a run-down single-family house similar to the others except for a single-car garage, which seemed to take up too much of the house's total space.

There were bikes lying on the tiny patch of grass and an assortment of balls by the front door. Three different scooters leaned against the garage door, all the same height; Chloe guessed there were other kids living in one or more of the houses nearby. She thanked the driver and got out of the car.

She stood in front of the house, wondering what to say. She remembered when she'd found out her mother died, when her grandfather had told her she would be raised by her dad. She was young and didn't appreciate the significance at the time. It wasn't until later in life that her father told her that her mother had committed suicide because she was blacklisted and couldn't find anywhere to continue her research. She hoped her dad was happy, wherever he was.

"Where'd he go?" Fisher asked. This was the first time Chloe had felt violated by his presence.

Fisher sensed Chloe's anger and asked her how it felt.

"I'll learn to deal with it," Chloe said. "And I haven't heard from him since he went down south to live near the water."

When the front door opened, Chloe realized she had been standing in front of the house for far too long. A pretty young woman with disheveled hair stood in the doorway, a quizzical look on her face. Chloe approached and said she had news about Richard.

"He's dead, isn't he?" the woman asked.

"Yes," Chloe said. She appreciated the directness of Richard's former partner. "He wanted me to give you and the children this." Chloe handed over the photo.

The woman took a look at it, holding it for a long moment. Chloe didn't think her time was spent reminiscing; rather, it looked like the woman couldn't decide whether to tear the photo up in pieces now or keep it to throw away later.

"He never should have gotten mixed up with those edited bastards," she snarled.

Chloe nodded.

"I told him, don't poke them or they'll strike out. That's why I left him in the first place: I knew I couldn't depend on him."

A young boy and a girl ran from upstairs, past the front door and out the back. A larger boy who was chasing them stopped at the front door and looked at Chloe. "Who are you?" he asked, curious.

"Came to give us this," his mother said. She shoved the photo in his hand.

The boy looked at the photo before shoving it in his pocket.

"What do you say?" his mother said to him.

"Thanks," he said. An automatic answer.

Chloe wondered what the boy's mother had told him about his father.

"Do you need anything else?" the woman asked Chloe.

Chloe looked at the boy, ignoring his mother. "I'm going to get the person who did this to your dad." She wished someone had told her the same thing when she was younger.

The mother pushed him away. "Go play with the others."

The boy stared at Chloe before leaving. His mother glared at Chloe before closing the door in her face.

Chloe walked away, confused. The interaction with Richard's family hadn't been what she'd expected and, worse, had stirred up emotions she had long since buried. Before she got far from the house, she heard a small voice call out for her to wait. She turned around and saw the boy running towards her, the picture still in his hands. She knelt down.

"Will you take care of the bad people? That's what dad said he was going to do."

Chloe nodded. "I'm going to get rid of them."

"Good," the boy said. He stood still for a moment then ran up to her, gave her a hug, and ran away.

Fisher hadn't missed the exchange. "How are you going to do that?" he asked.

"I'm going to take over every edited mind on that island."

"You want another Richard? Their blood will be on your hands."

Chloe thought for a moment. "I need to talk to Shada."

CHAPTER TWENTY-SIX

CHLOE RANG the bell and stood in the middle of the driveway, in front of the gate, so the sisters could see it was her outside their safe house. She looked around, paranoid a random officer could be passing by. It wasn't long before she heard a buzz and the gate slid to the left, allowing her to pass. As soon as she was through, it began closing, not ever getting far enough open for a car to pass through. The front door was thrown open as she walked up.

"Sorry to barge in on you like this," Chloe said.

"Don't say sorry! We're glad to have you," Sikya said in the doorway. She stepped aside and allowed Chloe to enter, closing the door and following her into the kitchen. Shada stood up from the kitchen table, crossed the room, and gave her friend a hug.

When they parted, Chloe told them about running from the police, how they wanted her because of her involvement in Piper's death. "Ruby said she would tell them to leave me alone, but she hasn't gotten around to it yet," she said with scorn.

Shada nodded. Sikya asked why she'd risked coming to the city.

"I've got some bad news," Chloe said.

Shada sat back down, and Sikya sat in the chair opposite her sister. Sikya gestured for Chloe to sit as well, but Chloe shook her head, preferring to stand.

Chloe came right out and said it. "Richard's dead."

Sikya gasped. Shada blinked twice, and Chloe wondered if Hollis ever took control of her friend's body anymore.

"I liked him," Sikya said, her voice full of sadness. "He was always so nice. What happened?"

Chloe told the sisters about the plan to upload another mind into Richard, about running him through the process of retaking control, and about how he'd jumped off the building.

"I tried to jump off a building in the city," Shada admitted.

Sikya stared at her sister. "Because you couldn't control your body?"

"It seemed hopeless. This was before the serum, before I learned to keep Hollis from controlling my body for good without it."

"You don't take any serum?" Chloe asked. She had trouble wrapping her head around negating Fisher's attempts at control without her injections, even though Fisher seemed to be resigned to his fate. Hollis, from her understanding, posed a bigger challenge.

"I ran out a while ago," Shada said.

Chloe's respect for Shada grew.

"What did you tell Richard about gaining back control of his body?" Shada said.

Chloe gave Shada a brief overview of the steps she had learned from Shada.

Shada sat for a moment, deep in thought. The other two women waited for her to speak again. "I've been wondering how important it is for whoever receiving the upload to be hijacked into first. I think that's the key. We were both able to find the light before the permanent uploads; he was thrown into the deep end and asked to swim. To be honest, I'm surprised he was able to get enough control to jump off the building in the first place."

"I'm not," Sikya said.

Chloe and Shada looked at her.

"What?" she said. "He was a stubborn guy."

Chloe nodded in agreement. She spoke after a break in the conversation. "One thing I've been talking about with Alfie," Chloe said, directing her words to Shada. "Do you think it's possible to upload multiple minds into the same body?"

"All edited into one unedited? I've been wondering that too."

Sikya's face gave away her surprise.

"Yes, edited into unedited," Chloe said.

"Are you considering taking on another one?"

Chloe admitted the idea had crossed her mind after speaking to Richard's son. "My first thought was to force more edited minds into unedited bodies. But I don't want anyone else to die, so then I thought, what if I host them?"

The mind inside Chloe's head began to protest but found himself silenced.

Shada folded her hands on the table. "With the serum, it might be possible."

"You could do it, with the serum," Chloe told Shada.

Shada shook her head. "I don't want anything to do with WestCorp. Look how they've forced me to live! Nothing good can come from working with them again."

"Alfie suggested you take on Ruby's mind. With both Hollises inside your mind, you could take over the company."

Shada smiled at Chloe. "There's already one target on my back, why invite more?"

Chloe now took the seat at the kitchen table that had been

offered to her. She leaned forward, both hands on the edge of the table. "The target was placed there by Ruby!"

"And Piper," Sikya added.

"Whom I took care of," Chloe said. "Since that one was my fault. But this would rid you of the Ruby problem!"

Shada admitted Chloe was right. "But I would never make it onto the island."

"Let me worry about that," Chloe said. She told Shada about the group meeting she'd been brought to by Richard and Tony. "I'm sure they'd help."

"There are a lot of variables to consider," Shada said. She wasn't convinced.

"Then, when you're in control, you can help teach unedited humans how to take control of edited minds instead of letting them come onto the island for the negative edits."

"Negative edits?" Sikya asked. "What do you mean?"

Chloe told the sisters about Ruby's plan to edit the unedited to be angry and impulsive. "She's offering them for free," she said.

"Why would she do that?" Sikya said.

"Her plan is to convince them the negative edits were designed and implemented by Michael Hollis," Chloe began.

"And then she'll tell them he currently resides in my head," Shada said.

"She's going to blame the whole thing on you? If I didn't know the two of you, I'd never believe the uploads were possible," Sikya said.

"It wouldn't be hard to convince them she's on their side. She could wait until a predetermined number of the negative edits were completed, then say she wasn't aware of the switch, throwing Alfie under the bus as well."

Chloe marveled at Shada's ability to grasp Ruby's malevolent intentions; she hadn't mentioned Ruby's desire to get rid of

Alfie and didn't realize this option was available herself. "How can you put the pieces together so well? She does want to get rid of Alfie . . ." Chloe said, her voice trailing off.

"I've spent a lot of time with a Hollis," Shada said, tapping her forehead. "One large maneuver to eliminate all of her enemies, seems like something they'd do," Shada said.

"It's disgusting," Sikya said. She leaned back in her chair and massaged her temples.

Chloe excused herself to go to the bathroom. On her way back, she stopped in the hallway when she heard the sisters speaking in hushed voices.

"She needs to be stopped."

"She's gone too far."

"What am I supposed to do? This is all you."

Chloe assumed they were talking about Ruby. She reentered the kitchen and sat back down.

"So will you help me?" Chloe asked Shada.

Shada's head tilted when she looked at her friend. "I don't know. How would we get Ruby to upload in the first place?"

Chloe thought for a moment. "We could tell her the upload was to reunite her and her husband, that it would be a quick hijack, but really it's permanent. Alfie would help—he'd have to help, if he wants to continue his work."

Sikya glowered at Chloe. "You think they'd just let her walk onto the island?"

"It would work if I'm in custody," Shada said. "I don't want to do it that way, but it would work."

Sikya's eyes opened wide. "Use you as bait? Are you insane?"

"There has to be a better way," Chloe said. "I just came up with that off the top of my head."

The three of them sat in silence, thinking. "What if she has to upload into you?" Chloe ventured.

Sikya urged her to elaborate.

"Well, if she was about to die, and the only way she could go on was to upload into another body, I doubt she would hesitate."

A thin smile crept onto Shada's face. "And I'd be there, waiting."

"All we'd have to do is get you onto the island. We could probably do it in the bunker."

Sikya crossed her arms. "I don't like it."

"Now, I'm not agreeing, but what then?" Shada said.

Chloe said Alfie would help with Shada's takeover of West-Corp, then they could begin teaching the unedited how to take over edited minds.

"I'm not sure that's a good idea," Shada said.

"Why not? The unedited could finally take over. It's what we deserve."

"If I'm in charge of WestCorp, the edits could be distributed evenly, to those who want it, without the need to take over the edited that already exist."

"You'd provide more edits?" Sikya asked.

"It's an option. Look, I'm not agreeing to anything, I'm just thinking through the possibilities."

"Well, if you decide to go through with the plan, we would know for certain if it's possible to upload multiple minds into the same person. Then I could do it myself."

Shada's eyes bored through Chloe as if she could see Fisher in the recesses of her friend's mind. "You're going to do it anyways," she said.

Chloe blushed. It was the first time she'd felt seen since she was a girl, and she wasn't sure she liked the feeling. "Nothing's planned," she said. "But if you don't capture Ruby, I will. And I'm going to need your help keeping everything under control."

Shada nodded; Sikya scoffed.

"So either way, you want her on that island," Sikya said.

"I guess so, yes."

"You refuse to leave her alone!" Sikya said before storming off. Chloe and Shada stared at the ceiling as they heard Sikya's footsteps come from above.

"She'll get over it," Shada said. "I'll let you know. Don't tell Alfie I'm considering it. I don't want him getting any more ideas."

Chloe promised she wouldn't, then got up to leave. "You might not need the serum, but I do," she said, informing her friend she was headed back to the island.

Shada smiled. "Don't bother trying to get on without it, you'll need it when you upload that second mind."

CHAPTER TWENTY-SEVEN

CHLOE WOKE up Monday morning dreading the start of another hectic week. Her day was spent escorting fresh-faced unedited from the city to the staging warehouse, feeling guilty the entire time. In order to get through the ordeal, she kept reminding herself that steps were being taken to upend West-Corp's scheme, that soon Ruby would pay for her deception. The one good part of the day was when Ruby told her the police investigation had been taken care of. "Better late than never!" she said with artificial cheer before retreating back into her office.

Chloe shook her head. After spending the afternoon waiting for Ruby to end their day, she headed to Alfie's office.

"Come in," Chloe heard after she knocked on the scientist's door.

Alfie asked Chloe to give him a few minutes to finish what he was working on, telling her that then he would be "all hers."

Chloe watched his facial expressions go through a range of emotions, from confusion to indifference, understanding to anger, as he worked. It occurred to her he might not be edited, or if he was, his edits weren't as numbing as the standard.

"I was just looking over the results of last week's edits," Alfie said.

"And?"

"About what you'd expect. They were all successful, and the newly edited have shown some worrying signs of impulse control. There's already been an attempted murder: one guy walked in on his wife sleeping with another man."

Chloe wondered if the couple he was talking about was the same one she had escorted to the warehouse on her first day a week ago.

Alfie turned to Chloe after a final click of his mouse. "What brings you in?" he asked.

"I talked to Shada," Chloe said. "She's said she wants time to think about taking on another mind."

"She'd better decide soon. She's our best candidate."

"She doesn't want anything to do with WestCorp. She's upset about going into hiding in the first place."

Alfie nodded. "You think she'll do it?"

"I think so. She's just being obstinate."

"OK, keep on her. We need her."

Chloe told Alfie the plan she and Shada had discussed. "Either way, we would need to get her to the island."

"You think you could handle uploading Ruby?" Alfie said. It seemed to be the first time he'd considered the possibility.

"If she doesn't do it, what choice do I have?"

"Wounding Ruby and not killing her will be difficult," Alfie said. The statement was more of a spoken thought, not intended to spark a debate or poke holes in the plan.

"There are people in the city who have that kind of training. They're itching for the chance to help."

Alfie raised an eyebrow, and Chloe told him about the group Richard had belonged to. "One guy, Tony, was with Richard all the time. He'll want revenge."

"You've been busy," Alfie said, impressed.

Chloe smiled.

Alfie leaned back in his chair and stared at the ceiling. Chloe wanted to ask him what he was thinking but trusted he would tell her when he was ready. After what seemed like forever but couldn't have been more than a few minutes, his gaze returned to Chloe. "If you're going to upload another mind into you, we should make sure it's possible by uploading a mind less . . . intelligent."

"Couldn't that make it more difficult to upload and control Ruby? She'd then be the third."

"That's what I couldn't decide. It seems to me there's a better chance at controlling her if you already know what it feels like to partition once. Keep them organized. Then, when she gets inside, you already know what to do."

Chloe wasn't sold but trusted Alfie's judgment. "Do you have someone in mind?"

"The head gatekeeper," Alfie shot back right away. "He's bred for size and strength, not his ability to think. Should be simple enough."

Butterflies erupted in Chloe's stomach. Those massive humans were imposing. She calmed herself down with the reminder that Fisher was more of a challenge than one of them would be.

"I would hope so," Fisher said in Chloe's head. "Everyone knows they're slow. Impossible to have a conversation with."

Fisher's confidence killed the butterflies once and for all.

"So don't expect me to talk to him," Fisher told Chloe.

"The two of you will be separate, don't worry." She looked at Alfie. "Fisher," she said as an explanation for her silence.

"Understood," Alfie said.

Chloe appreciated that he didn't ask the details of their back-and-forth.

"Having the gatekeeper would also give us a way to know the best way to get Shada and Richard's friend—Tony, was it?—onto the island."

Chloe confirmed his name was Tony.

"I should be able to take back control faster than with Fisher, right?" Chloe asked Alfie. She had a plan brewing.

"I don't see why not. Unless Fisher tries to take back control again, which is always a possibility."

Fisher told Chloe he had no intention of trying again. "I like experiencing the world. Last thing I'd want to do is give you a reason to banish me from the light."

"I ask because I want to take the poison before the next upload." She knew there was a chance Alfie would advise against it, but her bloodwork would give her away if she did it without consulting him.

Alfie thought about it for a moment. "You have the antidote, right?" he said.

"I do."

"I'll leave that decision up to you. I don't see a reason, but then again, if you can't take back control, you'd be lost inside your own body. I can understand why you'd take steps to make sure that doesn't happen."

Chloe would be taking the poison before the upload.

"When should we do this?" Chloe said. "Ruby's got me busy all week."

"It could be Saturday morning," Alfie suggested.

"These weekends fill up fast," Chloe lamented. "Yesterday I stayed inside all day just to recover."

"Do you have a better idea?" Alfie said.

"No, I was just complaining. It has to be then."

The confused look on Alfie's face reminded Chloe he wasn't used to dealing with someone who wasn't edited to be happy all the time.

"Assuming this works, we can make plans to capture Ruby. Whether it's in you or in Shada doesn't matter; we'd know it is possible to hold two minds inside."

"We'll need plenty of serum," Chloe said.

Alfie agreed. "There's plenty already made. We're good there."

"What happens when we capture Ruby? I know we said Shada would take over the company if she's the one to do it, but if she doesn't agree and I have to do it, what then?"

Alfie thought for a moment. "Not sure. I guess we'll have to sort that out when it happens. The people on the island could hold some sort of vote, I suppose."

"Whoever's in charge needs to fix the people who received negative edits," Chloe said.

"It shouldn't be a problem. They might lose the memory of their time spent since the edits, but I should be able to get them back to normal."

"Or perform the standard edits, if they want?"

"That's an option too."

"It would go a long way to rebuilding trust. Once this all gets exposed, the people of the city won't appreciate what we're doing here."

"I know. You're beginning to sound like a leader yourself."

Chloe ignored Alfie's probing compliment. "If others express interest in permanent uploads after finding out about me and Shada, we could match them up with edited volunteers," Chloe thought out loud. In reality, she wanted to force the edited into unedited hosts but didn't think a strong stance would be given space by Alfie.

"That was my initial plan," Alfie said. "Fisher had to be tricked because we needed to see if the process worked. Sorry," Alfie said. It was the first time he had addressed Fisher instead of Chloe.

Chloe sensed Fisher's indifference even though his mind never communicated the sentiment outright.

"What I'm curious about is how much access to the uploaded minds you'll have," Alfie said. "If we can perfect the process, and upload many more into you or someone else, could they form a sort of collective consciousness? What would their life span look like? Would they ever be able to exist without the serum?"

Chloe considered his questions. Part of her wanted to volunteer right then and there to receive more than just three minds, to upload as many as possible until she knew more than any other human in history. The internet held the world's data; a collective consciousness would hold both data and experiences. "I hadn't thought about that," she said, a small phrase that didn't betray her thoughts.

"Taking it to the logical conclusion: if there were multiple humans, each containing multiple minds, they could work together to control the future of WestCorp and the city. They could upload into another body when their body expired, giving long-term stability to civilization."

Chloe laughed. "You have too much faith in people."

Alfie asked what she meant.

"They would kill each other! Only one would be left standing. Whoever creates the collective consciousness first would have to be the only one."

CHAPTER TWENTY-EIGHT

AT THE END of the week, Chloe still wasn't one hundred percent sure she was ready to go through with the second upload. Some days she was determined to see it through, while others she worried about becoming lost inside her body. Fisher's continued protests to the introduction of a third mind into her body forced Chloe to double down on going through with the procedure, confidence inspired by his negativity. Her own doubt would creep in when she hadn't heard from him for a few hours. In a twist of irony, if he kept his opinion to himself, she wouldn't regain her determination, but each time he told her it was a bad idea, her resolve was strengthened.

One concern she had was that the two minds would team up against her. She wasn't sure how it would work, and even Fisher claimed he would never do such a thing, but she couldn't shake the notion. At these times, she was grateful for the serum and knew she had access to her body in a way the two edited minds would never understand.

Alfie informed the head gatekeeper, Valhall, that Ruby wanted to reward him for a job well done. It was common knowledge there had been no breaches in security, a fact

Chloe attributed more to the lack of threats than anything the oversized man had done or implemented. Other than the searches outside the train, there didn't seem to be any other security measures in place, and she was certain that with a little creativity she would be able to figure out a way for Tony and the rest of his group to get onto the island. When she thought about using a boat to get the group to the island, she considered the possibility that a more telling indicator of Valhall's success was the absence of boats off the island's shores, both private and commercial. She hadn't seen a single craft in the water her entire time on the island; maybe this was his triumph.

Chloe was sent to collect Valhall and bring the man to Alfie's lab early in the morning. She had wanted to stay out of the buildup, preferring to prepare herself for the additional mind's upload into her body. Alfie convinced her that by bringing the head of security herself, it would make the plan more believable, since everyone knew Chloe worked for Ruby.

Outside the nondescript building on the side of the island closest to the city, Chloe took a deep breath, opened the door, and walked into the barracks where the security guards lived. The dim lights showed a common area filled with chairs, sofas, and table games. Everything seemed to be stained or broken, signs of heavy use. There were three guards gathered around a television, their eyes glued to the screen and their backs to her. They were seated on normal-sized metal folding chairs. Each chair had at least one warped leg. In a corner of the room was a pile of discarded chairs, their legs bent past the point of being useful. Meal containers and remnants of old food were piled onto tables and stacked on the floor.

Chloe waited for the three men to notice her, but they provided no recognition. She cleared her throat and they continued to ignore her. Tired of beating around the bush and wanting to get the upload over with, she stood in front of the television, blocking the game they were watching from view.

"What are you doing?" the guard closest to her, on the right of the group, said. He leaned over to the right to try to see around her. "We're watching that!"

"I'm looking for Valhall," she said. It was her first time speaking the name, and it felt strange on her lips.

"I'm Valhall," the man in the middle said. "Now move out of the way!"

Chloe didn't budge. "We have to go," she said.

"Get her outta here, Val!" the third guard said.

"Fine, fine," Valhall said. He got up and stood behind his chair. Chloe stood still for a moment longer, grinned at both seated men, then walked back around them. She stood next to Valhall, behind his chair, while he continued to watch the game.

"Let's go," she said. When she spoke to him, she had to look up, since the top of her head didn't even reach his shoulder.

He looked down at her. "This is turning out to be more trouble than it's worth. I don't care about some useless award."

"Be quick about it and you'll be back here in no time." She felt like she was dealing with a child, not the head of security.

"Told you they're impossible to talk to," Fisher reminded Chloe. He was ignored.

Valhall tapped one of his friends on the shoulder and raised a hand to the other. "I'll be back," he said.

They both grunted.

Chloe hadn't considered the size of her target when she'd used her personal transport vehicle to get to the barracks. With a glance, she knew there was no way he would fit inside. She turned to Valhall. "Do you have a vehicle here? All I have is this thing," she said, pointing to her ride.

Valhall laughed. "I've sat on toilets bigger than that!" He pointed to a garage door. "In here," he said. He opened the door and walked into the dark room. Inside was a pair of oversized golf carts. The sides were exposed to the elements, and there wasn't a windshield.

The cart could've held two of the guards, or four normal-sized humans, so Chloe had plenty of room on each side of her when she sat down. She instructed him to drive them to the lab.

Alfie was waiting for them outside. He extended a hand and congratulated the head of security for a job well done. "Ruby considers you a valuable asset and regrets she couldn't make it today."

"Where is she?" the guard asked. His eyebrows crept closer together.

"She got called into the city at the last minute."

"I didn't see a flight plan," Valhall said.

Chloe could see then why he was in charge. She wondered if the constant suspicion had been edited into his DNA.

"It was within the last few minutes. Don't worry, everything's under control." Alfie extended an arm and guided the guard, who looked to be about one and a half Alfies in both height and width, into the lab.

Chloe followed behind the two men, trying to guess whether the guard ate one and a half times more food.

Alfie led them to his personal lab. Chloe noticed the machine used to upload sitting between two stainless steel tables and saw that the associated, modified helmets had been brought in. Valhall kept asking what they were doing there, that he'd prefer a nice meal over anything else, but Alfie insisted he would be pleased with the surprise and that he had to wait. "Not much longer now," he said. He asked Chloe to step outside.

Chloe's eyes searched Alfie's for a sign of what was about to happen. The scientist kept a blank expression. She walked out, shutting the door behind her, and pressed her ear against the door to hear inside. She heard nothing. Less than a minute later, at Alfie's instruction, she walked back in and saw the guard lying on one of the tables, next to the machine that would upload his consciousness. The helmet was already on his head, and his feet hung off the edge of the table.

"He doesn't need to be awake for this?"

"Everyone who uploads is sedated beforehand. This time, I just gave it to him earlier. Much larger dose than everyone else's though," Alfie said.

"How long do I have?" Chloe asked.

"I'd like to start within the next few minutes," Alfie replied.

Chloe retrieved the bag she had left at the lab from a cabinet under the counter. She withdrew a vial of poison, the antidote, and the picture of her grandfather. This upload felt larger than the previous, somehow more involved. When Fisher had been captured, she'd already known it was possible, since Shada had done it, but now the weight of her decision came bearing down on her, and if she wasn't so far into the process, she would have considered backing out. Looking at her grandfather, at the lines in his face, and remembering the time the picture was taken, she tried to conjure up the comfort the picture had brought her in the past. The feeling wouldn't reproduce; it hadn't after she had been hijacked, and since then she'd accepted a permanent upload. What the picture did do, however, was give her a lens with which to view what she was about to do, gave her hope about the future she was taking a small step to create.

After placing the antidote in her pocket, she unscrewed the vial of poison and drank it in one swig. It was bitter, but the taste didn't linger. She took note of the time: half past seven. She had until half past three in the afternoon before the effects would set in.

Chloe climbed onto the other stainless steel table and looked at Valhall. Next to him, she felt like a child. Her feet didn't come close to the end of the table, and her shoulders left plenty of space on each side, unlike the security guard, whose body took up the whole table. She put the helmet on her head and lay down.

Alfie rolled his chair between the two tables and punched the buttons on the machine. "Ready?" he said.

Chloe closed her eyes and brought her chin closer to her chest.

CHAPTER TWENTY-NINE

"Time to take back over," Chloe heard Fisher think. The darkness was all-encompassing, and his voice issued from all around her, as if she inhabited a sphere made of speakers.

She knew what she had to do.

Chloe found the faint sliver of light and allowed herself to see around it—since looking right at it would cause it to disappear—then drift towards it. As the circle grew, it took over her entire field of vision. Through the aperture, she saw the lab. She was seated on the edge of the table, and Alfie stood in front of her body, trying his best to calm Valhall, who had woken up in a different body without knowing he would be switched.

"What's going on?" she heard herself say. The words boomed from her mouth and were slurred, as if her tongue was too large. She attributed it to the lingering effects of anesthesia.

"Give me a minute and I'll tell you," Alfie said. He took out a penlight and shone it in each of her eyes.

The field of Chloe's vision shifted as the man in charge of her body turned to see his mind's previous lodgings lying on the adjacent table. Chloe found her breath; it was fast and shallow.

"That's my body!" Valhall, with Chloe's voice, said.

"I know, I'm figuring out what happened," Alfie said. He turned his back and consulted a chart lying on the counter.

Chloe assumed he was using his act to buy her time. This was why Alfie insisted that edited humans know what was about to happen. If the host wasn't able to take back control, a frantic mind could cause damage to themself or those around them. Sedating the host's body wouldn't work, because that would affect the host's ability to take back over. She got to work decreasing the speed of her breaths.

Valhall began to calm down. Even though Chloe hadn't taken back control of her body, she had still been able to affect behavior. She wondered if Fisher ever did the same thing to her. Could he have calmed her down or stimulated her without her knowing?

"I haven't, but it's an interesting idea," Fisher said.

Chloe still wasn't used to the fact that none of her thoughts were ever private.

While in control of her breath, Chloe sensed Valhall was close to jumping off the table and breaking equipment in the room. This was a good sign; awareness of the body meant she was one stop closer to taking control.

"Put me back!" Valhall-in-Chloe demanded instead of taking action.

Alfie turned to face Chloe. "It's going to take some time for me to figure out what happened. I won't be able to put you back right away, so you'll have to wait."

"How long?" Valhall-in-Chloe snarled.

"Could be hours. No later than tonight," Alfie said. There was a hint of mischief in his eyes.

Chloe made her body take a deep breath. She felt her stomach expand, then her chest. She was pleased with her ability to sense her body once more, and it helped her lose the sense of disorientation the darkness had produced.

Alfie smiled. He seemed to know the large, exaggerated breath was a signal from Chloe.

"Let me give you something to help you relax." Alfie walked forward holding a syringe.

Valhall recoiled, not trusting Alfie at all. He twisted on the table so Chloe's legs dangled from the side, and he was about to push himself off when Chloe took total control of her body, freezing herself in place.

Alfie seized the opportunity and shoved the needle into her right arm.

There was still some serum in her veins from the morning dose, but the additional vial boosted the effects. Chloe felt her connection with the world around her increase. She could sense Alfie's heartbeat resonating through the inanimate pieces of scientific equipment in the private lab, creating within them purpose that wouldn't exist without his presence. She became aware of her own heartbeat and followed it to the end of the line, through her limbs to the furthest reaches of her extremities. It didn't take long before she knew she was back in control for good.

Chloe swung her legs back to their original position, looked at Alfie, and smiled. "What was my time?" she said.

Alfie looked down at his watch. "From when you woke up? Minutes."

Chloe jumped down from the table. When she did, her legs seized up and she fell, face-first, onto the floor. She was able to use her arms to slow her fall. She climbed back up to a seated position on the floor.

"Was it the sedative or was it Valhall?" Alfie said, concerned.

"Not sure," Chloe said. She climbed to standing and used the table for support. Out of nowhere, the hand she used to grip the table tried to rip the table over on its side, but she regained control before it could succeed. When Alfie rushed to her side, she kicked him in the shin. He doubled over for a moment before popping back to vertical, pulling air through his nose in deep, long breaths.

"That hurt," he said through gritted teeth.

"I don't know why it happened," Chloe said. "There wasn't a thought for me to block. It happened right away, like an instinct."

Alfie backed up and leaned against the counter. "They're bred, and trained, to respond to threats without thinking. To be fast. Looks like he might be faster than you."

Chloe placed both hands on the table and closed her eyes. Controlling Fisher had been a cakewalk compared to reining in Valhall. With Fisher, once she had taken back control the first time, he had more or less stopped trying, except for the one time when he had reached out to Piper. Valhall, on the other hand, couldn't help but lash out. She knew she would have to stay present with her body, in a constant state of vigilance. She inhaled, feeling the air fill up her lungs. She knew her breath was the key. She should have learned her lesson after the Piper incident, but now she couldn't forget: control of her breath would keep control of her body.

She stayed still for dozens of breaths, making sure she was aware of her body so Valhall wouldn't have the chance to take over any of her limbs. She wasn't sure she could maintain awareness of both her breath and her heartbeat at the same time, and leaving either one unaccounted for could allow for one of the minds inside her to take over. It seemed Valhall posed the greatest threat, so she ignored her heartbeat, which meant there was more space for Fisher.

She reached out to Fisher. "Do you sense him at all?" she asked the edited mind inside her head.

"No words, just anger and impulse. Best of luck," he said, chuckling.

Chloe looked at Alfie. "I need to leave the island," she said. "And get to Shada. She can help me."

Alfie nodded and didn't ask any questions. "Let me help you get what you need from your room," he said.

"No, I don't need anything else from my room. I just need to get to the city."

"What if he takes over again?"

"It's not so weird in the city," Chloe said with a laugh. "There's all sorts of characters walking around the subway. Some lady talking to herself, moving around with jerky motions, won't even be looked at twice." She thought for a moment. "Do you have some serum here? I'll need two doses."

"Staying the night?" Alfie asked as he retrieved two vials and a syringe. He handed them to her, and she placed them in one of the pockets of her backpack.

"Might be," Chloe said as she walked out the door.

Alfie walked a step behind Chloe through the lab, in case she lost control again and had the urge to strike out. He helped her into a transport then took a second, each of them riding alone. While on the trip, Chloe looked out at the bay around the island, surveying the horizon for boats. She felt relief when she didn't see any and somehow knew there was a system in place to deal with intruders if she had. She wasn't sure why these feelings and beliefs sprang up—she hadn't cared about the island's security before she knew Valhall would be uploading, but it was a gut feeling that couldn't be ignored. When she tried to ask Valhall about the security measures in place, she was met with silence.

Alfie kept his distance as he walked her through the atrium and to the tram platform below. Passing by the two guards posted at the bottom of the stairs induced a sense of pride in

Chloe, along with the confidence that everything would be taken care of in the event of an attack. She remembered Richard's gun, left with the guards when the unedited man had been brought to the island. While maintaining her awareness of every breath she took, she asked for it back.

"He forgot it when he left," she said as an explanation.

The two guards couldn't care less about who the property was given to, as long as it wasn't allowed past them onto the island. They handed it over before resuming their own conversation.

Chloe placed the gun into her bag right before her head jerked sideways. The two guards didn't notice, but if they had, Chloe would have pretended she was trying to crack her neck. She heard Valhall's voice inside her head for the first time. "This bitch has me trapped!" he screamed.

If she hadn't been forced to take back control of her neck, and therefore her head and face, she wasn't sure she could've stopped him from screaming with her own voice.

Chloe got on the tram and watched Alfie recede in the distance as it pulled away. She was certain the next time she saw him she would have full control of the mind inside her head, including access to his knowledge and memories. She tried to ask Valhall how the station would handle multiple intruders coming on the tram and got no response.

She felt the antidote in her pocket and knew she would have to wait until she could get past the silence before she considered herself safe from being lost inside her mind.

CHAPTER THIRTY

CHLOE WAS on edge around so many people. She couldn't explain the feeling, or why it was happening, but wave after wave of anxiety poured over her while she navigated the train system on her way to Shada. Since she'd never had issues with anxiety in the past, she attributed her heightened awareness to the presence of Valhall and his constant search for threats, although without him communicating with her in any way, she wasn't positive he was aware of his surroundings.

In the hub beneath the center of the city, Chloe took note of every exit and studied the train system's employees for signs of recognition. Every traveler who walked by was scrutinized. The presence of the implanted head of security didn't account for her awareness of police officers; she was wary of them herself, since the last time she'd seen any they were pursuing her.

The train departing the hub was crowded, with every seat filled and still more people left standing. When a fellow traveler sat down next to her, she worried her body would strike out. Instead, she seemed to collapse within herself, wary of the person's presence.

Chloe did her best to use the awareness of her breath to stay grounded, but she couldn't shake the confusion about how Valhall could affect her internal state to such a degree. Part of her wished she could go back to her uncaring attitude, her confidence that everything would turn out all right, but another part knew Valhall's constant searching was necessary. It meant there was something she could push back against, that she could take steps to negate him, instead of being lured into a false sense of security. She didn't want a repeat of what had happened when she'd first captured Fisher and he had surprised her by taking over and talking to Piper.

While she rode the train north, Chloe realized Fisher might be able to help her. Could he block out Valhall's manipulation of her senses by controlling her body himself? She knew how to block him. It would be a tenuous form of control, but better than nothing.

"I can try," Fisher said.

Chloe felt Fisher take control of her hand. In the past she would have blocked him, but this time she let him take it, knowing she could end the test at any time. Fisher moved Chloe's hand onto her thigh and tapped it twice.

"Now try to find my breath," Chloe told Fisher. Her chest rose as he took a massive inhale. When he allowed her body to exhale, the beginnings of a sense of calm lapped at the shores of Chloe's nerves, taking part of her anxiety with it.

"It's working," she said. She allowed the edited mind to take ten long, slow breaths. Fisher must have been aware of Chloe's plan to take back control of her breath, because he held the last inhale longer than normal. Chloe was about to force the exhale when the air was released.

"Just wanted to make sure you were still there," he said, laughing inside Chloe's head.

"Don't worry, I'm not going anywhere."

Chloe took stock of her situation. The man in the seat next

to her, short and wearing athletic gear, wasn't a threat. This realization caused her body to relax, and she took up more of her seat. The mass of people standing in the center of the aisles, holding on to either the pole running through the center of the car or the poles going from the tops of the seats to the ceiling, stirred up slight feelings of claustrophobia but none of the worry their presence had elicited before. There was still a strange pull to inspect and memorize the various exits, an awareness she appreciated because it made her feel prepared.

By the end of her train ride, she had relegated Valhall's ability to affect her body to third, behind Fisher's, with hers given priority. Fisher didn't like having to do anything.

"I was happy just seeing the light," he grumbled.

"Well, we won't be able to enjoy the world if we are always looking for threats," Chloe countered. "But it is necessary to have him searching for us. Just in case." She wasn't sure she'd ever referred to the combination of Fisher and her as "us," and she hoped she wouldn't regret placing trust in him.

"You won't," Fisher responded.

She responded, without direct words, by thinking about how Shada would be able to help her take control if she ever needed it.

"You have a lot of faith in your friend," Fisher responded. "I'll show you it's all right to have faith in me too. My body's most likely gone, and I'm not going anywhere. We might as well work together to get through the rest of your natural life in a state where we are both content."

"Maybe I'll let you take over and navigate the world while I rest," Chloe said. She liked the idea of Fisher using her body to perform the tasks she didn't want to do while she could turn off and exist in the background darkness. She knew why she hadn't thought of allowing Fisher to perform some of her less-desirable tasks before: she didn't trust him. But an ability to cede control to the uploaded mind could prove beneficial to both of them, another benefit to uploading she hadn't considered. Had Alfie foreseen this possibility when he performed the uploads? She wouldn't put it past him.

By the time Chloe got off the train at Shada's stop, she was confident in her ability to maintain an equilibrium with both Valhall and Fisher. She called the safe house, and Sikya was at the station within minutes to pick Chloe up. On the ride to the house, Chloe kept her backpack on her lap and felt the vial of antidote in her pocket, wondering if it was the right time to take the dose. She almost took it in the car, but she didn't want Sikya asking questions.

When they got to the house, Chloe found Shada seated at the kitchen table, staring out of the window with a mug in front of her, looking like a stereotype. Chloe laughed. "Deep thoughts?" she said.

"Always," Shada responded. She smiled.

Chloe slung the straps of her backpack over one of the chairs at the table then stood next to her friend. They gave each other one-armed hugs without Shada standing up.

"Any news?" Shada asked. Her eyes inspected Chloe's face.

Chloe shook her head. "Not from me," she lied. "I was going to ask you the same thing. Did you make up your mind about Ruby?"

"I'm not going to do it. But I'll go to the island with you and help you keep control. I have some thoughts on how you might be able to get it done."

"I'm all ears," Chloe said. She tried to sound nonchalant, but inside she was dying to hear what her friend might suggest.

"First, let's take some time doing some breath work." Shada got up and led Chloe into the living room. All of the furniture had been moved to the sides of the room, leaving the middle wide open. Shada sat cross-legged in the center.

When Chloe went to sit down, she found the tightness of her pants restricting. She pulled them up and tried to sit down again but was uncomfortable seated.

Shada watched her friend before offering a suggestion. "Sikya, can you grab some shorts from upstairs?" Shada called out to her sister.

Sikya ran upstairs and came back with the shorts. She handed them to Chloe and told the two of them she would leave them alone.

Chloe changed out of her pants, folding them and leaving them on the table.

Shada guided Chloe through a meditation session. Chloe wondered if her friend had been taught by someone, read books, or taught herself. Whatever the case, she found an increased awareness of her body when they were done. She thought being around Shada could be part of the effectiveness of the session, that somehow their bodies had resonated with each other, imparting Shada's control onto Chloe. Whatever the reason, she was also aware she needed to use the bathroom. She excused herself, left, and changed back into her pants when she got back.

"You were going to tell me your thoughts about uploading two minds?"

"Right," Shada said. She had been staring off into space, and Chloe's question pulled her back.

"You and Fisher get along, right?"

Chloe nodded. She had a good idea of where the question led.

"She's good," Fisher said, impressed, in a space Chloe alone could hear.

"And you know how to control him. So, when Ruby gets in there, just create a simple hierarchy. Allow Fisher to take more control than Ruby, with you always having the most."

Chloe pretended to consider Shada's advice. In reality, she was ecstatic she had come to the same conclusion on her own.

"As long as you have fifty-one percent, I don't see why you couldn't maintain the upload of multiple minds," Shada said. "In a way, it mirrors real life. As long as you keep fifty-one percent of reality, the rest of the world can have the other forty-nine and you won't lose your identity."

CHAPTER THIRTY-ONE

CHLOE WANTED to start the process of getting back to the island now that Shada had agreed to be part of the plan to capture Ruby. She was able to get a hold of Tensen through Sikya, who had his private number. When she asked him for Tony's phone number, the mayor hesitated for a moment before giving her the information. He asked her to repeat the numbers back to him, which she did before thanking him and hanging up. She called Tony and asked if he could meet her at the safe house that afternoon. "Could you bring everyone else too? We're going to need them."

Tony didn't ask any questions before agreeing. In fact, he'd seemed to be expecting the call. "We'll be there around two," he said, then hung up.

Chloe confirmed Shada was still all right with going to the island that afternoon. "We'll be escorted by Tony and his friends."

Shada told Chloe she didn't even have to ask. "It's not like I have anything else to do," she said.

Chloe and Shada spent the early afternoon trying to figure

out how to communicate with Valhall. Or at least get him to communicate with words instead of impulses and reactions. They needed to find out the best way to get Shada onto the island and, if they could, find out if there was any way Tony and his team could join them in infiltrating WestCorp. Their main concern was getting weapons onto the island, since Richard had been forced to forfeit his when he had gone with Chloe. Without the guns, there wouldn't be much use for the team to be there.

"Then why get them to come at all?" Sikya said. She looked over the top edge of her book. Most of the time she was silent, content to listen to her sister and friend try to untie the knot they found themselves entangled in, but when she heard something she had a question about, she didn't hesitate to ask.

"To make sure we get to the tram in one piece," Chloe explained.

Sikya furrowed her brow. "Tensen's mayor now," she said. "We can tell him to make sure the police don't bother us looking for you. They might even be able to provide an escort."

"It's not the police I'm worried about," Chloe said. She lowered her voice. "WestCorp has been performing a substantial number of edits over the past two weeks."

"Aren't people always getting edited on the island?" Sikya said, interrupting.

"She's not talking about the standard edits," Shada said to her sister.

Sikya's face turned from confusion to recognition then settled on slight embarrassment.

"We never know when Ruby's going to tell them Shada's responsible for their new . . . outlook on life," Chloe said. A gnawing feeling in her stomach made her stand up and rearrange her pants.

"They're going to be pissed," said Sikya. "Why would she tell them to come after her now?"

"Why does she do anything?" Chloe said. She sank down in her chair and put a hand to her stomach. It was in knots; she was overcome with worry. Could it be Valhall? The thought hit her like a ton of bricks.

"Ruby's already told them you're responsible," Chloe said, her tone neutral. It was as if she was tapped into a source of information outside herself, plugged into the universe around her, even though it was just the head of security locked away inside her mind. She wondered if this was how Shada felt.

Shada, who was seated next to Chloe on the floor, crawled over and sat down in front of her. "My name is Shada Gray," she said.

Chloe felt her head try to jerk to the side and knew Valhall was responsible. The look on Shada's face gave away her concern.

"Let them," she said, her hand reaching out and touching Chloe's leg.

Sikya, on her chair, let the book fall onto her chest.

Chloe let Valhall take over and instructed Fisher to pay attention in case he was needed to help take back control.

"Get her!" Valhall-in-Chloe yelled. He lunged out with Chloe's body and pinned Shada on the ground, fingers wrapped around her throat. When Sikya scrambled out of her chair to help, Shada told her sister to wait.

It didn't take long for Shada to reverse their positions. She ended up on top of Chloe, her hands pinning Chloe's shoulders down instead of wrapping around her neck.

Chloe saw her field of vision shift as her head swiveled left and right.

"It's nice to meet you," Shada said. She was calm, somehow calmer than before, a woman in complete control of herself.

"They're coming for you," Valhall-in-Chloe said.

"Who's coming for me?" Shada said.

"You know."

Shada smiled. "I want to hear you say it."

"The other city-dwellers who thought they were getting something for free." Valhall-in-Chloe laughed, a deep, booming laugh that didn't belong to her body and had never been issued from her mouth before.

Shada stayed still, deep in thought. Chloe was tempted to take back control but trusted her friend would let her know when the time was right.

"Do you know the best way to get someone onto the island?" Shada asked.

"If I did, why would I tell you?"

"If you don't, I'll have Chloe take back control right now," Shada said.

Chloe's new laugh reverberated off the walls of the rearranged living room. "There's only two ways onto the island: the tram or the helicopter. Unless you plan on taking Ruby's helicopter, picking up your people, and coming back without anyone finding out, looks like you're coming up from below."

"It's happened before," Sikya said.

Valhall snapped Chloe's head to look at Sikya. "You mean the one who killed himself? We knew he was coming and let him in."

Chloe was shocked.

"Alfie told us he was part of an experiment. He was to be allowed onto the island without his weapon." Valhall laughed. "You think we'd let someone on we didn't know was coming? The second they step on the platform beneath your precious city, we know all about the people who are on their way."

Valhall turned Chloe's head back to Shada, and Chloe watched her friend digest the information.

Shada's eyes narrowed, then closed. Chloe felt a slight awareness of her own heartbeat; then, as it grew stronger, she became aware of the resonation of its rhythm with her friend's. It wasn't long before Chloe was back in control.

Shada opened her eyes. Chloe blinked twice then smiled.

"It's me," Chloe said.

"That wasn't Fisher, was it?" Shada said.

"It was like you were possessed!" Sikya said.

Chloe realized she had never told Shada about Valhall, and that she had figured out Chloe had a third mind on her own. "No, it wasn't."

"Who is it?"

"Head of security. Alfie uploaded him this morning." Chloe sat up and wiped her eyes. "I haven't been able to read his thoughts."

Shada closed her eyes. She spoke with them closed, as if working through a problem. "It seems like he doesn't think before he speaks. Definition of shoot first, ask questions later. Without that lag, that censor of himself, there's nothing for you to read." Shada opened her eyes. "Try letting him control your throat. Your vocal cords. But keep control of your mouth. It might allow you to hear what he would say if given the opportunity."

Chloe did what Shada suggested and was amazed to find the stream of slurs he was trying to release. She looked at Shada, amazed.

"I think you'll have to ask the questions out loud, since he isn't used to an inner dialogue," Shada suggested.

"What do you want to know?" both Fisher and Sikya asked Chloe, one inside her mind and one sitting in the room with her.

The image of Richard's son approaching her in the street popped into her mind. "Do you want me to upload your friends in here with you, or should I leave them for someone else?" Chloe said.

Chloe heard Valhall threaten to rip the limbs from her body while she squeezed her mouth tight. She took back control of her throat, and the screams stopped. She didn't miss the glance shared between the sisters.

Sikya looked terrified, Shada resolute.

CHAPTER THIRTY-TWO

Tony ARRIVED at half past two with three additional people. They were all dressed in black. A light mist was falling, and as soon as the team walked into the house, they brushed drops of water from their clothes. Chloe recognized the woman with the ponytail, but she couldn't remember if she had seen the two men. When Tony made the introductions, Chloe found out the woman's name was Cora and the two men were Gustavo and Tim. She had a feeling she wouldn't remember their names.

"Is everyone ready to go?" Tony said.

Shada had changed clothes before they arrived, taking off her comfortable loungewear, and was now wearing jeans and a T-shirt. She told the team she was ready.

Chloe said she needed a minute. She didn't need to change but still took her backpack with her into the bathroom. She laid out two vials of different sizes on the sink and stared at them. One held the serum Alfie had given her, and the other was the antidote. After spending time with Shada, she was convinced she had gained enough control over Valhall that she didn't have to worry about losing herself inside her body, and since seven of the eight hours before the poison took effect had already passed, she unscrewed the cap of the antidote and drank the blue liquid down in one swig. It was bitter and had more of a chemical taste than she remembered. She stared at the vial. Could the antidote go bad? It had worked the last time after having been untouched for so long, so she doubted it had a shelf life. If it was ineffective, it would have to have been a bad batch, which, unless both poison and antidote were bad, she knew wasn't the case. Maybe the seal was broken? She stared at the lid, looking for cracks and finding none.

Enough time passed that she began to doubt the taste was as different as she first thought. She attributed her second-guessing to paranoia.

The vial of serum, still sitting next to the sink, was larger than the antidote. She worried Valhall could still strike out at someone around her, making the serum necessary, but as long as she stayed in control of her breathing, she thought she could control his impulses. Plus, if she allowed him to communicate with her, in the way discovered by Shada, his impulses might not build up and erupt unannounced. Deciding it was more important to have Fisher around, she put the serum back in her bag.

When she threw her backpack back over her shoulders, the gun the guards had returned to her shifted inside her bag. She took off her backpack, withdrew the gun, and put the backpack back on.

"How can I get a gun onto the island?" she whispered, alone in the bathroom. A question for Valhall. She listened for his response.

"You can't," he replied. "The guards won't allow it."

"What if they are busy?" she asked.

"They won't be too busy to search you."

Chloe thought a distraction was necessary. Or maybe a sacrifice. The presence of Shada might be enough to keep their attention, letting her slip onto the island with the gun. If not, she would have to forfeit the weapon and come up with another way to force Ruby to upload, although she couldn't shake the thought that a mortal wound would provide the most incentive. Alfie might be able to help with that. It was something she could worry about later, once she was on the island and knew if she still had access to the weapon.

She walked back into the kitchen, where everyone else was gathered, holding the gun pointed to the ground.

"Where did you get that?" Tony said. His eyes were wide, as if he had seen a ghost. He must have recognized the weapon.

"The guards took it from Richard before they let him onto the island. I got it back when I left this morning," Chloe said.

"And what do you intend to do with it?" Tony asked.

"I need to get it onto the island."

Cora, the woman with the ponytail, rushed forward and held her hand out. Chloe handed over the gun. Cora checked to make sure the safety was on, told Chloe to turn around, and shoved the muzzle down the back of her pants after lifting her backpack out of the way.

"You'll have to hope they don't search you."

Chloe felt Shada's stare and lowered her eyes, embarrassed. She had a feeling her friend knew her plan.

"There's a way to get past the guards," Chloe said, hoping her confidence wasn't transparent. "I'll take care of it."

Cora looked at Tony, and Tony nodded.

"Will we be going with you to the island?" Tony asked.

Chloe considered telling the group of them to come as well. More people meant a larger distraction. She felt Valhall try to take over and let him try to speak but stayed in control of her mouth. She found out that a group of this size would be seen as intruders, and there would be reinforcements waiting when they got to the station below the atrium. If it was just her and Shada, there was a good chance they would encounter the two standard guards, but with more guards waiting for them, the chances of getting the gun onto the island fell.

"No, it'll just be me and Shada," Chloe told Tony. "We need your help to get onto the platform in case there are people in the hub who want to harm Shada."

Tony agreed. "Is everyone ready to go?" he said to the group.

Everyone, including Sikya, said they were. Sikya had packed a large duffel bag, and it sat on the ground next to her.

Shada told her sister she wouldn't be able to come to the island. "I know," Sikya said. "But I don't want to be in this house alone while you're gone. This is everything we brought," she said, gesturing towards the bag.

"Where are you going to go?" Shada asked.

Sikya admitted she wasn't sure, then suggested she go back to their old apartment.

"Why not stay at my old place? Nobody would think to look for you there," Chloe suggested.

Sikya looked at her sister. Shada shrugged. "Can you think of any reason why that wouldn't work?" Shada asked Tony.

"Not from my perspective. It's probably a good idea to switch locations anyways." He looked at Chloe. "Where's your place?" he said.

"Half an hour from here. Takes forever on the train since it has to go through the center of the city first, but with you driving it'll be quick."

Tony reviewed the plan. He said they were going to take two cars to Chloe's apartment. The first car would stay with Sikya at Chloe's, while Tony and one of the men would escort Shada and Chloe all the way to the platform below the hub. "Sound good?" he said when he finished.

Everyone agreed.

Two black SUVs left through the front gate of the safe house at a quarter to three. Chloe and Shada sat in the back of one, with one forgettable man driving and Tony riding shotgun. Sikya rode in the other, with Cora and the second man, either Gustavo or Tim.

CHAPTER THIRTY-THREE

CHLOE WATCHED her old neighborhood pass from inside the SUV. The weather contributed to the gloom, clouds overhead tinting everything gray. It was the ignored part of the city most well-respected citizens avoided at all costs, but it was her home. She missed the place, even the uncertainty of her walks home, when she crossed paths with all types of people and had to figure out what threats they might pose. There was a sense of pride at having made it out of her previous conditions and an understanding she would never have to live that way again.

This was all sterilized from inside the vehicle, behind two men charged with her and Shada's safety. For a moment she considered getting out and walking, to taste danger once again, but knew it couldn't happen.

In the alleys were homeless people inspecting piles of trash that materialized every night, their eyes bloodshot and faces gaunt from both lack of sleep and indulgence in various substances. There were rats walking on the sidewalk without a care in the world, staying far enough from people they couldn't be kicked but never running away to the dark. The groups of people who sat in front of abandoned buildings watched the two black SUVs pass, curious for a moment before returning to their conversations.

The two-car convoy came to a stop outside of Chloe's building. Tony told Chloe to accompany Sikya to the apartment, to let her in and make sure she was settled, before coming back out and continuing to the train station. "We'll drive around the block," he said to both her and the driver, not wanting to stay in one place with Shada in the vehicle.

Chloe thought it was a useless precaution, since the windows were tinted and nobody could see who was in the back seat, but she nodded and got out of the car before it rolled away. Sikya, Cora, and either Gustavo or Tim exited their vehicle and met Chloe on the sidewalk.

"Let's go in first," Cora told Chloe. She turned back to Sikya and her comrade. "You two follow."

Chloe led the group up to her apartment. The door was locked. A moment of panic set in when she realized her keys were still in her backpack in the SUV, which was circling the block, but she kept a spare on top of the light fixture opposite her door. She retrieved it and gave the key to Sikya after she unlocked the door. "This is the only spare, so don't lose it," Chloe said.

Sikya nodded, her face serious. "I won't."

The apartment had been ransacked.

"Wait here," Cora told Chloe and Sikya. She told Tim, using his name, to watch her back, and together they entered the studio apartment, searching for threats. It took less than a minute for them to designate the apartment as safe. "Come in," Tim said with a nod of his head.

The first thing Chloe noticed was the various stages of death of her plants. Some were brown and withered to near-nothingness, some drooped and looked like with a little water they could be revived, and some seemed not to have noticed her absence at all. Her ivy had reached out for the window, towards the sun, and had somehow been able to extend a stem across a span the length of an arm. Its tips rested on a book Chloe kept on her windowsill. She was thankful whoever went through the room—she guessed it was the police—hadn't bothered to dig up the plants, because nothing was hidden in them.

The dresser drawers were all pulled out, and the clothes Chloe had left behind were tossed on the floor. Her mattress was twisted on the box spring, its sheets left in a pile in the middle. She peeked inside her bathroom. The mirror had been left ajar and the drawers beneath her sink were emptied, leaving extra toiletries and cleaning supplies on the floor.

Sikya touched Chloe's arm. "You need to go. I'll take care of this," she said.

As much as Chloe wanted to clean up the mess and leave a comfortable place for Sikya, she knew her friend was right. The car couldn't circle the block forever. Chloe tried to apologize. "It wasn't like this when I left," she explained.

"I'm sure it wasn't."

"We'll make sure she's settled before we leave," Cora said. Tim nodded.

"Take care of the plants," Chloe said. "You might be able to save this one." She began walking towards one of the plants that still had a faint green hue, but Sikya stopped her by standing in front of her. "Go," Sikya said. "I'll save it."

Chloe thanked Sikya and left. While she waited for Tony's SUV to circle back around, a man on the far side of the sidewalk called out to her. "Hey!" he yelled.

She ignored him.

"Hey, you! You out here all alone?" the man said. He had on a stained coat, and even from across the street Chloe could tell it had been a long time since he'd seen a shower. The man stepped into the street, making a beeline for Chloe. He looked both ways and so did Chloe. He watched the black SUV turn the corner and timed his approach to coincide with the moment the SUV passed by her. When the SUV stopped and Chloe climbed in, she looked through the tinted windows and saw a mixture of confusion and surprise on his face. She laughed.

"Do you know him?" Shada asked.

"Sure don't," Chloe said. She leaned back in her seat, and the SUV pulled away.

Being home must have lured Chloe into a false sense of confidence, a space where her defenses were down, because Valhall took over and began to speak. The words rushed out before Chloe could stop them. "Chloe's going to force all the edited into unedited bodies," Valhall said, using her voice. Chloe took back control right away, but the truth was out. She was furious with Fisher, who was supposed to stay present so Valhall couldn't take control, but she knew right away he had allowed Valhall to speak.

Shada stared at her friend. "That wasn't you, was it?" she said.

Chloe was taking long, slow breaths and didn't want to interrupt them to answer.

"You don't want to just take over Ruby. You want to take over all of them," Shada said, her voice low. Chloe couldn't tell if she was angry, because the words were said as more a statement of fact, a new development to be accounted for. "What makes you think other unedited can handle hosting an edited mind?" Shada said.

Shada leaned forward and told Gustavo to drive to the train station closest to Chloe's home. Gustavo looked at Tony. Tony turned back towards Shada. "There are too many threats," he said.

"Do it," Shada said.

Tony stared at Shada, then turned to Gustavo and nodded. Gustavo made a U-turn and drove in the direction of the station.

"What are you doing?" Chloe said. Her breath was now under control, and she made sure Valhall didn't have room for another outburst. She cursed Fisher once more. He didn't respond.

"We need to ride the train," Shada said.

Chloe waited for Shada to provide an explanation. It never came. "Why?" she said.

"You think the unedited are wonderful and you've demonized the edited. It's not so black and white."

"I'm not saying it is."

"Was the edited mind inside you lying about your plan?" Shada asked.

Chloe considered lying but knew her friend would be able to tell. "No," she said, hanging her head. "All the edited will be gone by the time I'm done. I made a promise to get rid of them."

"And that's why we're going to the train station. I want you to see the difference between the facilities controlled by unedited and those controlled by edited and tell me again they haven't done at least some things right."

"You're on their side," Chloe whispered, appalled.

"I'm on no one's side," Shada snapped. "I just know they aren't all bad. They've done good things as well."

"If you aren't on their side, why are you protecting them? Stop listening to Hollis and help me get rid of them," Chloe said. It was hard for her not to yell.

"We can't ignore the fact that the technology exists. It's not up to us to control it; people have to be given their own choice. It's about free will. You're trying to close Pandora's box after it's been opened."

Chloe was about to reply when Gustavo announced their arrival at the train station. He parked the SUV, and they all got out. Chloe had her backpack slung over her shoulders, and the other three carried nothing. Gustavo made sure the doors were locked and inspected the area where he had parked. His lips pinched together; he was forced to accept the vehicle might not be there when he returned or, if it was, odds were it would be vandalized.

Shada pointed to the tent community below the tracks. "These are the unedited. These are the people you want to elevate by eliminating an entire population of edited."

Chloe had seen many of them at regular intervals, had watched the kids grow taller as they aged. "They just need to be given a chance," she said.

"Not at the expense of others."

The four of them climbed the rusty stairs up to level of the train tracks, then paid to enter even though the turnstile was stuck open. Chloe's mind raced to come up with a response to Shada, to continue their debate, but when she looked at Shada's relaxed face, she couldn't imagine her friend thinking anything at all.

Chloe led the group to her usual spot on the platform and stood waiting for the train. "They made their fortune at our expense," Chloe said. She thought of Richard, then the memory of her grandfather the hijacks had stolen from her.

Shada looked at her friend. "An eye for an eye makes the whole world blind."

"What's that supposed to mean?"

"It means that your plan makes you the same as them, not better."

"They have to pay!" Chloe yelled. Right away, she descended back into her breath, kept it steady so there was no room for Valhall to reemerge. She was tired of arguing with her friend and resolved to keep her mouth shut.

"Look at the shadow from the pillar," Shada said. The sun

had, for a moment, peeked through the clouds. She must have been tired of arguing as well and found something in the physical world to focus on. "It makes a right angle with the tracks."

Chloe nodded.

"And points right at the clock."

She looked at the large analog clock, broken ever since she could remember, and saw the time: 3:41. She looked at her cell phone and saw the same time displayed. The synchronicity of the moment wasn't lost on her. She felt lucky to both be on the platform and notice the clock at the same time. It had to be fate, and she believed she was on the right path.

The shatter of glass on the tracks drew Chloe's attention. "What was that?" she asked.

Shada shrugged.

Chloe grew suspicious of her friend. For some reason, she thought that the shatter could have been the vial of serum in her backpack. She tore her backpack off her shoulder and found the serum right where it should have been. She looked at Tony and Gustavo, looking for some hint in their eyes they knew what had happened.

Neither of them looked at her.

The sun disappeared back behind the clouds, and the train pulled up, empty. They were the first stop on the trip into the heart of the city.

CHAPTER THIRTY-FOUR

THE TRAIN FILLED up with more passengers as it approached the hub in the center of the city. At first, a handful of people boarded. When they got on, they took seats far apart from one another, everyone leaving the seat next to them empty. The exceptions were Shada, Chloe, and their two male companions. The four of them sat in two rows of two seats, next to each other, with the two women closest to the window. Every stop added more passengers, groups of young men who chattered then giggled at their own crude jokes and elderly women who sat with their purses on their laps, patience evident in their posture. The seats filled up when they still had a few stops to go before their destination; more people would board than the number who disembarked, taking their place and forcing the leftovers to stand.

Tony and Shada sat in the row behind Chloe and Gustavo. Over the speaker, a voice announced that the next stop was the center of the city. Chloe felt Tony's face next to hers. He'd leaned forward to talk to Gustavo.

"Don't look, but have you seen the woman sitting at ten?" he said, referencing her position using the face of a clock.

Gustavo leaned his head closer to Tony but kept looking forward. "She's been staring," he said. "You think she recognizes Shada?"

Chloe leaned over Gustavo and into the center of the aisle, pretending to look out the window to the car in front of theirs. Through her peripherals she saw the woman the two guards referred to. Chloe's first thought was that the woman looked like a mother. The hair around her full face was frazzled and looked like it had been colored in the past. She was wearing tights and sneakers and had a large bag with her that looked like it came from a grocery store. Her eyes were locked on Shada.

"What harm could she do?" Fisher asked Chloe. Chloe ignored the edited mind inside her so she could remain in the moment and listen to Tony and Gustavo. She wondered why she hadn't noticed the woman herself and thought maybe Valhall had given up viewing the world through her eyes to search for threats.

Tony reminded Gustavo that, even untrained, she was still a threat. "Remember, she's still a two-hundred-pound primate. If she's been edited to be angry enough, she could make life very difficult."

"PCP," Gustavo said, referring to the drug.

"Exactly," replied Tony.

Gustavo asked about the plan.

"Well, if she doesn't do anything, we leave her alone."

"Maybe she thinks Shada's pretty," Chloe joked.

Neither man laughed.

"But if she makes a move, I want you to subdue her while I take the two of them to the platform," Tony said.

"And stay on the train if necessary?"

"We can't risk her getting off the train. If she's been edited, her anger might make her continue to attack, keeping you occupied off the train as well."

Gustavo paused.

"Don't even think about tranquilizing her," Tony said.

"I wasn't! I was thinking about choking her out."

"It won't happen fast enough. I can handle taking these two to the platform on my own."

Gustavo looked like he took Tony's assessment as a challenge but didn't press the issue. "But what if there are others?"

"That's an order," Tony said.

Gustavo nodded, all business.

The doors opened at the center of the city. There were lines of travelers waiting to board outside every door. About half the passengers on board the train began to get off. Chloe's group waited until they would be the last, then got up and rushed to get off. Tony made sure he was between the seated woman and Shada. As they passed the woman, she screamed.

"This is all your fault!" she said while rushing forward.

Gustavo, ahead of Tony and Shada, was prepared. He turned and grabbed the woman, one arm around her neck and the other hooked under her armpit. "I got her," he said.

Spittle collected at the corners of the enraged woman's mouth. "You think you can take advantage of us," she snarled. She thrashed against Gustavo's hold. "Let me go!" she yelled.

The other passengers did everything to ignore the unfolding scene. Some looked down, and others out the window. The few who couldn't ignore got up and moved to a different part of the car. Most of the people waiting outside the door Chloe was about to exit went left or right, to enter through others doors, while a handful of braver individuals squeezed past, as if the screaming woman and the man holding her were an obstacle they had to tolerate.

"Go, I got her," Gustavo said.

Tony ushered Chloe and Shada off the train. They turned around as the doors closed and watched the woman struggle.

Gustavo let her go once the train got moving. She threw herself against the glass and yelled at Shada, but her words couldn't be heard through the door. The last thing Chloe saw was Gustavo's stern face waiting for the woman's wrath to turn towards him.

"Let's keep moving," Tony said.

Chloe led the way, with Shada behind her and Tony bringing up the rear. They rushed through the station at a jog, fast enough to draw curious looks from everyone in the crowded hub.

Feelings of anxiety bubbled up in Chloe's stomach, like words that needed to be said, and she knew it was Valhall. Instead of allowing him to lash out, she let him take over the formation of words while keeping her mouth shut.

"Get out of here!" Valhall wanted to yell. Self-preservation overrode his hatred of Chloe.

Chloe didn't need to ask why. Everyone's attention, ill-intentioned or not, increased the chances of a threat.

Bypassing the escalator, she led them down the adjacent stairs, clearing two at a time. They passed another level before arriving at the private platform, breathing hard. They were alone. Nobody else was traveling to WestCorp on a random Saturday afternoon.

The screen lit up, telling them the train would arrive in eighteen minutes.

The three of them walked to the center of the platform. Chloe sat down on a concrete bench, which Shada used for support, while they both caught their breath. Tony was quick to recover. His focus was on the staircase leading to the platform.

Chloe knew, from the change in the time remaining until the tram arrived, that it took her two minutes for her breathing to return to normal. She realized her decision to communicate with Valhall, to release the built-up anxiety from his unsaid words, had saved her from dealing with him trying to take over while she didn't have complete control of her breath. She followed Tony's gaze and watched the staircase as well.

A pair of small feet appeared on the step just below the ceiling. Tiny sneakers, blue jeans. The feet went one step down, exposing the child up to their knees. Instead of continuing down the stairs, the child bent over; Chloe saw the messy dark brown ponytail of a young girl. The child's eyes got wide. "Mom!" the girl yelled. "Are these the ones you're looking for?"

Her feet disappeared.

When twelve minutes remained, the young girl and her mother stood at the bottom of the stairs. The mother yelled at Shada from behind Tony, who had stopped her from advancing onto the platform and now held the woman at gunpoint.

"All I wanted to do was provide for my daughter!" the woman yelled. Her child vacillated between sharing her mother's anger and being scared of the man with the gun in front of her.

The woman's screaming continued for five minutes, until the tram was seven minutes away. She hurled every obscenity she could think of at Shada, then at Tony for preventing her from attacking.

Chloe was grateful the gun kept her in place.

All of a sudden, the woman turned and ran back up the stairs. Her child struggled to keep up. Chloe could hear indistinct shouts from above. Tony listened, then turned back towards Shada and Chloe. "She's telling everyone up there that you're down here."

Chloe attempted some quick math, trying to determine how many people had received the negative edits and the likelihood of them being in the hub at the same time. She got lost in the numbers.

With just two minutes remaining, a group of five people, not counting the daughter, walked down the stairs. Their steady march struck more fear into Chloe than if they had run, and she felt her face flush red. Her stomach turned over, and she allowed Valhall space to communicate again. "Get out!" he wanted to yell.

There was nothing she could do but wait.

Tony swept his gun from left to right, taking steps back as he did so, threatening the group to stop their advance, but there were too many of them. Chloe took a look at the clock and saw the timer display just one minute remaining. She looked back at Tony and saw his chest rise with a deep inhale before he holstered his weapon. The mother was the first to run forward. Tony caught her with a straight arm and knocked her down. In the space it took for him to knock her down, another member of the group, a middle-aged man, rushed forward. Tony lunged out, grabbed the collar of his shirt, and yanked, pulling him to the ground as well.

Chloe had no doubt Tony could handle their attack, if they were all attacking him, but since they just needed to get past him, he was fighting a losing battle. The remaining three rushed forward, all with hate in their eyes, and Tony was able to grab one, leaving two free.

Shada and Chloe prepared to stand their ground. The tram was set to arrive at any moment, and they needed to somehow get on without their attackers. Chloe stood in front of Shada and prepared to fight the two young women who were barreling towards her.

They tried to run past Chloe, one on each side, their anger making Shada their sole focus. At the last moment she crouched, stuck out her arms, and held the two attackers by the waist.

"Let us go!" they demanded, striking her back with their fists.

"Get out of here," she yelled. They were Valhall's words.

Chloe screamed. Tears streamed down her face.

Out of nowhere the two attackers were pulled back. Gustavo had returned. They had been at the platform so long he must have been able to get off the train, turn around, catch another, and run down to the platform.

The tram pulled up, and Gustavo yelled for the two of them to get on while he held the attackers.

Chloe and Shada got onto the tram and watched as Tony and Gustavo fought to keep the five edited humans from getting onto the tram themselves. It was a strange sight, watching two experts struggle without having to worry about their own safety.

Their angry screams ceased as soon as the doors closed.

CHAPTER THIRTY-FIVE

CHLOE REACHED a hand up to her face and wiped away her tears. The liquid on her face smeared. She looked down at her hand and saw blood, bright red, on the back of her hand.

The poison she'd taken that morning was starting to kick in.

Chloe shook her head, confused. She'd taken the antidote. She thought back to her time in the bathroom, her inspection of the bottle. Was the antidote compromised? Had it gone bad with a broken seal? She hadn't noticed anything unusual. She cursed herself for not bringing a backup dose with her.

She felt faint and used one of the seats on the tram for support, leaving blood on the stainless steel.

Shada stared at her. "You should sit down," she said.

Chloe didn't need to be told twice. Her stomach roiled. She attributed it to Valhall but didn't want to hear what the island's head of security had to say. Fisher's voice crept into her mind. "We aren't going to make it, are we?"

She knew there wasn't much time left once blood began leaking from the eyes. She wasn't sure that, even if she did have another dose of the antidote, it would do any good. Chloe looked at Shada, at the two thin scars that descended from her eyes, and chuckled to herself when she realized that the two people in the world who had captured a mind inside themselves had experienced blood running down their cheeks. A strange coincidence even Alfie couldn't have predicted.

The knot in her stomach continued to tighten, and she wasn't sure if it was because of Valhall or due to her impending death. She allowed Valhall to talk, not bothering to control her mouth.

"Someone switched the antidote," Valhall-in-Chloe said, the voice deeper than normal.

Shada nodded, an admission. Chloe felt like the air was taken out of both her and the tram as they both sped beneath the city.

"You . . . why?" Chloe croaked. She felt light-headed and lay down on the floor of the tram after placing her backpack on a seat.

"You had to be stopped," Shada said. There wasn't a hint of second-guessing in her friend's voice, no regret at the permanence of her decision.

"Stopped? We were in this together!"

"You wanted to eliminate the edited. They're humans too. You seem to have forgotten that."

Chloe closed her eyes and felt the tram shift on the tracks side to side as it traveled.

"When?" Chloe said.

"You were in the bathroom and left your pants in the living room. I put the antidote in a small jar and replaced it with glass cleaner. At the time I thought it was the poison."

"But it was blue."

"I never knew what color the poison and antidote were. I thought you had too much confidence after the capture of your first mind and didn't want you to take it before uploading Ruby."

Chloe thought for a moment. "This was before you knew about the third mind," she said.

"Correct, and I didn't know you had poisoned yourself earlier. But once I found out you'd captured the guard, I guessed I was in possession of the antidote. I was going to give it back until I found out about your plan to make the edited pay."

"No! That's not fair. This was all for the unedited."

"The lengths you are willing to go . . . you don't even realize what you've become."

Chloe had no response. After a pause in their conversation she said, "Give it to me and we'll go back to the city."

"I don't have it," Shada said.

Chloe knew where the antidote was. She opened her eyes. "You threw it onto the tracks," she said.

Shada closed her eyes and nodded.

Chloe thought she should be more upset at her friend for allowing her to die. Instead, she felt a wave of relief wash over her. She remembered her grandfather's farm, being next to the old man as he picked an orange from the tree, and hoped the sense of comfort the memory used to bring would rush back once she drew her last breath.

Shada sat down and looked at her friend. Chloe felt more liquid leak from her eyes and knew her time was drawing to an end.

"You have to capture as many minds as possible," Chloe told Shada.

"It doesn't work like that," Shada said.

"Do this, for me. I'm not saying you have to eliminate the edited, but the more minds you can gather, the more you can help. Think about your sister, create the world for her."

Shada took a deep breath. Chloe wondered if Hollis needed to be subdued or if the breath was to control her own emotions. She hoped it was the latter.

"Alfie will help. He's the only one who knows it's even possible," Chloe said.

Shada looked like she wanted to argue but instead told Chloe she had no intention of working with the scientist. "You put too much faith in him."

"What other choice do you have? You're already headed to the island."

"I know," Shada said. It was the first time in a long time Chloe sensed uncertainty in her friend's voice.

Fisher couldn't believe Chloe still considered Shada a friend. "She's the one who let you die!" he yelled inside her head.

Chloe explained to Fisher that Shada was doing what she thought was best.

"And still you defend her," Fisher shot back.

Chloe blocked her mind off to the edited mind, choosing to spend her last moments in reality instead of in her head.

The tram pulled out from beneath the city and began its climb to the height of the tracks over the bay. Shada looked at the island in the distance. "They're going to be waiting for me," she said.

It occurred to Chloe that Valhall might be able to reverse the train. She had to say the question out loud in order to find out. "Is it possible to send the tram back to the city?" she said.

Valhall answered right away, without pausing to think. "Of course."

Shada looked confused for a moment before she realized her friend was communicating with the voice inside her head.

Chloe gathered her strength, turned over, and crawled to an interface next to the door. She managed to stand up and rested a hand against the wall for support. "Reverse it," she commanded.

She waited for Valhall to take control of her hand, but he didn't take the initiative.

"Shada's going there to attack Ruby. You're supposed to protect the island," Chloe said.

Appealing to Valhall's sense of duty did the trick. He pressed a series of buttons on the touch screen and the tram slowed, then stopped, midway between the island and the city. A few more commands, followed by a prompt for a code, were entered, and the tram began to go back the way it came.

Chloe collapsed. Shada kneeled down next to her.

"I'm sorry," Shada said.

"You did what you thought was right."

"There are people on the platform who want revenge," Shada said. She retrieved the gun from the back of Chloe's pants.

"Tony and Gustavo are there to help you," Chloe said.

Shada returned to Chloe's side but didn't say anything.

Chloe closed her eyes. The strength it took to keep them open was too much to bear. She took a deep breath before appealing to Shada one last time. "Think about what you could do with multiple edited minds uploaded into you. You don't want to eliminate the edited? Then don't. But don't squander your gift. Do what you were made to do and change the world."

Shada looked out at the city they were fast approaching. "The city was created because humans worked together," she said.

"Let them work inside your mind to create the future," Chloe croaked.

Shada wasn't listening. She was talking to herself while Chloe was talking to her. "Without direction," she said.

"You can provide it. Both sides just need someone to bridge the gap," Chloe said.

A change in the air let Chloe know these words had punctured Shada's soliloquy. She focused on her labored breaths. Blood continued to leak from her eyes, never allowing the spilt blood to dry. The last thing she heard was the gun being cocked, then a shot fired and the shattering of glass. Air rushed in as the tram raced towards the city.

"Goodbye, Chloe," Shada said.

Chloe sensed she was the sole person on the tram. But she wasn't alone. There was Fisher, and Valhall, existing in the background of her consciousness. And her grandfather's smiling face waiting ahead of her. She exhaled for the last time and felt the comfort she had missed wash over her.

The skeleton of a memory persists long after the associated feeling has passed, a barren structure the mind can no longer fill. When Chloe's life ended, she was able to realize her ultimate dream, to leave the city and return to life on a farm, by bringing her memory back to life.

The decay of her body began when she drew her last breath. The collection of atoms that constituted her flesh would fall away, leaving just bones behind, until those too returned to the earth.

Death intensifies decay, but it's memory's sole protection against time.

THE EDITED GENOME TRILOGY

ABSOLUTION

Marcos Antonio Hernandez

CHAPTER ONE

THERE IS a distinct difference between killing someone and letting them die.

What if the person destined for expiration is in pain? Letting them die could be a mercy. And if the person will be the cause of someone else's pain in the future? The mercy extends to those who would be affected.

Time will tell, and time has no voice.

Shada watched Chloe on the tram, waiting for the poison present in her friend's system to take its toll. She had destroyed the antidote and knew there wasn't long before her friend found out.

Could death be the ultimate escape? Chloe would no longer have to struggle, no longer have to remember, and this in and of itself could be Shada's final gift to her.

The tram sped along the track towards WestCorp's island headquarters, where everyone's genomes were edited to make them happier, healthier, and smarter. Shada and Chloe were headed back to where it had all begun, where, excited at the prospect of their new futures, they'd first arrived to have their own genetic codes edited. Instead, they'd both ended up hosting the minds of now-dead edited humans. Shada reminisced about this trip, the first time they'd met. Chloe, her face dotted with piercings, had been ready to escape the rat race by signing a contract for twenty years of employment on the island in exchange for her edits. Shada's future playing the sport she loved had been ripped away because of a small mutation in her DNA, and she was prepared to sign the same contract and work for the company to help her sister and begin paying down her debt.

The certainty of being happier because of the edits was icing on the cake for both, a way to gain control over their emotions by eliminating the negative ones from existence. But they'd never thought experiencing those negative emotions would be desirable for those who were born without them.

Shada was pulled from her memory when she heard Michael Hollis, the former leader of WestCorp whose mind now resided in her body, cackle in the furthest recesses of her mind. She wondered if he'd influenced her decision to toss the antidote, Chloe's antidote, onto the tracks. Together, they were on their way to kill Michael's wife, Ruby. Could Hollis's captured mind, inside Shada, have been scheming a way to save the woman's life?

Shada wasn't sure she had made the decision on her own.

Tears of blood leaked from Chloe's pale blue eyes, and she wiped them away with the back of her hand. Shada's friend, who had submitted to the implant of a second mind, realized the poison was taking hold, and she looked at Shada with confused eyes.

"You should sit down," Shada said.

Chloe studied Shada's face and a thin smile spread across her lips. Then she said, in a deep voice Shada recognized as the edited mind in control of her friend's body, that someone had switched the antidote.

Shada nodded.

Chloe placed her backpack on the seat next to her with a dull thud from the weight of the gun inside. She then lay on the floor of the tram with her hands across her chest. "Why?" she asked.

"You had to be stopped," Shada replied.

"Stopped? We were in this together!" Chloe said.

"You wanted to eliminate the edited. They're humans too. You seem to have forgotten that."

Once Chloe's plan had been put into motion, her death seemed, to Shada, the most obvious way to terminate it. If Shada hadn't taken action, she felt she would be no better than the edited, whose plan was to force the unedited humans to destroy themselves.

Chloe closed her eyes. A moment passed, then she croaked, "When?"

Shada knew she was referring to how the antidote had gotten switched. She told her friend how she had taken the antidote while Chloe was in the bathroom, then confessed to throwing it on the tracks. She knelt down next to Chloe, who opened her eyes. More blood leaked out and caught in her eyelashes, macabre red mascara.

"You have to capture as many minds as possible," Chloe urged.

A wave of nausea washed over Shada. She already had two minds residing in her body, hers and Michael Hollis's, and the thought of trying to maintain an equilibrium with a third, or fourth, was a burden she didn't want to bear. "It doesn't work like that," she said.

"Do this, for me. I'm not saying you have to eliminate the edited, but the more minds you can gather, the more you can help. Think about your sister, create the world for her."

Shada bristled at the mention of Sikya and took a deep breath to focus herself.

"Alfie will help. He's the only one who knows it's even possible," Chloe said, referring to Alfie Reynolds-Grant, the head scientist for WestCorp and the intellectual leader on the island.

"You put too much faith in him," Shada said.

"What other choice do you have? You're already headed to the island."

"I know," Shada said with resignation. She thought about Ruby Hollis, left in charge of the company when her husband's mind was captured by Shada. Ruby had been hunting Shada in search of revenge and would be grateful when her quarry showed up on her doorstep.

Shada looked through the window as the tram emerged into daylight and watched the approach of the distorted outline of the corporation's compound as they crossed the bridge that spanned the bay. "They're going to be waiting for me," she said.

"Is it possible to send the tram back to the city?" Chloe said, her eyes on the ceiling.

"Of course," Chloe said right away, in a deeper voice.

Shada knew her friend wasn't talking to her, that she was communicating with the captured mind of the island's former head of security, trapped inside her head. Together, she and Chloe had figured out that speaking questions out loud was the best way to get answers from the gatekeeper, whose modified DNA made him unable to maintain an internal dialogue. Shada appreciated the beauty of WestCorp's design, to make sure any of the massive security personnel's thoughts were said out loud. In possession of superior strength and size, they could wreak havoc for the island's inhabitants if they were allowed to plot amongst themselves.

Chloe set her jaw, turned over, and clawed towards an interface next to the door. She stood up and leaned against the wall for support, smearing the surface with blood. "Reverse it," she said.

The tram continued to barrel towards the island while Chloe stood still.

Going back to the city didn't solve Shada's problem. When she and Chloe had pulled out of the station, they'd left behind a group of people who wanted to tear Shada apart. Ruby had edited them, for free, to be angry and impulsive, then informed them Shada was to blame. A powder keg of people had been sent back to the mainland city to find and destroy her, with the fuse lit by Ruby. The one reason returning to the city was better than returning to the island was that Tony and Gustavo, members of a group dedicated to combating the spread of West-Corp's reach, had stayed behind on the platform to fight the horde. Their efforts had given the two women time to escape. Shada might have a chance of survival if those two were still alive.

"Shada's going there to attack Ruby. You're supposed to protect the island," Chloe said to the mind of the gatekeeper in her head.

A moment later, Chloe's hand rose up and pressed a series of buttons, stopping the tram, before another series of buttons sent them back in the direction from where they'd come. She collapsed.

Shada kneeled next to her. "I'm sorry," she said, and meant it.

"You did what you thought was right."

Shada realized she had a third option. Her choice of where to go wasn't black or white, life or death, and she wished she could have discovered a third option for Chloe before she'd destroyed the antidote. "There are people on the platform who want revenge," she said as she retrieved the gun from Chloe's backpack before returning to Chloe's side.

"Tony and Gustavo are there to help you." Chloe closed her eyes and sighed. "Think about what you could do with multiple edited minds uploaded into you. You don't want to eliminate the edited? Then don't. But don't squander your gift. Do what you were made to do and change the world."

Shada felt tears well up, and she turned before they could fall. The buildings along the water's edge cast shadows onto the bay, imposing pillars of metal she would have to pass beneath if she wanted to return. "The city was created because humans worked together," she said, her voice drifting off. It struck her how the sprawl had grown over generations to become an amorphous blob. "Without direction," she added. How much better could it be if someone had taken charge?

"You can provide it. Both sides just need someone to bridge the gap," Chloe managed to choke out. Her breathing was labored, and the strain from trying to take in oxygen turned her into a pale white specter writhing on the floor, her closed eyes making her form seem even less human.

Shada stood, cocked the gun, and fired at the window. Air rushed through the shattered glass. She stood on a pair of seats and kicked away enough glass for her body to pass through the opening. She looked back at her friend, said goodbye, and jumped.

CHAPTER TWO

WIND RUSHED past Shada's face as she fell. The sudden acceleration caused her breath to catch in her chest. She tried to keep her feet pointed below her, but the speed she'd acquired from riding the train tilted her body backwards. Time stood still for the few seconds of her free fall, and the moment she hit the water, she felt a sharp slap on the back of her legs and her backside.

She plunged deep into the water and threw her hands out to the side in order to arrest her descent. The cold water almost ripped the breath from her body, but with a conscious effort, she was able to keep the air in her lungs. She kicked out the instant she reached her maximum depth, and all four limbs scrambled to work together on her swim back to the surface. She sensed she must be close to the air above and fought the instinct to open her eyes. Her efforts to resurface continued longer than she felt possible, but still surrounded by water, she had no choice but to continue. Panic set in, and she heard Hollis laugh.

An exhale when her head emerged was followed by a shallow inhale and a mouthful of water. Treading water, she opened her eyes, allowing the world around her to come into focus. She was closer to the city than to the island, in the long shadows of the tallest buildings. She was grateful, because she knew nothing good could come from arriving on the island. If she could make it to the city, she at least stood a chance. She took one last look at the island before she began to swim towards the city and witnessed a craft surface halfway between her and land. It was white, with a bubble on top, and as the vehicle sped to her location, she saw the bubble withdraw. Although the boat was far in the distance, she could tell there were two people on board, speeding towards her.

Shada swam towards the city's shoreline. While in motion, she took stock of her situation and noticed her frantic strokes were unsustainable. She had the composure to realize that with a more controlled cadence, she could save energy without sacrificing the time it took for her to cover the distance, so she focused on being smooth and gliding through the water. She knew that this would give her the best chance of success to make it to the city while leaving some energy for her to deal with capture if the boat caught up to her before she reached safety.

The boat caught up with her while the shore was still far off. It blew past her, and the driver positioned the craft perpendicular across her path.

"Climb onto the boat," one of the men on the boat said to her with the confident air of someone used to being in charge. The boat's passengers were both middle-aged men, clean-shaven, and wore matching dark long-sleeved shirts and dark baseball caps.

Shada studied their faces and checked Hollis's memory for any recollection. He didn't know who they were, but she found out their uniform was worn by members of the WestCorp coast guard.

"You don't really have a choice," Hollis said to Shada, the dialogue occurring inside her mind.

Shada shook her head in response to the captured mind, convinced there was another option. The two men on the boat assumed her gesture was directed at them. The man who wasn't driving reached down, pulled out a wide-barreled weapon, and pointed it at her. "We can do this the hard way if you want," he said with a sneer.

Shada laughed despite her exhaustion. Keeping her head above water was wearing her out, and she knew she couldn't do it for much longer. She was grateful she'd learned to swim when she was young but knew she was so out of practice that her inefficiency was forcing her to work harder than necessary. "Are you going to harpoon me?" she said, even though she didn't see a projectile emerging from the barrel.

The driver of the boat laughed. The man holding the weapon told her, his tone serious, he would shoot the net over her. "Hopefully you don't drown. But don't worry, we'll fish you out."

"Wouldn't be the first time," the driver added.

It was obvious to Shada she had to climb on the boat, but she wanted to maintain her defiance a bit longer. She stared at the two men while treading water, and after a few seconds gave them a tiny nod. The man let the end of the weapon fall as Shada began to swim towards the boat. When she reached the edge, they grabbed a hold of her, one hand beneath each of her armpits, and pulled her up. The moment she collapsed into the boat, a small gun was pressed against her upper arm, the trigger pulled, and she felt the sharp pain of a quick injection. Her surroundings faded from sight.

Shada had no idea how much time had passed before she heard Hollis say, "That was unpleasant." Her eyes were still closed. She'd had no sense of awareness before hearing the captured mind communicate with her, and she wondered if Hollis had been active while she was passed out or if he'd come back from the darkness the exact moment she did. A sobering thought gripped her: What if Hollis became the first object of her awareness every time she woke up? He had access to the space between sleep and wakefulness, between dreams and reality, and if he wanted, he could haunt these times without restriction.

"Sounds like a lot of work," Hollis replied.

Shada hated when he listened to her internal dialogue. She had learned how to keep her thoughts hidden from him, but in her transition state she didn't use the skill. She never bothered trying to block his access to the sensory input of the world around her and wasn't sure she could if she tried. Hollis wasn't able to keep his thoughts hidden from her, evidenced by her ability to probe the full catalog of his memories. As far as she knew, her own memories stayed inaccessible to him, unless he was thumbing through them while she slept, in which case she would never find out.

Red mixed with multicolored spots filled Shada's field of vision, the light beyond her eyes illuminating the blood in her eyelids. She opened her eyes narrow enough that her eyelashes provided a filter against the brightness, and all she could discern was whiteness. She consulted Hollis, asking him instead of probing his knowledge base if he knew where they might be.

"No idea. Definitely on the island though, they wouldn't let you go," he replied.

Over the course of the next several minutes, she worked up to having her eyes open but never readjusted from her original position of lying on her right side. She discovered she was in a small padded room. The floors, walls, and ceiling in her field of vision were all a bright white and composed of padded squares.

She lay still and took stock of her body. She could tell how weak she was and assumed it was from the events leading up to and on the tram, capped off with the plunge into the bay and subsequent swim. Without any knowledge of the time that had elapsed since those events, she couldn't be sure. Her weakness could just as well be from lack of movement over a long period of time. Or, since the facilities on the island were able to upload a mind into another body, could her captors have kept her unconscious while someone else had control of her? She doubted it, since either she or Hollis would have become aware, even if in the background, but the possibility scared her into greater alertness.

Shada decided the reason for her physical weakness didn't matter, that it was a state to be dealt with, and since there were no physical threats present to deal with, she would worry only if it became an issue.

Sitting up, she realized her clothes had been changed. She was now wearing a white gown, like a patient in a hospital. An inspection of her surroundings revealed that the padding's sole deviations were a small handle and space for the doorframe. Shada crossed her legs and began counting her breaths, focusing on both the inhale and exhale, reconnecting with her body, her way of making sure she kept control of her limbs away from Hollis. When the implanted mind had still been new, before she knew what she was doing, she'd thought Hollis had gained control for good, shutting her off from her own body. She'd responded by trying to kill herself. It didn't work, and in the end she became better for the experience, but she never wanted to let her guard down and lose control again.

Ten breaths passed, then twenty, and over time she lost count, absorbed in being in the present moment, experiencing the sensations passing through her body as they arose. A click rang out, and she opened her eyes.

"Shada. Welcome back," a woman's voice said.

Shada didn't need the captured mind inside her to confirm that the voice belonged to Ruby.

CHAPTER THREE

SHADA LOOKED around the padded room, trying to find a microphone, or a speaker, or a camera. Finding none, she stayed facing the direction she was sitting and talked to the open air around her.

"What do you want?" she said.

"You took something that belongs to us," the bodiless voice of Ruby replied.

Hollis laughed. "I didn't belong to anyone, not even her," he said.

Nobody but Shada could hear his response.

Shada didn't say a word. Her first instinct was to disengage, to wait and see what the woman who held her captive wanted. She heard Ruby sigh into the microphone.

"Look, I know Michael was uploaded into you. But I need to know how much you know about what we do here. Can you read his thoughts? Or have you kept him locked away, banished in the basement?"

Shada wished she knew where the camera was so she could stare into it and still not say a word.

"We can do this the easy way, or the hard way," Ruby said,

exasperated. She sounded like a woman at wit's end, tired of the game.

Something in Ruby's voice made Shada decide to cooperate. She'd never planned to be back on the island and had no energy to resist any longer. "I can," she said, admitting she could access the memories of the former leader of the island corporation.

There was a momentary silence before Ruby spoke again. "Where did we meet?"

"I believe you were in Chloe's body and brushed my cheek when we were in Hollis's office."

"Not you and me, idiot," Ruby snarled. "Michael and I."

Shada delved into the catalog of Hollis's memories, searching for the first time they met. "You two were in school together, on the island. You were a few years younger than him, but he knew who you were. Your meeting was arranged by WestCorp as a potential match, for breeding purposes. You had two children and raised them in a house by the water."

Shada's account of Michael and Ruby's past was met with silence. It must have been enough to satisfy Ruby, because when she spoke again, she asked Shada what her favorite flower was.

Hollis himself supplied the answer. "She never liked flowers, thought they were frivolous," he told Shada. Shada relayed the message to the empty room.

"So you know everything about WestCorp," Ruby said, her voice trailing off.

"Or can find out. To be honest, I haven't bothered to investigate because I don't care. I tried to leave what you do, or did, on the island behind. I assume there have been some changes since you've been in charge."

"There have been a few," Ruby admitted.

"He didn't know about this room, for one," Shada admitted.

"It's new. Built in case we got a hold of you. If you wanted to leave the island behind, why did you come back?"

It was a good question, one Shada couldn't provide a clear answer to. "Chloe thought it was important."

"But she died on the way here," Ruby said.

"She did." From the tone of Ruby's voice, Shada guessed the woman didn't know she was the one who'd allowed Chloe to die by destroying the antidote. She again wondered how much time had passed since she'd been pulled from the water and if the tram car holding Chloe's body had been returned to the island, the body removed, and the window fixed.

There was a click, and Shada knew the conversation was finished. She sat up and returned to counting her breaths. The breath work was a gateway into the true source of her control over Hollis: the ability to find her heartbeat and follow its resonance to every limb in her body. The low dose of modified LSD provided by Alfie, designed to allow Hollis to maintain control, had exposed Shada to the concept and resulted in Hollis losing control of her body for good. The resonance of her heartbeat had first surfaced in the presence of other unedited humans, the synchronization making her own heartbeat easier to detect, but after practicing while she was in hiding from WestCorp, she had learned to focus on its steady rhythm alone and without the drug.

After an unknown length of time, the door opened, and one of the massive humans bred to be a security guard—the same type of edited human whose mind had been Chloe's second upload—walked in. He appeared unsure of his footing; each step was taken with a deliberateness bordering on caution. Shada realized he was bracing himself for action every time both feet were on the ground, assuming she might run or attack, even though he was bigger than Shada by half. In his hand was a large clear glass containing a thick white liquid, which he held out to Shada without saying a word.

"What is it?" Shada asked. She took the glass for the simple reason it was held out for her to take.

"Drink," the giant grunted.

Shada smelled the liquid and detected sweet hints of vanilla. Still seated, she looked into the guard's face. His features were oversized, like the rest of his body, with an enormous round nose, deep-set eyes, a heavy brow, and a large mouth. He nodded with his chin and raised his eyebrows, urging Shada to drink. He didn't smile, but Shada felt the gesture was his form of connecting.

There were four large mouthfuls of liquid to consume, and Shada took them one after the other. The taste wasn't bad, but it had a certain thickness she found off-putting. The guard stayed until Shada finished the drink, then took the glass back with him when he left.

Shada felt sick to her stomach from all the liquid, so she lay down to let it settle. She stayed there a long time, satisfied with existing, and felt herself drifting off to sleep. Whoever was monitoring the prisoner must have been able to tell, because a loud beep rang out from the direction of the door. Nobody ever entered.

It wasn't until the third time this happened that she realized they were keeping her awake. She wondered if, as she got more tired and closer to falling asleep regardless of interruptions, there would be an escalation of methods to complete their assignment. She got her answer after two more occasions of being thrust into wakefulness.

She was determined to fall asleep despite the beep, but the door opened as she drifted off. The change in stimulus was successful, and her eyes watched the opening door while her head stayed still. She assumed it would be one of the massive guards again and was taken aback when she recognized the normal-sized man who walked into her small room. It was Alfie Reynolds-Grant, the head scientist, the man who'd uploaded Hollis's mind into her body and insisted she call him by his first name.

"Alfie!" Shada exclaimed, sitting upright so fast she became dizzy. He had shaved off his beard, but his gray hair looked to be the same length and still had thin wisps sticking out at odd angles.

"Hello, Shada," Alfie said. In his hand was a small gun, the same type as the one used by the men on the boat to tranquilize her.

Shada scrambled away. Her limbs were heavy and movements sluggish. The last time she'd received an injection of this kind, she'd lost track of time and woke up in the padded room.

Alfie approached Shada, staring at her with the kind eyes of a grandfather.

"What's that?" Shada asked, her chin gesturing to the weapon in his hand. The juxtaposition of it in contrast with his demeanor kept her on high alert, uncertain about how to respond.

"Just a quick injection," Alfie said. He took a step forward, and Shada slid along the wall. "Please don't make this more difficult than it has to be," Alfie said. "I can always call one of the guards in here to hold you in place."

Shada's skin crawled at the thought of being touched by one of the massive humans. She set her jaw and withdrew from the wall she was pasted on. When she got close, Alfie held out the gun, and Shada put her upper arm up to the end of the barrel. Alfie pulled the trigger.

Her heart began to race, and her first thought was to get it under control so that Hollis couldn't take over her body. She didn't make any effort to hide her reservations from Hollis, who assured her he wouldn't waste a takeover of her body in a room where he couldn't "do a damned thing."

"What was that?" Shada asked Alfie, her eyes wide. He had made his way to the door and was halfway through.

Alfie paused, leaned back to look at her, and said, "Stim," before walking out.

CHAPTER FOUR

Shada, sitting against the wall farthest from the door, began a series of rapid breaths in order to give her body somewhere to expend the excess energy caused by the Stim. She consulted with Hollis about the injection device that had twice been used on her, asking him outright instead of taking the time to probe his memories. "They used the same thing to knock me out on the boat," she said.

"It was a prototype when I was still around, simmering on the back burner, to be developed if we needed increased control over visitors from the city," Hollis informed her.

Shada focused on her breathing while waiting for the captured mind inside her to continue.

"The Stim was a different project. The ultimate goal was to create a method for physical labor enhancement, one that each person could shoot into themselves whenever they felt their body was slowing down. Workers would require less sleep and experience maintained or increased output. I suggested we package the substance in independent vials workers could inject themselves, since everyone experiences fatigue at different rates based on food consumption, sleep, and baseline fitness."

"If everyone had an injection gun, it wouldn't be hard to use it on themselves," Shada thought, in response to Hollis.

Before Hollis could respond, the door to Shada's room flung open and a massive guard filled the doorframe. Shada, still taking rapid breaths, met his gaze. The guard grinned with delight and seemed to enjoy watching Shada struggle with the Stim's effects. "Let's go," he said, tilting his head to the right before turning around.

Shada didn't wait for another invitation. She stood up and walked out, following the guard out the door and turning left. She passed a second guard stationed outside her room to the right, and the man began following her. Walking barefoot between the two large humans, she recognized Hollis's underground bunker. She was led to the elevator that would take her to the island's surface; the heavy footsteps of the guards reverberated off the high stone ceilings of the cave.

"They've been busy down here," Hollis told Shada.

"I wonder what they did with your body," Shada thought, communicating with Hollis by thought. The upload of Hollis's mind into Shada had been performed down the hall in the opposite direction, leaving his former body an empty shell. In theory, it could still be kept alive, but what use could someone have for the brain-dead body of a man with a terminal illness?

"Who's to say they haven't kept it warm for me to come back to?" Hollis said with a laugh.

The guards in front of and behind Shada had no idea she was communicating with Hollis. All they heard was her heavy breathing.

The two guards and Shada took the elevator to the surface and walked outside to a sun that was low in the sky. Around the entrance to the bunker was a square area surrounded by a chain-link fence with barbed wire above, and there were four more guards outside the enclosure, one at each corner. Against the fence on the side closest to the sun lay a medium-sized dog, dusty brown with flecks of gray around its face. When it saw people emerge from the bunker, its head lifted and tail wagged.

Shada stopped when the guard in front of her stood on one side of the door. The guard behind her pushed her forward. "Exercise," he said.

She didn't need to be told twice. Turning to the right, she set off at a jog with Stim coursing through her veins. The dog, sensing it was time to play, joined her as she ran back and forth, touching one side of the chain-link fence before turning around and heading towards the opposite side. Each time she turned around, the dog jumped up and got ready to play, under the impression that when Shada turned around the game was about to begin. During one of these jumps, Shada discovered her canine companion was male.

This routine continued until the sun had risen in the sky. By then, her legs felt weak, but pure energy still coursed through her veins. She dropped to the ground and performed push-ups, with the intention of continuing until her arms gave out, but the dog wouldn't leave her alone and kept trying to lick her face. She gave up and began playing with the animal instead. She had never seen a dog outside of a cage on the island, and she wondered if they'd brought it out just for her.

The two of them created a game where she would slap her hands against the ground, and the dog would respond by leaning forward onto his forepaws, keeping his hindquarters high in the air, at which point Shada would crawl forward until their heads came into contact. Over time, the dog got worked up and yelped, at which point one of the guards stationed at the bunker door spoke up for the first time since she'd first walked outside.

"Jax!" the guard said.

The dog's tail dropped, and it slinked away.

"That's enough for today," the guard informed Shada. "Time to go back inside."

Shada stood up and became aware of her dirty hands, feet, and knees. The guards must have noticed too, because instead of taking her back to the padded room, they continued through the bunker to the end of the hall, through the large open space that housed the kitchen and large table, into Hollis's bedroom, which was adjacent to the room where the initial upload had taken place. The door to the upload room was closed, so in theory Hollis's body could still be behind the door.

The guards ushered her into Hollis's bathroom and commanded her to take a shower. She removed her gown and bathed, taking pleasure in watching the brown water disappear down the drain. When she finished, she found her soiled gown had been taken away and a fresh one was hanging on the back of the door.

Shada expected to see the guards outside the bathroom, waiting in Hollis's bedroom, but they weren't there. She was about to look through the space, both out of her own curiosity and to give Hollis the chance to look at his old stuff again, but a woman's voice called out to her from outside the bedroom.

"Shada, are you finished in there?" It was Ruby, her voice full of a sickening artificial sweetness.

Shada's jaw clenched, and a tide of rage surged to her extremities. She didn't allow the feelings to linger, afraid she wouldn't be able to maintain control over Hollis, and she took ten slow breaths to calm down and stay present before walking out.

Ruby was seated next to Alfie in the two chairs closest to Hollis's bedroom. The black stone wall behind them glittered from where the light caught its jagged edges, reminding Shada of numerous stars looking down on her from the night sky. The guards stood on each side of the door to Hollis's bedroom. Ruby gestured to the seat across from her. "Sit down," she said.

Shada knew she had no choice in the matter. Flanked by the two guards, she approached then sat down in the seat she was told to occupy. Both guards stood behind her.

"How are you doing?" Ruby asked.

In an instant, Shada checked in with her body and found the Stim was still keeping her in an elevated state. "What do you want?" she said.

Ruby turned to Alfie. "All business," she said. "I like that."

Alfie shrugged.

She turned back to Shada. "I'm going to need to upload into you to talk to my husband."

Shada stared at Ruby. Unlike Chloe, Shada had never wanted to upload another mind. Her apprehension must have been painted on her face, because Ruby tried to assuage her fears.

"It won't be permanent, not at all! I like my body," Ruby said. "It can be quick, but I need you to agree to it."

"Why? You could just knock me out."

"If you're knocked out, Hollis will be too," Alfie said.

"You could restrain me."

"I've considered it," Ruby admitted. "But you've already demonstrated the ability to keep control over Hollis. If you choose to maintain control and keep us separated, it would be a waste of both our time for me to go inside."

Shada checked in with Hollis while waiting for Ruby to continue. He was curious about what his wife could want to discuss.

"Alfie will make sure we don't go past the agreed-upon length of time. We can do it right there," Ruby said, gesturing to the room where Michael Hollis had uploaded into Shada.

Both Shada and Hollis were curious about what was behind

the closed door, to see if his body had been removed. "If Alfie can guarantee it will only be for an hour," Shada said. "And you'll let me sleep after."

"Two," countered Ruby.

Shada crossed her arms and leaned back.

Ruby studied Shada's face before her shoulders fell and she agreed to one hour. "And no more beeps."

"Let's get it over with," Shada said. Alfie stood up and led Ruby to the upload room, telling Shada he'd call her in when everything was set up.

CHAPTER FIVE

WHATEVER HOPE Shada had had that Ruby would scream at the sight of her husband's brain-dead body evaporated as soon as Alfie and Ruby opened the door. The room was small, so there was no way a dead body could be missed. Minutes ticked by before Alfie told Shada to come inside.

The guards attempted to follow Shada into the small room, but a look from Alfie told them to stay outside. "I'll call you if you're needed," he told them.

Ruby was lying on the same table her husband had been on the last time Shada was inside the room. She already had the modified helmet with its multicolored wires over her head. Her eyes were closed, her arms folded on her chest. With her wrinkles still visible on her resting face, Shada found it hard to believe this was the woman who held her captive.

"You know what to do," Alfie told Shada, using his lips to gesture to the second table.

Shada climbed onto the stainless steel table and put the second modified helmet over her head. Her gown had ridden up and exposed the skin on the backs of her legs to the cold table, but she didn't bother to adjust herself. "One hour," she said.

"One hour," Alfie replied, pushing a series of buttons on a computer between the tables.

Shada crossed her arms over her stomach and closed her eyes. "Let's get this over with," she said.

She didn't have to wait long. Moments later, Alfie initiated the upload, and Shada was plunged into darkness. The process was designed so that the mind of the person being uploaded into would be shoved to the background, forced to exist in a vacuum, while whoever uploaded was free to use the new body as they saw fit. Shada had figured out—and shared the knowledge with Chloe—how to come back from the darkness then use the breath to take initial control back from the uploaded mind. That's what she did the instant she found herself surrounded by darkness.

It was like looking out from the bottom of a well towards a small circle of light in the distance. Instead of moving towards the light, the light had to be allowed to grow larger, like looking at a star in the sky using peripheral vision to sense the absence of darkness instead of staring directly at the light. Once the light grew large enough, the world could be seen through her own eyes, and hearing came once the darkness at the periphery disappeared. With hearing came a small recognition of the breath, and once the breath could be controlled, the body was back in the control of its original owner.

It had taken Shada days to figure this out the first time, and it had almost cost her her life. Chloe had been able to replicate the process twice and seemed to be comfortable doing so. This time, with both Ruby and Michael Hollis uploaded into Shada, and therefore neither of them able to slow her down, the process of coming back from the darkness was instantaneous.

"That was fast," Hollis remarked. "She just got in here!"

"Leave us alone!" Ruby screamed.

"It's no use, honey, she's in control now," Hollis said to his wife. He asked Shada not to hold the outburst against her.

"I don't need or want her forgiveness!" Ruby said, continuing her tantrum.

Shada severed the communication between the two voices in her head and looked at the room around her. Alfie was staring at the monitor. He seemed to sense Shada's gaze and didn't look up from his work.

"It's you, isn't it?" he said.

Shada could tell Alfie was aware of who was in control. "How'd you know?" she asked.

"You're missing that extra sense of wonder," he replied. "When a new upload sees the world through someone else's eyes for the first time, they look around as if seeing the world brand new. You're just looking at me, annoyed."

"She doesn't like not being in control," Shada told the scientist.

"I can imagine."

Shada checked in with the couple. Hollis was silent, waiting for Shada to allow space for him to communicate with his wife, experience having taught him that it was useless to rebel.

Ruby, on the other hand, hurled obscenities at Shada, a stream of insults that Shada found amusing.

"Are you done?" Shada said, interrupting her.

"You agreed, you backstabbing—"

"Stop. It's time for you to agree to something. Let me off the island, and I'll let the two of you talk."

"Let you go?" Ruby said, stalling for time. One thing Ruby didn't realize about being a guest in Shada's mind was that the host could read her thoughts, so even though she was trying to come up with a lie, Shada knew the truth.

"You wanted me to show you it's possible to upload a second

mind," Shada told Ruby. "You have someone in mind you want me to take off your hands."

"Stay out of my head!" Ruby yelled.

"You know, you're the one in my head," Shada countered. "If I agree to upload this other mind, then you'll let me go?"

Ruby gave up pretending to keep her thoughts hidden. "Yes," she said. "If you can do it, I can have Alfie figure out how to do it with others."

Shada probed Ruby's thoughts once more and found out that the mind she wanted implanted into Shada's head was speaking out against actions taken by Ruby and the trajectory of the company under her control. Shada then withdrew and allowed the couple to communicate with each other.

Michael and Ruby Hollis began by discussing all that had occurred on the island since Hollis had left, a rundown of the business since his upload. Shada felt sad that this was the state of their relationship, that they had no personal news to share with each other, and she decided to leave them alone until their time was up.

During the next hour, alone in the room with Alfie, Shada spent her time focused on her breathing, alternating between sitting up and lying down with her eyes closed. The Stim still present in her system wouldn't let her stay in one position for long, and when she was tired of paying such close attention to her breath, she would watch Alfie monitor the status of the upload on the computer monitor. Every time she checked in with the conversation occurring in the background of her mind, she found they were discussing past events at WestCorp and ways Ruby could have better handled the situation. Shada was brought up towards the end of their time together, with Hollis asking what was to be done with her. Ruby didn't go into specifics with her husband but told Hollis she "had a plan," and that he didn't need to worry, which Shada knew from reading

Ruby's thoughts stemmed from the proof that it was possible to capture another mind.

"I know you'll get it taken care of," Hollis said. "Just remember, I'm still in here," he added.

Ruby said she knew, and the conversation died, as if they could tell Shada was listening. In the physical world, Alfie informed Shada it had been an hour, and he told her to lie back down and put the helmet back on.

"Let's get her out of there," he said.

A moment later, both Ruby and Shada sat up and removed their helmets.

"We should talk," Ruby said. Her voice contained none of the anger and frustration she couldn't contain while uploaded.

Shada wondered if there was a constant difference between her internal state and her exterior presentation. "You do know I'm your prisoner, right? You just show up and I don't have a choice whether I want to talk to you or not."

Ruby slid off the table and began to leave. "I'll come back soon," she said before walking out.

Shada was led back to the padded room. She sat in the middle of the room, alone in her amazement at how well she had been able to maintain control of herself with two minds uploaded into her body. She made sure to keep these thoughts hidden from Hollis, because she wanted to sort through how she felt without interference before having to deal with Ruby again.

Had Chloe been right to suggest she upload multiple minds? She had to assume Ruby and Michael Hollis would possess the most potential to disrupt her control, and she had been able to keep their conversation in the background. If there were minds left to their own devices in the background, could they be used to figure out how to create a world where edited and unedited humans could coexist without her involvement? She had never wanted the burden, and didn't think it possible, but after experiencing the ease with which she'd held two minds apart from herself, she couldn't help but extrapolate to three, and four, in the future, all working together for a common goal.

Shada fell asleep in a corner of the padded room. This time there were no beeps to keep her awake. She lost all track of time —not that she was able to track the days in the windowless room —and she was woken up by a guard entering and telling her that Ruby was on her way to see her.

"Let's go," the guard said. He didn't sound rude, even though his direct method of communication could seem so if taken at face value. The words themselves were said with softness, as if he would say more if he could, but he lacked the language to elaborate.

Shada was led back to the large table and given another glass of the thick vanilla meal replacement while she waited. It was finished by the time Ruby arrived, flanked by two more guards.

Ruby sat across from Shada and folded her hands on the table. The two women looked like children compared to the four guards that stood around them.

"So you really did take my husband with you when you left," Ruby said.

Shada nodded. "I really did."

"And you showed you can keep hold of two minds as well."

Shada was about to reply that Chloe could do the same thing, but she wasn't sure whether Ruby knew the extent to which her friend had plotted to eliminate the new leader of WestCorp. Chloe had been Ruby's personal assistant and was working the entire time to destroy the company from the inside.

"Get to the point," Shada said. It was as if Ruby wanted Shada to agree with everything she said, not content to impose her will on someone she knew she couldn't control. At a certain point, the cards had to be laid down so Shada could make a decision about how to act. Whether she agreed or not was a different matter.

"I'm here to discuss your freedom," Ruby replied. "And the taking of another mind with you when you go."

"Did Alfie have anything to say about this?" Shada asked.

"Says there shouldn't be any problems," Ruby replied.

Shada knew Chloe's second upload had been performed without problems, but in time her friend had still ended up dead.

"Do I have a choice?" Shada asked.

"In theory, you could say no, but she's already in there with Alfie," Ruby said, looking at the closed door of the upload room.

CHAPTER SIX

SHADA TURNED around in her chair and stared at the closed door of the upload room. She shook her head. "There's something wrong with you people," she said.

"Funny, we say the same thing about you."

"Let's get this over with then," Shada said, sliding her chair back and standing up. Part of her, a small part, was pleased with herself for saving the mind of someone whom Ruby detested. If she died, her knowledge and memories would evaporate into nothingness, but instead they were now being added to Shada's collection.

The four guards stayed still as Shada walked over to the upload room and opened the door. Alfie looked up from his work, a thin smile on his lips. He nodded to her before putting his head back down and resuming his preparations for the upload.

The woman lying on the table had on the same style gown Shada wore. Her wrinkled arms and legs were spotted with age, and her white hair stuck out from beneath the helmet already covering her head. Her breathing was steady, and she didn't acknowledge that Shada had entered the room.

Alfie, his eyes still down, must have sensed Shada's gaze, because he explained the woman was in an induced coma. "Her body's out, but her mind is still active," Alfie said.

Shada lay down, covered her head with the helmet, and didn't have to wait long until Alfie made the switch. She recovered her senses right away but stayed still so that she could get a sense of how much resistance the woman would have now that she no longer controlled a body.

"What's your name?" Shada asked. She blocked Hollis from their communication. She thought it would be harder to keep the two minds separate during the permanent upload, but her organized mind did it by default.

A small voice responded, full of trepidation. "Marnie," she said.

"Do you have a last name, Marnie?" Shada asked. She could tell she had access to the woman's memories but chose not to probe, at least not yet.

"Marnie Compana," the woman said. "Where am I?"

"You were uploaded into my body," Shada told her.

"Uploaded?"

The uncertainty in the woman's voice made Shada uneasy. "Didn't you know this was going to happen?"

"The doctors told me I needed to be put into a coma, so my body could heal. I assumed I would be going into the dream station."

"The dream station?" Shada asked. She had never heard of the device.

"It's a way for older people to pass the time once we're past working age."

"People on the island?"

"Yes." Something about Shada's question caused Marnie to pause. "Wait," she said, "you aren't edited?"

"No, I'm not."

Shada allowed Hollis into the thought-conversation. "Hollis is edited."

"I am," Hollis said.

"Hollis? As in, Michael Hollis? I assumed you were dead."

"My physical body died, but my mind lives inside this unedited woman."

"What's her name?" Marnie asked Hollis. Then, aware that Shada could also hear her, she redirected the question. "What's your name?"

"Shada Gray. I grew up in the city."

"So you're unedited."

"Correct."

"And who are you?" Hollis asked.

"Marnie Compana." Her response to Hollis was all business, like she was talking to a superior. "I was on the team that works with the city's government, until they phased me out due to age. They put me into a coma, and I assumed I would be taken to the dream station, but instead I woke back up in here."

Shada probed Hollis's memories and discovered that the dream station was how the majority of older edited humans passed their time. Instead of uploading into another person's body, they would spend anywhere from two to six hours inside the device, their minds experiencing everyday activities in a body that wasn't broken down. For most, it was how they passed the time until they died, the one thing they looked forward to each day. As edited humans, they would have been content with simple existence until their death, but this was a way for West-Corp to test the possibility of further productivity for mental tasks.

"This was Ruby's plan," Shada told Marnie.

Marnie laughed. "Doesn't surprise me, she wanted me out of the picture. I knew what she was doing to those poor unedited. They came thinking they were getting the standard edits, the ones everyone on the island receives, and instead they were edited to be worse versions of themselves."

"If you were phased out of your job, why would she care if you knew?" Shada asked.

"Just because I wasn't working day-to-day doesn't mean I didn't have any influence. My protégé came to me to discuss their misgivings with the direction of their work, and I told them to talk to their superior and to stop working if they thought it was best. Of course they didn't listen; the edits allow us to stay in ignorant bliss. Ruby must have found out about my advice and taken steps to drown out the voice of reason."

Shada knew she could discover the identity of the protégé by probing Marnie's mind but chose to let the woman keep the knowledge for herself.

Marnie continued. "Makes me wonder if I even needed to be put into a coma or if it was Ruby's idea. I was sick, no doubt about it, but didn't feel any worse than normal."

"Sounds like something she would do," Hollis admitted.

Shada opened her eyes, ending the meeting of the three minds that occupied her body. She sat up, and Alfie studied her face.

"Everything all right?" Alfie asked, as if he was unsure of who he was talking to.

"Everything's fine," Shada replied.

Alfie's shoulders relaxed the moment he comprehended that Shada was the one in charge. "How'd she take it?"

"She's surprised," Shada said. "But offered no resistance. I haven't even felt her try to take control of my limbs, but if she did, I could stop her."

"Fisher was the same way. Once Chloe took back control, he accepted their arrangement, as far as I'm aware."

Shada didn't want to talk about Chloe. The guilt involved made her second-guess herself, and with multiple minds now under her control, the last thing she needed was a crisis of confidence. "Is Ruby still here?" she said.

"Still outside. It's been all of five minutes."

Shada took the helmet off and set it on the table. "Good, I want to talk to her."

"I believe she wants the same thing."

Shada strode back out into the open space outside the upload room. Two of the guards, the ones who had been with Ruby when Shada arrived, were still standing behind the leader of WestCorp. The two who'd escorted Shada were on the far side of the room, on the opposite side of the massive table, helping themselves to whatever food was in the kitchen. Based on the limited amount of trash on the counter and their empty hands, they hadn't found much.

"Shada?" Ruby said, as if questioning the unedited woman's ability to gain back control over her own body.

"It's me. Marnie's here too."

"Good to hear."

Shada placed both hands on the back of the chair opposite Ruby. "Happy?" she said.

Shada stared at the older woman and watched Ruby close her eyes and nod.

"Marnie put her nose where it didn't belong, that's all. By doing so, she made herself the leading candidate for my second permanent upload test."

"You went in and talked to your husband. That should've been proof enough of what I can do."

"Paying a visit and moving in are two different things. Are you able to keep control over both of them? What's it like? We never talked about my visit, and I'm so curious. I'd upload another mind into myself if I could."

The thought of Ruby displaying enough self-awareness to

keep multiple minds organized made Shada laugh. "I'd like to see you try. Let me in, see if you can keep control."

Ruby was amused by Shada's suggestion.

"Now that you've seen for yourself it's possible, I'm free to go, right? You said this upload was in exchange for my freedom."

"Correct, a deal's a deal. You got rid of a thorn in my side, and now I'll help you. You are free to go."

Shada stood up straight and looked at the stone ceiling above. "Finally!" She looked around. "Now where's my stuff? I'm leaving."

"There's one more thing," Ruby said.

Shada glared at the seated woman. "What?" she said. She had read Ruby's mind while the woman was uploaded and knew there hadn't been more to her plan.

"Let me rephrase: a few more things. There are others on the island who continue to . . . disagree with my methods. You'd think since everyone is edited to be happy, nobody would bother trying to change the status quo."

Shada wondered if Ruby had been able to withhold information from her or if she had thought of this added wrinkle after spending some time alone. Whichever the case, Ruby was dangerous, but if she could keep her thoughts hidden from Shada while uploaded, Shada had to be more cautious when dealing with her in the future.

"What does this have to do with me?" Shada asked. There was no way she would agree to upload another mind, no matter how much Ruby tried to sweeten the deal.

Ruby leaned forward in her chair. "I want you to convince others from the city to come onto the island and leave with the minds uploaded into them."

CHAPTER SEVEN

RUBY STARED AT SHADA, waiting for an answer. The hungry look in her eyes made Shada's hair stand on end.

Shada knew there were unedited inhabitants of the city who would jump at the chance to upload one of the edited minds into their body. One member of the resistance, Richard, had been brought by Chloe to try to accept an edited mind into his body. Shada and Chloe were the only two living humans who had been able to undergo the procedure, and both had been subjected to a temporary occupation before the permanent upload. There must have been something about the experience that prepared them to receive a permanent upload, because Richard, as soon as he regained the tiniest bit of control, ended the experiment by jumping off the roof of a building on the island.

It also helped that Shada had told Chloe how to take back control, sharing her own process with her friend and making sure the procedure was understood. Richard had to hear about the steps secondhand through Chloe, one step away from the source, lessening his chance for success.

Shada knew Tony and Gustavo, Richard's comrades in the

resistance, would jump at Ruby's offer. In their eyes, it would be their chance for revenge, resulting in one less edited human in existence. The acquisition of a lifetime of knowledge and experience that could be referenced and drawn upon whenever needed was a delightful bonus. What did Ruby know about the resistance? She herself didn't know much; it had been Chloe who had the most experience with them. The group had been used by the city's new mayor, Mayor Tensen, to escort Shada and her sister, Sikya, into hiding. The group took care of the logistics. Their plan had worked, until Shada had chosen to come back to the island with Chloe and left Sikya in Chloe's apartment.

What a mistake that had been.

All these thoughts passed through Shada's mind in an instant, and she nodded to Ruby. "If I agree to bring them, then I'm free to go?"

"Correct."

Shada's thoughts turned to Marnie. The woman had taken the transplant of her mind without resistance. If others pushed back, it would be harder for the unedited members of the resistance to control their own bodies, assuming they agreed to the procedure. "I'm not sure they will be able to walk out of here in control of their own bodies," Shada told Ruby.

Ruby leaned back in her chair. "I've thought about that. There are two things working in favor of this new cohort. One, they'll have you to guide them through the steps. I understand you were the first to pull it off, and I'm assuming you told Chloe how to do it?"

Shada nodded.

Ruby continued. "And two, I'm going to tell the edited minds it's their chance for immortality. Might even use Michael as the example. This prospect alone should be enough to convince the selected individuals to go along with the procedure."

"Why are these individuals speaking out against you?"

"They're the ones who advocated for the negative edits," Ruby said with sadness. "I never should have listened to them. You'd be helping all the unedited people by taking their opinions off the island."

Inside Shada's head, Marnie called Ruby a liar. "She's the one who wanted to perform those edits!" she said.

Until Marnie spoke up, Shada hadn't been sure if Marnie was able to experience the outside world or if she was still stuck in the darkness. Shada also knew Ruby was lying but didn't bother contradicting her.

"If they are speaking out against you, why would they trust you enough to go through with the upload?" Shada asked. It was more of a question to herself that she spoke out loud. She realized she could say the same thing about herself. Here she was, entertaining a discussion about the plan, even though she felt Ruby was a snake in the grass ready to strike at any moment.

Ruby sighed. "Everyone wins," she said. "They get taken off my island, and the people who agree to the procedure gain the experiences and knowledge acquired over a lifetime."

"Why not just put them in a coma?" Shada asked. "They won't say a word."

Ruby considered the question for a moment before responding. "It would look too suspicious. If it's their own choice though, nobody would point fingers at me." Ruby looked at the guards around her before continuing. "And I can't just upload all these minds into you, because I don't know what would happen to Michael. To be honest with you, I want to see if your results are repeatable, to see if anyone can learn the skills you and Chloe demonstrated or if the two of you are unique. If I can figure out how to pull off a successful upload with another unedited, then Alfie can develop the technology to make it happen for anyone who wants the procedure."

"And what if I don't agree? I could force Hollis into the darkness right now and you'd never hear from me again," Shada said.

In her mind, Shada heard Hollis curse his wife's name.

"Well, I'll just have to tell the people who receive negative edits that it was Sikya's fault they ended up worse than before."

Shada was stunned. She had nothing more to say. With a threat to her sister now on the table, she knew she had no choice. The disgust in her stomach was as clear a sign as any that it was time to leave the island. With her head down, she informed Ruby she would find people willing to receive the upload. "How many do you need?" she asked.

"Seven," Ruby said as she stood up from her chair. The two guards who had come with her snapped to attention. She beckoned for the two guards who'd retrieved Shada from the padded room to take Shada to get her belongings. "They're in the room next to where you've been staying," Ruby explained, as if the padded room hadn't been used for Shada's imprisonment. Then she left, her footsteps echoing down the long hall towards the elevator.

Shada glimpsed Ruby and her entourage getting onto the elevator in the distance before she was led into Hollis's study. Hollis begged Shada to fight for some time in there alone so she, and by extension he, could look through his former collection of books. She ignored him, wanting to get off the island as soon as possible.

Her clothes were folded on the desk, the same ones she had been wearing when she'd jumped from the tram into the water, and before she put them on she smelled them to see if the scent of the bay was still present. To her surprise, they smelled like industrial cleaning supplies. She was grateful to shed her gown and got naked without warning the guards or waiting for them to leave.

Wearing her laundered clothes, Shada was led up the elevator and to the surface of the island. As they passed through the chain-link fence surrounding the exercise area, the dog lifted its head and watched her leave with sad eyes. It seemed this animal was used to disappointment and decided to take it without wasting the energy to stand up. As Shada was escorted to the tram, she remembered Chloe's backpack and wondered what had happened to it. She assumed the gun was lost, sitting somewhere in the bottom of the bay, but what had happened to the rest of the stuff? Shada didn't even know what was in the bag but wouldn't mind having it so she could keep something that had once belonged to her friend.

Her two escorts, bred to be muscle and not to think, wouldn't understand why she wanted the bag if she asked where it was, and she didn't feel like explaining herself. They could have taken her to someone who knew, but that would delay her departure, and she felt like she should take advantage of her opportunity to leave the island before her situation changed.

The three of them walked through the food court in the atrium at the center of the island and descended onto the platform below. Shada felt a mounting concern about the humans who had attacked her the last time she was in the city. She had no idea how much time had passed while she was on the island, though once she'd woken up, she'd felt like it was a few days at most. So the group Tony and Gustavo had held back would be gone, but what if she ran into others who wanted revenge for the edits they'd received to make them angry and impulsive, edits Ruby had blamed on Shada? She would have to keep her head down until she could get in contact with members of the resistance. They would be able to help, once they knew she was back. And when she talked to them again, how would she suggest they go along with Ruby's plan and receive the edited minds? She was lost in thoughts of their future interaction while she watched the guards on the platform disappear as the tram pulled away.

Luck was on her side when she walked through the terminal in the heart of the city on her way to board another train bound for Chloe's old apartment, to where Sikya had been left behind. Not a single person paid her any attention. If they had, and had their thoughts on revenge, she wouldn't have known, because she was too busy trying to organize her experience on the island without leaving room for the two edited minds inside her to surface.

Shada struggled to keep feelings of guilt from surfacing while she walked the few blocks between the train station and Chloe's old apartment. She had been responsible for her friend's death, but it was with the ultimate goal of saving lives. She reminded herself that edited lives were worth just as much as unedited ones; since Chloe disagreed, she had to be stopped. She was pulled back to reality and made aware of the conclusion of her trip when she heard movement behind the closed door of Chloe's apartment. The rustling stopped when she knocked on the door.

"Who is it?" Sikya called out.

"Shada."

The door opened with a rush, and Sikya stood there staring at her sister, breathing hard and pregnant.

CHAPTER EIGHT

SHADA STARED at Sikya's swollen stomach in disbelief. The last time they had seen each other, when Shada and Chloe had departed together for the island, there hadn't been any men in Sikya's life, as far as Shada was aware. "When did this happen?" she said.

"About six months ago," Sikya said, patting her stomach with a smile. Her face showed signs of the weight gain, the fullness of her cheeks framing her glistening eyes. Her black hair was pulled back in a ponytail. She was shorter than Shada by half a head, but they were built the same. Anyone who saw them could tell right away they were sisters. Sikya rushed forward and embraced her sister. "Where in the hell have you been?" she said.

"On the island," Shada said. She felt her sister's stomach press against the top of her hips. It dawned on her how much time must have passed before she had been allowed to wake up. The room might not even have been built when she was pulled from the water, and Ruby could have ordered the padded room's construction after Shada was in her possession.

Sikya pulled back and held Shada at arm's length. "We thought you were dead," she said.

"Who's we?" Shada said. She looked into the apartment, looking for the man who had impregnated her sister.

"Tony. We sort of became a thing." Sikya stepped back and put an arm on the edge of the door, inviting Shada to enter.

"Is he here now?" Shada asked as she stepped inside. The numerous plants Chloe had cared for were still thriving throughout the space, on the walls and most available surfaces. She couldn't elaborate what quality about the apartment suggested two people lived there—it could have been the way the pillows and covers were scattered on the bed or the coffee mugs on the edge of the sink, something she couldn't remember her sister doing—but she could tell Sikya didn't live there alone. Or if she did, Tony was there often.

"He's at work," Sikya said.

The sisters sat on the edge of the bed, and Shada launched into an account of where she'd been since she left her sister behind. She told Sikya how Tony and Gustavo had stayed behind on the platform to fight off the people who were coming for Shada, how Chloe had died on the train, and how she had woken up days before trapped in a padded room.

Sikya listened while Shada talked, waiting for Shada to finish before sharing her story. "When Tony got here, he said the group of people stopped fighting once the tram pulled away," Sikya said. "His face was bruised, and his arm had to be kept in a sling for a few days. He came back here to check on me, and that night was the first time he spent the night. A few weeks later, I found out I was pregnant."

Shada digested the information, calculating how long it had been since she'd left with Chloe.

Sikya told Shada she'd been gone for seven months. She left space for Shada to respond but was met with a fog of silence.

"I'm going to put some hot water on, do you want some tea?" she said, getting up by leaning to the side and using more arms than legs in order to accommodate her stomach.

"Sure," Shada said.

Sikya asked if Shada knew how Chloe had died when she sat back down.

"She took poison before her second uploaded mind, and I threw away the antidote," Shada responded.

"It wasn't them?" Sikya said, referring to the inhabitants of the island, the employees of WestCorp. "It was you?"

"She never made it to the island. I couldn't let her. She wanted to eliminate them all and make a new world ruled by the unedited." Shada waited for her sister to chastise her, but the words never came. Shada continued, "She couldn't see that what she wanted was the exact same thing Ruby wanted, to get rid of an entire group of other people just because they were born under different circumstances."

As Sikya nodded, the kettle on the stove began to whistle. She got up, made two cups of tea, and sat back down after handing Shada her cup. The chamomile-infused steam surrounded the pair.

"They're people too, and they deserve the chance to live," Sikya said with a softness bred by the prospect of bringing another life into the world. "And so you rode the train onto the island and that's where they captured you and held you the past seven months?"

"No, I used the gun Chloe had brought to shoot the window and jump into the bay. I thought I could swim back to the city, but one of WestCorp's boats picked me up. The last thing I remember before waking up was being tranquilized on the bottom of the boat."

"They kept you unconscious," Sikya said, horrified.

Shada told Sikya about the edited woman that had been

447

uploaded into her. "Marnie was put into a coma and woke up when her mind was transplanted into my body. I bet they kept me in a coma too," Shada said. A surge of anger welled up, and she paused to take a series of ten calming breaths before Hollis or Marnie could capitalize on her reactive state and take over any part of her body.

"Marnie?" Sikya said.

The awareness of the older woman inside Shada perked up, but she never tried to take any action through Shada's body.

"Marnie is the second mind I uploaded. She's in here now," Shada said, tapping her skull. "Ruby wanted to get rid of her because she spoke out against the negative edits."

Sikya took a sip of tea. "You shouldn't have accepted another one. Look how much has happened after you accepted Hollis's proposal!" She shook her head. "I swear you don't want to learn your lesson."

"I didn't have a choice! Ruby said it was how I had to earn my freedom."

"I don't trust that woman one bit," Sikya snarled, her protective instincts coming to the forefront.

"Well, I shouldn't have either, because she added another stipulation before she let me go: I have to bring other unedited members of the city to the island to accept more of the edited minds she no longer wants on her island."

Sikya set her mug on the floor and stood up with a fair bit of effort. "You have to do what? Why would you ever agree to that?"

"She said she would create more of the vengeful humans that came after me."

"So? We dealt with them once, we could've dealt with them again! We could've gone into hiding again, or left the city altogether."

"And go where? There's no hope outside the city; no food,

no water. And no city will accept us without documentation, which I'm sure Ruby can make sure we wouldn't get."

"Still, we could have tried!"

"She wasn't going to have them come for me this time," Shada said, looking at the ground. Her words were heavy, and she had trouble looking at her sister while she spoke. "She was going to have them come for you."

Sikya's eyes grew wide and her face flushed red. "I'd love to see them try! Tony would never let anything happen to me. To us," she said, her hands on her protruding stomach.

"Well, nothing's happened yet," Shada said. "This is the first place I came after the island. But I don't think it's such a bad idea."

Sikya's jaw dropped.

Shada continued. "I would teach whoever receives the upload to control the mind, and they'd then have an entire lifetime of knowledge and experiences of WestCorp. This could be the chance for peace! Ruby wouldn't want to stir up trouble because of all the inside knowledge we would have of her company."

"You two are a lot alike, you know that?"

Shada glowered at her sister. "Go on," she said.

"Both of you play with people's minds like they don't matter. What if they kill themselves, like Richard? Or worse, what if they don't and are forced to suffer through the rest of their existence trapped inside their own body, like some sort of sick purgatory?"

Shada lowered her voice. "I'll teach them how to make sure that doesn't happen."

"And what makes you so special?" Sikya said, tearing up. "How do you know it's even possible to do what you are suggesting?"

"I taught Chloe."

"Before you killed her," Sikya said.

Shada set her own mug on the floor and folded her hands in her lap. "She took the poison herself."

"But you destroyed the antidote."

"You don't agree with what I did? You want her to get rid of all edited people? You don't think they deserve the chance to live?"

"You know I don't think that, Shada!" Sikya began to sob and collapsed onto the floor. She cried until all her tears were used up. She looked at her sister and apologized. "I'm sorry I get worked up so fast," she said.

Shada shook her head. "It's fine."

Sikya stared at Shada. "I'm scared," she said.

"Scared? Of what? I told you, I won't let Ruby come for you. That's why I need to bring people to the island."

"I'm scared for Tony," Sikya continued. "And Gustavo. And the rest of the resistance. Because I know they are the ones you are going to ask to accept the edited minds."

CHAPTER NINE

Tony drove through an industrial part of the city and turned into a large parking lot behind a row of clean white warehouses. Some bay doors had cars parked outside, and some had tractor trailers backed up to loading docks. Although there was no movement outside, Shada had the sense that if the large doors were pulled up, or the trucks pulled away, each space held a flurry of activity within. The sense of stagnation and rust Shada had expected when Tony informed her they were going to this part of the city was replaced by a pleasant sense of surprise at the unexpected modernity.

Sikya was in the passenger seat, and Shada rode in the back. They had been alone in the apartment for a few hours, catching up on what had happened while Shada was on the island, when Tony walked through the door. He'd crossed the studio apartment in a few long strides and embraced Shada, grateful she had returned. She'd told Tony where she had been in the previous months and informed him about the need to keep Sikya safe by finding unedited people willing to upload edited minds. Over dinner that night, Tony had told the sisters to stay in Chloe's old apartment and that he would stay at his own place. This was how Shada found out they weren't living together full time, but that Tony was there enough to walk in without knocking.

Shada stared at the ceiling for a long time during her first night in the apartment, in a bed shared with Sikya, sleepless while thinking about Chloe. Shada had spent the night next to her friend before they had gone to the island to receive the edits, before they had been offered the chance to accept the uploaded mind of an edited island inhabitant. And now her friend was gone. Shada's guilt subsided sometime in the middle of the night and she was able to get a few hours of sleep, and in the subsequent nights, she was able to fall asleep before her sister, comforted by the safety she felt being with her once more.

After a few days stuck inside, with food brought by Tony—a similar situation to when the two sisters had lived in the safe house while Ruby hunted Shada—Tony informed Shada the resistance was going to meet to hear Shada's plan. They left the next day. He had tried to leave Sikya behind in the apartment, but she refused, saying she wasn't going to let the two of them make plans that would affect her without being present.

Tony parked the car outside the warehouse at the end of the row, the empty spaces blocked from view by an all-black trailer parked in front of the loading dock next door, and the three of them got out, climbed up the metal stairs, and went inside. Shada expected to walk into a massive space but instead found a small room, an office space with thin carpet and bare drywall painted white. There was a wooden door opposite the entrance. Something about the way the sound reverberated in the room made Shada believe the room they were in was a small section inside a much larger space.

The three of them were the first ones to arrive. Chairs were arranged along three of the walls; the wall between the two doors was left bare. Sikya took a seat in a far corner of the room and sat down with a sigh, leaning back to allow plenty of space for her stomach. Tony told Shada to sit down as well, gesturing to the seat next to Sikya.

Gustavo was the next person to arrive. His black hair was longer than Shada remembered. When they saw each other, Gustavo crossed the room as Shada stood up, and he gave her a hug. More people arrived, and fifteen minutes later, with most of the seats occupied, Tony announced everyone was present. By Shada's count, there were twelve people, not counting herself and her sister. There were people of all types, from clean-cut white men to dark-haired women with tattoos and piercings, which reminded Shada of Chloe. Tony stood in front of the bare wall and thanked them all for being there.

"We haven't met since Chloe was here. I'm sure you've all heard by now, but Chloe is no longer with us." He paused, giving space for anyone to react. "She died on the way to the island."

Hollis laughed inside Shada's head before telling Shada it was her fault. She tried to ignore him but couldn't stop the guilt from bubbling up. She began counting her breaths, with the intention of taking ten. When she got to seven, she began feeling better, but Tony's mention of her name disrupted her focus.

"Shada was the first person to capture a mind," Tony said.

The entire group turned to look at her. One man, older and sporting neck tattoos, had hungry eyes that sized her up with more primal thoughts in mind.

"It was Hollis, the founder and former leader of WestCorp," Tony added.

Shada didn't know he was going to divulge this information, and she was left stunned. She shook the feeling, figuring if she was going to be asking these people to upload a mind into their own bodies, it didn't matter if they knew her secret.

"She's here now because she needs our help," Tony said.

"Shada, do you want to come up and let everyone know what you've got in mind?"

Shada had never enjoyed public speaking. Silencing her reservations, she stood up and joined Tony up front. She ignored the stares of the man who looked at her like a piece of meat and instead focused on the rest of the group.

"We have an opportunity for peace," she began. She then went on to describe how Ruby wanted to get rid of seven people from the island, and that these seven minds would need to be uploaded into seven of those present.

"Why doesn't she just kill them?" asked a shorter woman who had the sides of her head shaved.

"I asked her the same thing. She said she wants to know if it's possible to repeat the procedure Chloe and I went through, to upload a mind into an unedited body. They want to develop the technology."

"So you expect us to help WestCorp carry out their research?" the man with the hungry eyes said. He leaned back in his chair and crossed his arms.

"In exchange for the knowledge and experiences of their employees, yes. Think about it: if we know what life is like on the island, which is possible with the memories of the uploaded minds, then we would be better informed if we ever wanted to take the fight to them."

Tony cleared his throat, and everyone looked at him. "We all want to get rid of WestCorp, that's why we're here. If the upload works, why wouldn't we just use the knowledge to bring them down from the inside?"

The group nodded their heads and murmured their agreement.

"It's an option," Shada said. "I'm suggesting we use the acquired knowledge to shape WestCorp's future projects only after we agree to them. It might be a more effective strategy. What luck have you had trying to get rid of them?"

The group bristled, not used to their methods being called into question.

In the back of the room, Sikya raised her hand.

"What's the real reason you want these minds captured?" Sikya said.

Shada knew Sikya was referring to Ruby's threat to let edited humans loose in the city and blame Sikya, but she also felt Sikya was too trusting of what motivated the group. She sighed. "The minds Ruby wants us to capture are the ones who advocated for the negative edits in the first place, making the humans who came after me." She wanted to call upon their desire to help the unedited, not require their allegiance to her sister.

Shada knew this was a lie, one that Ruby had provided, since Ruby was the one responsible for the negative edits. It pained her to see the look of disappointment on her sister's face.

The lie turned out to be the spark that lit the group on fire. It started with one member of the group, a young white man with a military bearing, who stood up and proclaimed nobody deserved to be edited in the first place, let alone edited to be worse. "I'll accept a mind," he said.

One by one the group stood up, each of them saying they'd be willing to travel to the island and receive the upload. All except the man with the neck tattoos who seemed to desire Shada. He stayed with his arms crossed, his skeptical eyes darting to each member in turn.

"Doesn't anyone remember what happened to Richard?" he said. "He was taken to the island and accepted a mind too. Where is he now? Dead."

"That's different," Tony said.

"How so?" the man shot back.

"Chloe's the one who taught Richard how to control the mind," Shada said.

"Didn't she learn from you?"

"She did. But it's different coming from me."

The man squeezed his lips together and frowned.

"You don't have to agree, just don't stand in our way," Gustavo said.

The two men stared each other down until the seated one seemed to realize he was the lone dissenter. "Oh, what does it matter," he said, uncrossing his arms and pushing against the chair to stand up.

Tony told Shada to choose.

Shada first decided on Tony and Gustavo, with an apologetic look towards Sikya. She then chose four women, wondering for herself if women were more predisposed to accepting the upload of another mind, before making the young man who'd first stood up her final selection.

Tony adjourned the meeting when she sat back down. "The rest of you can leave," he said. Everyone that hadn't been selected filed out, and the man who had been staring at Shada didn't give her a second glance.

Everyone who remained looked at Shada. "When should we start training?" Tony said.

"Close your eyes," Shada told the room. They all obeyed. "Now count ten breaths."

The room was silent except for the sounds of rhythmic exhalation. When they were done, they opened their eyes, awaiting further instruction.

"Do that as many times as you can during the course of the day. We'll meet again tomorrow, and I'll walk you through the steps."

CHAPTER TEN

Shada stood in front of the seven members of the resistance who would be going to the island. They were seated in two wooden church pews, four in one and three in the other, the rest of the church empty. The group had been ushered in by a young priest, or priest-in-training, who couldn't have been more than thirty. When she entered, Shada couldn't look away from a depiction of Christ on the cross, blood dripping down his face from the crown of thorns. She had been to church before, when she was young, but never when it was empty. The rest of the group strode in and sat down without so much as a second glance at the altar.

"I'm going to assume you practiced counting your breaths," Shada began. The group nodded, and she began pacing left to right, gathering her thoughts.

"So. The procedure will take place with you lying on one table and whoever is being uploaded on the other," she said. "You put a helmet on your head, Alfie or whoever is in charge will count you down, and the next instant you'll be plunged into darkness."

The woman with the sides of her head shaved blinked twice.

"The closest thing I can use to describe what it's like is being at the bottom of a well. None of your senses are available in this darkness, and it can feel like you'll be there forever. Trust me, you won't. Look for the light at the top of the well. It will be faint, like a star you can sense is there that disappears when you look right at it. Use the periphery of your sight to keep track of the light, don't focus on it."

"I thought you said we won't be able to see," the military man said.

"You can't at first, but this light will show up. It's the window back to your senses. You won't have access to your sight until you allow the light to take over your field of vision. Now, if you can keep the circle of light in your awareness, it will grow larger. This is when it's most important to not focus on it, just let it grow. I believe this is the step Choe and I were able to get through, which made us successful, and what Richard had trouble with."

Tony's and Gustavo's eyes fell at the mention of Richard's name. He had been the leader of their trio, the guy the mayor had called when he needed to protect Shada, and his loss still stung the two men.

"Now, assuming you can allow the light to grow, you'll be able to see the world through your own eyes. Then you can focus on the objects outside, until the darkness disappears altogether. When this happens, you should be able to hear the world as well."

Hollis and Marnie, their minds trapped inside Shada's head, marveled at the clarity of Shada's process. Marnie in particular wondered why she didn't have to go through this step to experience the world outside Shada. Shada informed her that she'd allowed her access so they could communicate.

"Chloe likened it to floating up from your feet to your head, and if you tried to force it, you'd fall back down."

Shada could tell this analogy resonated with the woman with long dark hair and deep-set eyes.

"This is where the breathing comes into play. It's one thing to witness the world, another to control your body. Nobody pays attention to the automatic process, so this is where it's easiest to gain access. Keep trying to find your breath until you can control each one. The person uploaded into your body won't know or register your presence."

"Is this when we take back over?" Gustavo asked.

"You could, but not yet. I tried to take over then, and Hollis was able to resist."

"And how long does all this take?" Tony said.

"Depends on the person. Now, I can do it in an instant, but the first time could take a few days."

There was a noticeable shift in the seriousness of the group. The thought of being out of control of their own bodies didn't sit well.

"The icing on the cake, what will allow you to take back control once and for all, is a serum developed by Alfie. I'm sure he'll administer it, but I don't know how soon. It's a modified form of LSD, and it allows you to sense your heartbeat."

A thin black woman raised her hand and began to speak before she was acknowledged. "This is getting weird," she said.

"Trust me, it's even weirder to go through it. But once you find your heartbeat, you can follow its resonance to every limb in your body. Keeping track of this is what will give you back full control." Shada scanned the group, waiting to see if anyone had any questions or comments. When nobody did, she continued. "To summarize, observe but don't try to force yourself back into the light and it will come to you, find your breath, then find your heartbeat and follow it to the rest of your limbs."

The process still didn't sit well with the black woman. "Sounds very . . . transcendental," she said, as if a transcendental process couldn't be trusted.

"Have you ever taken LSD before?" Shada asked.

"No," she replied. The rest of the group shook their heads as well.

"Well, it can be unsettling. But remember, it's unsettling for the person who is in charge of your body as well."

The woman with the side of her head shaved asked how Alfie would know the right time to administer the drug.

"He won't. If I had to guess, he'll give it to you soon after the upload. Or at least I'll tell him to. Don't try to skip steps though; this is the process that worked for me and Chloe."

The group all agreed, but Shada knew it was a lot for them to digest, made even more unpalatable because they were accustomed to and trained for action; the process Shada described required an acceptance of stillness.

Tony checked the time and stood up. "I think this is a good start. We should get going."

"This isn't a start, this is the whole process," Shada replied.

"That's it?" the black woman said.

"If we can do this, we'll be able to take back control of our own bodies?" the military man said.

"This is the worst-case scenario too," Shada said. "If they don't even try to keep control, there's a chance you won't have to do a thing. Be careful though: if you don't lay the groundwork, the uploaded mind could surprise you and take back control when you least expect it. That's what happened to Chloe," Shada said. The edited mind in Chloe had managed to get the word out that Shada had captured Hollis, which led to Shada being hunted by Ruby in the first place.

Tony stood and walked sideways along the pew, past the three pairs of legs between him and the aisle. Gustavo stood up and joined him. "We've got to go," Tony said. "The mayor's waiting for us."

The other five members of the resistance all looked at Shada, curious as to her business with Mayor Tensen. With her parting words, she told the group they would go over the process again, but in the meantime they should be thinking about the steps they needed to take before heading to the island. Then she left the church with Tony and Gustavo.

Mayor Tensen had reached out to Tony about seeing Shada. The trip to his new office—new for Shada, as he had been in his current position for the better part of a year—took twenty minutes from the church, since both locations were still downtown. The three of them walked past the building's security on the bottom level, rode the elevator up to the fortieth floor of the high-rise, then had to pass through another guard station in order to get to the mayor's corner office. It had a wide view overlooking the bay and, in the distance, WestCorp's island.

The mayor stood up from behind his mahogany desk and came around to greet Shada with a hug, as if they were old friends. She wasn't sure how to feel about his newfound familiarity. He then shook the hands of Tony and Gustavo.

"How have you been?" Tensen asked.

Shada, wary, told him she'd been fine. "Just getting used to being back after losing a few months," she said.

Tensen laughed but didn't seem surprised, as if it was an inside joke the two of them shared. How much did he know about WestCorp holding her hostage? It occurred to Shada to approach the authorities about WestCorp instead of getting revenge in her own way. Something about Tensen held her tongue, as if she suspected he would never be her ally. Even if she did somehow convince Tensen to go after WestCorp— which was a stretch, since the company was the reason his city was even relevant—she wasn't sure enough action could be taken before Ruby took action against a pregnant Sikya.

With all this in mind, Shada waited to see what Tensen would say. The mayor walked back around his desk, sat down, and gestured for Shada to sit across from him.

"I wanted to bring you in here today to talk about peace between the city and WestCorp," he said.

Shada was right; asking for Tensen's help would have been a waste of time.

He went on to describe how it would be best for everyone involved if they moved on from Shada's capture and imprisonment, that they should leave it in the past. "I've arranged for you and Sikya to live in one of the city's houses for visiting diplomats, a gated five-bedroom house. I can arrange for these two to be paid to protect you and Sikya." He used his chin to gesture to Tony and Gustavo. "All you need to do is leave WestCorp alone."

Shada stared at the mayor. He smiled, but she didn't return the gesture.

"Think about it," he said. "Chloe tried to take them down once, no reason for you to make the same mistake." The mayor leaned back in his chair, folded his hands across his stomach, and adopted a pastoral air. "Speaking of Chloe, how did she die?"

"She poisoned herself," Shada said. She left out her own involvement.

A look of shock crept over Tensen's face. "I'm sorry to hear that," he said. His response seemed genuine. He took a moment to absorb the news before clapping his hands together once and leaning forward. "So, what do you think about my offer? Leave WestCorp alone in exchange for the house? Live there as long as you'd like."

Shada thought for a moment. Her first instinct was to tell

Tensen she would think about it, then let the decision drag on long enough until a suitable path became clear.

Hollis had been listening and offered an alternative. "Lie. Take the house and tell him you'll be there in a few days. That way, all the people who accept the edited minds can live under one roof, with you there in case they need your help. He doesn't need to know about your business on the island."

Shada asked Hollis why he was helping her.

"I'm helping Ruby. This guy doesn't know anything about the arrangement between you two, so don't tell him. Just accept the house and get out of here."

Shada looked at Tensen. "Sounds reasonable to me," she said. She wasn't aware Tensen had been worried until she saw his face relax with relief.

"Perfect! I'll make sure Tony receives the access codes by the end of the day."

CHAPTER ELEVEN

───────────────

THE TRAM STOPPED beneath the center of the island. The seven members of the resistance stood and waited for Shada to lead the way. She walked at the head of the group and tried to reconcile her decision to go back into the lion's den when the last time she'd been here she had lost months of her life.

There had been some pushback from Tony about Shada accompanying them on the trip. He said the seven of them should go by themselves, since they were the ones about to receive the uploads, and there was no need for Shada to put herself in harm's way.

Shada countered by telling them she was the one tasked with bringing them to the island. What she didn't tell him was that if they showed up without her introduction, she worried the scientists might try to perform edits to make the members of the resistance angrier and more impulsive. The last thing she wanted to deal with was a well-trained security force let loose on the city with revenge against Sikya on their minds.

The two WestCorp guards stationed at the foot of the stairs at the end of the platform stood to their full height when they saw the group disembark, each of them a full head taller than any of the visitors. Their eyes narrowed as they scanned for threats. Each one gave Shada a small nod of recognition before subjecting her to a cursory pat-down. They told the seven resistance members to place all firearms into a small bin. When nobody stepped forward to deposit their weapons, since Shada had told them to leave their weapons behind in the city, the guards began searching each person, their large hands groping men and women alike. Satisfied nobody was armed, they let everyone pass.

Shada led the group up the wide staircase and into the atrium above the platform. They emerged in the center of a food court, with edited humans walking and seated throughout, eating everything from noodles to burgers. It was clear none of the first-time island visitors expected such a modern, communal space, and their eyes scanned the room as they took it all in. Shada, who had come to the island on the tram numerous times before, remembered the first time she'd arrived and her disbelief at the comforts the edited were provided. She led her group to a rectangular table large enough to fit everyone and told them to sit down, that she'd be back in a moment.

A woman approached Shada from the direction of the information desk. "I've told Alfie you're here," the woman said.

Shada hid her surprise, but it took a second for her to understand how the WestCorp employee knew who she was there to see. There were cameras on the tram, and when she had first come to the island, the onboard computer had asked the purpose for her visit. She hadn't been questioned again, but she assumed it was because her face was recognized; now it seemed whoever she'd had the most interaction with was also notified of her arrival. As she walked back to her group of unedited, she wondered how interconnected the island was, if somehow the system knew she was tasked with bringing more people to the island so when they showed up on the tram with her there was no need to ask for their purpose. Could the cameras and micro-phones be recording it all, creating a vast database of every interaction on the island in order to ensure its smooth opera-tion? It could be how Ruby knew about Marnie's conversation with her protégé.

Shada asked Hollis why the tram's computer hadn't asked why she was coming to the island with seven people from the city, and he told her it already knew the reason.

"Did Ruby tell it to expect me and seven new people?" she asked him with her thoughts. She pulled a chair from beneath the table and sat down on the same side as the three men, across from the four women.

"Didn't have to. It's always listening."

Shada wondered how much data the island had acquired about her, and how much she had produced. With a clear enough picture, could it guess what she would do next?

"That's the goal," Hollis replied.

Shada kicked herself for not closing off her personal thoughts from the mind trapped inside her.

"What are we waiting for?" Gustavo asked. His eyes were locked on the burger restaurant.

"Not sure, but Alfie knows we're here."

"Is this food specially made for the edited? Like, we could eat it too, right?" he said.

"We can eat it too. This is where everyone on the island comes to eat. It's their cafeteria."

"That's amazing," said the woman with the sides of her head shaved.

The edited humans in the food court couldn't be bothered with the newcomers. They went about their business, focused on their own tasks. Each unedited member of the resistance studied the island's inhabitants, trying to understand their enemy. Shada knew the people presented just like everyone in the city, that her cohort was wasting their time trying to distinguish a difference.

They didn't have to wait long for Alfie to show up. He had on his white lab coat, its bottom edges fluttering around his knees as he walked. He smiled when his eyes met Shada's.

"Welcome to WestCorp!" he told the group, sounding more cheerful than Shada had ever seen him.

The group muttered their greetings.

Shada went around the group and introduced each one to Alfie.

"Tony, Gustavo, and Mark," she said, pointing to the three men in turn.

"Vick," said the woman with the sides of her head shaved. "Kren," said the thin black woman. "Ophelia," said the woman with deep-set eyes. "And Sophie," said an Asian woman with short, jet-black hair.

Alfie laughed. "Pleasure to meet everyone. Did anyone want to get something to eat before we get started?"

Shada found his welcoming manner unsettling. To her relief, everyone, even Gustavo, said they weren't interested in a meal at the moment.

"Right this way then!" Alfie said.

Alfie led them down the long corridor to the lab. They passed by the decorative artwork attributed to children of increasing ages Shada had seen on her first trip to the island. She wondered where all these children were kept because she hadn't seen a single one during her time on the island. A fear gripped her: What if they were all sequestered away in a manner similar to how she had been kept in the padded room? Their edits would keep them happy, even as they grew up to become a contributing member of the island community, never knowing their treatment was abhorrent.

Shada asked Marnie where the children were, not wanting

to deal with Hollis's potentially cavalier attitude towards children in captivity.

"They're on the far corner of the island," Marnie said.

Shada asked if they were allowed to go outside.

"Of course," Marnie said with a laugh. "Why wouldn't they be?"

Shada chuckled to herself and shook her head, drawing a few quizzical stares from Gustavo. He seemed to always be aware of where she was and took steps to be near her.

Alfie led everyone into a conference room in the lab building and told them all to take a seat. "I'm going to assume Shada told you why you're here," he said.

The group all nodded.

He then explained that there would be a one-hour hijack, a test to make sure they could take back control. "Then, we'll proceed with the full upload."

The group of unedited humans looked at Shada. When she didn't offer any objection, neither did they. Seven scientists, all wearing white lab coats, then walked in and led each of the seven members of the resistance out of the room.

"They'll be back," Alfie said when he was alone with Shada. "Why don't we take a walk?" He sounded more cheerful than she had heard him before.

That ended the moment they walked outside.

"They seem nice," he said, as serious as Shada had ever seen him.

"They are."

He didn't seem in a rush to get his thoughts out. It was as if he wanted to take the full hour and not leave too much time at the end, preferring to start in silence than end in it.

The pair made a full lap around the building. When they got back to their origin point, they turned and walked around in the opposite direction. On the back side of the building, at the direct middle of the wall, Alfie spoke again.

"Don't trust Ruby," he said, his eyes still forward.

If it hadn't been so silent, Shada wouldn't have been sure the scientist had spoken.

"I don't," Shada said. She took a page from Alfie's book and didn't turn her head either. She pushed both Hollis and Marnie into the darkness, shutting off their ability to experience the outside world.

"Whatever angle you think she's taking, expect it to change. I don't even think she knows what she's doing until it's done. That erratic nature makes it tricky to come up with a plan."

"Be ready for anything, got it," Shada said.

"And now that she won't have anyone speaking out against her, who knows what she'll be able to get away with."

Shada didn't respond.

They turned two more corners than went back inside. Within fifteen minutes, the rest of the group had rejoined them in the conference room.

Alfie sat at the head of the large table and reviewed the reports supplied by his team of scientists. While viewing each one, he nodded, pursed his lips, and furrowed his brow. Shada thought he might see something that worried him even though her own inspection of the group's current demeanor led her to believe all hijacks had been successful. When she realized he'd responded the same way for every candidate, she attributed his gestures to signs of approval. Once the last file had been inspected, he arranged them in a stack, held them up, and used the table to line up their edges.

"Everything looks good to go!" Alfie said. "Now, let's get these minds uploaded."

CHAPTER TWELVE

"WHO WANTS A BEER?" Gustavo called out from the kitchen.

"I'll take one," Mark, the member of the resistance who looked like he came straight from the military, yelled back.

"Me too," Vick called out. The sides of her head were still short but she would need to get a haircut soon if she wanted to maintain her hairstyle.

"Do you all want one?" Tony said, addressing the group. They were in the living room of the house Mayor Tensen had provided, spread out on the two white couches, two white chairs, with Ophelia seated on the floor next to the fireplace. "Well, I know you don't," he said to Sikya.

Sikya pretended to be angry with the father of her unborn child. "You mean I *can't*," she said before telling him she was fine for the time being. "I might get some water later."

The rest of the group who received the uploads all nodded. Everyone but Shada. She didn't drink, not wanting it to affect her ability to control the two minds uploaded into her. She had her reservations about the ability of everyone else to maintain control of the uploaded minds while under the influence of alcohol but a single celebratory beer wouldn't hurt. If they tried to keep drinking she'd have to speak out.

"Bring out seven," Tony yelled, assuming Shada would be drinking one as well.

Gustavo brought the drinks out in two trips, setting them on the coffee table between the couches. Tony took it upon himself to hand them out. Shada shook her head when he held out the bottle brought for her. "I'm fine," she said.

Confusion on Tony's face gave way to recognition. He informed the rest of the group that they would be limited to a single alcoholic drink. "Just to be safe," he said.

"I've got this guy under control," Gustavo said, tapping his head with his index finger. "Nothing to worry about!" He laughed while trying to get Shada's attention.

Shada averted his gaze.

Tony was insistent. "No reason to put ourselves in a situation that could affect our success," he said.

Gustavo didn't push back again.

The group had taken a tour of the house when they first arrived. They looked through the five rooms and discussed who would be sharing. Tony and Sikya took a room, Gustavo and Mark another, the four women split two rooms, and Shada was left with her own. The decision to give Shada her own space wasn't ever discussed, and nobody questioned the decision. Each room had a single bed and Shada wondered if the bed would be shared or if one member of the room would be sleeping on the floor.

In addition to the five bedrooms, there was a kitchen with an island counter that could seat five on barstools, a dining room with a dark brown table large enough to seat fourteen beneath a crystal chandelier, and a study with a dark brown desk that matched the dining room table. The study had a bookshelf that was barren save for a few books left behind, paperback thrillers that could have also been left behind in a beach house.

In the basement was a small theater that could seat eight and a room with a pool table and bar. After Gustavo handed out the beers he suggested they head downstairs. "Lets get a game of pool going," he said. "We can play doubles. Shada, want to be my partner?"

Shada agreed, then Gustavo asked who wanted to be their first victim. Ophelia raised her hand and looked at Sophie, asking with her eyes if the woman would be her partner. Sophie declined, saying she was terrible at the game. "Vick?" Ophelia ventured.

Vick shrugged. "Why not?" she said.

Everyone went to the basement. While the two pairs played pool the other five lingered at the bar, with Sikya seated on one of the two barstools. Shada and Gustavo won the first game, and the team of Tony and Kren beat them on the next. Mark and Sikya said they had no interest in playing, and Sophie made no indication her mind had changed about partaking in the fun. The three teams kept a cycle of games going, with the winner staying on each time, and no team was able to string together more than three wins in a row. Everyone switched to drinking soda since there was plenty in stock for mixers, although Gustavo mentioned the various types of liquor and seemed to hope someone else would push for a shot or two. His comment was ignored.

The people not playing pool discussed their experiences with the upload. They had spent almost a week on the island, able to leave after five days. Each person had taken back control of their body by the end of the second day, a fact which inspired pride in Shada about the effectiveness of her method. The biggest issue members of the group had was her description of the light from the bottom of a well, which some of the group said was more confusing than helpful. Kren in particular said she made a breakthrough when she focused on the light instead of keeping it in her periphery.

"I'm just glad you were able to find what works for you," Shada said when she found out.

Everyone agreed that finding their breath gave them hope in their ability to take back control and that the uploaded mind never sensed their presence when they found it. The consensus was that it was a hack to keep themselves from getting lost in their thoughts, and it set them up well for when Alfie administered the serum. Within hours of the dose, each member of the group was back in full control of their bodies. No edited minds had tried to move the host's limbs since.

Shada was concerned about the uploads being completed without any resistance. Of course, Marnie hadn't tried to control any of her limbs, and Fisher hadn't tried to control Chloe, according to Alfie, but the fact that all seven uploads went off without a hitch made Shada uneasy. Her time on the island was spent in one of the dorm rooms for visitors, a barren space with just a small bed, wooden desk and wooden chair. There were numerous discussions with Alfie, the most memorable being when they discussed what uploading multiple minds into Shada might look like.

"I'd imagine you'd have to spend a lot of energy just to control them," Alfie ventured.

"Or, since there were so many vying for an increased presence, they could cancel each other out."

They were outside, walking along a gravel path between the building where she was staying and the lab where the members of the resistance were learning to suppress the edited minds uploaded into them. Alfie never said there was a chance their conversation would be recorded indoors, and Shada never pressed the issue, but whenever the two of them spoke inside

Alfie had a different air about him, an energetic disposition Shada didn't experience on their walks.

"I wish I had another body to keep the uploads in," Shada had said. She was feeling guilty about bringing the group of unedited to the island. "Like a container I alone could open."

"That would be a massive hard drive," Alfie said, his voice trailing off.

"You mean if we kept the minds on a computer?" she said.

Alfie ignored her response. "I don't even know how I would begin to figure this out, but you may be on to something. I'll have to talk to the guys underground."

She asked Hollis who the guys underground were and he told her that's what people called the employees who worked in the server room.

Alfie ended their conversation telling her he would let her know if he came up with something. "With any luck, we won't need to map one brain onto another, we can keep the blueprint in storage until it's contents need to be viewed."

Shada didn't understand. "What do you mean?" she said.

Alfie lifted both hands, balled up into fists. "Right now we map one brain onto another, using the host brain as a sort of template. Like carving a statue from a block of stone. But what if there's no stone? We would have to print it, layer by layer, until we got the complete statue."

"When you first explained the uploading process to me you said your ultimate goal was to design a mind from scratch, like an artificial intelligence. Isn't this the same?" Shada asked.

"This isn't a design, it's a recreation. Building the artificial intelligence would be like building a large block of stone, layer by layer, and figuring out what we wanted our stature to look like afterwards. Massive computational power that could be taught to perform however we wanted. This is like building a pre-existing statue instead, no teaching necessary. But much more complex."

Alfie's gaze clouded over, lost in thought. Shada tried to get him to elaborate but he didn't offer more information about his idea. When they got to the seven members of the resistance they found they had all taken back control of their bodies. From then on Shada was busy making sure everyone was taking steps to maintain a hold on their bodies, staying present in reality. She hadn't gotten time to talk to Alfie again.

Back in the basement, Shada heard her name called out. "Shada," Sikya said again. The rest of the group was looking at her when she came out of her memory.

"I think it's time to go to bed," Shada said. "For me, at least," she added, aware she wasn't in charge of the rest of the group. Though she did ask them not to drink. Even thought they had all come to an understanding, she thought it was best to say it out loud.

"We should all go to bed too," Tony said.

The group took a second to clean up before everyone went to their respective rooms. Shada put on a pair of athletic shorts and a t-shirt before climbing into bed. The sheets were softer than any she had slept in and the pillow was the perfect hardness. She fell asleep in no time.

In the middle of the night she was shaken awake by her sister. "Shada, get up," Sikya said.

Shada sat up with a big breath and looked around, alert and heart racing. "What's wrong," she said. She was upset at herself for not hearing the door to her room open, feeling like it was a lack of vigilance on her part.

"Come downstairs."

Tony was in the kitchen with Gustavo and Ophelia. In the middle of the night her eyes seemed even more sunken than before. Her defeated posture didn't help.

"I stayed awake to keep watch," Tony said. "And found her sleepwalking."

Gustavo walked forward with an open laptop in his hand. "She wasn't sleepwalking, she was using this to access a secure communication channel," he explained.

Shada's stomach dropped.

"I stopped her before she could send the message," Tony said.

Sikya alternated between looking at Gustavo and Tony. "Who was she calling?" she said.

Shada answered her sister, not needing the two men to tell her what was going on. "WestCorp."

CHAPTER THIRTEEN

OPHELIA RESTED her elbows on her knees and hung her head. "I don't remember anything," she muttered.

Tony and Gustavo looked at Shada. She wondered when she'd become the de facto leader of the group. Although Tony had made the call on his own to stay awake, keeping an eye out for threats, once he'd stopped Ophelia, it seemed his role in the matter was finished.

Shada studied Ophelia. Something made her believe the woman, but the fact remained she had tried to call WestCorp to report their location, as discovered by Gustavo.

"Check with the edited mind, see what they say," Shada told her.

"He said he doesn't remember."

Shada thought it was interesting that Ophelia also had a male mind uploaded into her body, just like she did. "Well, there's no way neither of you remembers. Someone was in control of your body."

Ophelia's eyes filled with tears. "I swear it wasn't me. I went to bed, just like everyone else, and the next thing I knew I was sitting in this chair, being shaken awake by Tony."

"I believe you," Shada said.

Sikya couldn't hide the surprise on her face. "You think the edited mind took over her body while she was asleep?" she asked.

Shada heard Hollis laugh. "Can't put anything past Ruby," he said.

"We all got control of our bodies back before we left the island," Tony said, thinking out loud. He turned to Shada. "Did you think it would take longer?"

Shada leaned against the counter across from Ophelia and crossed her arms. "No, I didn't. But I assumed the uploaded minds were weaker than the one that went into Richard, or that my ability to teach you to take back control was more effective than Chloe's." She paused. "I think they might have been planted. Or at least this mind was," she said to the room.

The five of them fell silent, a silence that was absorbed into the noiseless house in the middle of the night.

"Ophelia," said Shada.

Ophelia lifted her head and stared at Shada with bloodshot eyes.

"Don't ask if they took over. Go in and find out yourself."

Ophelia nodded, closed her eyes, and took a series of long breaths. She looked peaceful, like she was deep in meditation, but Shada knew how hard it was to access the memories of an uploaded mind for the first time. While Ophelia searched, Sikya met Shada's gaze. Shada closed her eyes and nodded, instructing her sister to be patient. It was a full eight minutes before Ophelia opened her eyes again.

"He was told by Ruby to allow me to take back control at first, then wait until we were settled before trying to contact the island."

"It's just like with Chloe," Shada muttered.

Tony and Gustavo shot Shada an inquisitive look, but she

didn't elaborate. She asked the two men to look into the memories of the minds uploaded into their bodies as well, to see if there was a similar conversation with Ruby buried in the archives.

After minutes of silence, both men reported the minds inside them had been tasked with infiltrating the resistance.

"Ruby didn't share her ultimate plan," Gustavo said.

"Mine says he thinks Ruby wants to eliminate the resistance. He was told to wait until he'd witnessed the entire group together before attempting contact."

"Ophelia was confirming the edited minds made it to the city," Sikya ventured.

Shada cursed herself for not looking into the identities of the minds before they were uploaded. She assumed they were all like Marnie, older and waiting for their natural expiration, and had spoken out against Ruby, drawing her wrath. She never considered they were working for Ruby, with Ruby, to take down the unedited resistance from the inside. Hadn't Alfie told her not to trust Ruby? His words of advice echoed in her mind.

Tony tasked Gustavo with waking up the rest of the team and told Sikya to go back to bed. She protested until Shada told her there was nothing she could do. "This could take a while," she said. "I'll let you know what happens."

When the entire group was in the kitchen, Shada asked them to all dive into the memories of their uploaded minds to find out if they had been instructed to offer little resistance to the host's attempts to take back control. "Find out if the minds inside you are planning to establish contact with WestCorp in the future."

All eyes fell on Ophelia as they realized this was why she was the first one in the room, and why she was so upset.

"Why wouldn't we have found this out before?" Vick asked Shada.

"You didn't know what questions to ask. It's like an encyclopedia. Lots of information, but if you don't know where to look, impossible to know it all."

The team fell silent as they searched the memories stored inside them. It took some longer than others, and Shada had to kneel in front of Mark and guide him through the breath work before he was able to access the memories of the mind uploaded inside him. In the end, all the team members reported the edited were in fact sent by Ruby and told to allow the team to take back control with minimal resistance after the initial upload.

"Ruby wanted it to be a surprise when they took back over," Sophie said.

"We need to find out who we're dealing with," Shada declared. She told the group to find out the former identities of the minds that were uploaded into them and write down their previous roles in WestCorp. "In particular, find out how old they were," she said. Based on her experience with retired West-Corp members, Shada guessed they were easier to control and posed less threat.

The group all closed their eyes. Kren was the first to break the silence. "They don't know their age because their birthday wasn't celebrated."

Shada thought for a moment. "See if they spent time in the dream station before uploading." She knew from Hollis that the only people who used the artificial sleep machine were the ones with nothing to do, that the productive members of the island were expected to work and therefore didn't have the time to spend in another reality.

All the team members said the edited minds hadn't used the device, that this was the first time they'd experienced anything outside of their own bodies.

Shada's stomach dropped when she considered the possibility that Ruby might have selected her strongest supporters on the island. "Find out their opinions of the unedited, in particular how they feel about nonstandard, post-birth edits."

The group dove back into the archives of the edited minds. One at a time, their eyes opened, and they each sat in silence until the last member of the group came back to the room. Vick was the first to speak. "This one doesn't care about what kind of edits WestCorp provides, she trusts Ruby's judgment."

The other six nodded in agreement, each discovering the same sentiment.

A wave of guilt crashed over Shada. She'd been betrayed by Ruby and had led the members of the resistance, including the father of her sister's baby, into a trap.

"What should we do?" Gustavo asked.

Tony spoke up before Shada could say anything. "We need to make sure nobody can contact the island. We'll sleep in shifts, a group of three and a group of four. If we limit ourselves to six hours a night, it should be manageable."

"Not ideal though. Less sleep means there will be more time awake, draining mental energy," Shada said.

"But also less time for the edited mind to take back over," Tony countered.

"From now on, everyone needs to remember the uploaded mind allowed you to take back control. Imagine a scenario when you'd need to fight back, and practice the breath work with that added focus," Gustavo said.

"Should we take the serum?" Tony asked. Alfie had sent the group back with a considerable stockpile, but Shada had told them not to use it since they had been able to maintain control over themselves without it. She herself didn't use it and had imagined the group was at the same level as her. Now she wasn't so sure.

"Yes, take the serum and begin your training all over again, with the knowledge that the minds inside you are lying in wait," Shada said.

"And what if the minds inside have heard this entire conversation? They'll know what we're trying to do," Vick asked.

"Practice accordingly," Shada responded.

"Will we have to keep this up forever? Afraid to sleep out of fear they will take over, always waiting for them to show up?" Kren said.

Shada sighed. "For now, yes."

Kren's eyes narrowed. "What do you mean, for now?"

Shada told them about her conversation with Alfie, about their idea to create an external server for uploaded minds. "The edited minds could be stored in there, leaving you alone again."

"They would live forever," Vick said.

A look of disgust swept over Sophie's face. "Why should they get to be immortal? Shouldn't we be able to upload too?"

"In theory, you could upload when you die, if you wanted."

Everyone in the group fell silent.

"What would be the point of uploading and living in a computer?" Mark said.

"Could I upload into someone else?" Gustavo ventured.

"I'm not cursing someone else with this," Mark said.

"You know what would be nice? If we could upload into a blank human. Or swap with them," said Vick.

"Where are you going to find a blank human?" Sophie shot back.

"You'd have better luck uploading into a robot," said Kren.

Something in Shada clicked, and she realized the group might be on to something. "They're called androids," she said.

CHAPTER FOURTEEN

NOBODY LEFT the house for the first few days after Ophelia's nighttime attempt to contact WestCorp. Their groceries were delivered, and teams of two took turns cooking for the group, with Tony joining Sikya and Shada in a group of three. There wasn't a strict schedule or assignment of who cooked the meals; a loose volunteer system emerged where everyone contributed. The group spent each evening in the basement, some watching a movie and the rest in the pool room, even if they weren't playing. Mark turned out to be the best player of the group, and nobody was surprised to learn there had been a table in his childhood home.

Four days after the discovery of Ruby's plan, Tony and Gustavo left to meet with the rest of the resistance. They told the group beforehand there was a chance their identities would be discovered by WestCorp, if they weren't able to block the edited minds inside them from witnessing the meeting, but that extra precautions would be taken when they slept to prevent communication with the island. None of the resistance chose to skip the meeting, but it was conducted in a public place so their warehouse location would remain secret.

Ophelia moped around the house. Everyone tried, in their own way, to cheer her up, but she couldn't recover from the guilt of putting the group at risk. She never played pool, just sat and watched in silence, and when she watched movies, she had a far-off look in her eyes, as if she could see the screen but wasn't processing the story. Shada wondered if Ophelia would be able to take action in the event of a threat, but Tony assured her Ophelia's demeanor wouldn't interfere with her work.

A week after Tony stopped Ophelia from sending a message to the island, Shada received an unexpected one. Alfie contacted her by sending the message to Tensen, who relayed it to Tony, who delivered it to her.

FOUND COMPUTER ENGINEER. COME TO ISLAND WHEN READY.

"Tensen called me and asked what the computer engineer was for, said he thought you agreed to stay away from West-Corp. I told him I'd get back to him after I talked to you," Tony said.

Shada was surprised Alfie had followed through with their discussion. She was still interested in the storage device but never imagined it had landed on the scientist's list of priorities. His message left her with more questions than answers. Had the computer engineer already solved the storage problem? Did Alfie want her to come to the island to test if she could upload one of the minds inside her into the device? Or did Alfie want her to upload the engineer, joining Hollis and Marnie, so he could work on the problem while inside her mind?

She told Tony to tell Tensen the truth. "Tell him we're making an advanced storage device," Shada said.

"He'll be able to guess it's for the uploaded minds," Tony said, who guessed its purpose as well. He closed his eyes and took a deep breath, followed by a slow exhale, before opening his eyes again. The members of the group all adopted Shada's attitude about the minds uploaded into their bodies: pretend they don't exist.

"Even if he guesses, what can he do?" Shada asked.

"He could tell Ruby, if she doesn't already know. WestCorp contributes so much money to the city that Tensen does everything he can to keep her happy," Tony said with disgust. As a member of a group that proclaimed itself to be for unedited rights, it had to be tough to know his boss was in bed with the enemy.

"I'll worry about her when the time comes." The leader of WestCorp was a sore subject with Shada after her lies about the edited minds that the group had uploaded.

"Are you going to go back to the island?" Tony asked.

"That's the plan."

Sikya approached Shada about the message from Alfie that evening. Shada didn't wonder how her sister found out; she assumed Tony would tell her and had braced herself for the conversation.

"Another upload?" Sikya said. They were alone in Shada's bedroom. Shada had just finished a session of breath work when her sister knocked on the door and asked to come in.

"All the message said was he found a computer engineer. How do you know they're going to be uploaded?" Shada asked. She herself wasn't sure what Alfie had in mind.

Sikya tilted her head and stared at her sister. "Because I know you. If the project was going to be completed in the real world, Alfie could have taken care of it himself and wouldn't need you to go back."

Shada squeezed her lips together and nodded. "Alfie and I never discussed uploading another mind. If the engineer was uploaded, how could they test their work? I think the message meant that he'd found someone to work on the problem, and that I can come back to the island because it's been solved."

"What problem is that?"

"How to store uploaded minds outside a body."

Sikya's jaw dropped. "If it works, could we clear everyone here, get them back to the way they were?" Tears welled up in her eyes, and she wiped them away with her fingertips.

Shada was sure her sister missed the way Tony used to be. "In theory."

"Would you upload Hollis, and what's her name, into the device?"

"Marnie," Shada said. She hadn't given any thought to clearing the uploaded minds from her own body, but now that the potential had been vocalized, she knew she would keep them. They had become a part of her, a part she didn't want to get rid of. "I don't think so. I've got a firm hold on them, and they weren't sent to lie in wait for my defenses to drop. I've known from day one what they can do and haven't had any problems yet."

"Then why go to the island at all?" Sikya asked.

"He could want me to test the device. If it works, we can send the others. They deserve to sleep in peace."

"You should consider leaving those two inside the device as well," Sikya said, her chin pointing to Shada's head, her word choice not matching her rabid tone.

Shada knew her sister wanted her to get rid of the uploaded minds, but if Sikya used strong language, Shada would double down on her decision to keep them. "I'll consider it," Shada said, a lie, since her decision was already made.

"What happens if Alfie does want you to upload the engineer and you lose control with him in there? Have you considered that?"

Shada laughed. "It hasn't been an issue yet," she said. "Hollis was the most difficult, for me and perhaps anyone. Compared to him, Marnie was a breeze. Even if the engineer gets inside and wants to take over, Hollis will put up a fight. I think—and I could be wrong—that the more minds uploaded, the less of a chance any one of them takes over. If anything, I would present like a person with multiple personality disorder, each identity coming to the forefront for a period of time before they lose control to the next."

Sikya tilted her head back and stared at the ceiling in frustration.

"And that's the worst-case scenario. Odds are I keep control of them and nobody notices a thing." Shada waited until her sister looked at her, then met her gaze. "Trust me, I'll be fine."

Sikya looked away. "There's no reason to keep poking West-Corp. We should get Tensen to help, trust the authorities. If they knew what WestCorp was doing, they would be shut down."

"Ask Tony how he feels about Tensen," Shada said, knowing the doubt he held about the mayor's loyalties. "I met with Tensen. He knew they took me hostage and he asked me to let it go! You really think the city has the power to stop WestCorp? WestCorp owns the city. The money they provide is the only way the city sustains itself. Tensen knows that."

"But he's on our side," Sikya said, referring to those who fought for the advancement of unedited rights.

"Was on our side. When money wasn't involved. I don't trust him."

Their conversation was interrupted by Gustavo knocking on the doorframe. "You two should come downstairs, you'll want to see this."

The sisters exchanged a curious glance before leaving the room. When they got downstairs, they found everyone crowded around a laptop, with the news playing onscreen. Ruby was front and center. The leader of WestCorp was at a podium addressing the media. Shada recognized the island in the background.

"What's this about?" Sikya asked.

Gustavo informed her that Ruby was offering free post-birth edits beginning the next day. The banner at the bottom displayed the information in text.

"This isn't good," Tony said. Some of the group nodded in agreement, and some ignored Tony and kept their eyes on the screen, their jaws clenched, shaking their heads in anger.

Ruby's announcement bothered Shada. There was a scratchiness inside her that wouldn't go away. What did the woman want? The last time free edits had been provided, the resistance had to protect Shada from vengeful recipients of the procedure. Shada wondered if these edits were of the same variety, that the people subjected to the change would be told the members of the resistance were responsible and would hunt them down.

"Sounds like something Ruby would do," Hollis said. "Since she hasn't heard from any member of the group."

For a split second, Shada wondered if they should have allowed Ophelia's attempted communication to succeed but altered the message she sent.

"Too late, what's done is done," Marnie said.

Shada agreed. No point in second-guessing the group's decision. She knew one thing for certain: if the storage device did exist, they needed to use it. The members of the resistance would be needed and couldn't be expected to stay locked away in a house, afraid to sleep.

"I've got to get to the island," she told the group. Everyone turned to her and stared.

CHAPTER FIFTEEN

SHADA'S DESIRE TO go back to the island came as a shock to them all.

Gustavo looked as if he had been betrayed. "Wait, you want to get edited?" he said.

Tony hadn't told anyone but Sikya about the message from Alfie, so Shada filled everyone else in. "I believe he's found a way to store a mind outside the body. I need to find out for sure, so we can store the minds you've all uploaded onto the device."

Ophelia's face brightened for the first time since her uploaded mind's attempted betrayal of the group, a spark of hope lighting up her darkened eyes. Vick and Kren both looked at their feet. Sophie was shocked.

"What if we want to keep it?" Sophie asked.

"That's your choice," Shada said. "I would never force you to do anything."

"If you're the only one, you'll have to find a way to sleep without putting the rest of us at risk," Gustavo said.

Sophie grew defensive. "And what if I don't?"

"If you don't, then why would we let you stick around?" Gustavo shot back.

"That's not up to you to decide. The group would have to make that decision," Mark said. "If she wants to keep her uploaded mind, I'll keep mine as well, and we can help each other."

The two of them looked at each other, and Shada wondered if they were harboring a secret romance.

It was decided that Tony would accompany Shada on her trip. She wanted to go by herself but was told it was too risky. Mark thought Shada shouldn't go at all, that two of the team members should go talk to Alfie instead.

"The message was for me," Shada said. "There's a chance the storage device isn't even done, that he needs me to help finish the project."

"What would he need you for?" Vick said. "If you could have solved the problem, you wouldn't need the computer engineer."

"If the engineer needs to be uploaded, who better than her to accept another mind?" Sikya said. Her attitude towards Shada's trip had changed the moment it was decided Tony would join her, and Shada knew she wanted Tony back the way he was before. He would be able to sleep without worry, and Sikya would still be safe because they had fulfilled their end of the bargain.

"Agreed. If the message was for Shada, then she has to go," Tony said. "We'll be back as soon as possible."

Nobody pushed back again.

Tony and Shada left within the hour. Ruby's announcement had come in the early evening, and it was already dark by the time the pair left the house. Shada had been stuck inside for days, and being outside again felt like leaving her protective bubble. They decided to take the train into the heart of the city, where they would then catch the tram to the island, so the vehicles could be left at the house in case they were needed by those left behind.

Shada was surprised at how many people were walking towards the train station with them. Not many people lived in that part of the city—since the houses were so large and expensive, not many could afford to live there—but the few who did were streaming from their residences, with more joining as they went.

"Ruby said the edits won't be offered until tomorrow," Tony said.

"Maybe they're lining up," replied Shada.

The underground train station was full when they arrived. There was one attendant, since normal travel volume at that time didn't require more, and she was busy helping people get their tickets and pass through the turnstiles. When Shada and Tony got onto the platform, they were met by a sea of people waiting for the next train to arrive. A display said it would be there in eleven minutes.

"There's no other reason all these people would be out at this time," Tony said. "Everyone's going to the island."

"I can't believe everyone wants to be edited," Shada said, looking around. "I wonder if Ruby's expecting this kind of volume." She hoped the edits Ruby was providing were the standard type, to make everyone happier, healthier, and smarter. If not, if Ruby was going to edit them to be angry and impulsive, the people still at the house would soon be in danger.

Shada remembered those who'd blamed her for their not receiving the standard edits. They had hunted her down and almost got their hands on her before her trip back to the island with Chloe. Did any of them still roam the streets? Could they be here, on the platform with her? She hoped they'd learned their lesson from their first experience with WestCorp and were staying far away.

Tony must have sensed her fear, because he shuffled closer to her, his eyes scanning for threats.

They boarded the train together when it arrived. Every seat was taken, and the remaining passengers had to stand squeezed together in order for everyone to fit. The passengers were silent.

Shada studied the people packed in the train with her. Her heart sank when she saw children, some still in pajamas. She hoped their parents weren't taking them to the island and told herself they were on the train for some other reason, any other reason, like going to the hospital because they were sick.

"Stop lying to yourself," Shada heard Hollis say. "Those kids will be edited alongside their parents."

Shada closed her eyes and counted ten breaths instead of engaging with the edited mind inside her. She hoped the children would get off every time the train stopped at a different station. They never did. Each platform they stopped at was filled with people, and since nobody disembarked, their car wasn't able to accept more passengers. The closer someone was to the heart of the city, the longer they would have to wait, if they wanted to take the train. Of course, they could always walk, and Shada had a feeling these people would get to the tram any way they could.

The entire contents of the train spilled onto the platform when it pulled to a stop beneath the heart of the city. Shada looked inside the train before it pulled away and saw a solitary older woman, homeless by the look of her and the amount of luggage she had. She must not have heard about the free edits, and Shada imagined how confused she was after being joined on her trip by so many people before being left to continue on alone.

There was a line to get to the lower level where the tram that would take them to WestCorp departed. It stretched up the stairs and went out the entrance. She wished she had a special pass, one that said she had business on the island and wasn't there for the edits, but who would look at it? She remembered the information desk at the end of WestCorp's tram platform. It was worth a shot. "Come with me," she told Tony.

WestCorp employees were on the platform maintaining order, distinguishable by their smiling faces, khaki pants, and white polos. There were queues where each of the tram doors opened, and unedited inhabitants of the city stood five deep in each. Shada asked a WestCorp employee if she could get to the island sooner since she wasn't going for the edits.

"Sorry, everyone has to wait in line," a smiling man with salt-and-pepper hair told her.

"What about those who need to commute to the island tomorrow morning?" she asked.

"All meetings have been rescheduled."

"What if I'm edited and need to get back?"

The man's smile broadened, showing off straight white teeth without imperfections. "All edited were told to stay on the island or risk being left in the city. These people are our first priority," he said with a wave of his hand.

An older unedited woman, in her late sixties or early seventies, smiled at what was taken for superior customer service.

Shada shook her head and began walking the length of the line. The gates were kept open as the line stretched through them, and Shada asked a station employee if they were still ticketing. "No ma'am, WestCorp paid to keep these open."

The line stretched down the city blocks approaching the station. Tony and Shada took their place at the end as more people stood behind them. She had never seen a line so long and wondered how long it would take to move to the front.

Hours went by. At first, they had moved a few steps every fifteen minutes, but towards the middle of the night their progress stalled and never began again. She thought people would leave the line, but those around her sat down on the sidewalk instead, not willing to lose their spot. Close to dawn, word reached them that there was a one-in, one-out policy, since the island was full, meaning that one tram car would depart for the island as soon as a full one arrived.

The line moved again as the sun rose. Everyone knew this meant the first edited people were coming back to the city, and all eyes turned towards the station. Sirens rang out within minutes of the line making progress, and emergency vehicles raced towards the entrance to the station.

"What's going on?" everyone seemed to ask at the same time.

Word trickled back that there were people upset with waiting so long they'd begun vandalizing the area around the entrance, hoping to scare away those waiting in line. Shada's heart sank at her suspicion that the destruction was committed by those just returning from the island.

Twice more the line moved forward, meaning two more trams had returned. Shada and Tony were now three blocks from the station's entrance and could see a line of cops, in full riot gear, who had set up on the far side of the street.

The sound of glass breaking rang out in the early morning hours, followed by an explosion. Shada stepped into the street and could see flames on the far side of the station. Nobody abandoned their spot in line, convinced the damage was done with the sole purpose of scaring them to do so.

Shada watched as the cops scattered and began trying to apprehend those in front of the station who were rioting. One young man evaded them and ran down the street towards her. Tony pulled her back into line and placed himself between her and the street.

As the young man approached, Shada saw his ecstatic eyes

and was shaken by the grin on his face. He seemed to enjoy being chased. The cops behind him yelled for him to stop.

The young man reached in his pocket, pulled something out, then slammed it into his arm. He threw it to the side, where it landed on the ground next to Tony.

It was a clear, finger-sized vial, with WESTCORP written in black on the side.

"So they used my idea," Hollis said.

"Guess so," Shada thought in reply, staring at the vial that had been full of Stim moments before.

CHAPTER SIXTEEN

SHADA EXPLAINED to Tony what the vial had contained. "It keeps you wired. They gave it to me when I was on the island so I wouldn't sleep. I've never had so much energy in my life."

Tony turned back from watching the police's pursuit of the young man. "You think they gave the stuff to everyone coming back from the island?" he said.

"It wouldn't surprise me. All that extra energy would have to be burned somehow, that's why they are vandalizing the city. It's only going to get worse as more people return."

The line marched forward and stopped half a block closer to the entrance. "I think we should go back," Tony said.

Shada cocked her head. "Why? Once we get onto the island, you can get the edited mind out of you. You'll be back to normal."

"Assuming that the storage device is even finished. You don't know that for sure."

Shada nodded, agreeing that Tony presented a fair point.

"Plus, what if Ruby told them to hunt us down, like she did for you? We're sitting ducks out here," Tony said. He kept leaning into the street and looking towards the station, monitoring the destruction from afar.

Thick black smoke rose in the distance. Tony told Shada a car up ahead was burning.

"We need to get out of here," he said again.

"Now that we're making progress? Come on, we've already been waiting all night."

"The closer we get to the station, the larger the chance one of them spots us."

"Assuming Ruby told them to go after us," Shada said.

The line moved forward again. They were now two blocks away. Shada leaned into the street as well and watched another batch of people with fresh edits stream from the station. There were dozens of them, and after taking one look at the scattered police officers and the destruction caused by those who came before, they ran in every direction, looking for something to destroy themselves. It was as if they'd walked into the city and were unleashed to join in the fun.

One pair, a man and a woman, left the fresh destruction behind and ran down the street in the direction of Shada and Tony. Tony stepped out into the street when they got close.

"Hey!" he called out to them, getting their attention.

The two individuals stopped in their tracks. Their heads tilted to the side and they blinked twice, as if they were animals in the wild who had just spotted their prey. They leaned forward and walked towards Tony, crouched, ready to pounce. Tony pulled out his pistol.

"What did I tell you?" Tony called over his shoulder.

Inside Shada's head, Hollis laughed. "Shouldn't have stopped that girl from contacting WestCorp," he said.

Marnie responded. "Don't distract her. You do know if she gets killed, we do too, right?"

Shada closed her eyes, took a deep breath, and blocked both minds from communicating with her.

With a curse, Shada stepped out of line and stood next to Tony. At the sight of Shada, the woman stood up straight, turned around, and yelled in the direction of the station entrance. "Over here!" she said.

One new arrival heard her, and when he saw two of his fellow edited being held at gunpoint, he turned around and yelled for more of the edited to follow him. Five more, farther away, heard his call, and instead of continuing to break windows where they were, they began walking towards Shada and Tony.

"Agree we've got to get out of here?" Tony said.

"Agreed."

Tony walked backwards, his gun still on the approaching pair, and Shada did the same. They were waiting for the opportunity to run. The edited man who'd communicated to the other five jogged forward until he was with them. The three of them could rush at any moment.

The gun went off before any of them could make their move. One of the men collapsed in a heap, writhing on the ground and holding his leg. A second shot rang out, and the second man fell as well. Both had been shot in the leg.

The woman with them didn't bother to inspect if they were all right. She lunged forward, sprinting at Tony and Shada as fast as she could. Tony fired a third time and the woman collapsed in a heap, clutching her side. The five edited in the distance began sprinting.

"Run!" Tony said.

Shada sprinted away as fast as she could. Tony, behind her, instructed her to turn right down a side street, through the line that stretched off into the distance. They ran for a block then turned left. Shada continued for as long as she could down the street parallel to the one they had stood on the entire night before she slowed to a walk and turned to see if they were still being pursued.

All five new arrivals turned the corner, running as fast as they could, the taller, thinner ones in front, the slower ones behind.

"Could use some of that Stim right about now," Tony said through heavy breaths.

"We'd never stop running," Shada replied.

Tony told Shada to go into an apartment building. The entire city seemed to be shut down, its inhabitants all waiting in line for their free edits. Soon, they'd be joining the pursuit for Tony and Shada as well.

Inside the apartment building, Tony and Shada found the staircase and began climbing. They were on the third floor by the time they heard footsteps below. On the fifth floor, Tony told Shada to exit the staircase.

"We've got to find somewhere to hide," he said. Shada could tell Tony was focused on keeping control over his breathing, scared the mind inside him would use the danger as an opportunity to take back control of his body. When Shada tried the door of the first apartment inside the hallway, Tony told her to keep running until they turned a corner. "In case they look into the hallway from the stairs," he explained.

They found an unlocked apartment and rushed inside, shutting the door behind them without a noise. The air was stale, and the furniture belonged to another decade. They assumed it was empty until a weak woman's voice called out from the back. "Diego? Is that you?"

Tony followed the voice to the back bedroom. He popped his head inside and held a finger up to his lips. When Shada looked in, she saw a white-haired skeleton of a woman, so old her days couldn't involve much movement. She assumed Diego was the elder's son, or caregiver.

The woman's eyes, fearful at the sight of Tony and the gun in his hand, pleaded with Shada for protection. "What's going on?" she asked Shada. "Why does he have a gun?"

Shada knelt next to the woman's bed. "We're here to protect you," Shada said. "Diego sent us. He's on the way to get edited now."

"Diego's always so thoughtful! I'd go too, but I can't leave the apartment," the woman said, resting her head on the pillow with a sigh.

Tony and Shada spent the day with the woman. There was no sign of their edited pursuers, or Diego, but Tony kept his weapon ready. The woman had plenty of canned food. Shada and Tony ate one meal, wanting to leave as much food as possible for their host because they didn't know how long she would have to last on her own. Both of them knew if Diego was edited, he wouldn't be coming back for her, he'd be hunting for them and the rest of their group.

They decided to wait until nightfall to try to make their way back to the house Tensen had provided. They discussed the possibility Tensen would tell Ruby where the group lived, and they convinced themselves that Tensen would keep their secret safe. They hoped. Both Shada and Tony referred to the group as a whole, but each knew they both prioritized Sikya's safety.

Travel across the city was slow without the train. They took care to move between buildings so they could hide if necessary and made it more than halfway back on the first night. Their day was spent hidden in the chemical storage room of an industrial cleaning company, and their projections put them back at the diplomat's house in the middle of the second night.

Their plan didn't account for the barriers.

The first barrier they encountered was a pile of cars stacked up in the street. Bright lights accompanied by the rumble of heavy engines streaked by on the far side. A block over was another barrier, this one built from concrete dividers. It was as if the city had spent the day erecting walls to keep everyone apart, dividing itself into sections. Shada assumed it was the work of the unedited locals and not the returning edited, even though the new arrivals were the ones with Stim and could have worked the hours necessary to get the job done.

Shada and Tony were forced to travel through buildings to get past the barriers, instead of running through streets and using buildings as way stations. They managed to get past the first set of barriers by moving through a convenience store and kept looking for the vehicles they'd heard before, not knowing if they belonged to the city or the edited. Not being able to travel through the streets made their trip take much longer than expected, and they got back to the neighborhood of the safe house right after dawn. The street outside was abandoned; to limit their exposure, they approached the house from the rear, hopping between backyards.

They knocked on the back door and Kren answered.

"Where have you been?" she exclaimed when she saw them.

Within moments, everyone was at the back entrance, even those who had been asleep, grateful to see Shada and Tony alive.

When Sikya rushed forward and gave Tony a hug, Shada felt both happy her sister had found someone and sad she wasn't the first one Sikya embraced. Her place in Sikya's life had been taken. Sikya pulled away from Tony and hugged Shada.

Shada was quiet while Tony told the group how they had been standing in line when the riots began and had to come back. It didn't take long for his own questions to begin.

"Has anyone come here looking for you?" he asked.

Gustavo told him no. "We wanted to leave, to look for you, but we thought you might show up here, so we stayed put."

"Good," Tony said. "The edited are coming back to the city to hunt us down."

CHAPTER SEVENTEEN

"The reports say the unedited are rioting to scare people from getting WestCorp's free edits," Gustavo told Tony and Shada. "It's all over the news."

Tony shook his head. "The people coming back from the island were the ones rioting. They got to work as soon as they left the station."

"They've been Stimmed," Shada added. "With all that extra energy, Ruby just had to point and off they went."

"Stimmed?" Sophie asked. She twirled a pen in her fingers while she sat at the kitchen table.

"A compound WestCorp developed so their workers could push past their physical limits. No need to sleep," Shada explained. "They gave it to me when I was held hostage to keep me awake. I've never felt so energized."

Sophie nodded then stared at the pen crawling across the back of her hand.

"Tensen instituted martial law," Sikya said. She didn't bother to hide her frustration. "Accepted money and support from WestCorp to get the city back in order."

Gustavo and Tony met each other's gaze. "He's gone off the

deep end," Gustavo said. "He doesn't care about the unedited anymore, if he ever did in the first place."

"I think he did before Ruby got into his ear," Shada said. "That woman is an expert manipulator."

"He divided the city into districts: Alpha, Sigma, and Theta. Said his goal was to keep the riots contained to specific areas," Sikya said.

"We had to pass by some of the borders," Tony said. "Looks like they were made of whatever was available: piles of cars and concrete. The area around here seemed untouched, but we need to get out of here. If anyone finds out where we are—"

"Or if Tensen tells Ruby where we are," Gustavo interjected.

"We'll have some serious problems."

"Where should we go?" Kren asked.

The group fell silent while they tried to come up with a solution.

"Could we go to the warehouse?" Ophelia said.

"In theory, yes, but it would present the same challenges as here: we're trapped if they find us. Both the warehouse and here could work as long as nobody finds out where we are."

"Are you worried somebody would give up our location?" Ophelia said. "We already sleep in shifts; I don't think it would be one of us."

"It's more about the lack of exits. If we'd had time to prepare, we could have made an escape tunnel, but that's not an option now."

Gustavo suggested they take the high ground. "If we find a high-rise and stay in the upper levels, we could see everyone coming into the building. We could cut off the elevator and block the staircases."

"And if they found us all they'd have to do is wait," Vick said.

Gustavo looked down at the floor, thinking. "What if we go to Tensen? He has a ton of security, his office is high up, and if we're there, we can make sure he doesn't say anything to Ruby."

"All he'd have to do is get a single message out. That's going to be difficult to stop. His priority is the city, and WestCorp has him convinced they are helping," Tony said.

Silence descended on the group. "Instead of going up, we could go down," Shada said.

Everyone looked at Shada. Kren was the first to speak. "What do you mean?"

"The tunnels. If we need places to run, it would make sense to be in a series of tunnels. We could split up if we needed to and pick where we come back onto the surface for supplies. Not much light, and probably smells terrible, but it could work."

"The tunnels," Tony said, chewing on the thought. "It does work."

"What made you think of that?" Gustavo said with a chuckle.

"I was just thinking about escaping, how it would be nice to be near a train."

Gustavo was impressed. Shada's face flushed.

"We could enter at the train station, walk until we found somewhere to set up camp," Tony said.

"What if we don't want to go?" Vick said. Her nose was turned up.

"Then you can stay on the surface and wait to be found. The way this city is being torn apart, it's not if, it's when."

She was quick to backtrack. "I was just saying, in case someone didn't want to go."

The group decided they would wait until night to leave under the cover of darkness. Tony and Shada excused themselves and went to sleep, their first proper rest in days. Everyone else took turns sleeping in shifts in preparation for their long night, even though some of them had just woken up when Tony and Shada arrived back at the house.

Packing for the journey took place throughout the day. Everyone carried two bags when they left, one filled with their own personal items and a second with items the group would need: food, toiletries, and cookware. Everyone was responsible for as much water as they could carry. The plan was for them to travel in three groups of three and meet up at the train station, each group traveling along a different route. Shada and Sikya were placed in separate groups, since it didn't make sense for one member of the resistance to guard two of them. Tony made sure he went with Sikya, and they took Kren with them. Gustavo stayed by Shada's side during the assigning of groups, and the two of them were joined by Sophie. Ophelia, Mark, and Vick made up the third group.

Since Sikya was pregnant, they had her group take the shortest route to the station, a straight shot that avoided open road. Mark, Ophelia, and Vick left first, making an arc out to the left before turning back in the direction of the station. Shada's group's route was the mirror image, an arc to the right, and Sikya's group left last. If anyone was watching the house, the hope was they would follow the first two groups instead of going after the slow-traveling Sikya.

The trip went by in a blur. The next thing Shada knew, all nine travelers were underground, in the darkness of the tunnel between the station and the heart of the city. Vick handed out glow sticks. Everyone cracked them and used the meager light to inspect their surroundings. The tunnel was filthy, filled with a variety of paper trash, and a thick layer of grime covered the concrete walls. Sikya covered her mouth with her shirt. The light from the glow sticks didn't reach the ceiling, but it illuminated the numerous pillars, casting shadows into the dark spaces beyond.

"Let's start walking," Tony said. "If anyone hears a train, let us know so we have plenty of time to get out of the way." Pregnant women weren't known for being quick on their feet.

"The trains have stopped running," Gustavo said.

"Part of the whole martial law thing," added Kren.

"So we shouldn't hear anything. But if we do, give the rest of the group a heads-up."

Tony and Gustavo led the way, with Shada and Sikya right behind them and the rest of the group in the rear. Every so often, Tony would point to the ground without saying a word, calling Gustavo's attention to something without stopping to investigate. It took Shada a few times to realize there was evidence of other people who had traveled through the tunnel before them.

A flickering light up ahead made Tony stop the group. He told Mark and Vick to investigate while everyone else stayed back. It turned out to be a group of unedited squatters who had come down to the tunnels when the riots began. "They said to keep walking, then turn left down a side passage. There's an area where we can set up," Mark reported.

The area the group was directed to was at the intersection of three walkways. Each walkway was large enough to accommodate the tallest workers, but the intersection of the three opened up to a high ceiling. A large wall on one side was covered in graffiti. Nobody objected when Mark said, "This will work."

The group cracked open a prepared meal, the last home-cooked meal they expected to eat for a while. There wasn't any use in saving food for later since there was no way to keep the leftovers from spoiling. The men ate more than they would have under normal circumstances so the food wouldn't go to waste.

Tony, Kren, and Sophie were assigned the first watch, a person for each walkway leading into the space. They were tasked with keeping an eye out for intruders in addition to making sure none of the group woke up and tried to contact WestCorp.

From where Shada lay, she could see Tony's back as he sat in the middle of the passage that faced the wall. She had trouble falling asleep, since she had slept the entirety of the previous day, and she hadn't eaten enough food to make her eyelids heavy. She guessed an hour or so went by while she focused on her breathing. She watched as Tony turned around to inspect the group. She squinted to hide the whites of her eyes, kept her face relaxed, and witnessed Tony stand up and walk away without making a sound.

He was gone too long for a bathroom break. No, he left, then came back while everyone but Shada was fast asleep.

CHAPTER EIGHTEEN

SHADA SLEPT through the changing of the guard. When she woke up, Tony, Kren, and Sophie were fast asleep. Ophelia, Vick, and Mark were posted at the three entrances to their space. "Where's Gustavo?" she asked Sikya.

Sikya was lying on her back, her hands on her stomach. "He said he'd be back before he walked off. He's been gone for a while now," she said. She beckoned Shada over with her head and whispered, "Come here."

Shada crawled over.

Sikya took Shada's hand and placed it on her stomach. "Can you feel him?"

"It's a him? When did you find out?" Shada said. Her eyes fell as she waited for a kick.

"I just know it's a boy," Sikya whispered, as if she didn't want to scare the child inside her.

Shada felt a series of rumbles beneath her hand. She looked at her sister and smiled. "He's dancing in there!"

"Has been all morning."

They lay next to each other while the others slept. Shada debated whether or not she should tell Sikya about Tony's nighttime trip. She still hadn't decided what to do when Gustavo came back and knelt down at their feet, off the blankets, on the cold concrete floor. He looked at his watch. "They'll be awake soon. We should get some food ready."

Shada pulled out a camp stove and boiled a large pot of water. With it, they made instant oatmeal and coffee. The smell woke up the three sleepers, and once they were awake, the three who stood guard were able to leave their posts and join them.

Shada waited until everyone finished eating before she said what was on her mind. "We should find somewhere else to set up," she said.

Ophelia was collecting everyone's trash. "Why? We just got here."

Shada didn't want to share her concern that Tony had given up their location. Instead, she said it would be best if they found somewhere with more space, so they didn't have to live in such close quarters. "We could set it up so people could sleep apart from everyone else, a room with one door if we can find it. Those who are asleep wouldn't be disturbed, and one person would be enough to watch them, instead of three," she said.

"I found a group of people in a blocked-off train station half an hour's walk from here when I was out exploring," Gustavo said. "We could take a corner of the platform and find a bedroom for when some of us"—he gestured to the seven resistance members—"need to sleep."

Everyone looked at Tony. He let the suggestion digest for a moment before agreeing with the move. "Pack everything up then, we'll head out soon."

Whenever Sikya tried to help, a member of the group told her to sit back down. They'd packed light, so it didn't take long to be ready to move. Gustavo led the way down the tunnel, with the same reminder as before to keep an ear out for trains. There still wasn't a single sign that any of the trains were running.

The tunnel curved to the right. The space ahead became more illuminated as they walked, until the entrance to the station ahead could be seen, a circle of light in the distance. It reminded Shada of coming back to reality for the first time after being hijacked. She realized she hadn't heard from Hollis or Marnie for some time. Instead of checking in on them, she left them alone, content with them staying in the background.

Tony told the group to stop at the entrance to the station. "Get your eyes acclimated to the light," he instructed.

Shada got a whiff of sewage while she waited for her eyes to adjust. Hollis started complaining, so she blocked him from using her senses to experience the world. She wished it was possible for someone to do the same to her so she could escape the stench too.

There were three groups of people on the two platforms. One group was in each of the far corners, and the third group was set up in the middle, on the right side of the station. Both entrances were blocked off, one with piles of furniture and one with broken concrete rubble that had bent rebar sticking out at odd angles. A boy, no more than nine, was playing with a rubber ball on the right platform. The ball rolled in the group's direction. He chased it down and saw the nine people waiting in the shadows. His jaw fell, and he froze. Shada saw Sikya, ahead of her, flash the boy a smile. Without grabbing his ball, he turned and ran. He reached a woman in the middle of the platform—his mother, judging by her age—and buried his face in her side, clutching her around the waist. She rubbed his head. He turned to the where the group stood and pointed. His mother hurried over to a group of seated men and leaned in close to one of them.

The next thing Shada knew, four men were walking towards their location, baseball bats in hand.

"We should go out there," Gustavo said.

"Did you already meet them?" Sophie asked.

"Nope, I stayed here and watched them for a minute before coming back."

"Let's go introduce ourselves," Tony said. He led the way into the light of the station, both hands raised.

The four men stopped their approach when they saw the number, and quality, of people who showed themselves. Shada and Sikya both used their hands to shield their eyes, but the other members of the resistance strode forward, tall and proud-chested.

"Hello!" Tony said, doing his best to sound welcoming.

"Hello," said the man in front, the one who had been informed of their presence. "What can we do for you?"

Tony hopped up onto the platform and the rest of the resistance followed. Shada kneeled on one leg and offered her bent knee to Sikya to use as a step, which Sikya refused, and Ophelia reached down to help the pregnant woman climb up. She managed to get both knees onto the platform, then stood up one leg at a time. Shada was last to get onto the platform; she placed both hands on the edge and threw a leg up before standing up to join the others.

Tony waited until everyone was on the same level before kicking the boy's ball back to him. "We were wondering if we could set up camp here," he said. He looked around. "We could take that corner," he said, pointing to the end of the opposite platform. "And guard against others coming in from the tunnel."

By now, the rest of the women and children on the platform had gathered behind the group of men. A man on the far platform called out, "Everything all right over there, Jimmy?"

"Everything's fine," Jimmy, the leader of the small group, responded.

"She's pregnant," a woman who appeared to be Jimmy's wife called out.

"I see that, honey," Jimmy said.

One of the men whispered into the leader's ear. Both pairs of eyes fell to the waistbands of the resistance members, noticing their weapons for the first time.

Jimmy's face fell for an instant before he flashed Tony, and the rest of the group, a smile. "Make yourselves at home!" he said. He lowered his voice. "But take the end of the platform on this side, you don't want to set up in that far corner."

Tony thanked the man, and Gustavo oversaw the setup of their camp. Four of the group were instructed to put their belongings along the wall closest to the tunnel, and the other five were told to put their stuff along the wall closest to the entrance, the one blocked off by piles of furniture. He put the camp stove, food, and water in the corner, explaining he didn't want the other groups to see how much and what kind of food they had. "Food and water are going to be the biggest things for us to worry about," he said. "Carrying it down from the surface isn't going to be easy, for anyone."

The young boy, who was curious about the newcomers taking the space where he played with his ball, was lingering nearby. When he heard Gustavo talk about water, he said the water fountains in the middle still worked. "That's where we get our water from," he added, before chasing his ball back towards the area his family occupied.

Shada looked at the group, pretending she was seeing them for the first time. They were all thin, sinewy, and it was clear from their matching outfits and the hard looks on their faces they were not people to be messed with. With this in mind, she informed the others she would walk over to the camp and introduce herself to the neighbors alone. Just inside the edge of the middle camp, she saw the water fountain on the wall near the blocked entrance. Part of it had been removed so larger containers could be filled.

Jimmy came out to meet her. "Do you need something?" he said, his voice cold.

"Just wanted to introduce myself," Shada said. In her mind, Shada heard Hollis add, "So she can drink your water."

Jimmy stood still before the boy's mother rushed forward, scolding him. "Where are your manners?" she said. She looked at Shada. "My name is Caprice," she said, walking forward and extending a hand.

"Shada," she replied with a smile.

"I'm sure you've seen my little guy, James, running around. Just tell him to leave you alone if he bothers you."

Shada laughed. "I'll keep that in mind."

Marnie communicated to Shada through shared thoughts. "They seem nice," she observed.

Caprice gave Shada a tour of their encampment, the one in the middle of the platform. The one in the farthest corner was Caprice's sister's family. The two camps were mingled most of the time, so when Caprice was finished the first tour, she showed Shada the setup on the far end as well. There were three other men in the two camps, two women, and a couple of surly teenagers who didn't look Shada in the eye. All their names were shared, but Shada retained none other than the first family she'd had contact with.

"Across there is Tim and his family. We don't go over there."

"Any particular reason?" Shada said, doing her best to sound curious without being intrusive.

"They use the corner of the platform as their bathroom instead of going off into the tunnels. It's gross over there; best to just stay away."

A white sheet hung in the far corner. The stench near the tunnel made sense now.

"I noticed a water fountain . . ." Shada said, her voice trailing off.

"Right." Caprice paused. "We don't share it with them." She pointed across the station with her head. "But since you've got a pregnant woman with you—"

"She's my sister," Shada said.

Caprice smiled, appreciative of sisters who stuck together. "Then you guys can use it. Fill up containers for emergencies, while it still works."

"We appreciate it," Shada said. "Let me go back and let them know."

"We'll talk soon!" Caprice said as Shada walked away, sounding like they were friends who had just had lunch together.

The boy stood near the wall of the platform, halfway between his family's two camps. There was just enough room for him to play without going near the edge. He waited until he was sure Shada was paying attention to him then kicked the ball in her direction, so slow there was little risk it would fall onto the train tracks. Shada kicked it back. The boy smiled and left her alone to walk through the middle camp and back to her own.

CHAPTER NINETEEN

THERE WAS nothing for the group to do but exist once their space was organized. They had light, shelter, and water, and meals required two people, at most, to prepare. The members of the resistance performed body-weight exercises to pass the time.

The bathroom situation was the first problem to be addressed. Sikya asked Gustavo if she should share the same area in the far tunnel their neighbors used as a bathroom. Shada overheard the question and said she thought Caprice would show her where to go.

"Let's just find our own spot," Gustavo said to Shada. "I don't want us to have to walk across the platform every time we need to use the bathroom." He looked at Sikya. "Let's go into the tunnel and see if we can find a good spot."

Sikya looked uncomfortable at being joined by a man. Sophie offered to go with Sikya. "I can stay with her while you find somewhere for us to sleep," she said to Gustavo.

Gustavo agreed, since it would save a later trip. Tony helped Sikya down onto the train tracks and watched the three of them disappear into the shadows.

Shada was on edge the entire time her sister was gone. She

could tell Tony was too. When Sikya walked back into the light a half hour later, she crinkled her nose at the smell coming from the opposite platform. Both Shada and Tony helped pull her up from the tracks.

"We should build a set of stairs," Tony said, thinking out loud.

"You don't want to do this every time?" Sikya said. Her breathing was heavy.

Tony let out a relieved laugh, able to relax now that Sikya was back.

Shada took her sister by the arm and made her sit down with her back against the wall. Tony lingered around them, waiting to see if there was any way for him to help.

"If we stay here for a while, I don't know if I can keep doing that. This guy's getting bigger by the day," Sikya said. She tapped her stomach; she could have been referring to her belly or to the baby inside.

"There's a maintenance room a short walk from here where we can sleep," Gustavo reported. Everyone could hear him, since they lived in such close quarters. "Took me a while to get the door open, but it will work well."

"It took you a while because you had to wait for me," Sophie said with a smirk.

"Right, she picked the lock in no time at all. I was going to shoot it if I had to."

"And where are we supposed to go to the bathroom?" Ophelia asked.

"There's an open space just inside the tunnel. Past the pillars on one side of the track," Sophie said.

"Whoever goes has to bring someone else with them," Tony said. He looked at both Shada and Sikya. "One of us, to keep an eye out. Just in case," he said, referring to the members of the resistance.

"I can't go to the bathroom unless you hold my hand," Gustavo said. His expression didn't change.

Tony chuckled and shook his head. "Only you," he said.

Gustavo grinned and gave Shada a wink.

Gustavo and Shada turned away from the group and joined Sikya with their backs against the wall. She was watching the boy play on the far side of the middle camp.

"I wonder if this guy will play sports," Sikya said, tapping her stomach.

"I'm sure he will," Shada replied. "I'll be the one to teach him!"

Sikya looked at Shada with tears in her eyes. "Will there even be sports to play for unedited people?"

"Of course there will be!" Shada said. She wasn't as confident as she sounded, but she wanted to cheer up her sister.

"The world is changing. I don't want him to have to deal with WestCorp just to have a future," Sikya said, her voice full of sadness.

The sisters and Gustavo sat in silence. Shada was the first to break it. "I'm going to get back to the island and stop the edits," she declared. "This little guy doesn't need to grow up in a world like this."

"How are you going to do that?"

"Not sure," Shada admitted. "I'll blow up the lab if I have to."

Gustavo stared at Shada. "What about storing the minds on the device? Alfie can't do that without a lab," he said.

"Well, what's the point of getting the edited minds out of everyone if there's no city to return to?" Shada said.

Neither Gustavo nor Sikya said another word.

Marnie told Shada she should spend the night with Gustavo, and Hollis accused Marnie of having a crush on the mischievous man. "It's clear he likes her," Marnie said. "They're both young and strong. Why not?"

Shada read Hollis's thoughts and learned about his disgust at the prospect. She hadn't considered how getting physical with a man might not be something Hollis would want to witness, and she communicated, through her thoughts, that she'd block him out if it ever happened.

Marnie told Shada to leave her alone. She wouldn't mind seeing the act occur.

"Bet you wouldn't," Hollis responded.

Shada took ten controlled breaths and ignored the two bickering minds.

Over dinner that night, the group discussed how soon they would run out of food. Kren calculated they had enough for the next four days. "I think we should make groups of two or three, head to the surface at night, and see what we can gather," she said.

"Three," Tony said. "Two can carry most of the supplies and the third can protect them."

Gustavo suggested they make a trip in two days. "That way, if the first group doesn't find anything, we can take another trip before we miss a meal."

Everyone agreed. There was an awareness of Sikya and the life growing inside her that nobody vocalized. They could go hungry if necessary, but she couldn't.

Tony said they needed to decide who would keep watch over the room while the first shift slept. Tony, Kren, and Sophie had taken the first watch the previous night, and the task would fall to one of them. Tony said he would prefer to stay on the platform with Sikya, and nobody disagreed. Kren offered to watch the door while Mark, Vick, Ophelia, and Gustavo slept.

"And who's going to guard the second shift?" Tony asked, talking to the four who would sleep first.

Mark offered to do it, and nobody had any objections.

With the first shift of sleepers gone, Shada and Sikya were joined on the platform by Tony and Sophie. They both had to stay awake until it was their turn to rest. Shada tried to sleep but found the constant light distracting. She tossed and turned, and when she faced Sikya, she saw her sister was wide awake as well. They exchanged a thin-lipped smile before Shada closed her eyes and counted ten breaths.

She was woken up by a gunshot from the tunnels.

By the time Shada had opened her eyes and sat up, Tony and Sophie were already on their feet, heading towards the noise. At the end of the platform Tony stopped, leaned over as far as he could, and looked into the darkness.

"Kren!" he shouted. The name echoed off the walls in the tunnel until it was replaced by silence.

"We have to go," Sophie said.

Tony looked back at Sikya and told her he'd be back before leaving with Sophie.

More gunshots rang out soon after they disappeared into the tunnel. Shada could sense the distress her sister was under, her own nerves responding to her sister's elevated state. A few tense minutes passed before six of the group emerged from the tunnel and jumped onto the platform. Tony told Mark and Vick to cover the entrance to the station. The two of them nodded, turned around, and kept their weapons aimed at the shadows.

"Kren stayed back to cover us," Gustavo told Shada when he saw her counting those who had returned.

A series of gunshots rang out, and Shada knew, deep down inside, she would never see Kren again.

Tony helped Sikya stand while telling her, "We have to move."

Sikya stood and began gathering her things. Tony told her to leave it all. He grabbed her arm and pulled her towards the far end of the platform. Everyone from the other camps had already fled into the tunnel.

Gunshots rang out close behind them. They were near the water fountain when Sikya screamed in pain and fell to her knees. Tony knelt beside her.

Shada watched as her sister reached down between her legs, and her hand emerged covered with blood.

"Were you shot?" she asked.

"No," she said through gritted teeth. "The baby—" Her words were choked off by a groan.

Gustavo pulled on Shada's arm. "Come on, we've got to get out of here," he said.

"No! Not without her," Shada said.

Gustavo overpowered her. "Let Tony take care of her. You've got to get back to the island, remember? Nobody else can do it."

Shada struggled to get back to Sikya's side.

"It's what she would want," Gustavo yelled.

An earsplitting explosion forced everyone to look back at the tunnel. Where Shada had been lying down asleep just minutes before was now a crater. Rubble was everywhere. The mangled bodies of Mark and Vick were on the floor, their limbs at odd angles. Shada watched as WestCorp forces, identifiable by their white polos and khaki pants, streamed into the station. They all wore black body armor vests and black tactical helmets. There were at least a dozen of them.

CHAPTER TWENTY

SELF-PRESERVATION TOOK over and Shada began to run. Gustavo led the way, crouching behind the left-behind gear in the other camps as he went. The shouting and the gunshots behind them blended into one cacophonous mess of sounds.

The next thing Shada knew, she was in the tunnel with Gustavo, Sophie, and Ophelia. Tony had stayed behind. The three remaining members of the resistance took up positions behind cement pillars with their weapons aimed at the entrance to the tunnel. A WestCorp member jumped down from the platform and ran into the shadows. Three gunshots rang out, and he fell forward in a heap. Gustavo fired once more, ensuring the pursuer never stood up again.

Shada looked further into the darkness of the tunnel. The rest of the displaced platform dwellers had their eyes wide open as they watched the action unfold.

After a series of frantic gunshots on the platform, another person jumped down and began running into the tunnel with their hands up.

"Don't shoot!" Tony said. He dove into the shadows on the

dark side of the wall that separated the platform from the tunnel.

Shada rushed forward without a second thought, ignoring her own safety. "You left her behind!" she said. She punched Tony in the face, and was about to again, when he caught her hand.

Another series of gunshots rang out, and three more members of WestCorp fell to the ground just inside the shadow of the tunnel.

"Stop!" Tony said to Shada. "Listen, she told me to! She couldn't move, and she wanted me to help you get to the island," Tony said.

Shada tried to strike him with her other hand. "Why did you listen to her?"

He was about to answer when a man's voice from the platform yelled into the tunnel. "Give up the fight!" he said.

Shada froze.

"You're resisting the inevitable. We're the future, you just haven't recognized it yet. Help us save the city."

His words were met with silence. Shada knew he was talking to her, that this message was from Ruby.

"Everyone is getting edited; you can too. No questions asked. We'll forget about the men you killed."

"We won't!" Gustavo shouted.

In the dim light, Shada saw Tony shake his head in frustration at his comrade's outburst.

"If you're still listening, we don't expect you to come out. We'll take care of the pregnant one on the island; she'll be given the best care."

Shada's blood boiled at the smirk she imagined was on the man's face.

"And you can show up whenever you like to receive your edits. It's time to join the future!"

"This is all your fault," Shada whispered to Tony.

"My fault? She told me to leave her behind!"

"You shouldn't have listened to her," Shada hissed. "Where did you go when you left? You went to tell WestCorp where we were, didn't you?"

Tony was shocked at Shada's sudden accusation. "What are you talking about? I never went anywhere."

"The first night, when you stood guard. I watched you walk away."

Tony paused for a moment before closing his eyes. "I dozed off," he admitted with a sigh.

"And when you did, your implanted mind took control and walked away from the group to tell WestCorp where we were. She trusted you!" Shada hit him in the chest. "We trusted you."

Everyone else in the tunnel was silent. They could hear the retreating footsteps of the team from WestCorp as they walked away on the platform. Gustavo stepped forward, stood in the shadow of the tunnel, and reported seeing their attackers leave the station. "They've got Sikya with them," he said.

Shada didn't want to watch in case she got the urge to run through the station to try to take her sister back by herself. "We should've kept moving," she said, more to herself than to Tony.

"We hadn't even been there a night," Tony said, looking at her.

"But it was long enough for them to catch up with us!"

Tony was still grappling with the knowledge he'd put the group at risk. "I woke up in the same position as when I shut my eyes. I could have sworn it was just a second," he said, shaking his head.

"That's all it took to put us in danger."

Tony absorbed the weight of his mistake. "Did you tell the others?"

"No."

"Are you going to?"

"I might."

"Let me tell them," Tony said.

As mad as Shada was, she couldn't deny how much she respected his courage.

Their private conversation was interrupted by Gustavo telling Jimmy to wait before entering the station again. "They could have left people on the far side of the wall," he said.

"I don't care," Jimmy said. "I'm going back to get my stuff."

Gustavo looked into the shadows towards Tony and Shada. Shada wondered if he could make out any more than their outlines in the darkness. "A little help?" Gustavo said.

Tony stood up and walked into the middle of the tunnel, in front of Jimmy. "We'll make sure it's all clear." He looked at Gustavo and used his lips to point to the far wall. He and Gustavo stood on each side of the tunnel, both looking across the span at the platform beyond the far wall. They crept forward, alternating between looking onto the platform and looking at each other, with subtle head nods indicating that the platform on their comrade's side was clear. When they had inspected each corner, they gave the all clear. Gustavo waved the other groups into the station.

The bodies of three dead WestCorp attackers were left on the platform, close to where Shada had tried to sleep next to her sister minutes before. Shada looked at the spot where her sister had fallen; there was blood on the ground. Not much, but enough for her to wonder if her sister's child would make it to term. Caprice didn't let James leave her side while she inspected their camp. Tim and his cohort settled back into their space as if nothing had happened, making Shada wonder how much chaos they'd seen on the surface before descending underground.

Tony told Gustavo to help him with Mark's body and asked

Sophie and Ophelia to take Vick's, telling them he wanted to leave their bodies, along with Kren's, in the room Gustavo had found for them to sleep in. "When this is all over, we can come back and give them a proper burial," he said.

The somber survivors nodded. While Shada was alone on the platform, she couldn't shake the worry that WestCorp was waiting in the shadows for them, that the group was walking into an ambush, and she waited to hear the gunshots that would signal a second round of fighting.

To occupy herself, she began collecting all salvageable supplies, the things that had survived the blast that killed Mark and Vick. In the corner, their food and water had fallen over but was still intact. The bags that were closest to the tunnel were all damaged beyond use. She gathered their remaining supplies near the blocked-off entrance to the tunnel, arranging them into small piles on the platform floor.

A loud noise rang out from the far side of the platform. Shada jumped, thinking it was the first shot of a gunfight, before realizing the sound had come from the wrong direction. In the far camp, Caprice's sister stood up with a frying pan in her hand and a sheepish look on her face. "Sorry!" she yelled to all.

The four surviving members of the resistance emerged from the tunnel, weary and slow-moving. Their climb onto the platform seemed to take forever. Everyone assembled around the pile of gear Shada had created while they were gone.

"I've got something to tell you guys," Tony said.

Shada turned away to give the tears welling in her eyes time to reabsorb.

"It was my fault they found us," he began.

"No, don't say that. We all chose to set up camp here," Gustavo said.

"But how'd they know to look for us in the tunnels in the first place?" Sophie asked.

"Exactly," Tony said with a nod to Sophie. "They knew because I told them."

If Gustavo had been shot at that exact moment, he couldn't have looked more surprised. Ophelia's understanding eyes stayed on Tony's face, urging him to continue.

"Shada said she watched me walk away when I was supposed to be keeping watch at the first camp," Tony said. "I remember dozing off for a second, but I snapped awake right away. Or so I thought." Tears began streaming down his face. "I could've sworn it was only for a second!" He closed his eyes and wiped his cheeks with the back of his hand.

When Shada put a reassuring hand on Tony's shoulder, she heard Hollis laugh. "Guy gets your sister taken and you feel bad about a few tears . . . you unedited are too much!"

Marnie was quick to jump in. "Don't you see he already feels bad enough? She's going to need his help if she's going to get her sister back."

"He'll help get her back either way," Hollis said. "It was his mistake, he'll fix it. There's no reason to worry about making him feel better."

Shada took three deep breaths and silenced them both. She didn't care to hear either of their opinions about her actions, and for the first time she wished she wasn't under the constant scrutiny of these inner voices.

"What do we do now?" Sophie asked. Ever practical, she wanted to figure out the next step, not caring to analyze those previous. Ophelia looked like she wanted to give Tony a hug but maintained her distance, and Gustavo still looked shaken that the leader of their small group was the one who'd put them in danger.

"We have to get to the island," Shada said. Now that West-Corp had her sister, she was going back whether they went with her or not.

Tony looked at Shada and nodded. "I'm with you," he said. "Let's go get her back."

Gustavo also agreed to make the trip. "And once we get her back, we can find a way to stop the edits and save the city."

"And get these uploaded minds out of our heads and into the computer," Ophelia said. "If we want to," she added, looking at Sophie.

Sophie studied the faces of the other four members of her group. Sensing their resolve, she said she would join them too. "I don't want to miss out on the fun," she said with a smirk.

CHAPTER TWENTY-ONE

BEFORE THEIR DEPARTURE from the barricaded station, the group emptied the contents of the bags Shada had salvaged. They took stock of what had survived and repacked the available gear into four duffel bags, one per person. Since they were heading to the island instead of setting up camp again, they didn't need food, kitchen supplies, or toiletries. They made sure to pack their weapons and ammunition, even though Shada knew these items would be confiscated by security the moment they tried to step onto the island. Everyone had extra clothes, and Tony reminded them to keep a pair of socks they could change into on top, since they'd be on their feet for the foreseeable future.

Shada found Caprice and told her they were leaving. "Feel free to take everything we leave behind," she said. "There's some food left, and cookware."

Caprice thanked Shada before telling her she was sorry about what happened to her sister. "I don't know what I'd do if anything happened to mine," she said, turning to look at the other camp.

Shada didn't mention that they were on their way to get her back. All Caprice knew was that they had decided to move on.

"Best of luck," Shada told Caprice. James walked by holding his ball. "Hope he stays out of trouble."

"Everything will go back to normal once we're back on the surface," Caprice said. "We just have to wait out the storm."

Shada marveled at the woman's inability to grasp the fundamental transformation the city had undertaken. She wanted to grab Caprice by the shoulders, to shake some sense into her and convince her things would never be the same again, but she realized hope was the one thing keeping the transient wrinkles in her face from becoming permanent evidence of constant worry. "It'll pass soon enough," Shada said. She returned to her section of the platform, grabbed her bag, and nodded in the direction of the far tunnel, indicating to the group it was time for them to set out.

They walked for hours, each step taking them closer to the heart of the city and the tram that would take them to the island. There were thirteen stops between them and their destination.

Shada tried to picture how they would get onto the tram without waiting in line so they could limit their risk of exposure to the edited humans returning from the island. Was there a way they could get to the front of the line as soon as they showed up? They could hold the mass of unedited back at gunpoint, but WestCorp could stop the tram from running, leaving them in an extended standoff with a massive disadvantage in numbers.

She hoped the WestCorp employees at the tram had been told to expect her after their message had been delivered.

"See how hope can make it easier to take one step at a time?" Marnie said.

Shada was appreciative of the insight but wasn't a fan of the edited mind commenting on her thoughts.

Some of the stations they passed through were exposed to the night air, even though the tracks between them ran through underground tunnels. The half moon was in a different location in the sky each time they surfaced. The buildings on the sides of the station grew more prominent as they approached the heart of the city, over time becoming too tall for them to see more than a few stars through thin cloud cover.

They emerged from underground and walked beneath a broken bridge on their approach to one of the exposed stations, stepping over rubble from the collapsed middle. The skyscraper on their right had numerous windows overlooking the tracks. "Keep your eyes open," Gustavo said with a nod to the array of glass.

Twice, Shada thought she saw eyes following their movements. She found darkness both times she focused on their location and was left wondering if she'd imagined the feeling of being watched.

The walls of the station were covered with turquoise tiles, the most distinctive station they had passed through on their trip. The station had the same layout as the one they had been in when WestCorp attacked, with two sets of stairs in the middle of the platform, one on each side, that rose up from the station's platform to the surface above. A dog in the corner of the platform was gnawing a bone. He growled before taking his bone up the stairs to find another private location to enjoy his prize.

The group left the moonlight behind and entered the darkness of the tunnel once more. As they got closer to the heart of the city, they found more and more evidence of previous human presence: tattered rags, discarded food wrappers, and evidence of small fires. There was even an abandoned pillow and blanket.

The last station they passed through before their destination was underground. In the tunnel on the far side, they found a handful of people seated in the shadows on each side of the tracks. Shada kept her eyes ahead of her, worried they were edited and would come after her and the group, like the edited who had chased her and Tony on the surface.

Not one of them moved.

Gustavo cracked a glow stick and held it up high, searching their faces.

"Look at them," he urged the others. "They're all sick."

Shada saw unresponsive eyes set in hollow sockets. Their skin was pale, and each one of them was bent in half, clutching their stomach. Their sunken cheeks looked as if they were sucking air through straws. If it wasn't for the rising and falling of their chests, they could have been dead.

A young man pointed to a cracked pipe with a container positioned beneath to collect dripping water. "Don't drink it," he said.

Gustavo used his glow stick to look into the container before showing the rest of the group. Flecks of metal floated inside. Concerned their own water was contaminated, they withdrew their personal containers and inspected them. Each person's water was clear. Shada wondered if Caprice and her family would have to resort to drinking tainted water from an underground pipe if, or when, their water fountain got turned off. James had no chance of thriving if the storm never passed.

Tony told the rest of the group they had to keep moving, that they were close, and to ignore the people on the sides of the tracks. A short walk later, they saw the light of the station at the heart of the city. Both sides of the platform were filled with people.

The five travelers walked into the light. The people closest to the tunnel were aware of the emergence of the group but turned away after a quick glance. A sense of relief washed over Shada when she realized everyone was unedited and waiting for their chance to get to the island. They climbed onto the plat-form at the first possible opening in the mass of people.

The station presented an extraordinary amount of stimula-tion after the trip through the dark tunnel. The artificial lights were incongruous with the hour, and a new ecosystem had developed to service the long-waiting unedited. There were food vendors, small stands where books and magazines were sold, and signs for private bathrooms for which use could be purchased instead of using the facilities provided by the station. Most clusters of people were asleep, but some of the older men were gathered in a group, each clutching a small paper cup of what Shada assumed was coffee.

Shada led the group through the waiting unedited to the staircase that led down to WestCorp's private platform. People even waited on the steps, their heads resting against the wall as they rested.

The WestCorp employee closest to the stairs, one of many dotting the platform, greeted Shada and her group when they arrived. He was wide awake and smiling, average height, average weight, and had an average face punctuated by a thin beard. "Good morning!" he said to Tony, even though Shada was the one in front.

Shada wanted to punch him in the face.

"Mornin'," was Tony's gruff reply. "We need to get to the island."

"So does everyone else. Please wait in line. As soon as another group comes back, the line will start moving again."

He inspected the group, still grinning, before addressing Tony again. "Is there anything else I can do for you?"

Shada stepped between the employee and Tony. "Yes. Talk to whoever's in charge, Ruby if you have to, and get us on the next trip. We were told by one of you to come to the island."

The WestCorp employee blinked twice before requesting a

moment and walking away. At the information desk on the far side of the platform, he leaned over the counter to talk to a seated woman in private.

The unedited who were awake stared at Shada and the members of the resistance. They nudged those closest to them and used their eyes to direct attention to the five people not standing in line. Those people then nudged the people in front of them, and they repeated the sequence until the unedited who were next in line to board the tram were wide awake and staring at Shada, Tony, Gustavo, Ophelia, and Sophie.

Shada felt like she'd just walked into the lion's den. She could tell the members of the resistance were on edge as well; their eyes searched for threats, and their taut postures prepared them to spring into action at a moment's notice. Sophie made her intentions clear by resting her hand on the grip of the handgun at her side.

CHAPTER TWENTY-TWO

THE WESTCORP EMPLOYEE came back a few tense minutes later. If he noticed the stare-down between the various unedited, he didn't acknowledge it. He made a beeline for Shada and her group, with that grin still pasted on his face, and said they would be on the next trip to the island.

"That's not fair!" one of the unedited near the front of the line yelled out.

"They just got here! We've been waiting for days!" another said.

One woman, a teenager, left the line and rushed towards the WestCorp employee closest to her, a middle-aged woman. Shada couldn't hear their exact words but watched as the employee smiled then gestured with an open hand to the back of the line.

"I just came over to talk to you!" the teenager exclaimed.

"The line begins back there," the employee said, loud enough for everyone around to hear.

The line shifted as the abandoned spot was filled, like a snake moving a single coil.

The teenager pulled her arm back to strike the WestCorp

employee. Her arm then passed through open air and she lost her balance. Two male WestCorp employees came from nowhere, grabbed the teenager, and escorted her away.

Shada and the members of the resistance were taken to the front of the platform to wait for the tram to arrive. They stood with their backs against the wall, facing the horde of angry unedited. An hour passed, then two, and Shada would have fallen asleep if it wasn't for the constant threatening glances thrown their way. She assumed the rest of the group was exhausted as well after their overnight journey.

It occurred to her there was no reason for the others to stay awake. It wouldn't matter if anyone woke up under the control of the edited mind, since they were heading to the island and to Ruby. She was about to suggest they take turns resting, leaving some of the group awake to monitor the unedited surrounding them, when the tram pulled up.

The five of them were given an entire tram car to themselves. This drew more loud protests from the people waiting for their turn to get edited, but not one of them left their spot in line, having learned their lesson from the impulsive teenager.

Tony told everyone to rest their eyes the moment their tram began to move. "There's nothing the edited can do if they take over your body on here," he said. Even though the trip was short, they could catch a quick refresh before they got to the island.

When Shada closed her eyes, she saw Chloe's poisoned body lying on the ground in her mind's eye. She remembered the sound of the gunshot, and the glass breaking, and her breath caught in her throat as she recalled jumping from the moving tram into the water below. She tried counting to ten breaths, hoping the memory would go away, but when it persisted, she opened her eyes to escape into the present.

The pull of eyes burning into the back of her head caused

her to turn around. Some of the unedited in the next car had their faces pressed against the glass separating the two cars and appeared to be trying to kill her with their gaze. Was it possible to cause physical harm if enough people focused their hatred on a single person?

The tram emerged from the underground tunnel that ran beneath the city and rose to the level of the bridge. The city in the background was bathed in the red of the rising sun. Shada turned away from the city, away from the murderous unedited, and watched the island approach.

Shada's car, at the front of the tram, entered the station beneath WestCorp first. The opening doors woke up everyone but Gustavo. The unedited rushed to get out after their eternal wait. Everyone wanted to get their edits first, not knowing they would be led into a massive warehouse with enough tables to accommodate them all. Shada shook Gustavo awake and told her fellow travelers to wait until the other cars had emptied before they disembarked. A few of the unedited stared at them, looking like they might approach, before they rejoined their cohort and headed towards the staircase and its guards.

"Please step off," a robotic voice commanded.

Tony looked at Shada, and she tilted her head towards the platform. They all got off, and she told them to wait until the rest of the unedited had passed through security at the foot of the staircase. "We don't need to get near them," she said.

Everyone wanting edits was past security in minutes. Nobody had to be searched off to the side, and any confiscated items were left behind without a fight.

The group of five was alone on the platform with the two guards, one on each side of the platform.

"What are we going to do?" Sophie said. Shada ignored the question at first, assuming it was meant for Tony, but when

Tony didn't respond, she looked at Sophie and saw the woman's eyes were on her.

"We've got to talk to Alfie. He'll tell us where Sikya is," Shada responded.

Shada wondered why there wasn't more WestCorp security. Didn't Ruby know they were coming?

Tony must have been thinking the same thing. "Where is the welcome committee? I thought we'd have to shoot our way in," he said.

"Maybe they assumed we came to get edited," Ophelia suggested.

"Let's just get past these two, and we can figure out what to do in the food court," Gustavo said. His speech was slow, each word measured, as if he hadn't quite woken up yet.

"But if we don't blow past these guys, they're going to take our guns," Sophie said.

"Let's get as far as we can before we start negotiating," said Tony.

Ophelia laughed at Tony's euphemism.

Sophie pushed back. "If they take our guns, we won't have anything to negotiate with," she said.

Gustavo started walked towards the two large guards. They stood in the distance like two massive pillars supporting the island on their shoulders.

Shada and the others were quick to follow behind, assuming he had a plan. The guards told them to place their bags on a conveyor belt, alongside a bin that was for their belongings, so they could be taken through a metal detector.

Without hesitation, Gustavo threw his bag on the belt and took his guns from their holsters, placing them into the designated bins. Sophie's eyes were wide with disbelief.

"You know we have to keep these," the guard working the

metal detector said, holding up one of Gustavo's guns before starting the conveyor belt.

Gustavo shrugged. Sophie looked like she was going to scream.

The other guard patted down Gustavo and let him pass. The guard working the metal detector looked up from the screen at Gustavo, then at the others. His eyes narrowed. "We'll be keeping the bag," he said, as if tempting someone to offer resistance to his statement. A slight smile crept onto his face, as if he'd relish a fight.

"That's fine," Gustavo said, carefree. He was waved through and began climbing the stairs instead of waiting for the others.

"Gustavo!" Tony said. When his comrade didn't respond, Tony joked that he must be hungry.

Ophelia and Sophie laughed, but Shada grew suspicious.

The rest of the group passed through security in the same way Gustavo had, each forced to leave their bags and weapons behind. Tony made sure Sophie didn't resist. Once everyone was through, they climbed the stairs together.

The food court had been transformed. There was now just one place to eat, a burger spot in the corner, and the rest of the spaces except one were used to process the unedited arrivals from the city. The last space had a large sign above it that read DEPARTURES, with shelves stocked with small vials of Stim to be handed out to those headed back to the city.

Shada, Tony, Sophie, and Ophelia walked around the entire space, inspecting every line of unedited waiting to be processed and enduring their angry stares. Gustavo was nowhere to be found.

"Where the hell did he go?" Tony said. "Let's find Alfie and find out where they're keeping Sikya."

Shada didn't know what they would do if they found her sister. Negotiate her release? It seemed like their lone option, since they were trapped on the island without weapons. Following Gustavo had been a terrible idea.

The departure station was the one place where a WestCorp employee could be approached without navigating past a group of unedited. Shada marched to the counter and asked if they could tell her where to find Alfie.

"Scientists are to stay in the lab until everyone is edited," the employee said, as if they had been forced to recite this rule over and over again until it was committed to memory.

"Even Alfie?" Tony asked.

"He's a scientist, right?" came the reply, with a grin.

Shada shook her head and turned away. She tried to leave the atrium, to take a transport vehicle to the lab, but was stopped by two guards stationed outside. She then tried to lead them down the long hallway, to get to the lab on foot, and found two guards also blocking this path. They were told to wait with the others, that they would all walk to the lab together.

Shada, Tony, Ophelia, and Sophie passed through processing then waited with the other unedited outside the hallway that led to the lab, all of them with paperwork in hand. The unedited stared at them, frozen by the uncertainty of what to do now that Shada and the three members of the resistance were within arm's reach.

Two WestCorp employees emerged from the hallway. They began inspecting everyone's paperwork, nodding when each person could pass. When they were almost to Shada, they stopped and turned to the far side of the atrium, towards the corner that housed the burger restaurant.

Shada turned to see what had stolen their attention.

It was Ruby, her chin held high in the air, with Gustavo at her side.

CHAPTER TWENTY-THREE

Ruby was wearing an all-black outfit accented with bright pink high heels. She strode through the space with the confidence of a woman who was positive she would get what she wanted. Together with Gustavo, dressed in all black himself, she stood out among the run-down unedited from the city and the employees of WestCorp dressed in khakis and white polos.

Gustavo searched the crowd, his head on a swivel.

Shada turned around, nudged Tony, and used her chin to gesture towards Ruby.

"What the hell," Tony whispered.

Ophelia and Sophie, standing behind Shada and Tony, gasped when they saw Ruby and Gustavo. Shada held a finger to her lips, telling them to be quiet. She gestured for the group to follow her, and she left the line.

A WestCorp employee exited an elevator ahead. Shada closed the distance with a few large steps, walked inside, and held the doors open for the others.

She let the elevator doors shut after they were all inside.

"I can't believe Gustavo turned on us!" Sophie exclaimed when they were alone.

"He didn't," Shada said. The button for the second level wouldn't light up when pressed because a key card was required. "They didn't have this before," she said, looking around. "They really don't want anyone leaving the atrium."

The elevator stayed still. It was just a matter of time until they were discovered.

"What do you mean he didn't?" Sophie hissed. "You saw him with Ruby!"

"It wasn't Gustavo," Ophelia said. Her voice was soft, and she seemed preoccupied, as if seeing Gustavo with Ruby had triggered her own memories of losing control.

"It was, I just saw him!" Sophie said.

Shada looked at the buttons above the door, hoping the floor beneath her would soon move and the light corresponding to another level, any level, would blink on, just not the one where they were.

"The edited mind inside him took over," Tony said.

Sophie leaned against the interior of the elevator. "When he fell asleep on the way over," she said.

"I had a feeling when he walked up the steps without us," Shada said.

"Why didn't you say anything?" Tony said. "We could have been more careful."

"If there was going to be a welcome party, Gustavo walking away didn't change anything. Ruby has to know we're here; the trams keep record of everyone who comes to the island."

"Maybe she thinks we really are here to get the edits. Think she just wanted to talk?" Ophelia said.

The sudden descent of the elevator interrupted their conversation. Shada assumed they would end up back on the platform below the atrium, and she pictured their next series of moves. They would climb the stairs once more, somehow get past Ruby, talk to Alfie, and find out where Sikya was being kept. But how would they get her off the island?

It occurred to Shada that Sikya might be in Hollis's private bunker. It was secluded and had the medical equipment she would need.

The elevator's speed, and the length of time it traveled down, seemed far too long to cover the distance between the platform and the atrium. Shada consulted the edited minds inside her, asking if there was anything else beneath them besides the platform.

"It's where—" Marnie said before she was cut off by Hollis.

"Don't tell her, she'll find out soon enough," Hollis said, laughing.

The lit-up button above the elevator door changed with a loud beep, showing U1. The now-lit button was right next to the one corresponding to the ground floor, misaligned with the length of their descent.

A set of doors behind the group, unnoticed by all up to this point, opened up. When Shada turned around, she saw rows upon rows of white pods, each large enough to keep a person inside, in a massive, low-ceilinged room that disappeared into the horizon. Above each pod was a single hanging light bulb. Most of the bulbs closest to them were off, but some were lit, interspersed throughout the grid, and the ones in the distance all shone bright. Fluorescent lights ran down each aisle between rows, creating lines on the ceiling that stretched off into the distance away from the elevator.

A wizened old man stood right in front of them. His thick glasses were too big for his face, and his wool socks were pulled up so high the darker-colored heel could be seen halfway up his calf. He studied the group, blinking twice, before he turned around and shuffled away, leaning on his cane as he went. "I'll just go ahead and stay for another hour," he said with his back turned.

Shada, Tony, Ophelia, and Sophie stepped off the elevator and looked around in awe. There was an empty desk right next to the elevator. Shada watched the old man climb into a white pod a few rows away. The single light above him went out soon after he shut the lid.

Through Marnie, Shada found out they were among rows of dream stations, where the elder edited humans went to pass their days after WestCorp no longer had use for them. Someone was supposed to be at the desk to assign users to unoccupied stations.

"The ones with lights off have someone inside them," Shada told the group after learning the information from Marnie.

"Inside them?" Sophie said. "What are they?"

"Right," Shada said, annoyed at herself for assuming everyone knew what the pods were for. "These are the dream stations, where retired edited go to escape reality."

"Instead of hijacking an unedited body," Ophelia said.

The elevator came back to life behind them. They heard it rise up and pass through the ceiling.

"Do they know we're here?" asked Sophie.

"Not sure, but I don't want to be standing here if they do," Tony replied.

Shada told everyone to hide inside a station. They rushed to the closest illuminated pod. When they found it empty, Tony told Sophie to get inside. Sophie flexed her jaw before climbing in, putting her duffel bag down by her feet.

Shada set the dial beneath the handle to an hour. Along the seam where the lid met the base, they could see a faint purple light begin at Sophie's feet and work its way up to her head, extinguishing when it reached the end of the pod. The single bulb above the pod grew dark the moment the purple light went out.

The process was repeated in another part of the room for Ophelia, before Shada and Tony went to a third available pod. "Climb in," Tony told Shada.

"No, I'll be the last one," she said.

They stared each other down.

"How are you going to turn off the light above?" Tony asked.

Shada licked her fingers and unscrewed the bulb just enough for the electrical connection to sever. "Like that," she said.

"Perfect," Tony said. "You lie in here, and I'll do the same thing before I climb into one of those over there," he said, gesturing to the side of the room farthest from the elevator.

Shada smiled. "Get in, Tony," she said.

Tony's head cocked to one side, searching Shada's face. She waited, focusing on her breath to slow her heart rate. Tony squeezed his lips together and climbed in, his duffel bag positioned between his legs.

"Leave it off, I want to hear when they come for us," Tony said.

Shada, her hand on the pod's lid, nodded. "You got it," she said before closing the lid. She walked around Tony's pod and set her bag on the floor without a noise. Then she climbed over the white pod, draping her body over it, and reached down for the timer from above.

"Shada?" Tony said from inside.

She felt him push against the lid and went limp so all her weight would be used to keep it shut. She set the timer for four hours.

When the purple light began at Tony's feet, Shada heard him scream her name. He pushed against the lid, struggling to get free, until the light extinguished at his head and his movement stopped.

"Sorry," she said before climbing down.

Shada hurried back to Sophie's and Ophelia's pods and changed the setting of the timers from one hour to four. She apologized both times.

She was close enough to the elevator to hear its descent. She turned and ran away as fast as she could, sticking to one side of the room, an aisle out of direct sight of the elevator. Over the sound of her breathing, she heard the beep that accompanied the opening of the elevator's doors, so she crouched down while continuing forward. There had to be another way out, and she intended to find it.

She heard Ruby yell out, "Find them!"

She kept running, amazed at the length of the room. She felt like she ran the length of the entirety of the island and wondered if she was deep enough underground to run beneath the water around the island. A timer beneath one of the lone dead light bulbs ahead of Shada went off, and when the buzzing stopped, the light above came back to life.

Shada saw a thin, age-spotted hand lift the lid of the pod, the interior hidden by the surrounding machines. She ran past, hoping the person didn't see her. She waited to hear if the dreamer yelled out, but all she heard was her breathing.

At the end of the room were double doors with small windows set at head height in the middle of each. She pushed through and found an old metal staircase. It had cracked, decayed brown tile and green metal latticework beneath each railing. There was a door opposite where she'd entered at the bottom of the stairs. She looked inside and found the remains of a collapsed building. It was tight, but she could have navigated through the rubble if she didn't have her bag with her. To throw her pursuers off her scent, she left her bag just inside the rubble, hoping it would seem like she'd left it behind before crawling through.

Shada ran up the stairs, covering two at a time. She lost track of how many times she turned the corner and started a new section. She felt how little she had slept and eaten in the past two days. From her playing days, she knew there were extra reserves the body could call on at the end of the game, when it was all on the line, but she also knew these wouldn't last forever. She counted her breaths in order to escape from the monotony of the climb and to make sure the edited minds inside her, in particular Hollis, didn't take advantage of her exhausted state to try to retake control of her body.

She passed by a source of daylight at the bottom of a window well and slowed down, knowing she had returned to the surface. The staircase ended at the top of the next set of stairs. There was a single door, with a single window at head height. She looked through one corner of the window and saw a woman rushing down the hall, her head down and white lab coat fluttering at her feet.

CHAPTER TWENTY-FOUR

SHADA PUSHED OPEN the door at the top of the stairs and walked into the lab's hallway. The section of the lab she was in was older than the parts she had been to before. The floors were a dull off-white with brown specks, and the walls were a mustard yellow with thin cobwebs up near the ceiling. She hoped her lack of white coat wouldn't draw attention from any of the WestCorp employees. She stood tall, doing her best to seem like she belonged there.

Her first thought was to figure out where she was. She knew she was in the lab, but which part? She didn't recognize any of the rooms around her. She peeked into the closest room. It was empty, with a variety of glassware scattered on the counters. The shelves above each counter held bottles of all different shapes and sizes, all labeled with a uniform sticker and the writing in the same color ink.

"This is the chemistry wing," Hollis said before Shada could search his memories. "Where they worked on the Stim, at least when I was still in charge."

When Shada withdrew from the room, she found a man in a

lab coat walking down the hallway in her direction. She got ready to pretend she was lost.

"Can I help you?" the scientist said. He smiled when he spoke. It seemed he enjoyed talking to another human, even though she was a potential trespasser.

"I'm looking for the room to get edited." She pulled her paperwork from her pocket, hoping to convince him she had gotten lost, that she was at the lab to receive her free edits. This seemed easier than convincing him she was edited as well.

"It isn't hard," Marnie told Shada. "Just smile. Nobody can tell the difference."

The scientist didn't even glance down at the paper in Shada's hand. "You're a long way from the rest of the unedited," he said.

Shada couldn't tell if the man was suspicious or not. That smile did more to mask his thoughts than if he'd tried to remain impartial.

"Can you tell me how to get back to them?" Shada asked, doing her best to sound innocent. She reasoned that Alfie would be with the unedited, overseeing their edits.

"Sure. You must have been walking for a while; we aren't even close."

"I'm very lost," she said with a laugh.

The scientist told her to walk in the direction from which he'd come. There, she would find another hallway running perpendicular to the one they were in. "Turn left, then keep walking until it ends too. A right turn will take you to where the edits are taking place."

Shada thanked the man and set off. She turned around every few steps, to see if the scientist was watching her walk away, but he continued at his steady pace until he turned off the hallway, either down another or into a room.

There was a definite change in the quality of the building

when she left the chemistry wing. The walls became newer, stark white, and matched the white floors, which had been buffed to a shine. The air smelled of sterility, a mix of bleach and lemon soap. As she continued on the scientist's suggested path, there were more and more scientists rushing between rooms, each of them carrying manila folders stuffed with papers.

The low rumble from a large crowd of people reached her when she got to the end of the hallway and turned right.

Shada recognized where she was. The first time she'd come to get edited, before the edits were free, she was led to the large warehouse room, ahead of her on the left, where the unedited were now gathered. This was before she and Chloe had been asked if they would accept an uploaded mind into their body so WestCorp employees could experience the world in an unedited body. She also knew where Alfie's personal lab was. She made her way there, hoping to find him and find out where her sister was being kept.

The door to Alfie's lab was unlocked. Shada walked in without knocking. He wasn't inside, but she could tell this was where a lot of his time was spent; on the counter was trash from prior meals next to scattered paperwork and evidence of chemical experiments he hadn't bothered to clean up.

She guessed he was with the unedited, either preparing them for or performing their edits. Even if she left the lab and found him, what was she supposed to do? Tap him on the shoulder and ask for a private word? No, she needed him to come to her. Her sister had already been gone long enough, and she didn't have time to wait.

The bottles of chemicals drew her attention. Shada inspected each one, not sure of what she was looking for. A gallon jug of benzene caught her eye. It had a large "flammable" symbol on it.

There was a momentary pause when Shada was hit by the

potential consequences of what she was about to do. But her sister was worth it.

Shada assembled all the chemicals in a pile on the side of the room farthest from the door. She opened the jug of benzene and poured it out over the containers. Her eyes watered from the fumes. She kept them closed until the jug was empty, then backed away, looking for a way to spark the blaze. She was searching for matches or a lighter when she found an old Bunsen burner and a long piece of rubber tubing. After locating the gas line and connecting the rubber to one end, she set the burner, unlit, on the ground. She still had the same problem as before: How to spark the blaze?

The smell of benzene began to overwhelm her as it suffused throughout the room. She looked in the cabinet where she'd found the Bunsen burner and found a striker, a piece of flint and steel at one end of a pair of tongs that when squeezed created a spark. She tested it out and saw a small spark. A momentary fear gripped her, soon followed by relief, when she realized she had created a spark in the midst of the fumes.

She turned on the gas and fell to her hands and knees, lighting the Bunsen burner before more fumes crept from the pile of chemicals. By using the rubber tubing to force the burner along the ground, she was able to get it close to the benzene. Nothing happened.

Impatient, she twisted the rubber tube, knocking over the burner. The benzene ignited in a bright flash, causing small colored lights to appear in Shada's vision.

She hurried to turn off the gas so the flame wouldn't travel through the rubber tube to the gas source. Once the gas was off, she turned over the stainless steel table closest to the door and waited for the containers holding the other chemicals to melt, hoping some of their contents would explode.

The fire alarm and sprinkler system kicked into action. A

torrent of water rushed down from the ceiling, and Shada worried the fire would be extinguished before it could catch anything else on fire. She watched one container melt without its contents bursting into flames and was about to stand up when a plastic bottle erupted in a fireball. She pulled her head back behind the table just in time.

The door burst open, and Alfie rushed into the room. He was drenched. The howling fire alarm overhead was deafening. Shada rushed the older scientist and pinned him against the wall, her hands around his throat.

"Where's Sikya?" she screamed. Water was dripping down her face.

"My work! Let me put out the fire!" Alfie responded. He tried to push himself off the wall, but Shada was stronger than him and forced him back down. "The fire extinguisher!" he yelled.

"Where is she?" Shada said. She was losing control and she knew it. She forced herself to exhale so she could keep Hollis and Marnie from taking over her body.

Alfie squirmed. "In Hollis's bunker. She's safe, the baby's safe. Now let me go!"

This time, when Alfie tried to pry himself free, Shada didn't stop him. She watched him rush to the far wall, grab the fire extinguisher, and position himself right in front of the fire.

A glass bottle exploded right before he squeezed the trigger. Flames and glass went everywhere. Shada got a few cuts on her arms and legs but knew none of them were serious. Alfie, standing between her and the explosion, had taken the majority of the blast. He was on the floor, his torso burning. Shada grabbed the fire extinguisher and put out the flames on Alfie, then the chemicals, covering them all with a thick white foam. She dropped to his side. There were deep cuts all over his face and neck. Blood was pouring out from him, creating deep red lines in the foam, surrounded by bright pink.

"I would have told you where she was," he sputtered. Blood trickled from the corner of his mouth.

"I know," Shada said. Her guilt was almost unmanageable. She'd never meant to hurt Alfie, the one person who had helped her take back control. His motivation was science, not because he cared for her, but she didn't care about the reason. The fact was that he'd helped her and was now dying because of her.

It was Chloe all over again. Was she destined to be responsible for the deaths of those closest to her?

"I still have more to do," Alfie said. The sprinkler system, sensing the fire was no longer blazing, shut off.

"I know," Shada said again. She couldn't tell if the salty taste in her mouth was her own tears or water that had run down her unwashed face.

"Let me upload into you. We can rescue your sister together, then we can figure out how to continue my work," Alfie said. He was growing weaker by the second and didn't have much time.

Hollis tried voicing his objections, but Shada silenced him in less than a heartbeat. She had already been responsible for Chloe's death and wasn't going to lose Alfie too.

CHAPTER TWENTY-FIVE

"We'll never make it to the upload room," Shada told Alfie. Even if the lab was empty and she didn't have to navigate past other scientists, there was no way she could carry him that far. He was losing a lot of blood and could pass out at any second.

"Here," Alfie choked out. "Prototype."

Between the overturned stainless steel table and another table was a small monitor with an attached keyboard. Its back was covered by clear plastic, protecting the visible wires from getting wet. The fire and fire extinguisher foam had been far enough away that the machine was left untouched. Two long cables, covered in rubber, were attached, one on each side. The ends of the cables didn't end in helmets; they each ended with two electrodes, which was why Shada hadn't known there was a mind transfer machine in the room before Alfie told her.

Shada put her arms under the scientist, one under his shoulders and the other under his knees. Some of the foam stained with blood transferred onto her. She counted down from three, both to make sure Alfie was ready for the pain and to prepare herself for the exertion. After the count of one, she took a deep breath and pushed into the floor with her feet, standing up with him in her arms.

When she was halfway to standing, Hollis tried to take back over. Shada felt him open her hands. She was straining so hard she couldn't take back control. She used her arms to keep the dying scientist in place but couldn't rise any further.

Through squinted eyes, she saw her hands close. It wasn't her own doing, since her connection with the appendages was still blocked by Hollis.

"Leave her alone!" Marnie said.

Shada stood up with Marnie's help. She took small steps to the middle of the three tables and laid him down. She placed her hands on her knees, taking deep breaths. "Asshole," she said out loud, sure Hollis could hear. "Thanks, Marnie."

Alfie's head rolled to one side. His chest rose and fell with short breaths, but his body was otherwise limp.

Shada rounded the table Alfie was on and flipped up the table she had used for cover before. She attached the electrodes to Alfie's head, one on each temple, before attaching them in the same position on herself. She turned on the monitor between the tables and saw lines of white computer script begin filling the black screen from the top down. The oldest script disappeared at the bottom as more appeared at the top, seeming to go on forever. Eventually, a prompt appeared at the top of the screen: type T for transfer and S for storage.

Shada typed T, then selected L to tell the system the mind to be uploaded was coming from the left. A countdown from ten appeared on the screen, the lower number appearing above the higher one in a vertical line.

"Hold on," Shada told Alfie as she lay down. She felt Hollis attempt to take back control of her arm one last time, but she forced him into the background before he ever gained control of the limb.

Her world went black.

She allowed the light to take over her awareness. She soon recognized the ceiling above her bed, and the second the edges of darkness disappeared, she heard the blaring fire alarm. Then she was aware of her body once again. The scientist's mind was pushed back into the abyss. She heard him screaming in the darkness and told him to be quiet.

Marnie and Hollis were locked in a struggle for control that ended as soon as Shada was back. It was easy for her to block the two minds, like two small children trying to fight an adult and once the adult decided it was over, there was nothing the children could do.

"He tried to run the second you disappeared," Marnie said.

"Why are you helping her?" Hollis roared.

"We're stuck in here. Why fight it?" Marnie said. "We might as well work together."

"Work together to destroy everything I built? Never!"

Shada silenced both of them. She stared at the ceiling and focused on helping Alfie.

"Find the light and go to it," she said. "And you'll be able to see the world through my eyes."

Shada could sense Alfie understood.

"Do you see it?" Shada said a moment later.

"No," Alfie said.

Shada knew he was scared. "Give it time," she said.

"It's faint. Every time I find it, I lose it right away."

"Look around it, like looking at a faint star. It will grow brighter."

Shada waited until Alfie told her the light was staying in his awareness. When he reported it was growing bigger, she asked about the prompt for storage on the monitor.

"Was that in preparation for when the computer engineer

solved the problem?" Shada asked, not wanting to get her hopes up that the solution had been found.

"He already solved it. We can store minds on this device. It's the only one."

Shada felt a wave of excitement wash over her. Her first thought was to help Tony and give Sikya the family her sister deserved.

"Why didn't you have me store your mind on the device instead?" Shada asked.

"I can't continue my work from inside a machine," Alfie responded. "There's still a lot I want to do." He told her the circle of light was getting larger. "What happens next?"

"Once the ring of darkness disappears, you'll be able to hear the world too. Over time, there will be an awareness of my limbs as well, but don't bother trying to take over. If I don't block you, Marnie will."

"I won't bother. I'll have to guide you through my experiments." He then informed Shada he could hear the fire alarm.

"Welcome back," Shada said.

"You mentioned Marnie. Can I communicate with her? With Hollis?"

"Do it in the background. I don't need or want the distraction."

"Fair enough," Alfie said. "Can I see my old body?"

Shada turned her head to the side. Even this small action took an enormous amount of effort, and she became aware of how exhausted her body was. Thoughts of Sikya flashed through her head, and she knew she had to continue on and get her off the island.

Alfie's chest still rose and fell with each short sip of air. As they watched, his breathing became rapid then stopped altogether.

"I'm sorry," Shada told Alfie.

Alfie didn't say a word.

Shada heard a loud click and knew it came from the real world, that the noise wasn't in her head. She turned, sat up, and stared straight down the barrel of a gun. Gustavo's finger was on the trigger.

Ruby emerged from behind him, disdain on her face as she inspected the destruction of the lab.

"What did you think this would accomplish?" Ruby said.

Shada responded with silence. She watched as the leader of WestCorp knelt over Alfie, checking to see if he was still breathing.

Ruby shook her head when she realized the scientist was dead. "I thought you would come to get your sister. I never imagined you'd end up in here. What were you trying to do?"

Gustavo answered Ruby's question in a deadpan voice. "She came to stop us from editing the people from the city," he said. It wasn't Gustavo; it was whoever was uploaded into his body, having taken over during his nap on the tram.

Ruby laughed. "This didn't even make a dent! The edits will still continue, once we clean up all the water." She plucked the electrodes off Alfie's skull. Her face fell, and she looked at Shada. "He's in your head now, isn't he?" she said.

Shada didn't see the point in denying the truth. She nodded.

"Interesting way to try to stop me," Ruby said. "Were you trying to prevent us from developing better technology? It won't save the others from the city, but it could help those in the future . . ." Her voice trailed off. "The kid!" she said in a flash of recognition. "You want to make sure the future isn't any worse for your sister's baby." Ruby shook her head. "I admire your long-term thinking, but it still won't help." Ruby then told Gustavo to push Alfie's body off the table, holding her hands up and contorting her face, signaling she didn't want to get dirty.

Gustavo walked over and used his left hand to push the

scientist off the table while his right hand still held the gun pointed at Shada. Alfie's body fell to the floor with the loud crunch of broken bones, settling in a jumbled heap.

Ruby sat on the edge of the table that was covered in blood. "I can't let you keep Alfie," she said. "He belongs to WestCorp, and therefore belongs to me. You're going to upload him into my body," Ruby said. She looked at Shada, delighted, waiting to see what resistance awaited her.

Shada sighed. "What about Hollis? You don't have a problem letting me keep him."

Ruby looked like she'd been slapped. "I . . . I . . . I don't want him inside my head," she stammered.

"I think you like being in charge of WestCorp," Shada shot back. "What if I told you he doesn't have to be in your head, that he can stay on the island?"

Ruby's eyes narrowed. "Elaborate."

"This is a prototype for mind transfer," Shada said. "And storage."

Inside Shada's head, Alfie scolded Shada for giving away knowledge of the device. She silenced him.

"So you could upload Michael onto this machine," Ruby said, looking at the monitor. "And Alfie as well?"

"Sure, they can both be on there."

Ruby told Shada to put Hollis into storage. This time, when prompted by the monitor, Shada chose S and was shown another prompt: type L for left and R for right, accompanied by arrows.

Shada laughed, wondering who would be playing around with uploaded consciousnesses without being able to discern left from right.

She typed R, and a countdown began. She wondered how the machine would be able to determine which of the three minds inside her got uploaded. One appeared on the screen, and she pushed Alfie and Marnie into the darkness before joining them, leaving Hollis in control of her body for the final second.

When she returned to the light, she knew Hollis was gone. "There," she said to Ruby.

"Do the same thing with Alfie," Gustavo commanded.

"Let's not get ahead of ourselves," Ruby said. "Alfie doesn't do me any good inside a machine. I need him to continue his work." She inspected Gustavo. "And if we upload him into you, there's a chance your host will take back over."

"I wouldn't let that happen."

"Maybe not, but it's still a chance." Ruby paused for a moment. "The only option is to upload him into me. I'll continue his work myself."

The leader of WestCorp placed the two electrodes onto her temples and lay down in Alfie's blood.

CHAPTER TWENTY-SIX

ALFIE ACCEPTED that his mind would be transferred into Ruby, and Shada felt him try to take over her body during the countdown. The rest of the room was silent. Ruby's eyes were closed while she waited to accept Alfie's mind, and Gustavo held his gun pointed at Shada.

Alfie began to panic. "I can't find any part of your body," he said, communicating to Shada through thoughts.

"That's because I'm not letting you," Shada responded.

"Don't I have to be in control to transfer?"

Shada told Alfie he was correct, the way a teacher might tell a struggling student he was on the right path. She sensed the countdown was almost finished.

"You can't!" Marnie screamed when she realized what Shada was about to do.

"Try to work together," Shada told the pair of edited minds. Marnie tried to sacrifice herself by taking control of Shada's body, but Shada blocked her too.

She had made the decision to upload herself into Ruby, and there was nothing either of the uploaded minds could do about it. Her world went black.

Waking up in another's body was a new sensation. She expected to see the light in the distance, to wait for it to take over her field of vision, but instead she woke up with Ruby in the background. She remembered how Hollis had been in charge of her body after his upload, before she found the light and took back control. Now she would have to deal with Ruby's attempts to do the same.

Shada sat up. Seeing her previous body on the table next to her gave her the sense of being in a surreal dream. She noticed the thin red scars running down her cheeks from when Hollis had cut her face with a razor, attempting to make her cry tears of blood. It seemed like so long ago that she was in the bathroom without control of herself, and she promised herself she would look in the mirror more often so she would never forget.

"Ruby?" Gustavo asked. Whoever was in charge of the man's body should have known how long it took for the host to take back control from an uploaded mind. Either they forgot, or they had unfounded faith in Ruby's capabilities.

Shada, inside Ruby's body, ignored the question. She tossed her legs over the edge of the table, closed her eyes, and took a series of long, slow breaths.

She heard Gustavo tell Shada to stay down. Then, more people arrived in the lab. Ruby's eyes stayed closed, but Shada heard Gustavo tell them to wait. The additional people fanned out in the room, and Shada knew they all belonged to the island.

She was her own moment of calm in the eye of the storm.

Ruby discovered the circle of light and lost it every time she tried to focus on it. She went through the cycle of losing it and finding it countless times, iterations of a process independent of time. Frustrated, she screamed out Alfie's name.

Shada-in-Ruby smiled.

"She's back!" Gustavo said, mistaking the smile for his leader's return from the darkness.

The fire alarm stopped blaring, and Shada opened Ruby's eyes. She was surrounded by WestCorp employees, all dressed in khaki pants and a white polo.

Shada-in-Ruby looked at the body next to her once more. The head was turned in her direction, and they locked eyes. Whoever was in charge—either Marnie or Alfie—hadn't told Gustavo that Shada was the one who'd transferred. Shada felt a strange satisfaction knowing the two edited minds were on her side.

"Alfie! Let me come back!" Ruby screamed.

Shada was delighted Ruby still thought the scientist was the one in charge of her body.

Gustavo got the attention of the two WestCorp employees who were closest to Shada's body. He used his eyes to point at the body still lying on the table then tilted his head in the direction of the door, indicating it was time to get her out of here.

"Leave her," Shada-in-Ruby said. "I'm not done with her yet."

Ruby tried a different approach. "Alfie, let me back in so we can continue your work," she said in a sweet, delicate way. Shada could sense the rage present behind the words and wondered if Ruby realized that none of her thoughts or feelings would ever be secret again.

Shada closed her eyes, leaving the fire-ravaged room and its occupants behind. "Ruby," she thought. "I can hear you."

Shada got immense pleasure from Ruby's disbelief.

"You . . ." Ruby said. The woman's rage before was nothing compared to its magnitude when she heard Shada's voice from inside her own body.

"It's me."

"You're blocking me from taking back over my own body!" Ruby said.

"I don't have to; you don't even know how to get it back."

"You're scared if I regain control, you won't be able to take back over."

Shada thought the woman's amateur attempt at reverse psychology was cute. She opened Ruby's eyes and looked at Ruby's spotted, wrinkled hand, devoid of adornment.

"Allow the light to take over your vision."

"What do you think I've been trying to do?" Ruby snarled.

"You've been trying to force it. You have to allow it."

"What's the difference?" Ruby's mind grew still. "Why are you helping me?" she asked.

"I want you to see what I'm about to do." She waited for the light to take over Ruby's awareness.

When Ruby again saw the world through her own eyes, and heard the world through her own ears, she tried to scream out to the forces in the room whose feet could be seen through her peripheral vision. Shada never allowed Ruby to reconnect to her body, so these thoughts fizzled out before reaching her tongue.

"Do you see your hand?" Shada asked Ruby.

"Yes."

Shada withdrew her connection to the limb, allowing Ruby to take it over.

"Do you feel your hand?"

Shada watched as the fingers on the hand began to move. The thumb tapped the tops of each finger then made a fist. As Shada watched, the middle finger rose up, and the palm turned to face her.

Shada laughed before taking back control and relaxing the hand. She heard Gustavo laugh too, followed by the rest of the people in the room.

"Alfie's trying to take back over, huh?" Gustavo said.

"Idiot," Ruby said. Nobody but Shada could hear her.

Shada felt Ruby try to take back control of the hand. She let Ruby get close before forcing her back into the darkness.

"I can keep you there as long as I want," Shada thought.

"This isn't even hard for you, is it?" Ruby said, both frustrated and in awe.

"Not even a little."

"Are the others this good?" Ruby asked.

Shada probed Ruby's thoughts, searching to see if her deference was hiding a more sinister motivation. There was plenty of hate in the older woman's thoughts, but none of it scheming. "I've got the best handle on things," Shada said.

Ruby wondered if it was something to do with the fact Shada was unedited. She didn't have to communicate the thought to Shada, because Shada was aware of all that went through the woman's mind.

"Only one unedited ever had a problem with an edited mind," Shada said. "Richard. And I'm positive that if I was the one to teach him how to take back control, he'd still be alive."

"Let's find out what makes the unedited so good at controlling their bodies!" Ruby said. "Stay on the island, and we can study how to make you even better."

"It's not that we're good at controlling our bodies. We're good at controlling our emotions. Because we have them, we're born with them, and we learn to manage them our entire lives. WestCorp can't make this better; the skill is too delicate. All their fingerprints can do is destroy."

Shada knew it was time to get rid of Ruby for good. She looked up at Gustavo with Ruby's eyes. "Taking back control from one mind wasn't so hard."

Gustavo's eyes grew wide, as if he'd been slapped across the face. "I'm sorry it took so long for me to figure it out," he stammered.

Shada-in-Ruby laughed. "That wasn't an attack. What I'm saying is I don't see why I can't try to hold another! If she"—

Shada-in-Ruby looked at Shada's body on the table with all the scorn she could muster—"can control two, then so can I!"

Whoever had taken control of Shada's previous body, either Marnie or Alfie, inspected Ruby's face. Their eyes grew wide with worry as they stared, a frantic search to see if it was Ruby or Shada in control of the leader's body.

Shada-in-Ruby told her former self there was nothing to worry about. "We'll transfer Marnie, and you'll be left alone in there, free from the extra minds. Your body will be yours again," she said, pretending her own mind was still in her own body and not inside Ruby. She hoped none of the WestCorp employees would realize what she was about to do. A moment later she added, "After that, I'll take you to your sister. It'll be just the two of you!"

The other members of WestCorp all laughed.

Shada-in-Ruby lay down on the table and twisted so she could reach the monitor. She selected S, for storage, then L, to designate the mind was coming from her side of the monitor. The countdown began, and she rested her head on the table with her eyes closed.

"Wait!" Gustavo said. "It says S on the screen . . . that's the option she chose when she put Hollis into storage!"

Shada turned Ruby's head and opened her eyes. Gustavo allowed his weapon's aim to fall as he rushed towards the monitor.

Marnie or Alfie—whoever controlled Shada—shot up and lunged for the man. They fought as the seconds passed. Gustavo ended up on top, holding her down with his knee and both hands on the gun now aimed at her chest. He couldn't make it to the monitor in time to stop the countdown.

"Take those off!" he yelled to Shada-in-Ruby. His eyes fluttered between the two electrodes on her head.

Shada looked at the monitor and saw two appear on the screen. She closed her eyes and plunged into the darkness, forcing Ruby into the light.

CHAPTER TWENTY-SEVEN

THE AWARENESS of the room returned to Shada, her mind now the sole resident in Ruby's body. Gustavo stared at her.

"What happened?" he said, his eyes narrowed with suspicion.

Shada couldn't lie and say Marnie had transferred into her. She looked at the ceiling with Ruby's eyes, pretending to scan her internal state for signs of other consciousnesses. "I'm alone in here," she said.

"The monitor was set for storage," Gustavo said. "That's why I told you to take off those wires." He used his chin to gesture to both her temples.

Shada-in-Ruby nodded.

"But who got uploaded?" he asked. He put his left hand on the ground, using it to stand up, while his right kept the gun pointed at Shada's former body on the ground. Shada knew the weapon could be aiming at her in the blink of an eye.

"Alfie," Shada-in-Ruby said without hesitation. She got off the table and stood over her previous body. Both electrodes had been torn off in the struggle. "It's a good thing too, she wasn't even attached!"

Gustavo stood a step away, watching who he thought was Ruby help who he thought was Shada stand up.

Alfie or Marnie stared into Shada-in-Ruby's eyes, searching for some sign of recognition. Ruby's left eye displayed the slightest wink. "Let's try this again," Shada-in-Ruby said, loud enough for all around to hear. She helped her former body onto the table once more. "Ready to come live in my body?" she asked.

Either Marnie or Alfie shook Shada's head no.

"Of course not," Gustavo said. It sounded like he was rolling his eyes at the same time.

Shada ignored him. "You'd rather be stuck in there?" Shada-in-Ruby said.

"That one's old. Her time will come soon enough," Shada's former body said. The intonation of the voice was flat, similar to how Alfie spoke. "I want as much time as possible to finish what I started."

Gustavo laughed. "What can you do? Once you're off this table, you'll be thrown in with your sister, away from the rest of the world." He still assumed Shada was the one speaking from inside her own body and seemed to forget his suspicion about who was inside Ruby.

Shada-in-Ruby reattached the electrodes, whispering while their faces were close. "I'm coming back in. Alfie, you don't want to take over Ruby, alone?"

Alfie-in-Shada's head made the slightest shift from left to right.

Shada-in-Ruby stood up straight and turned around, addressing the group of WestCorp employees in the lab with her. "The girl makes a good point," she said. "I'm already old and don't have much time left."

Gustavo's head tilted to one side while he waited for her to continue.

"I think I'll take over her body," Shada-in-Ruby said.

"Your husband already tried that, and look where it got him. He's stuck inside a machine!" Gustavo replied.

Shada-in-Ruby looked at him and smirked. "Sounds like you don't think I can do it."

"It's not worth it."

"But I have one thing Michael didn't: the ability to upload. I'll get in there, then we can upload her mind into storage, leaving me alone!"

Gustavo looked around, aware that he was pushing back against the leader of the company in front of other employees. "She won't be the one who ends up in storage."

"What are you saying?"

"Shada's too good. If you go in there and try to put her into storage, she'll find a way to make sure you're the one going into the machine." He paused, took a deep breath, and seemed to come up with a solution. "Why don't we upload her mind now? Then you can take over her body."

Shada-in-Ruby didn't want to admit it, but his suggestion made sense. She set aside her reservations, agreed, then turned back to her former body. Gustavo expected both Marnie and Shada to be inside. "Don't make me run this more than once. I'll leave your body empty if I have to."

Shada watched as the eyes of her former body blinked twice. The face softened, and she felt deep inside that Marnie was now in control.

Marnie-in-Shada closed her eyes and dropped her chin twice, indicating she was ready to sacrifice herself.

Shada wished she could tell Marnie she would get her out as soon as she could, but there was no way to communicate without everyone else in the room hearing her. She initiated the upload. Seconds later, Alfie-in-Shada opened his eyes and let out a prolonged exhale.

"Finally rid of that filthy unedited!" Alfie-in-Shada said.

The scientist was playing along. Shada felt relief wash over her. Although she doubted Marnie would use such strong language, she also knew the sentiment was common among the edited. She hoped it was enough to convince Gustavo that Shada was in fact gone, leaving Marnie behind, alone.

Alfie-in-Shada's reaction seemed to be enough proof for Gustavo that Shada was gone. "Let's get you transferred over!" he said.

Shada-in-Ruby made sure the electrodes were attached to her own head then set up the monitor to transfer from left to right. She lay down on the table as the countdown began.

Shada didn't want to kill Ruby, but the upload would leave the older woman's body an empty vessel, devoid of life. Without a mind, and with no hope of regaining one, there would be no point for the body to exist. She knew they could keep it alive, for a time, with the technology on the island. How long would it take for the body to expire without any support? Days, from dehydration? Would it be a mercy to kill her sooner?

She thought about Chloe, and Alfie, and how their deaths had come about because of her actions. Both of those deaths had produced a sense of remorse; she felt nothing for Ruby. Not vindication, not relief, just nothing.

Shada's vision went black. When she found the light and opened her eyes, she was back inside her own body.

"Welcome back," Alfie said. "Remember, you're supposed to be Ruby."

Shada, back in her own body, opened her eyes. With just one mind inside her, Alfie, she felt like she could think faster than before.

"Gentlemen," she said, doing her best to sound both commanding and condescending at the same time. It was her best impression of Ruby. "Did everyone hear when our friend here questioned my decision?"

Shada sat up. Alfie laughed, knowing where the conversation was headed.

There were a few nods from the members of the group. "Well? Did you?"

Every WestCorp employee other than Gustavo said they'd heard him.

"Would you do me a favor and remove him from my sight?"

Gustavo, controlled by an edited mind, lowered his weapon to the ground with his other hand in the air, signaling he wasn't going to resist. Two men grabbed him, each one holding an arm.

"Where should we take him?" one of Gustavo's captors said.

"Take him to the bunker. Put two guards outside his door. The biggest ones we have." The two men led a shocked Gustavo away from the lab.

Shada liked giving orders and found herself enjoying the new role. She stood up and pulled the electrodes off of Ruby's mindless body. The woman looked frail as her chest rose and fell. The wrinkles in her face, kept hidden by makeup, made faint lines in her skin even when her face was relaxed.

The remaining WestCorp force, less than a dozen in total, stared at the two women. Ruby's lifeless body still commanded their attention, even though Shada was now in charge.

"Listen," Shada snapped. She jammed her index finger into her chest. "I'm in here now. Get used to it." She asked Alfie, through her thoughts, if it was OK to move the prototype; he said yes. "I need two of you to carry this," she said. She unplugged the monitor from the wall, lifted it up, and placed it on the table she had laid on during the uploads. She wrapped the long electrode wires around her hand and put them on top of the monitor. "The ones who aren't carrying it, guard it with your life."

The men scrambled to follow her orders.

"Wait for me in the hallway. And remember that my husband's in there!" she barked at the men as they left the lab.

Alfie agreed this was a nice touch. "What are you going to do with her?" he asked, referring to Ruby's former body.

"Not a thing," Shada said. She walked out of the lab, looking back once more before she locked the door from the inside and shut it.

She thought of Chloe. If she could leave her friend behind to die, she could do it to Ruby too.

CHAPTER TWENTY-EIGHT

THE MEN in the hallway stared at Shada for direction.

"We're going to the bunker," she said. She led the way through the lab building towards the exit, walking through the standing water left by the sprinkler system.

Outside the building was chaos. Scores of people milled about, waiting to find out what they should do. WestCorp employees had rounded up the inhabitants of the city and made them stand together, gathered around a single palm tree. Everyone was drenched.

Shada wondered if the edits had been completed or if the fire had interrupted the process before it began. She would deal with them later. Her first priority was Sikya.

It took three vehicles to transport Shada and her followers to the bunker at the edge of the island. The chain-link fence still surrounded the entrance, and the towering guards were posted outside. The dog inside the square lifted its head and stared at Shada's group as they approached.

"Hold it right there," one of the guards said while holding a hand up. He was one of two at the entrance, and there were two more posted on each corner.

Shada told them to let her group through.

The two guards at the entrance erupted in laughter. "Why should we listen to you? You were in here yourself not too long ago!"

They looked past Shada and her group, shaking their heads to themselves as if repeating the joke in their minds.

"Let us through," one of the WestCorp employees said. He lowered his voice to a hoarse whisper. "You don't know what you're doing."

"I'm doing my job!" the talkative guard said, looking at the employee with disgust.

"This is Ruby," another WestCorp employee chimed in. "She transferred her mind into this girl's body."

This revelation seemed to get their attention.

"Why do you think we're walking with her?" a third employee said. "We watched it happen. Just now, in the lab. Get out of the way or you'll end up at the bottom of the bay."

Shada wondered if people were ever actually thrown into the water surrounding the island or if it was an idle threat tossed around by the edited. Either way, their attitudes changed.

"Where's Alfie?" the guard said. "Get him here, and he'll tell us the truth." They were used to the scientist going in and out of the bunker, so he was someone they could trust.

"It's too complicated to explain. Just let us in!" a WestCorp employee said.

The guards didn't have the chance to wrap their heads around the situation before Shada walked between them. "I'm going in," she said.

The guards didn't stop her. They took a step back and allowed the other members of her group through.

The brown dog with flecks of gray in his face sauntered up to Shada's side. She reached down and petted his head while she walked. "Hello, Jax," she said. He ran away when they were halfway to the front door, trying to play, but when Shada didn't pay attention to him, he came back to her side and walked with her until they reached the concrete in front of the door. He must have been trained to stay away from the entrance, because he stood outside while Shada and her group went inside.

The elevator couldn't arrive fast enough. It seemed to crawl from the level below until it stopped at their level. The doors crept open as if they were peeling apart to reveal a secret that could escape if startled. Shada walked inside first, followed by the rest. The two men holding the prototype boarded last, facing the door.

Shada pushed her way past the men as soon as the elevator doors opened. She jogged down the bunker's empty corridor, stopping to search in every room. She paused at the padded room where she'd been held captive by Ruby. The door was open just a crack, and the light was on. Keeping a pregnant Sikya confined in the same room in which her sister had been kept seemed like something Ruby would enjoy.

Shada pushed the door open. The heavy door creaked and stopped halfway. The room was empty. She inspected the rest of the rooms and found nothing.

The two WestCorp employees in charge of bringing Gustavo to the bunker were seated across from each other at the long table in the open space at the end of the corridor. The expansive jet-black wall across the back glittered in the artificial light.

"Are you two the only ones here?" Shada asked, worried Sikya wasn't there.

"The guy you told us to bring down is in that room over there," one of the men said, pointing to the upload room to the right of Hollis's bedroom.

"There's a woman in the other room," the second WestCorp employee added.

Shada rushed into Hollis's bedroom.

Sikya was lying on the bed. She burst into tears at the sight of her sister.

Shada rushed to her bedside. "Are you all right?" Shada asked.

"I'm fine," she said as she wiped tears from her eyes. "Just thankful to see you."

"They didn't hurt you, did they?"

"No, they've been taking care of me."

"Told you she was fine," Alfie said, inside Shada's head.

"They left you alone down here?"

"A nurse comes a few times a day to check on me. She makes sure everything's all right and brings more food. Sometimes there are other people in the main area, but I just stay in here."

Shada leaned over and gave her sister a hug.

"Can we go back to the city?" Sikya asked when they parted. "These people give me the creeps. They're so cold. I don't know how you spend so much time around them."

"You get used to it," Shada said. "And yes, we'll get you back to the city."

Shada heard the clunk of something heavy being placed on the table outside the bedroom. "There are just a few things I need to take care of," she said. She walked out of the room and told the men to move the prototype into the upload room. She took a deep breath before walking into the room herself.

The glare on Gustavo's face told Shada the edited mind was still in charge of her friend's body. Not a word was spoken while the storage device was set up.

"The electrodes need to be attached to your head," Shada said. "Are you going to make me order them to hold you down?"

Gustavo looked at the others in the room and the few peeking in from outside. He shook his head no.

At a nod from Shada, one of the men stuck an electrode to each of Gustavo's temples. Shada selected S for storage, then R. Gustavo had the look of a man who would commit murder if given the chance.

The countdown began. Shada hoped with everything she had that the edited mind inside her friend didn't know to allow the real Gustavo to regain control of his own body, which would make the unedited mind the one that got uploaded. When the countdown ended, Gustavo's body went limp.

CHAPTER TWENTY-NINE

Seconds ticked by, then a full minute. Shada ordered everybody out of the room. When Gustavo opened his eyes, he looked at Shada and began uttering apologies with tears in his eyes.

"I couldn't take back control," he said.

Shada knew her friend was back. She walked to his side and laid a hand on his shoulder. "It's all right. You never have to go through that again."

Gustavo nodded, his breath catching in his chest. When he collected himself, he asked about the others. "Where are they? Are they all right?"

Shada told him she'd left them behind before she went to the lab. "I'll send some of the WestCorp employees outside to bring them here," she said, gesturing with her head to the door.

Gustavo's eyes searched Shada's face for an explanation as to why anyone from WestCorp would listen to her.

Shada walked to the door and stuck her head outside the room. She told the men to go to the dream stations, that her friends would be waking up soon. "There are three of them, two women and a man. Bring them here when they get out of the pods."

The men nodded.

"They won't want to come. Tell them Shada wants them to come to the bunker."

The men told Shada they'd be back soon and left.

"They think I'm Ruby," Shada turned and said to a stunned Gustavo. She then gave him a rough version of the events in Alfie's lab, finishing with the fact that she now had Alfie inside her and that Ruby, Marnie, Hollis, and the edited mind inside Gustavo were now trapped in the storage device.

Sikya, Shada, and Gustavo all sat down together to wait for the other three members of the resistance to turn up. Half of the WestCorp forces were there with them, and half were gone collecting the others. The elevator doors opened, and heavy footsteps could be heard walking down the corridor. All three of the unedited turned, hoping to see their comrades. Two oversized humans, the island's guards, emerged into the large space at the end of the corridor. Shada sent them away, saying their services were no longer required. They shrugged, turned around, and left.

Tony, Sophie, and Ophelia showed up an hour later. They seemed skeptical of their situation until they saw Shada, Sikya, and Gustavo sitting at the long table. Within moments they had crossed the space and embraced their friends. The looks of suspicion on the faces of the WestCorp employees disappeared with a stern look from Shada.

"What happened?" Tony said. "I could've killed you when I got out of that machine," he added, laughing.

Shada told them she would fill them in soon. "There's something we have to do first." She took each of them into the upload room one at a time and, after instructing them to give up control of their bodies during the countdown, put all the edited minds from their bodies into the device.

Once everyone but Shada was back to being the sole consciousness inside their bodies, she took them into Hollis's bedroom and shut the door. Inside, she told them about the events that had transpired in Alfie's lab.

"This is the second time I've heard this, and I still can't believe it," Gustavo said.

Tony was seated next to Sikya with his arm around her. "So now you're in charge of WestCorp," he said. "What's the first thing you're going to do?"

Shada thought for a moment. Then, frantic, she said she'd meant to stop the edits. "I can't believe I didn't remember!" she said. She rushed out of the bedroom and told the WestCorp employees to send the unedited back to the city. Inside her head, she asked Alfie how she would get a message out to those who had already been edited.

"There's a communications office," Alfie responded through thought.

Shada issued more instructions to the WestCorp employees. "Send someone to the communications office. Tell them I want everyone who was edited to come back to have the process reversed."

She hoped nobody had been edited in the short time she had been in charge. In her attempts to get to her sister and save her friends, she had forgotten one of the reasons she came to the island in the first place.

Alfie offered comfort. "Without me or Ruby telling them to start the edits back up after the lab was evacuated, nobody would take the initiative," he said.

Shada said she hoped that was the case.

Later that night, she found out Alfie was right. Everyone who had been in the lab when it was evacuated had stayed outside or gone back to the atrium. Since no edits were being completed, no one was sent back to the city, and no new unedited people had arrived.

Shada, Sikya, Gustavo, Tony, Sophie, and Ophelia ate dinner together then spent the night in the bunker. Tony and Sikya stayed in Hollis's bedroom, and Shada made space for herself in Hollis's study. Gustavo tried to sleep next to Shada, but she told him to stay on the other side of the room. She had no idea where Sophie and Ophelia slept.

Everyone left the bunker together the next morning. The morning sunlight reflected off the water surrounding the island. The air was crisp compared to the recycled air in the bunker. Jax the dog ran up to Shada's side and nudged Shada's hand with his gray beard.

"Get these fences taken down," Shada said to the guards posted outside.

They nodded. When they didn't move, she added, "Now," and they scrambled to disassemble the enclosure.

Jax joined the group, delighted to be outside the enclosure. They walked to the atrium, enjoying the sunshine, instead of taking a transport vehicle. The dog stopped at the entrance of the building when the humans walked inside. When Shada snapped her fingers, he hesitated before running to her side.

The space was full of unedited waiting to get back to the city. Undercurrents of anger swept through the crowd because they were going back without being edited. Everyone stared at the dog at Shada's side.

Shada and her group paused at the top of the stairs that led down to the tram.

"I'll come visit when I can," Shada said to the group.

Sikya stared at her sister in disbelief. "You're not coming back to the city with us?" she said.

"I've got to figure out what to do with this island and everyone on it. I'll be back soon."

Gustavo looked more pained than the others but nodded his agreement with the rest.

Sikya gave Shada a hug. "You'd better be there when the baby comes," she said.

"I wouldn't miss it," replied Shada.

The group split, leaving Shada at the top of the stairs. Jax, thinking everyone was going down, ran to the bottom and stood with his tail wagging while watching the group of humans descend. His tail stopped when he realized Shada was still at the top of the stairs. He paused for a moment before racing back up.

Together, Shada and Jax watched her sister and friends disappear into the crowd on the platform.

CHAPTER THIRTY

SHADA LOOKED at the city from her office. Fog covered the bases of the buildings, making the spires atop the skyscrapers seem like they were floating among the clouds. She had been in charge of the company for weeks.

At first, she'd wanted to dissolve the company once the edits of those terrorizing the city had been reversed. But collecting the edited had proved difficult. None of them trusted the company to reverse the procedure, and pockets of resistance dedicated to fighting WestCorp had sprung up all over.

When she had first heard about these groups, she'd laughed, thinking about how history had repeated itself. Now she was sad knowing her company was the object of their scorn when she was trying to help them. She wondered if Ruby had ever felt the same way.

The computer engineer who'd solved the storage problem walked into the office to tell her he had figured out a way to store the minds outside the one prototype. He told her he could store thousands on a server located on the island, and that they could be accessed anywhere connected to the island's network.

Shada asked if there was any way the stored minds could affect the island's other systems.

The engineer assured her they were useless outside of a body. "I made an alternate reality for them; they don't even know they're on a machine."

"Like a permanent dream station," Shada said.

"All I did was scale those up," the engineer replied.

Shada thought for a moment. "Do you think there's a way to get one of them a new body?" she asked the engineer. The thought of leaving Marnie in a reality with Michael and Ruby Hollis was repulsive.

"You want to upload them? Into who, other people from the city?"

"Not who. What. Androids."

The engineer thought for a moment. "You'd have to get other scientists involved. I don't know the first thing about robotics."

"But is it even possible?"

"I can't say for sure. What I can say is that it would take a long time, even with all the company's resources."

Inside Shada's head, Alfie said they should go for it. "Shada, this is the next step. Think about all the unedited people you could save. Their minds could live on the server after they die, and they could get into an android once we've perfected the technology."

Shada knew the first person she'd upload into an android would be Marnie. She told the engineer to take the steps necessary to begin the project.

"Will do . . . Mrs. Wes—er, Hollis."

Shada didn't miss the slip. Everyone on the island had gone from reporting to an aging Caucasian woman to taking orders from a young woman of color. She had heard the rumors, that her employees were calling her "Mrs. West" among themselves, but this was the first time anyone had used the name in person with her.

"I'm going to have everyone call me Ms. West," Shada said aloud, more to herself and Alfie than to the engineer.

The engineer looked embarrassed. "I'm sorry, I didn't mean anything by it."

"I'm serious, you can call me Ms. West."

"OK, Ms. West." The words seemed strange on his tongue. "Do you need anything else?"

Alfie laughed. Shada was the one person who could hear him. "You really want to be called Ms. West all the time? Like some teacher?"

"I don't want them to call me Shada, I know that much," Shada thought.

"So come up with a new name," Alfie said.

Shada, having just thought about Marnie, weighed the name on her tongue to see if it would work for herself. It didn't fit. "Barbie?" she thought. "Barnie?"

The computer engineer stared at her while her eyes searched the room, looking for her new first name.

"Marnie," she thought again. "Mable. Marble." Something clicked, and Shada focused on the engineer. "Amanda. Call me Amanda. First name basis from now on."

"Amanda West," Alfie said. "Has a nice ring to it."

Later that night, Shada wondered if it would ever be possible to duplicate consciousness. She was in the bunker, lying in what used to be Hollis's bed, and she wished she could have an android get her a glass of water. But if someone else's mind was inside the android, she would never be able to trust the machine. It would have to be her own consciousness, an exact copy, or as close as she could produce.

But if she did create the duplicate, what would happen when she died and her consciousness was uploaded onto the server? Would the duplicate be deleted? Absorbed? She felt a pang of jealousy for the duplicate that didn't even exist yet. It could rest and she couldn't.

This thought stuck in Shada's head as she drifted off to sleep.

Unedited minds would exist for eternity after they were uploaded. The edited, who had no problem with death and would therefore be uninterested in uploading their consciousnesses, would expire, never to exist again.

Were the edited the lucky ones?

Letting someone live and giving someone life are not the same.

INTERESTED IN READING MORE?

Find out more about the world Amanda West creates in *The Hysteria of Bodalís*! It's set in the distant future and based on the same mind-uploading technology Shada Gray/Amanda West experienced.

Get a copy FOR FREE by heading over to my website and subscribing to my email list.

authormarcoshernandez.com

Also, please help other readers learn more about this book by leaving a rating and review!